IN
FREEDOM'S
LIGHT

SHARON GLOGER FRIEDMAN

Renee,

Happy reading!

Sharon Gloger Friedma

IN FREEDOM'S LIGHT

A NOVEL

outskirts
press

For George, for Always

Conversos: Spanish or Portuguese Jews and their descendants who converted outwardly to Christianity during the Spanish Inquisition to avoid persecution or expulsion, though often continuing to practice Judaism in secret. Also known as crypto-Jews or secret Jews.

"On January 1, 2000, *The New York Times* ran a Millennium Edition. It was a special issue that featured three front pages. One had the news from January 1, 1900. The second was the actual news of the day, January 1, 2000. And then they had a third front page—projecting envisioned future events of January 1, 2100. …And in addition to the fascinating articles, there was one more thing. Down on the bottom of the Year 2100 front page was the candle-lighting time in New York for January 1, 2100. Reportedly, the production manager of *The New York Times*—an Irish Catholic—was asked about it. His answer was right on the mark. It speaks to the eternity of our people, and to the power of Jewish ritual. He said, 'We don't know what will happen in the year 2100. It is impossible to predict the future. But of one thing you can be certain—that in the year 2100 Jewish women will be lighting *Shabbat* candles.'"

"The Meaning Behind the Flames" by Rhona Lewis, Chabad.org

PART I

CHAPTER 1

Valencia, Spain, April 1785

"How could you be so foolish?" he roared at her, his dark eyes blazing with rage. Turning his wrath on the nearest object, Efren swept a vase from a walnut side table, scattering rose petals and shards of porcelain across the marble floor of the sitting room.

"For centuries the Amselem name has been respected in the royal court and the Catholic Church. My father is a physician in King Charles' court! Now there are whispers that you were observed refusing a cut of pork in the marketplace yesterday when no other meat was left. My God, Anica, what were you thinking? My family has denied its Jewish blood for generations and prospered. Any suspicion that we are secret Jews puts our lives in danger. One person," he said, slicing the air with his finger. "It only takes one person to accuse us, and we will be brought before an Inquisition tribunal. We'll lose everything, and Isabel will be an orphan."

His chest heaving, Efren sank into a chair and buried his lean face in his hands. When he looked up, his mouth was set in a grim line, the dark lashes that rimmed his lids wet with tears. He stared past his young wife and the crying infant in her arms, ashamed of his outburst. When he finally spoke, his voice betrayed his fear. "They are still torturing suspected Judaizers and burning them at the stake."

Anica clutched her daughter and sobbed at the realization that one moment of distracted carelessness had placed them in so much danger. "Mariana was ill, and I sent her home. I wanted to have a nice supper waiting for you, so I went to the marketplace. Isabel was crying, and I couldn't soothe her. People were giving me hard looks, and I was embarrassed. I could feel my breasts filling with milk, and I just wanted to get away. Oh, God, what have I done?" she cried, falling to her knees before him.

His anger was no match for the hold she had on his heart. The muscles in his jaw loosened and his face softened. Pulling his wife and child into his arms, Efren nestled his face into the nape of her neck, inhaling her sweet smell. "Anica," he murmured, repeating her name until her sobbing ceased.

"I am so sorry, Efren," she said, breaking from his embrace, her eyes shining with tears. "Are we really in danger?"

"I only know that there is gossip, and that cannot be good. I have business enemies who would be eager to seize on this and do me harm. We must be vigilant to any indications that we are under suspicion."

The whimpering baby in Anica's arms began to suck furiously on her fingers. "Isabel is hungry," said Efren, kissing his daughter's dark curls.

Watching Anica take Isabel to her breast, Efren was still stunned by his young wife's beauty. Raven-haired with dark, almond-shaped eyes the color of obsidian, her body sensuous and soft, she had beguiled him the first time he saw her at his family's Christmas ball. Accompanied by her widowed father, sixteen-year-old Anica Rezio had captivated him—and made him feel foolish for even thinking she would favor him. *Why*, he thought, as he observed the gaggle of handsome young men who swarmed around her vying for her attention, *would such a beautiful young girl be interested in a thirty-five-year-old man?* Efren smiled in spite of himself when he remembered how ardently he had pursued her, making up business excuses to appear at her father's home, ensuring invitations to parties he knew she would attend, seeming to appear by accident at the courtiers' salons she frequented.

He won her heart with patience and persistence, and they married the next year on Anica's seventeenth birthday. Happily giving up his former life of gambling dens and women eager to share his bed, Efren spent his days expanding his import-export business, and his nights in the arms of his beautiful wife. When Isabel was born a year later, he could not believe his good fortune.

Now, he feared it had run out.

❧✦❧

Her head resting in his chest, Efren ran his fingers through Anica's fine, silky hair, and whispered into the night. "I've always known that you practiced your Judaism in secret. Did you think I wasn't aware that you slipped away to the cellar before it turned dark to light the Sabbath candles? Or your aversion to eating pork, and that Friday night was the servants' night off?"

Anica could feel the hot flush of shame creep up her neck to her face. "I am sorry I kept that part of my life from you. My father's family converted long ago, and we lived as practicing Catholics. But my mother's ancestors were secret Jews, and she continued to follow as many of the Jewish laws and rituals as she could in secret. Not even my father knew. I was ten years old when she died, and all I have to remember her by are the candlesticks she used to light the *Shabbat* candles, and the observances she taught me. I would watch as she lit the candles and prayed over them, her hands covering her eyes, and I thought she was the most beautiful woman in all of Valencia. On Friday nights when my father was away on business, we would eat the *Shabbat* meal in the cellar so we wouldn't be discovered if someone came to the house unexpectedly. Mama always left out a special prayer book that had a cross embellished on its cover so that it appeared to be a volume of Christian blessings. She told me never to forget that I was Jewish. After she died, I was afraid I'd get caught lighting the candles, but I prayed every Friday night, holding her prayer book and my rosary in case I was discovered." Anica hesitated and took Efren's hand. "If you knew, why didn't you stop me?"

Efren let out a long breath. "Because I love you, and I kept telling myself there was no harm as long as you confined your praying and practices to the house when the servants were gone."

Anica sat up and circled her arms around her knees. "And now I have brought danger upon us. What are we going to do?"

"I'll go to the wharf first thing in the morning as I always do. Gossip and rumors travel fast among the merchants, and we'll know soon enough if we are in danger. I don't want you to leave the house tomorrow. If you need anything send Mariana."

Efren reached for Anica and pulled her into his arms. "You need to sleep. Isabel will be hungry again in a few hours."

Anica curled her body around his, and finally fell into a fitful sleep.

Slipping quietly out of bed, Efren padded across the cold stone floor and peered down at his sleeping daughter. Overwhelmed by emotions so strong they took his breath away, he sat by Isabel's cradle, watching the rise and fall of her tiny chest, waiting for the first pink rays of dawn to light the sky.

CHAPTER 2

Anica spent a restless day eager for Efren's return. Though she longed to take Isabel for a morning walk along the Turia River, Efren's admonition not to leave the house echoed in her ears. Seeking comfort in their garden, she inhaled deeply, breathing in the sweet perfume of the orange trees that framed the courtyard, and reveled in the carnations, roses, bougainvillea, and lantana that bloomed in a riot of colors. Sitting in the warmth of the afternoon sun, lulled by the hum of bees buzzing around the flowers, her eyelids grew heavy.

Anica woke with a start, finding Efren sitting in the chair beside her.

"I hope I didn't wake you. I know your sleep last night was troubled; you tossed about most of the night." His voice was solemn, his face obscured by the brim of his beaver top hat.

"I came into the garden for some fresh air. I must have fallen asleep," she said, blinking away the fog behind her eyes.

Efren removed his hat and raked his hand through his hair, dark and curling around his ears and neck. Peering into his face, Anica did not have to ask what he had learned.

She touched his cheek, her fingers tracing the edge of his beard. "It's as you feared, isn't it?"

He nodded slowly. "My cousin Alonso also heard rumblings among my rivals that we may not be true Christians. I don't know if word has reached the court or the Church yet, but Alonso said there are rumors that the Church is renewing its efforts to search out and prosecute secret Jews. I fear it is only a matter of time before we are accused of being conversos. My father's standing with the court may protect us for a short time, but we need to make plans to leave Spain."

Efren considered several avenues of escape, discarding some as too obvious, and others as too dangerous. Cognizant of the need to act quickly, he plotted their secret departure down to the minutest detail, praying that the necessary pieces would fall into place when it was time to leave. Fearful of discovery, and loath to worry Anica about the peril of his plan, he worked alone, late into the night, going over every aspect until he was sure his plan was sound. If they could stem the rumors for a while longer, they would be gone in two weeks, when one of his merchant ships would be loaded and ready to leave for Charleston, South Carolina.

To give the appearance that all was in order while he planned their escape, Efren arrived at the wharf each morning at his usual hour, making sure he was observed overseeing his outgoing shipments of spices and silk, and receiving the tobacco and cotton he imported from the American colonies. Mingling with the merchants at his regularly attended tavern, he conducted business over well-filled glasses of claret, and joked with the well-fed proprietor.

Anica too resumed her charitable functions, setting her face in a forced smile at social gatherings. Eager to appear as keeping to her normal routine, she spent several afternoons strolling along the *Paseo del la Almeda*, pushing Isabel in a wicker carriage, and greeting the other young mothers along the promenade. Hoping to look the model of a happy and devout family, Efren and Anica regularly attended church services, six-month-old Isabel snuggled in her mother's arms.

Two days before they were to leave behind everything and everyone they held dear, Anica paced the confines of their bedchamber, growing more anxious as Efren went over each detail of their departure one more time. They were to slip away to the wharf on the day of *Fiesta Corpus Christi* after Holy Mass, counting on the procession of decorated carts, giant-sized figures of Old Testament characters, and throngs of onlookers to provide cover for their exodus. One of Efren's ships, the *Águila*, was being loaded in preparation for their departure on the day of the festival. Hidden in the barrels of spices and crates of silk bound for Charleston, were their valuables and articles of clothing—secreted from the villa each night after the servants left.

"You will tell the servants that in addition to Friday, they do not have to come to the villa on Thursday so they can enjoy the *Fiesta*," said Efren, trying to calm his wife's fears. "That will give us two days before our disappearance is discovered. I will also allow my workers the day to enjoy the procession, and only Captain Lopez and the crew of the *Águila* will be at the wharf. They are being well paid, and I chose them because they have been with me for many years and can be trusted. By the time the servants and my workers return, we will be far out to sea."

Anica stopped pacing, and stood motionless, staring out the arched window at the silent courtyard below. "Mariana has been with my family since I was a child. She took care of my mother when she was sick. When my mother died, I would have been lost without her." Her voice was hollow, her face drawn.

"I am sure your father will find a place for her in his household."

The mention of her father brought tears to her eyes. "Please, can I just say goodbye to Papa?"

Efren looked away. He loved his father-in-law. He knew taking his only child and grandchild from him would break his heart. But it was Anica and Isabel's safety he was trying to protect, and he hoped the old man would understand. "We cannot let anyone, including our families, know that we're leaving. If they don't know anything, they can't be held accountable. Do you think it is easy for me to leave my parents and deprive them the joy of their granddaughter?"

Anica began to pace again, her hands fluttering to her face. "I am afraid that just the fact that we are gone will cast suspicion on our families."

"My father saved the royal princess when she had scarlet fever. The king won't allow anything to happen to him, and your father has done many favors for the royal family. There are debts of gratitude that can be called in," said Efren, trying to sound more assured than he felt.

"What do we know of this place? This Charleston in America? What will we do there? We do not even speak the language."

Efren took a deep breath in an effort to control his rising frustration. "My Uncle Philip owns a rice plantation near Charleston. I have written to him, and he will be expecting us. He is my father's older brother, and he will help us get settled. Captain Lopez speaks English, so we will have plenty of time to learn the language on the ship. Please stop worrying so much. We must remain calm and appear as if everything is normal if we are to avoid arousing any more suspicion. We only have two more days before we leave, but I still worry we are being watched."

CHAPTER 3

At the end of the day before they were to leave, Anica forced herself to smile as Mariana, and the other house servants, Paloma and Luisa, gathered their things. Excited about the holiday the next day, they were delighted to find that Efren had added two extra silver reales to their wages. With calls of thank you and good-bye, Paloma and Luisa made their way into the chilly night, leaving Mariana alone with Anica.

Slowly folding her apron and placing it on the kitchen sideboard, Mariana pushed away a strand of gray-streaked hair that had come loose from her tightly drawn bun, and smoothed her skirt over her round body. "You cannot fool me. I know that look. When you were a little girl it meant you were hiding something."

Caught off guard by Mariana's scrutiny, Anica hesitated, and then responded with a feeble laugh. "You know me too well. I just wanted to surprise you with the extra reales."

Mariana studied Anica's face. "*Mi cariña*," she said, her brown eyes growing moist. "I know something is wrong. You have not been yourself all week. You look sad all the time, and you eat next to nothing. You have become all skin and bones."

Anica started to protest, but Mariana shook her head. "I love you and Isabel like my own. Whatever you are about to do, take care of yourself and your precious baby."

Unable to hold back her tears, Anica stepped into Mariana's open

arms—arms that had offered comfort and love for as long as she could remember. When she tried to speak, Mariana pressed her fingers to her lips.
Wiping the tears from Anica's cheek, she left without another word.

They ate their last meal in their home in silence, each lost in swirling
thoughts and surging fears. Pushing her food around her plate, Anica finally
gave up all pretense of hunger. "She knows," she said in a near whisper.

"What did you say?" asked Efren, uncertain he had heard her correctly.

"Mariana knows."

"You told her?" he asked incredulously, his voice rising in anger.

"Of course not. How could you even think that? She has suspected
something was wrong for days. I should have known I couldn't hide anything
from her."

"Are we in danger of being discovered? Will she tell anyone?"

"Mariana would never put us in peril, and you know how much she
loves Isabel. I worry now that she is in danger too."

Efren reached across the table and took Anica's hands into his. "I know
you are frightened. I am too, but we have no choice. Although we haven't
been accused yet, my rivals are eager to find proof that we are Judaizing.
Rodrigo, my clerk, confessed he was approached yesterday by a stranger
who offered him money if he could provide evidence that I was a converso."

Anica's eyes widened. "Now there is one more person who is suspicious
about us."

Efren nodded. "All the more reason to leave tomorrow. Rodrigo has
been with me a long time, but I don't trust him. I laughed off the suggestion
and thanked him for telling me, but I am wary of his intentions. I suspect
what he really wanted was for me to offer him money to be quiet. I considered it, but I was afraid that to do so would have confirmed any suspicions
he might have, and he would betray us anyway."

Efren sat on the edge of the bed watching Anica nurse Isabel. The baby's
bow-shaped lips made little popping noises as she suckled furiously. When
Anica removed her from her breast to switch her to the other side, the angry
baby began to cry, her tiny hands balled into fists.

"She is always so hungry," marveled Efren. "No wonder she is so plump."

"Plump and feisty," smiled Anica, as Isabel eagerly latched on to her nipple and suckled contentedly. Sated at last, the infant's eyelids began to droop, and her mouth pursed as if to bestow a kiss. Nuzzling Isabel's cheek, Anica placed her drowsy daughter in her cradle, and slid into bed next to Efren.

"You smell like baby and milk," he whispered, stroking her hair and pressing his body to hers. Surprised at how quickly her body responded, Anica's breath caught in her throat, desire overtaking all her senses, her urgency matching his.

Lying in Efren's arms afterward, Anica tried without success to push aside her growing anxiety. She did not know which terrified her more—being discovered as a converso, or the voyage and uncertainties that awaited them. Her head grew heavy with thoughts of all that could go wrong, of the perils of weeks at sea, and of the danger of being caught. *Please, God,* she prayed as sleep finally found her, *keep us safe.*

CHAPTER 4

Fiesta Corpus Christi

Efren made a great show of escorting Anica—who held a sleeping Isabel in her arms—into Valencia Cathedral as it filled with worshippers attending the Holy Mass celebrating the blood and body of Christ. They took their seats in a pew near the front, where they were sure to be seen by the archbishop and the diocesan priests as they entered and took their places on the chancel.

Smoothing his white and gold brocade robe as he approached the alter, the archbishop scanned the faithful as they seated themselves, his gaze lingering on the Amselem family. Efren met his eyes and smiled. The cleric straightened the jeweled cross that rested his chest before nodding in Efren's direction.

Anica had no stomach for the dangerous cat-and-mouse game Efren was playing. A nerve began to pulsate in her neck, and fear rose in her throat tasting of bitter bile. Unable to concentrate on the archbishop's sermon, she stared, mesmerized as motes of dust danced a gentle ballet in the hued light streaming through the stained-glass windows above the altar. Sitting under the soaring vaulted arches of the Cathedral, with its vast baroque chancel and ornate frescoes, it struck Anica that she had never been inside a synagogue. Valencia's Jewish houses of worship were long ago made into churches, or stood in ruins in what remained of the city's old Jewish Quarters. *Were they,* she wondered, *this grand?*

Following the Mass, the archbishop and the priests led the procession of parishioners and large carts decorated in biblical themes past the *Miguelete* bell tower through the streets surrounding the Cathedral. Onlookers lined the procession's path, many jubilantly joining in the moving celebration as it passed. Mingling with the boisterous crowd, Efren and Anica edged their way to the group's outer fringe and ducked into the first side street they came to just as Isabel woke and began to cry.

"Good," said Efren, putting his arm around Anica, and guiding her down a narrow alley towards their villa. "If anyone notices us walking away from the procession, it will look like we are hurrying home to feed a hungry baby."

Isabel's wails grew louder. "At this moment, that is exactly what we are doing," sighed Anica.

Entering the villa, they were stunned to find Mariana waiting for them in the kitchen, a bulging cloth satchel at her feet.

"Mariana! What…what are you doing here?" sputtered Anica, as Isabel's hand found her mouth, and she began to suck noisily.

"My cousin is a priest. I overheard him talking about a family that was suspected of being *conversos*. He said he didn't know their name, but the husband had a young wife and was in the shipping business. I realized immediately he was talking about you, and it wasn't hard to guess what you were up to." She hesitated, fear shadowing her face. "I will be under suspicion once it is discovered you are gone. They will come for me, and I'm not strong enough to stand up to their methods of questioning. I have nothing to keep me here. My husband is dead, and I have no children. Take me with you, *mi cariña*. You are my family."

Anica exchanged glances with Efren, her eyes imploring his.

Efren took a deep breath and slowly released it. Everything Mariana said was true. Leaving her behind put her in grave danger. "Mariana, I must know if you understand that our journey is not without peril, and that we are leaving Valencia forever."

The tearful servant looked directly at Efren. "I'm in more danger if I stay, and I have nothing to stay for."

Efren nodded. "Then it is settled. You will leave with us."

Mariana's body sagged in relief. "Thank you *Señor* Amselem. I promise you won't be sorry. I will take good care of you and your family."

～✧～

"Hurry, Anica, we must leave, or we will miss the tide," called Efren, just as Anica entered the sitting room carrying a cloth shopping bag.

"I'm ready to go," she said, handing the bag to Mariana. Taking Isabel from her cradle, Anica paused for one last look, her gaze drifting from the intricately carved chest that had been a wedding gift from her father, to the porcelain figurines on the mantle, and Efren's favorite silk-covered arm-chair. "Everything we own will be confiscated, won't it?"

Efren grew impatient. "Delaying will not make it any easier to leave. Nor will dwelling on what is left behind. Let them have it all. It's time to go."

The streets were still filled with people following the Holy procession when they stepped out of the villa. As planned, they blended in with the crowd, Efren walking a few steps behind Anica and Mariana, so he could spot any trouble before it happened.

Careful not to draw attention to the bundles she was carrying, Mariana slowly shifted Anica's bag to her other hand.

"I'm sorry it's so heavy," said Anica.

"I am guessing the extra weight is your mother's brass candlesticks."

Anica's head whipped around in Mariana's direction, her face drained of color. "How long have you known?"

"You don't remember, do you? I am the one who gave you the candle-sticks and your mother's prayer book. When Debora became sick, she told me they were hidden in a panel in the chest in her bedchamber. She said the book and candlesticks had been in her family for generations. She made me promise that I would give them to you if she died. She said you would know what to do with them. I knew what they were for, but I loved your mother just as I love you, and I swore I would never tell anyone. And I won't."

CHAPTER 5

Anica walked in silence, stunned by Mariana's revelations. Terrified of being discovered before they reached the ship, she tightened her hold on Isabel, and tried to tamp down her rising panic. *So many things could still go wrong*, she thought, her mind ticking off the possibilities.

As if he sensed her fear, Efren was suddenly beside her. "We are almost there," he said, his voice low and reassuring. "I just have to stop at my office to retrieve some papers. The Águila should be ready and positioned to leave the harbor."

The briny smell of the sea and the cawing gulls wheeling above them signaled their approach to the wharf. As they drew closer to the harbor, the wind stirred the air, and it grew cooler. Anica shivered and wrapped Isabel's blanket more tightly around her, grateful that the infant slept as they made their way to the wharf.

"Ah, there it is," said Efren, lifting his hand, so that a gust ruffled the cuff of his coat sleeve. "I was afraid there wouldn't be enough wind to set sail."

Anica could feel the tension leave her body as the wharf appeared before them. The sight of the quay—ship masts jutting into the horizon, waves lapping against the seawall, men loading and off-loading vessels in spite of the holiday—gave her hope they would be safe. Her relief at getting this far pushed aside all regrets of what was being left behind. Viewing Valencia in the distance from the deck of the Águila was all she longed for.

The pulsating rhythm of the wharf engulfed them as Efren led the way to the old wooden building that housed his business. Guiding Anica and Mariana past officials inspecting cargo, and stevedores calling to each other while loading goods and supplies, Efren's eyes swept the area looking for any deviation from the normal activities of the docks. Only when he was convinced that nothing and no one appeared suspicious, did he escort Anica and Mariana to the two-story structure that served as his warehouse and office.

Efren unlocked the door, and stood aside to let Anica and Mariana pass through the doorway. "I just need to take a few things from the safe and we can..."

The words froze in his throat at the sound of Anica's screams. Rough hands grabbed his coat and pulled him into the building, sending him sprawling onto the dirt floor. Before he could rise, a booted foot stomped down on his chest, knocking the air from his lungs, and pinning him to the ground. Rodrigo glared down at him, knife in hand, his eyes cold, his thin lips stretched across his ferret-like face in a smug smile.

"I knew you were up to something. You think I am just some stupid little clerk, but you didn't fool me. Patting me on the shoulder and thanking me for telling you that you were under suspicion, as if I were a child," he said in a mocking tone. "If you want to save your skin and keep your wife and that screaming baby safe, you might want to consider making me an offer. A very good offer," he snarled, seizing Efren by the throat and yanking him to his feet.

Bent over, his hands on his knees, Efren began to cough, each choppy breath sparking bursts of pain in his chest. Focusing on the sound of Isabel's wails, he tried to locate Anica in the dimly lit room.

A flutter in the shadows told him Mariana was lurking nearby, unnoticed by Rodrigo. Slowly straightening up, Efren held out his hands to show he was unarmed. "I think we can find a way to resolve this situation," he said, inching towards Rodrigo.

"Don't come any closer," warned Rodrigo, flicking the air with his knife. We can discuss this 'situation' from right where you are. In fact, I am going to make it really easy for you. One thousand silver reales is all it will take to buy my silence."

Efren stared at the knife pointed at him and shrugged. "Unfortunately, I do not have that much money at my disposal."

"Unfortunate for you," said Rodrigo. Wetting his lips with his tongue, he took a step in Anica's direction.

Fury overtaking caution, Efren drove his shoulder into Rodrigo's stomach, slamming him into a wall, knocking the knife from his hand. "Don't even look at my wife," he growled, smashing his fist into Rodrigo's face.

Blood gushing from his broken nose, Rodrigo's rage roared back. With a renewed strength that caught Efren off guard, Rodrigo punched him in his bruised chest, sending him barreling backwards.

Efren landed on his back with an agonizing thud. Gasping for breath, he struggled against the pain in his chest that had turned to fire. He could hear Anica's screams, and he knew without looking that Rodrigo was coming toward him with the knife. Crawling to his knees, he kept his head low. Waiting.

Grinning, Rodrigo, slowly walked towards Efren. "You will pay me what I want, or you will pay with your life. And the life of your baby and wife after I have my fun." He bent low, and grabbing Efren by the hair, hissed, "Which will it be?"

"Neither," said Efren, looking past Rodrigo as Mariana emerged from the shadows. Before the clerk could react, pain exploded in his brain. Slumping forward, he landed on top of Efren.

Hands shoved Rodrigo from Efren's body. Mariana stood over him, gasping for breath, a brass candlestick in her hands.

Efren rose slowly. With one arm around Anica and Isabel, Efren drew Mariana to him. "We owe you our lives."

Mariana helped Efren roll Rodrigo to his side. Grateful for the man's groans, she pressed her hand to her heart, and gave a silent prayer of thanks. "I was afraid I'd killed him," she said in a shaky voice.

"He'll live, but I don't want to make it too easy for him to escape and alert the authorities." Ignoring the burning pain in his chest, Efren tied the clerk's hands and feet, and propped him in a sitting position against a wall. "I take no pleasure in doing this. I just hope that by the time he is found, we are far out to sea."

CHAPTER 6

The short walk to the waiting ship seemed an eternity. Pain radiated through Efren's chest with each breath he took. Pale and sweaty, his breathing growing more ragged, he refused Anica's pleas to stop and rest.

"There is no time. We have to be ready to sail when high tide ends, and the water begins to flow back into the sea. We need the current to help carry the ship out of the harbor."

Anica handed Isabel to Mariana, and put her arm around Efren's waist. Moaning in pain, he leaned on her as they picked up their pace.

The sight of the *Águila* waiting in the harbor—the open wings of its namesake eagle figurehead spread across the prow—filled Anica with hope. *Just a few more steps, just a few more minutes, and they would be safe.*

Anxious to sail with the tide, Captain Amadis Lopez, lean and tan, his face leathery from years at sea, paced back and forth on the deck of the *Águila*. Stopping to scan the dock, he spotted Efren and Anica slowly making their way through the crowded wharf to the ship. Hastening down the ship's ramp to greet them, he stared slack-jawed as Efren, pale and sweaty, broke free from Anica's grasp and stumbled.

"*Señor* Amselem," cried Lopez, rushing forward to catch him before he fell. "We must get you on board so you can lie down," he said, draping Efren's arm around his shoulder, and carefully guiding him towards the ramp.

"Just get us on the ship," said Efren, his voice raspy, his body shaking in pain. "Please make sure my wife and baby and Mariana are safe."

"I will do everything in my power to ensure their safety," said Lopez, turning to be certain Anica and Isabel, and his unexpected third passenger were close by.

By the time they reached one of the small staterooms used by occasional passengers, Efren felt like bolts of lightning were exploding in his chest. "You are right," he said to the anxious captain, "I do need to lie down." Coated in sweat, his legs weak, Efren lowered himself onto a berth with a grunt.

Sitting at his bedside, Anica watched Efren sleep, grateful for the laudanum the captain had provided to ease his pain. Haunted by irrational fears, she held his hand, afraid that if she let it go, he wouldn't wake up.

Her own sleep had been troubled—plagued by dreams of the previous day's terror so real that when Isabel's hungry cries pierced the air, Anica thought she was back in the warehouse. Now, listening to Efren's uneven breathing, she was overwhelmed by remorse. It was her fault that they were casting aside everything they held dear. She had endangered their lives, Mariana's, and possibly the lives of the loved ones they left behind.

"I am so sorry. Please, my love, forgive me," she said softly, touching Efren's face.

Efren's eyes fluttered open, and he squeezed her hand. "Anica?"

"Efren, thank God."

Trying to sit up, Efren gasped at the ripping pain in his chest, and fell back against his pillow. "Are we on the ship? Where is Isabel?"

"Isabel is fine. She is with Mariana in the stateroom next to ours. We sailed yesterday, almost as soon as we got on board."

Efren closed his eyes in relief. "I was so afraid we wouldn't get to the ship on time. I should have followed my instincts about Rodrigo. I was a fool to believe he wouldn't betray us."

Anica shook her head. "I am the one to blame. It was my carelessness that brought us here."

Rising up on his elbow to face her, Efren began to cough. Searing pain creased his face as he struggled to get more air into his lungs. When the spasms that rattled in his chest finally subsided, he was panting and covered in sweat.

Anica held a glass of water to Efren's cracked lips. Drinking in great gulps, he ignored the rivulets running down his chin.

"You need to rest. I am going to find the cook, and bring you something to eat. I'll be right back."

Efren grabbed her hand as she stood to leave. "We must put what happened in the warehouse behind us. Mariana must do the same. We'll start over in Charleston. It will be a new life for all of us, and I promise it will be a good one."

Mariana sat in her stateroom. With Isabel asleep in her arms, she took in the small quarters that would be her home at sea. Sparsely furnished, it held only a narrow berth, a single chair, and a small table that held a pitcher and a basin, providing little room to move about. To her surprise, she felt strangely comforted by the cabin's cocoon-like confines. *It holds no shadows; no places where unknown dangers could lurk*, she thought, the horror of the warehouse circling her brain in a never-ending ribbon of terrifying images. She did not remember how the candlestick got in her hand. Nor did she remember striking Rodrigo as he advanced on Efren. She could only remember the cold fear that ran through her when she thought she had killed a man, and it terrified her still.

"Not a good start to our journey," she whispered to the sleeping infant.

It was early morning days later when they sailed out of the Mediterranean Sea into the Strait of Gibraltar, portal to the Atlantic Ocean. Mid-May easterly winds, choppy waves, and the battling currents of the two bodies of water flowing into the Strait's funnel-like passageway churned the dark sea, pitching the ship as if it was riding the tail of an angry dragon.

In their stateroom, Efren clung to the side of the berth, gritting his teeth in pain with each roll of the ship. Frantic to reach Isabel, Anica moved unsteadily to her cradle, nearly falling as the ship dipped and then came up again. Clutching her screaming daughter, she steadied herself against the wall.

Mariana, who had joined them as soon as the turbulence began, reached out from where she was sitting and helped Anica ease into a chair. Her eyes wide, her stomach protesting every heave of the ship, she held tightly to Anica's hand, praying silently for an end to the torment.

When the turbulence finally eased, and the sea's tentacles released their fierce grip on the ship, Mariana, whispered "thank you." Sensing Efren's and Anica's stares, she pointed heavenward and smiled.

Entrance to the Atlantic Ocean accomplished, the ship's billowing sails filled with a steady wind, carrying them towards Charleston. The calm days at sea seemed to agree with Efren; by the second week of their voyage, he was eager to leave the stateroom for the fresh air of the deck.

"Don't fuss over me as if I were a child," complained Efren, as Anica placed a scarf around his neck, and helped him into his coat. As did all his clothes, it hung loosely on his much thinner frame.

"I just want to make sure you are warm enough. Are you certain you are up to this? You still seem to tire easily."

"I am fine. I just need to get out of this cabin or I will go mad."

Emerging from the lower deck, and blinking furiously in the glare of the mid-day sun glinting off the water, Efren cupped his hands over his brow, and waited for his eyes to become accustomed to the bright light. Despite the dull ache in his chest, he took a deep breath, and savored the crisp sea air, soft on his bruised lungs. He tilted his face to the sun, relishing its warmth. Laughing at a squawking sea bird perched on a yardarm high above the ship, he reveled in the siren song of the canvas sails whipping in the wind. The vast sea beckoned the ship like a seductive mistress, and Efren was filled with an undeniable surge of hope. Looping his arm through Anica's, he stepped onto the deck, certain at last that their voyage was taking them to a life filled with promise.

CHAPTER 7

Their daily routine at the mercy of the weather and the sea, they dreaded the days when storms churned the black sky with thunder and lightning, and cold pellets of torrential rain drummed a deafening rhythm on the deck. Forced to spend long hours in their cabins, they huddled together as the wind roared, and the waves broke over the ship, rocking it as if it were a child's toy.

It was the clear, calm days that allowed them the precious time topside they craved. Welcoming any chance to escape from the dampness and unpleasant odors of the lower decks, Anica and Mariana would bundle Isabel in blankets and spend as much of the day as they could on the main deck.

For Efren, time spent topside was a cherished gift. Eager to regain his strength after so many days in bed, he would stride around the main deck, taking in great gulps of sea air to expand his weakened lungs. Basking in the sun as it burnished his skin and replaced his sickly pallor with a golden tan, he could feel the pain in his chest slowly subsiding. His energy returning, he felt like a man reborn.

In the fourth week of the voyage, the fickle wind deserted the *Águila*, leaving its square sails draped limply on their masts like wilted petals. With the limitless, tranquil sea stretching before it, the ship drifted without purpose on the becalmed water.

"I cannot decide which is worse, the storms or this infernal quiet," said Efren, sitting in Captain Lopez's cabin. Their meal over, and the evening's

English lessons complete, Anica and Mariana excused themselves to put Isabel to bed, and the two men sat sipping Madeira.

The captain rose and refilled their glasses. "I did not want to say anything in front of Anica and Mariana, but this is not good. We have been a week without wind, and I am concerned that we will run out of food before we reach Charleston. If this goes on for much longer, I will have to cut the crew's rations. Ours too. We still have a few chickens left, and there are fish to catch when we can, but we are running low on the limes, biscuits, and salted meat that make up most of the crew's diet. I checked the water left in the remaining kegs this morning, and a few are fouled with algae. I am also afraid some of the cargo is ruined too. I saw rat droppings near the containers that hold the spices."

Efren stared into his wine glass, swirling the amber liquid before he took a sip. "I feel quite foolish. I was only concerned about getting to Charleston on time. I had no idea it could be this bad."

Lopez stood at the cabin windows looking out at the still ocean. "If all my years at sea have taught me anything, it is that the sea is as mercurial as a small child—sometimes pleasant, sometimes difficult. The wind will come, we just have to hope it comes soon."

Two days later, without warning, they woke to thunder and clouds so dark, they turned morning into night. Brilliant flashes of forked lightning split the sky, and cascades of blue-gray waves swept over the oaken boards of the deck. Howling like a wounded beast, the wind battered the pitching ship, flinging it to the top of the huge cresting waves, only to send it crashing back into the roiling sea. The crew scrambled to the deck, racing to their assigned tasks. Slipping on the slick, rain-soaked boards, they tied tethered ropes around their waists to keep from being thrown overboard. Groups of seamen secured the hatches to keep the water from flowing into the lower decks, while others climbed up the yardarms at the rear of the ship, straining to lower and tie down the billowing sails to prevent the masts from snapping. Fighting the stinging spray and biting wind, crewmen clambered up the eighty-foot main mast to lower the violently flapping topsails. On the main deck, the helmsman fought to remain standing in the onslaught of murky water crashing over the side of the ship.

Below, Efren, Anica, and Mariana listened in terror to the groaning boards of the bucking ship. Tempest-driven waves pounded its hull like gigantic fists, lifting it to mountain heights and dashing it back into the angry sea. Their stomachs churning, they clung to anything that would keep them from being tossed around the cabin, and watched in horror as chairs overturned, and a table went sliding across the stateroom floor.

Wild-eyed, Anica sat in her berth with Isabel cradled in her arms. Humming a lullaby to soothe the terrified child, her own body trembled, the metallic taste of fear filling her mouth. At any moment her lurching stomach threatened to empty its contents.

"This is worse than any storm we have endured," cried Mariana. "It feels like the ship is coming apart." Her face pale, she took deep breaths to quell her warring stomach. Fingering her rosary, she prayed loudly to make sure God could hear her over the bedlam of the storm.

"Amadis Lopez and his crew are seasoned seamen," said Efren, as the sliding table slammed into the stateroom wall, splintering on impact. "They will see us through this storm safely." His stomach lurched in violent spasms, and he could feel the acid burning the back of his throat. Retching into a basin, he silently swore he would never step foot on a sailing ship again.

The wind and seething sea raged into the next day. Working in shifts throughout the night, the exhausted and battered crew fought mightily against the savage squalls and driving rain that pelted their bodies. In their staterooms below, Anica—with Isabel in her arms—Efren, and Mariana lashed themselves into their berths.

On the morning of the third day of the storm, the constant drumbeat of the rain gradually turned to a gentle tapping on the deck. The remorseless, banshee-like wailing of the wind subsided, and slivers of sunshine poked through cracks in the drifting blanket of steel-gray clouds. As the angry ocean slowly gave way to calmer seas, the ship's mainsail was unfurled, embracing the wind in its canvas like a long-lost lover.

CHAPTER 8

By early afternoon, the ocean had settled enough for Captain Lopez to attend to his injured crew. Grateful no one had been swept overboard and lost to the sea, he moved around the main deck, dispensing laudanum for pain. With Anica and Mariana's help, he tended to the crew's bruises and sprains, cuts to the head, and slashed arms and legs, all sustained from the broken lines and loose pulleys whipping around in the wind. His men were battered and in desperate need of sleep, but Lopez knew it was a miracle it had not been worse.

The ship and its cargo did not fare as well. Despite the best efforts of the crew, the rear sails were ripped, riggings were torn, and the small jolly boat used to ferry passengers and cargo to and from the ship had been swept out to sea. Unable to withstand the fury of the ocean, broken hatches allowed sea water to flood the cargo hold, ruining containers of Efren's silk, and contaminating the barrels of spices.

Surveying the damage on the main deck with the captain, Efren shook his head, and exhaled a harsh breath. "Is it as bad as it looks?"

"We were fortunate the masts did not break. We can repair the sails and riggings, but it will take a few days, and the crew needs some time to rest." Lopez dropped his gaze. "I am afraid that much of your cargo is lost."

"We'll be fine," said Anica, trying to soothe Efren's anxiety. "Some of the containers are undamaged. We can sell whatever is salvageable."

"You don't understand. I was going to use the profits from selling the cargo to start my business in Charleston. I went down into the hold to see the damage for myself. What is salvageable may not even be enough to allow the captain and crew to sail back to Valencia. Because we left in secret, I did not insure the shipment. We will have nothing," said Efren, burying his face in his hands.

"We have Isabel and each other, said Anica, her voice barely audible. "Have you forgotten why we left Valencia? Whatever Charleston holds for us, it will not be the Inquisition and threats of torture and death."

Efren made a strangled sound low in his throat and reached for her, holding her tight in his arms. "I had so many plans for us. A new start in a new country. Now, I will have to go to my uncle and ask for his help. I am no longer sure of what awaits us."

Anica knew there would be no balm to heal his wounded pride. Accustomed to being in control, he was not a man who sought help easily. "We have come too far to doubt our future."

Efren looked away. "My Uncle Philip is twelve years older than my father, and he was doted on by my grandparents. When he was in his late twenties, he had a terrible argument with my grandfather over the time he was spending gambling in the taverns. He stomped out of the house that night and never came back. My father searched every tavern and brothel and could not find him. He did learn that Philip had won a lot of money at the gambling tables. Seven months later, my father got a letter from his brother that said he was in Charleston, had gotten married, and had invested in a rice plantation." Rubbing his temples, Efren searched for the right words to continue.

"I have only vague memories of him. I remember him as rather haughty, always concerned about how he looked, and who he was seen with. He was so unlike my father, yet they were close. My father was devastated when he left. When I wrote my uncle that we were coming to Charleston, I shared my plans to start my own shipping business, and assured him that we would be able to support ourselves. Now, I can only hope that he will extend his love for my father to us."

A knocking sound startled them. Anica opened the door to find Mariana,

Isabel in her arms. Sucking madly on her fingers, the baby's chubby cheeks were tear-stained and red.

"She is up from her nap and very hungry," said Mariana, handing the whimpering baby to Anica.

The sight of his daughter in Anica's arms had an immediate calming effect on Efren. Kissing Isabel's wet cheeks, he dismissed his regrets for all he'd lost, grateful instead for all he had.

CHAPTER 9

As if offering penance for the ferocity of the storm, the ocean remained serene for the rest of the voyage, with only occasional periods of rain to remind them of the weather's sovereignty over their lives. A steady wind billowed the sails, and the rich smell of the sea filled the air with the promise of a safe arrival in Charleston.

"If the weather holds, we should reach port in ten days' time," said Captain Lopez, signaling to the ship's steward to clear the table of their empty plates. "We have been fortunate that the ocean has remained calm enough for us to get all the necessary repairs done for a safe trip into port."

"Captain, as you know, most of our cargo was damaged in the storm. It was my plan to use some of the money I received from the sale of the silk and spices to fund your return voyage." Efren looked away for a moment. "I am afraid those plans may have to change. My uncle owns a rice plantation outside of Charleston. If you would be able to give me a few days to contact him, and get my affairs in order when we arrive, I will find a way to provide for you and the crew to return to Valencia."

The captain wiped his lips with a napkin, and met Efren's gaze. "*Señor* Amselem, you have always been good to me and to the men. Of course, we will wait."

Efren closed his eyes, and felt the tension leave his body. "Thank you." He paused, and cleared his throat to keep the emotion from his voice. "Thank you for your loyalty. I promise I will make sure you and the crew will have all the provisions you need before you embark."

Lopez smiled, and offered his hand. "I am always at your service."

Efren sat watching Anica get Isabel ready for bed. The sleepy baby rubbed her eyes, stretched and yawned, and snuggled deeper into Anica's arms. "My little princess is getting so big. I am already feeling selfish about her. I would like to keep her like this forever."

"You can do many things, my husband, but holding back time is not one of them," said Anica, kissing Isabel and placing her in her cradle.

Efren sighed. "But I can wish, can't I?"

"Yes, you can," she smiled. "Do you feel better about things now that you have spoken to the captain?"

"Yes and no. I was dreading that conversation, but I am relieved to have it over. I also feel as if I have let everyone down. I am not as confident as I sounded when I said that I would be able to finance their return trip. I am not even sure I will be able to put a roof over our heads and food on the table," he said, his eyes pools of despair.

Anica took his hand in hers, lacing her fingers through his. "I am not so foolish as to think that we will get through this easily, but I cannot believe God protected us that day in the warehouse, or that He brought us through the storms only to leave us hungry and without a home in Charleston. I know you will prosper in our new land."

CHAPTER 10

Charleston, South Carolina, July 1785

As Captain Lopez predicted, the fair weather and favorable winds that blessed their remaining days at sea hastened their arrival in Charleston. By the beginning of the seventh week of their journey, clumps of vegetation floating in the water heralded their approach to land.

Two days later, Charleston Harbor came into view. With a moderate breeze in its topmost sails, the *Águila* sailed past Sullivan's Island. Boarded by a pilot who would maneuver the ship through the dangerous sand bars at the mouth of the harbor, they entered the port on the incoming tide.

Efren and Anica stood at the ship's rail, eager for their first glimpse of Charleston. Trepidation mixed with excitement as they looked out on the harbor. The wharves were bustling with life; workmen loaded and unloaded ships, horse-drawn carts carrying goods to market crowded the area. Vendors cried out, hawking their wares. Seagulls and terns squawked and wheeled in lazy circles over ship masts, and warehouses dotted the docks. In the distance, they could see large houses lining the shore, and church spires rising into the sky like fingers reaching for heaven.

"Can you stand a few more days on the ship?" asked Efren, fidgeting with the lapels of his coat. "We'll have to remain on board until I contact my uncle, and I can make other arrangements for us."

Anica knew he was too ashamed to admit they did not have enough money for lodgings at an inn. "I do not mind at all. We can use the time to venture out into the city and get familiar with our new surroundings."

Efren clasped her hand and kissed it. "I will have Captain Lopez send a messenger to my uncle in Summerville. Hopefully, he'll come to us as soon as he knows we are here." His eyes searched the horizon as if he was seeking answers to all the unknowns that stretched before them. "Anica, I cannot lie. I am worried about the reception we will get from my uncle. He can be harsh. I was not concerned about that side of him when I thought we would manage on our own. But now that I come to him empty-handed, I'm not so sure of the kind of welcome we will receive."

On their first full day in port, hoping to distract Efren from the persistent anxiety that had settled over him like a shroud, Anica cajoled him into accompanying her, Mariana, and Isabel on their exploration of Charleston. Stepping onto land after nearly eight weeks at sea, however, proved to be a challenge. Feeling as if they were still on the rolling deck of the ship, the trio struggled to keep their balance. Their legs wobbly, they leaned into each other to steady themselves.

"We must look like a trio of drunks," said Efren, looking about to make sure their uneven steps weren't attracting attention. His gaze froze as he spied a coffle of slaves—their clothes in tatters and covered in filth. Their necks were encased in metal collars, their hands and legs shackled and blood-caked. The terrified slaves were prodded forward by two men, who laughed as they poked them with metal-tipped poles, urging them to walk faster. At the end of the line, a young girl of no more than thirteen or fourteen stumbled, nearly pulling down the muscular man in front of her. Quickly righting herself, she looked up and locked eyes with Efren. Tears leaving streaks on her dirt-covered face, she called out to him, her words lost in the clamor of the wharf.

His heart was pierced by the pleading look on the young slave's face. Feeling powerless to help, Efren put his arms around Anica and Mariana, and hurried them away from the wharf. They walked in silence; each trying to erase the vision of the human misery they had witnessed.

Efren spoke first, his voice rising in anger. "I was aware of the use of slaves in Charleston, but this! This abomination is no different than Spain." His face was florid, his breath coming in short bursts.

Alarmed by his uneven breathing, Anica placed her hand on Efren's arm. "I think we have seen enough for one day. I would like to return to the ship."

CHAPTER 11

The days passed slowly as they awaited word from Efren's uncle. By the evening of the fourth day, when rain kept them inside for hours, Efren was in a state of despair, convinced that his uncle had abandoned him. No longer able to contain his anxiety, he paced up and down their small cabin, the muscles of his lean face tight with worry.

"Anica, I do not know how we are going to manage. I have nothing to offer the few contacts I have in Charleston in return for their business. I don't know how much longer we can prevail on Captain Lopez and the crew to remain in port. I can see that onboard provisions are running low, and I am not sure how I will provide for more." Efren sat down hard on the berth, his head bent low. "I was so sure we would be able to make our way here."

Anica knelt, and taking his face in her hands, pressed her forehead to his. "Whether your uncle helps us or not, I know we will find our way here. You were a respected businessman in Valencia. You will be the same here. And do not forget what you saved us from. God only knows what would have happened to us if we had stayed."

"I do not share your confidence. My uncle is not going to help us."

After six days without a message, Efren gave up all hope. "We have lost everything," he said to Anica. "I have thought long and hard about this. I am going to sign the ship over to Captain Lopez. We will have to sell the few things we have of worth to buy provisions, so he and the crew can return home."

Anica's eyes widened in surprise. "Efren, if you do this, you will be fulfilling your own worst fear; we will truly have nothing."

"I don't know what else to do! I am responsible for their well-being. I will not be able to live with myself if I desert them. I will find any job I can to provide for us."

"I understand how you feel, but please, wait one more day," she implored. "Surely, one more day won't make a difference."

Efren stared at her in silence. He knew Anica was right, but he was honor-bound to provide for the men who had risked their lives to ensure their safe escape from the hands of the Inquisitors.

"Please, Efren. One more day."

Efren drew her to him. "I still cannot deny you anything. One more day."

After a sleepless night, Efren rose before dawn, and sought the quiet of the deck. An early morning fog hovered over the water, forming a blanket of white waiting to be warmed away by the sun. A light sea breeze stirred the air, creating small waves that lapped gently against the ship's hull. Nodding to the crewman standing watch, Efren leaned on the rail and looked out over the harbor, the glimmering lanterns of other ships moored along the wharves casting an eerie glow in the mist. Breathing in the familiar smells of the sea, he tried in vain to banish the doubts and fears bubbling up from the darkest places of his mind. Lost in his muddled thoughts, Efren did not hear Captain Lopez approach.

"*Señor* Amselem, you are up early. Are you feeling unwell?"

"I am fine," he answered in a hollow voice, still staring out at the sea. "I couldn't sleep, and I didn't want to disturb Anica and Isabel."

"I know how anxious you are to hear from your uncle. I hope you are not worried about arrangements for the crew. Most of the men are unmarried and have little reason to return to Valencia. None of them are complaining about the delay here. In fact, I think they are rather enjoying their free time on shore."

"What about you, Captain? Do you have a family waiting for you?"

Lopez shook his head. "I have been a seaman my whole life. Though some men do it successfully, it is hard to marry and have a family when you are away for so many months at a time. My parents died years ago, and my three brothers also travel the seas." He shrugged. "None of us married."

Efren turned to face his captain. "It must get lonely at times."

Lopez sighed. "It does. And I admit, after seeing the happiness your wife and Isabel bring you, I have had moments when I doubted my choice to remain unmarried." He paused and laughed. "Fortunately, it only lasts for a moment."

Efren, Anica, Mariana, and Isabel joined the captain in his quarters for their midday meal. Looking dolefully at the meager serving of cheese and biscuits, Efren knew that the lack of an ample table meant their supplies were almost gone.

"There is still no word from my uncle," he said, picking up and putting down a piece of cheese.

Anica and Mariana exchanged glances. Efren had been tense all morning, his temper flaring at the smallest provocation. Even Isabel, who was cranky and crying, did not escape his displeasure. Immediately ashamed that he'd raised his voice to her, Efren had stormed out of their cabin. Now, he looked drained of all energy.

"The day is not over yet," said Captain Lopez. "I have confidence that you will hear from your uncle."

Efren raked his fingers through his beard. "I have given up all pretense of hope. It appears he is disinclined to help me. If I do not get a message by the end of the day, we will need to talk. But for now, please excuse me. I am tired and would like to rest."

They watched him retreat from the captain's cabin, his shoulders hunched, his step slow.

Captain Lopez sat back in his chair. "Will he be all right if he does not get word from his uncle?"

Tears welling in her eyes, Anica shook her head.

Efren was still in their cabin when a coach drawn by two bay horses pulled up in front of the ship. Emerging from the leather-covered interior, the well-dressed passenger in a powdered wig shielded his eyes from the sun with his tricorne hat, and called out, "My name is Philip Amselem. I am looking for my nephew, Efren Amselem."

Captain Lopez looked at Anica and laughed. "I told you we would hear from him."

Her eyes misting, Anica hugged the startled captain and then Mariana. "I was beginning to believe my husband was right. Thank God he is here," she said, rushing to tell Efren.

Efren's knees nearly buckled in relief when he saw the captain talking to his uncle. In the twenty years that had passed, he could see that Philip had grown stout, his face fleshy. But even from afar, Efren recognized the man's imperious bearing, and he grew uneasy about his uncle's welcome.

CHAPTER 12

"I owe you an apology," said Philip, as they sat in the captain's quarters, sipping the good man's Madeira. "I was away from Bending Oaks, my Summerville plantation, attending to business in Darlington when your note arrived. I would have responded immediately otherwise."

Efren scrutinized his uncle. The powdered wig with its blue-ribboned queue and the fancy clothes of satin and velvet meant to convey wealth were incongruous to the heat of July, and he could see beads of sweat forming on Philip's brow.

Surprised by his uncle's preference to speak in barely accented English rather than his native Spanish, Efren put his newly learned use of the language to the test. "Thank you for coming all this way. It's good to see you after all these years."

"Of course, I would come to see you. And I am delighted to meet your lovely wife and beautiful daughter." He smiled, his hooded eyes lingering on Anica as he took a sip of wine. "You look well, while I have grown older and fatter," he said, patting the ample stomach straining against the buttons of his embroidered waistcoat, his plump legs stretching the stockings beneath his breeches. Distracted for a moment by a spot on his coat, he flicked the offending piece of dirt from his sleeve, providing a glimpse of the gold signet ring on his forefinger. When he returned his attention to Efren, his smile was gone. "We have much to discuss, but I do not wish to bore the ladies with talk of business. I would understand if they wished to excuse themselves."

Efren sat forward in his chair, caught off guard by his uncle's easy dismissal of Anica and Mariana. His dark eyes flashed in anger, and only Anica's calming hand on his knee kept him from directing his fury at the only person who could help them.

Nodding to Mariana, Anica rose. "It is time to put Isabel down for a nap. We will leave you to discuss your business. I am so glad we finally met," she said, her voice brittle despite her smile.

As soon as Anica and Mariana had departed, Philip's pretense of civility fell away. "Mariana. She is older of course, but I remember her when she was a servant in your father-in-law's house. I am surprised you would allow her to be a part of a family discussion."

Efren's face tightened, his fury simmering, teetering on the verge of boiling over. "Mariana saved my life when we escaped Valencia. She is not a servant. She is a member of our family, and will always be treated accordingly."

Philip glared at Efren, forming a steeple with his fingers and pressing them to his chin. "Ah yes, your escape." Furrows formed on his forehead. "I received a letter from your father informing me of the circumstances that led to your flight from Valencia. Your wife is an extraordinarily beautiful woman. I am just not sure she is worth leaving your family and sacrificing everything for a converso." His face contorted as if he had swallowed something rotten.

No longer able to contain his rage, Efren stood and pointed to the door. "If you are here to criticize my decision to come to Charleston, and to make me grovel for your patronage, I must ask you to leave. I love my wife, and I will not tolerate any attacks on her or her beliefs."

Philip eyed his nephew, and appeared to be contrite. "Please sit down. I did not mean to speak in such an unkind manner."

Efren swallowed, took a breath, and returned to his chair. Sitting with his arms crossed over his chest, he studied his uncle. Unconvinced of the sincerity of Philip's apology, he grew suspicious of his motive for offering one.

"I do not trust that man," said Mariana. "Your father had some business dealings with him years ago, and did not think highly of him. He always reminded me of a pufferfish, all blown up with self-importance."

Anica finished nursing Isabel and placed her in her cradle. "I share your distrust of him. His mouth says one thing, but his eyes say another. They are as soulless as a serpent's," she said with a shudder. "I do not think Efren holds his uncle in high regard either. Now that I have met him, I can't help wondering what price we will pay for his benevolence."

Entering their cabin an hour later, Efren sank down on the berth and stared straight ahead.

Anica's heart sank. Despite her misgivings about Philip, she knew that without his help, they would barely be able to survive in Charleston. "He's abandoning us, isn't he?"

A smile slowly crossed Efren's face. "I think my uncle Philip may need us as much as we need him."

"What do you mean? How could that be?"

"I'm not sure. When I told him that we had lost most of our shipment in the storm, he was angry. But once he'd had more of Lopez's Madeira and loosened up a bit, he was eager to extend his resources to us in exchange for use of the Águila and the crew to ship his rice to England. I have already spoken to the captain and the men, and they are willing to be a part of the agreement."

"Why does he need the Águila when ships come and go from the harbor every day?"

"I asked him the same thing, and he wouldn't answer at first. But after a few more glasses of wine, he admitted that he'd had a falling out with several of the shippers. He claimed they were shorting the number of delivered barrels, and then selling the rice they stole from him at a lower price."

Anica looked doubtful. "Do you believe him?"

Efren cocked his head to one side. "I have a feeling he is not telling me everything, but I don't see any other way to establish ourselves here. He has invited us to stay at his plantation, and the truth is we have no other place to go. I made it clear to him that Mariana will accompany us as a member of our family, and he agreed."

"And what else do you have to do to warrant his generosity?"

"I will handle the export of his rice, and look after things when he is away on business."

"That's not exactly helping you to establish your shipping business."

"I know. But it's a start to being financially sound again. He will send a coach and James, his coachman, for us in two days, so we have time to prepare to leave the ship, but there is something else you should know," he said, averting his gaze.

Anica stiffened. "What is so serious that you cannot look me in the eyes to tell me?"

Ashamed and miserable, Efren turned to her. "My uncle made it clear that you were not to practice any form of Judaism while living in his house. Please forgive me, but for the sake of all of us, I agreed to his condition."

Stunned, Anica stared at Efren, unable to speak. When she finally found her voice, it was taut with anger. "Then I do not want to live in his house. There is no Inquisition here. Why must I hide my faith?"

Efren closed his eyes and blew out a ragged breath. "Philip's wife, Mary, died three years ago from yellow fever. The doctor attending her was Jewish, and my uncle blames him for her death. He is irrational in his hatred of Jews. I know how much your Judaism means to you. I am not asking you to give up your faith. I am just asking you to wait a little longer to celebrate it openly. I don't see that we have any other choice but to accept his hospitality under his conditions. I promise I will do everything in my power to make sure we do not have to rely on him for a roof over our heads for long."

Anica's face remained stony. After their terrifying escape from Valencia, the grueling weeks at sea, and the tension of the past few days, she could not believe it had come to this. "What were you thinking when you consented to this arrangement?"

Efren jumped to his feet; his face flushed with anger. "I was thinking of you, Isabel, and Mariana! We cannot go back to Valencia, and we cannot succeed here without the help and contacts my uncle can provide. Anica, please, I have to know that you believe in what I am doing to ensure we have a future here."

Without a word, Anica removed her mother's brass candlesticks from the top of the dresser. Clutching them to her chest for a moment, she packed them away in her travel bag next to her mother's prayer book, and made her way to the cabin door.

Efren felt a rising panic, and his breath quickened. "Wait! Where are you going?"

"To get Isabel, and to tell Mariana that we will be leaving the ship the day after tomorrow."

CHAPTER 13

By late morning, their meager belongings were piled on top of the coach dispatched by Philip, ready for the twenty-two-mile journey to Summerville. Efren, Anica, and Mariana stood on the deck of the *Águila* one last time to say goodbye to Captain Lopez and the crew. Efren felt an unexpected surge of sadness as each member of the crew stepped forward to shake his hand, and say goodbye to Anica and Mariana. With great ceremony, the first mate presented Isabel with the small doll he'd made from canvas and stuffed with straw. Much to his embarrassment, he was rewarded with a hug from the delighted child.

Captain Lopez accompanied them to the coach. Shaking hands with Efren, he pulled him into a tight embrace, slapping him on the back. "We will work things out, my friend, do not worry. Four of the men who have families to go back to in Valencia have signed on with other ships, but the rest are staying on. They will work hard for you. You are a good man, and they know you will take care of them. I promise we will not let you down."

James flicked the reins, and the coach lurched forward. Turning onto East Bay Street, they were soon rumbling through Charleston's busy streets, the horses' hooves clattering loudly over the cobblestones. Ignoring the teeth-rattling bumps and constant jostling of the coach as they made their way out of the city, they looked out on the street scenes passing by, observing elegantly dressed Charlestonians walking arm in arm. Anica gazed wistfully at the vibrant markets, and the three-story homes with rooms that opened onto broad piazzas to welcome the cooling breezes of the sea.

"Perhaps we misjudged Charleston after our first attempt to see the city," she said. "It seems quite lovely."

"I'm sure it is for some, but not for others," said Efren pointing in the direction of a throng of people gathered before a raised platform. Standing on a block, a frightened Negro woman clutching an infant in her arms, a crying girl of three or four clinging to her dress, stared blankly at the crowd as the auctioneer called for bids.

Mariana gasped, and Anica instinctively tightened her hold on Isabel. Efren looked away, unable to meet Anica's eyes. Although his father opposed Spain's slave trade, he was certain his uncle depended on the labor of slaves to grow his rice.

The heat of the day was upon them when they left the Charleston city limits and made their way toward Philip's plantation. Away from the refreshing breezes of the harbor, the travelers welcomed the cooler temperatures provided by the shade of the massive pine and live oak trees lining the rutted dirt road that followed the Ashley River to Summerville. Lulled by the swaying coach, Isabel's eyelids fluttered, and she quickly fell asleep, her new doll clutched in her tiny hands. Mariana soon followed, her mouth slack, her face gentle in slumber.

"I wish I could just fall asleep so easily," said Anica, listening to Mariana's soft breathing.

"I wish there were something I could do to ease your fears."

Anica stared out at the verdant landscape and strained to hold back her tears. "I don't know why, but I cannot rid myself of the feeling that something bad is going to happen. I cannot tell you what it is, but I have this deep sense of impending calamity. Promise me you will be cautious in your dealings with Philip. I don't trust his motives."

Efren nodded, unwilling to admit he too harbored a deep distrust of his uncle.

Hours after leaving Charleston, James brought the coach to a halt in front of the brick tavern sited alongside the Ashley River Ferry landing. Two coaches and a wagon were already in line waiting to be ferried across the river to its north bank.

Eager to stretch their legs and escape the rising heat in the coach, Efren, Anica, and Mariana stepped out into the fresh air, grateful for the extra time the wait to board the ferry afforded them. While James tended to the horses and positioned the coach in the boarding line, Anica unpacked the basket of cheese and biscuits the ship's cook prepared for them. Efren returned from the tavern with mugs of cider, and settling Isabel on the blanket Mariana found stored in the coach, they sat in the shade of a copse of trees overlooking the river.

Mariana inhaled deeply. "This is nice. It is so good not to be bouncing."

Efren grinned. "We certainly did plenty of bouncing. Once we cross the river we shouldn't have to travel too much longer. At least I hope not. We only have a couple of hours of daylight left." He rose and brushed off the back of his tan breeches. "I'll ask James. I want to see if he needs anything."

Efren found James sitting on a bench near the coach, studying the swirl of gray smoke rising from his clay pipe. Seeing Efren approach, he stood and removed his hat. His scalp, glistening with sweat, peeked through sparse strands of dark hair. "Mister Amselem, anythin' I can do for you?"

"Actually, I was coming by to see if you needed anything before we got on the ferry."

"No sir. I fine. It shouldn't take much longer. Look like only a coach and a wagon ahead of us now. Once we cross the river, it won't be too long 'fore we get to your uncle's plantation."

"Well, then we have time to sit for a bit," said Efren, lowering himself to the bench, and indicating to James that he should sit too.

Taking the pipe from his mouth, James knocked it against the bench to empty its ashes, slipped it in his coat pocket, and joined Efren. Sitting forward, his elbows on his knees, he nervously fingered the piece of round copper that hung from his neck.

"It my freedman's badge," said James, aware that Efren was staring at it. He held it up for Efren to look at it more closely.

"My master, Mister Brick Hudson, he used to hire me out to do handiwork for others on plantations and in town. Most of the time I did carpentry.

The badge I had to wear then had a number and 'Charleston' on it, but where this here one say 'Free,' that there one be sayin' 'Servant.' Mister Brick, he let me keep some of what he got paid for my work. Sometimes he even let me keep all the money. That how I saved enough to buy my freedom. Took me nine years, but now this here badge prove that I be a free man. I be free for seven years now."

James paused, tucking the badge back into his shirt. "I don't live on the plantation no more, but my wife Mandy and our three children do 'cuz they still slaves. Mister Brick tole me he tole his son, Mister Tobias, to free them when he died. But when Mister Brick go to the Lord, Mister Tobias, he say that weren't true, and 'cuz there weren't nothin' in writin', my family still slaves."

Efren sat in silence, trying to absorb all that James had told him. "How old are your children?"

James spoke in a near whisper. "My oldest, Joshua, he twelve years old. Dinah, she eight, and my baby Gideon, he one year old. They live with their mother over to Mister Tobias' plantation down in Goose Creek. I tries to see them whenever I can, but I sure do miss my wife and my babies' sweet faces. I work for your uncle and anyone who hire me doing all kinds of jobs, and I savin' up to buy them their freedom."

Efren looked over at Anica and Mariana playing with Isabel, and a piece of his soul withered. *How long,* he wondered, *would it take James to save enough to purchase the freedom of his wife and children?*

When it was their turn to board the ferry, James steered the coach onto the broad, flat-bottom boat. On the opposite bank, the ferryman managed ropes as thick as a man's arm, and pulled the ferry across the wide expanse of water.

Sitting in the carriage, they watched the river come to life. Turtles sunned themselves on floating branches. An alligator slipped silently into the river, barely rippling the water as it swam away. Long-legged herons and egrets waded along the shore.

As James predicted, it was a short ride from the ferry landing to Bending Oaks. The approach to the plantation left no doubt about the inspiration for the plantation's name: rows of magnificent live oak trees, silvery moss hanging from their thick branches, formed a canopy so dense, only thin slices of pale sunlight filtered through their boughs.

Sensing they were near the end of their journey, the horses charged forward. The coach emerged from the bower of trees onto a sun-lit carriageway framed on either side by a rolling lawn of emerald green grass. Passing gardens rich in the colors of roses, azaleas, hibiscus, and hydrangea surrounded by clusters of palmetto trees, the coach came to a halt in front of a white, two-story mansion, its veranda fronted by four Doric columns.

"My uncle seems to have done quite well for himself," said Efren, surveying the immense property before him. "No need to worry if there will be enough room for all of us."

Anica leaned forward and looked out the window. "Apparently not."

Mariana just stared. "*Dios mio*," she gasped, "how do you keep such a big house clean?"

PART II

CHAPTER 14

Bending Oaks, Summerville, South Carolina, July 1785

Alerted to their arrival, Philip descended the front steps leading to the veranda, followed by two older black men who scurried to take the bags James was unloading from the top of the coach.

"Welcome to Bending Oaks," said Philip, shaking Efren's hand, and nodding toward Anica and Mariana. "I trust you had a pleasant ride, and that James treated you well."

"He treated us very well. I hope you appreciate what a fine driver you have in him," Efren said in a voice loud enough for James to hear.

The big man turned slightly, the hint of a smile playing across his face.

Ignoring Efren's remarks, Philip barked at the two men carrying the bags, his face dark with anger. He removed his hat to wipe the sweat from his face, revealing a wigless scalp covered in brown spots, surrounded by a narrow fringe of gray hair. "Dammit! Henry! Silas! Move it along! It's hot as blazes out here. You are worthless the both of you. I should have sold you years ago."

The two men lowered their eyes as they hurried past Philip. A few steps away, one of them stumbled, juggling the bags to keep them from falling.

"Silas, if anything is damaged," screamed Efren's uncle, "I swear I will take it out on your damn hide!"

Startled, Isabel began to cry. Anica looked wide-eyed at Efren. His face mirrored her dismay, but his eyes cautioned her not to speak. Her hands shaking, she took Isabel from Mariana's arms.

Turning his attention back to his guests, Philip's voice dripped with charm. "It's hot, and you must be very tired. Let's go inside so you can cool off and rest."

Welcoming the cooler air of the high-ceilinged entrance hall, they were unprepared for the opulence before them. A round marble-top table with a bouquet of dozens of freshly cut roses sat beneath a large crystal chandelier, its faceted prisms catching the final rays of the sun streaming through an arched window. A sweeping curved staircase, its balusters gleaming white, wrapped upward to the second floor, the stair runner matching the Persian rug that extended the full length of the hall. Lining the walls, portraits of stern faces in stiff poses stared down on them, their eyes seeming to look right through them.

Standing at the foot of the staircase, a young girl of sixteen or seventeen waited, her body tense, her head lowered.

"This is Ruth. She will take you to your rooms and get you whatever you need. After she finishes her daily chores, she is at your disposal," said Philip.

Her fingers twisting her long braid, Ruth stared down at her feet, the pink tinge of a blush overspreading her golden-brown skin. When she looked up, her large hazel eyes—dull and flat—darted around the room and settled on Isabel. Smiling shyly at the baby, Ruth's smile broadened when Isabel smiled back.

Philip snapped his fingers to get Ruth's attention. "She will behave herself and do as she is told. Isn't that right, Ruth?"

"Yes, sir, Mister Philip," she said, lowering her eyes.

"I am sure Ruth will be a great help," said Efren. "Isabel has already taken to her."

"Yes, well, go on, Ruth. Take them upstairs." He turned to Efren. "I suggest you rest before supper. We eat at seven o'clock. It will give you an opportunity to meet Margaret, my stepdaughter, and her husband Charles. They went riding this afternoon and should return shortly."

The astonished expression on Efren's face told Anica he knew nothing about Philip's stepdaughter. *Too many surprises,* she thought, as Ruth led them up the curved stairway, its mahogany banister smooth and polished to a glossy shine.

Out of Philip's sight, Ruth stood straighter, and the light returned to her eyes, highlighting flecks of brown against a sea of blue-green. When they reached the top of the stairs, Ruth guided them to the right. "The family's rooms are on the other side. This room is yours," she told Efren and Anica, pointing to a room at the beginning of the hall. "Miss Mariana, your room is the next one down."

Peeking into the bedchamber, Anica was relieved to see that their bags, including the satchel holding her mother's candlesticks, had been brought up to the room. Her eyes widened when she saw a crib draped in mosquito netting.

"This is lovely, Ruth. I am especially grateful for the crib. I wasn't sure where Isabel would sleep."

Ruth's face brightened. "I heard there was going to be a baby here, and I found the crib in the attic. I scrubbed it good to make sure it was clean, and my mama made the cushion for her to sleep on."

"Thank you, Ruth, and please thank your mother for us," said Anica, at the very moment the baby stretched out her arms to Ruth to be held.

Unsure of what to do, Ruth beamed when Anica nodded and placed Isabel in her arms.

"Looks like Efren was right," said Anica watching the radiant expression on Ruth's face as the baby laid her head on her shoulder and contentedly sucked her thumb. "Isabel has definitely taken to you."

CHAPTER 15

With Mariana settled in her room, and Isabel fed and napping in her crib, Anica and Efren sat on the edge of the large canopied bed, their legs dangling over the high mahogany bedstead. Exhausted and wishing the long day was over, Anica ran her hands over the pale-yellow satin bedcover. "Supper is in an hour, and all I want to do is sleep."

Efren stifled a yawn. "I have no enthusiasm for sharing a meal with my uncle tonight. I didn't know Philip had a stepdaughter, but I never knew much about his wife either."

"There is so much we do not know about Philip." Anica stood and walked about the room, pausing in front of the marble fireplace. "I hadn't expected him to own slaves. I don't like the way he speaks to them. They all seem terrified of him, especially Ruth. I hope I am wrong, but I sense that such a beautiful young girl has reason to be afraid in this house."

Efren frowned. "I don't approve of how my uncle treats the slaves either, but for what I hope is a short time, we are his guests."

Anica's eyes flared in defiance. "And as long as we are his guests, I will treat Ruth and the other slaves with the same courtesy I would treat any other person. Now," she said, softening her tone, "we have to find something clean to wear and get ready for supper."

Leaving Isabel asleep and under Ruth's care, Anica, Efren, and Mariana stepped into the hallway and regarded each other with a laugh.

"I think we do not look so grand," said Mariana, as she brushed a bit of dirt from the front of her light rose dress, and with little success, attempted to straighten the row of small white bows that adorned its bodice.

Anica fidgeted with the ruffles at the neck of her pale blue frock, and thought of the beautiful gowns that had been ruined during the voyage. "This is the best dress I have," she said, turning around so Mariana could adjust the dark blue sash around her waist.

"Considering that most of our clothes were ruined in waterlogged crates, I think we look fine," said Efren, pulling at the embroidered waistcoat beneath his gray jacket so that a missing button was less noticeable. "Come, ladies," he said bowing and offering each an arm. "It's my honor to escort two beautiful women to supper."

Silas met them at the bottom of the stairs. "Good evenin'. Mister Philip waitin' for you in the parlor," he said, leading them to a brightly lit room off the entrance hall.

Philip did not rise to greet his guests until he was fully satisfied they had taken in the lavishness of the room: the detailed frieze work on the molding, the elaborately embellished arches over the floor-to-ceiling windows draped in satin curtains, and the oaken sideboard with a silver tea set shining under the candles of a globe chandelier. Only when Anica's eyes remained fixed on the grand pianoforte in the corner, did he stand and welcome them.

"Please, come in," he said, placing his glass of wine on the doily-covered table beside an oversized settee. "I hope you found your rooms to your liking."

"Yes, thank you. They are lovely. Ruth made sure everything was perfect for us," said Anica, meeting Philip's gaze.

A scowl flicked across Philip's face and quickly disappeared. "I am glad you find Ruth so efficient. She is the niece of my late wife's house slave, Salina. Ruth has been in the house since she was a child. My wife spoiled her; made sure she spoke properly. Mary was especially fond of Salina. She even taught her to read and write. A dangerous thing in a slave. I sold her right after Mary died. Salina's sister, Lindy—Ruth's mama—is the house cook. Best cook I ever had. I'm not sure who Ruth's daddy is," he said, his lips stretching into a sneer.

Mariana pressed her hand on Anica's back as a warning not to provoke Philip.

"Nevertheless, Ruth has been most helpful. She said she would sleep outside our door in case we needed anything. I told her that wouldn't be necessary," said Anica, her tone unapologetic.

Looking from his wife to his uncle, Efren cleared his throat and quickly steered the conversation away from Ruth. "I see your stepdaughter and her husband have not come downstairs yet. Are we early?"

Philip pursed his lips. "No. They are late as usual. Please, sit down," he said, gesturing towards a damask-covered settee. "I am afraid Margaret takes after her mother in that respect."

"You do have to admit that women have more to do to get ready," said Efren, trying to lighten the mood.

"That may be true for most, but in this case, I am not sure it is Margaret who spent too much time at her toilette."

"What is it you are not too sure of?" asked Margaret, sweeping into the parlor, her green satin gown making swishing noises as she walked. Her honey-colored hair piled in an intricate design of curls, she paused and waited for Charles to dutifully follow her into the room, her fingers playing over the pearl choker around her slender neck.

"I was just saying I wasn't certain when you and Charles would be downstairs."

"We are only the tiniest bit late," said Charles, his hand fluttering to the lace-trimmed cravat tied loosely around his throat. "We rode further than we intended to, and it took us a little longer to get back," he added, adjusting his velvet coat so it hugged his slim body.

"Of course, you did," responded Philip, his voice thick with sarcasm.

"Now Philip, be nice and introduce us to our guests," purred Margaret, openly assessing Efren.

CHAPTER 16

Philip led the way to the dining room. The table, covered with a white linen cloth, was set with Delft China in a blue pattern that complemented the blue and gray damask wallpaper. Twin silver candelabras placed near the center of the table added to the glow cast by the room's crystal chandelier. Under the food-laden table was a Persian rug in vibrant colors of burgundy and blue. Yet, for all the room's splendor, it was the portrait above the marble-mantled fireplace that held Anica rapt.

Looking down from the oval-framed painting was a young woman of exquisite beauty. Dressed in a pale gold gown, her body was turned at a slight angle. Blonde ringlets fell delicately around her cheeks and brushed her bare shoulders. Her small, Cupid's bow lips offered a faint smile that suggested sadness rather than joy.

Anica stood riveted, lost in the disquieting stare of the woman's hypnotic green eyes. "Who is she? She is beautiful."

"She is my mother," said Margaret. "It was painted the same year she married my father, Duncan Hargret, and came to live here. She was from Boston. Her parents were killed in a carriage accident when she was eighteen, and she came to Charleston to live with her mother's sister, my great aunt Josephine. She met my father at a ball held in her honor, and they married soon afterward. I am not quite sure she was entirely happy living here in the South, but she loved my father, and she made Bending Oaks her home. Unfortunately, my father was not a well man. He died of consumption when

I was five." Margaret glanced wistfully at the portrait, her hard features softening in a rare unguarded moment.

"I lost my mother when I was young," said Anica. "I know how difficult
it is to lose a parent."

"Yes, well these things happen," said Margaret, her thin lips tightening;
the icy gaze of her pale blue eyes signaling the end of the conversation.

With only the meager mid-day meal they had consumed at the ferry
crossing filling their stomachs, the trio of travelers looked appreciatively
at the bowls of green beans, rice, sweet potatoes, and mashed potatoes and
gravy already on the table. At Philip's signal, Silas and Henry hurried to the
kitchen house and returned with platters of carved ham.

"I hope you enjoy ham. It's one of our favorite dishes, aged and smoked
right here in our smokehouse," said Philip, holding Anica's gaze.

Anica felt the blood rise in her cheeks. "I am sure it is delicious. But my
stomach is upset from all the travel, and I think I will eat lightly this evening.
I am sure you understand."

Philip nodded to Silas and Henry to begin serving. "Boys," he said to
the two gray-haired men, "give Mrs. Amselem a slice of ham just in case she
changes her mind."

Mariana fidgeted in her chair, afraid of what might come next. Her eyes
implored Anica to remain calm. Intent on keeping Anica from saying something she would regret, Mariana flinched when Efren threw his napkin down
on the table, his face red with anger.

"Philip, stop this nonsense, now," he hissed.

Silas froze, his arm midair, a slice of ham dangling from the serving fork.

Philip raised his hands as if in surrender. "Nothing to get angry about. I
just wanted to be sure that your lovely wife has enough to eat." His nostrils
flared; sweat glistened on his forehead.

Margaret eyed her stepfather, enjoying Philip's obvious discomfort.

Charles laughed and beckoned Henry to add more ham to his plate.
"Really Philip, I would have thought you'd be happy Anica doesn't want a
slice of ham. It leaves more for you to eat." He reached over and patted
Philip's ballooning stomach.

Philip scowled and batted Charles's hand away. "Silas, what are you waiting for? Bring that ham over here. I am starving, dammit. Why is my plate empty?"

They ate in silence; the only sound the clinking of the silverware against their plates. Philip remained sullen. His mouth set in a pout, his eyes shrunken and glazed, he ordered Silas to keep his wine glass filled, and emptied it with alarming frequency.

Throughout the meal, Anica could feel Margaret's eyes studying her as if she were a rare specimen. Aware of how plain her dress appeared in comparison to Margaret's satin gown, but refusing to be intimidated by the haughty young woman's scrutiny, Anica sat straighter in her chair and returned her stare. "Margaret, what do you do to occupy your time here at Bending Oaks?"

Flustered by Anica's directness, Margaret blinked rapidly and looked down as if seeking an answer to Anica's question amid the bits of food on her plate.

"I...I run the household for my stepfather," she sputtered.

Philip began to laugh. "Is that what you think you do? What she means is when she is not riding off someplace with Charles, or spending days at our Charleston house, or indulging in endless hours of fittings for new clothes, she is entertaining her silly friends."

Margaret made a sniffing sound and ignored Philip. "I apologize for our display of bad manners, and I hope you don't think all our meals are this contentious." She wiped her lips with her napkin and instructed Silas and Henry to serve dessert. "Something sweet to sweeten the mood." She smiled at Philip, but her eyes blazed with hate.

"What a long and dreadful night," said Efren, slipping into bed next to Anica and pulling the mosquito netting around them. "I thought it would never end." He was quiet for a moment. "I can't apologize enough for what my uncle did. Serving ham was a despicable affront to you."

Anica stared up at the elegant canopy that topped the bed. "This arrangement is worse than I thought it would be. I am afraid it is more than the *Águila* and Captain Lopez's crew that Philip wants from us; I just don't know what. Your uncle has been dishonest with us."

"I'll admit he is mean-spirited, but what makes you think he is dishonest?"

"You said your uncle wrote your father that he had invested in a rice plantation. From what Margaret told us, the plantation was her mother's when she married Philip. I can't help wondering what else he is hiding from us."

"I may find out tomorrow. Philip wants me to spend the day with him so he can show me the grounds and the rice fields. Charles will be joining us, so I'm afraid you and Mariana will have to deal with Margaret on your own."

"Despite his drunken state, I do believe your uncle was telling the truth about Margaret's daily activities. I doubt we will see much of her."

"Well, then, you will have a better day than I will."

CHAPTER 17

By the time they had finished breakfast and set out to see the rest of the plantation, the soft early morning rays of the sun had turned brilliant, its fiery fingers just beginning to heat the day.

"Let's do this quickly," said Charles. "I am already sweating. It's going to be impossible to breathe by mid-day."

Philip regarded Charles's satin waistcoat and scarlet jacket with scorn. "Of course, you are sweating. You're dressed as if we were riding to the hounds! Take off your jacket, you damn fool," he growled.

Charles' lower lip began to quiver. Without a word, he whirled around and charged back toward the house.

Efren started to go after him, but his uncle pulled him back. "Let him go. I can't stand the son of a bitch. We'll get more done without him. I assume you still remember how to ride."

"It's been a while, but I think I can manage."

"We'll go to the rice fields first, before it gets too hot. Then I'll show you around the slave quarters," said Philip, beckoning to a thin boy in torn shorts holding the reins of three horses.

"Daniel, you can put away one of the horses. Mister Charles isn't joining us. It's just me and Mister Efren. If he ever needs a horse, you make sure he gets one, you hear."

When the boy offered him a shy smile, Efren noticed a scattering of freckles against his light brown skin.

"Yes sir, Mister Philip. I gets Mister Efren whatsoever he wants."

Philip patted Daniel on the head. "That's a good boy. Now get along, and do your chores."

Efren watched Daniel run towards the stables. "How old is he?"

"Around eleven years old, I guess. He was born here on the plantation. He's a skinny little runt, but his mama, Viney, is big and strong. She's one my best field slaves."

"I am impressed that you know the names of all your slaves."

Philip mounted his horse and grinned. "Let's just say I know some better than others."

The sun was hot on Efren's face when they reached the rice fields. Dripping with sweat, his damp shirt clinging to his back and chest, Efren stared wide-eyed at the vast expanse of cultivated land, and the dozens of slaves laboring in the scorching heat. Standing in water up to their ankles, men and women—some with babies wrapped in cloth and tied to their backs—worked their way along the endless rows of gold-husked rice, their hoes making sucking noises as they withdrew them from the mud beneath their feet. Several small boys and girls stood in the muck, ringing bells and waving their arms to shoo away the birds that came to feast on the crop. Other children carrying buckets waded through the foul-smelling sludge, bringing drinking water to the field slaves.

"That's just one twenty-acre square of rice plants you are looking at. I've got four more," said Philip, wiping away drops of sweat from his eyes. "We drained the fields two days ago to weed the paddies. Got to make sure grass isn't choking the rice plants. We'll flood it again when they are done weeding. Then we'll drain the field in early September, give it a few days to get mostly dry, and begin the harvest."

Efren looked around for a water source. "Where does the water come from?"

"We tap into tributaries flowing from the Ashley River, and control the flow with rice trunks like that one over there," he said, pointing to a wooden sluice. "We flood the field when the tide is high, and then drop the gates to keep the water in. When we want to drain the field, we wait for low tide and open the gates so the water can flow out."

Efren watched the slaves swinging their hoes to the rhythm of their field songs. "Looks like hard work," he said, batting away the mosquitoes that attacked like warring hordes.

"I never said it wasn't. They've been out here since sunup. But unlike picking cotton, where slaves work all day long, these slaves have a set task and whenever they finish, they're done. They can do whatever they want afterward. Some of the lazy ones are out here all day. The faster ones can be finished by late afternoon." He squinted out over the field. "See that large black fellow over there? That's Earl, my field driver. He's been a slave here for years. He gets his instructions from the white fellow standing next to him. That's Jesse, my overseer. Jesse makes sure the crops are profitable and that there's no trouble in the slave quarters. Earl makes sure the job gets done out here. Any of these savages steps out of line, or fakes being sick, or tries to slow down the harvest by breaking tools, Earl will see to it that they never do it again. He knows how to use the whip, and he likes to use it."

Philip cupped his hands around his mouth and called out to Earl. "Come on over here, there's someone you need to meet."

Earl came trotting over, his loping strides surprisingly graceful for such a mountain of a man. Everything else about him, Efren noted, was menacing. The cheeks of his square face were pock-marked; a ragged, scar stretched from his hairline to the bridge of his nose. His muscular arms and chest strained against the cotton material of his shirt.

Efren studied the big man, sickened by thought of the punishment he could inflict.

"Earl, this is my nephew, Efren. He will be out here often, so make sure you remember who he is. Understand?"

"Yes, sir, Mister Philip. I sure do understand."

Efren glanced sideways at his uncle, surprised to learn he was expected to be at the rice fields at all.

As Anica expected, Margaret did not join them for breakfast. Instead, Anica and Mariana found Ruth waiting for them in the dining room. Smiling a soft smile that dimpled her cheeks, the girl's eyes darted towards a highchair set next to the table.

Following Ruth's glance, Anica gasped. "Oh, Ruth, it's beautiful. Thank you so much."

"I saw it up in the attic with the crib. You said you wanted Miss Isabel to have her meals with you, and I thought it might be good for her."

Overcome by a surge of tenderness toward Ruth, Anica placed Isabel in the young girl's arms. "Why don't you put her in her new chair, and we'll see how she likes it."

Ruth grinned with delight when Isabel wrapped her arms around her neck. "Let's see how you do, little one," she cooed, as she placed the baby in the delicately carved, oaken chair and pulled the hinged tray over her head. Isabel stared back at the three women staring at her, and began to gleefully slap her hands against the wooden tray, her sweet babble making them laugh.

"Looks like it is perfect," said Mariana. "I think you are going to make a wonderful mother someday."

Ruth's smile faded. Her hand grazed her stomach.

"Ruth, I am so sorry, if I said something wrong. I never meant to make you sad."

"No, Miss Mariana, you didn't say anything wrong. I just need to do my chores, that's all. I'll get you your breakfast now. My mama baked fresh biscuits and muffins this morning," she said, and hurried out.

"I am so sorry I upset her. She is such a sweet child."

Anica went to the window and watched Ruth slowly cross the yard to the kitchen house. "A sweet child who I fear may be having a child of her own."

CHAPTER 18

The mid-day sun radiated searing heat as Efren and Philip made their way back to the stables. "Is it always this hot and humid?" Efren asked his uncle, mopping his face with the sleeve of his damp shirt.

"No. It gets hotter." Philip grunted and dismounted his horse with great effort. "Just wait for August," he said, tossing the reins at Daniel. "Now, get down and let's go eat. We should be just in time for some of Lindy's fine cooking. Dinner is our big meal, so you don't want to miss it."

Efren shook his head, droplets of sweat flying from his face. "I need to wash up and change. I think the horses smell better than I do."

Philip pointed to a well near the barn. "Help yourself," he said, and headed toward the house.

Lying in the shade of a massive live oak tree, a sandy-colored dog, its once-dark muzzle now gray, growled low in its throat as Efren approached the well.

Efren stared at the dog, his hands on his hips. "What are you complaining about? You didn't spend the whole morning riding all over this plantation in this damn heat. Come over here, if you are so tough."

The dog rose slowly, and extending his front legs, stretched and yawned.

Efren lowered the bucket into the well and brought it back up, drinking the water in great gulps. His thirst sated, he poured the remaining water over his head, reveling in the feel of the cool water against his skin. When Efren finally lifted his head, the dog was standing beside him, its tongue lolling out of the side of its mouth, its tail wagging slowly.

Efren reached down and stroked the animal's head. "All right, it's your turn," he said, refilling the bucket and holding it as the old hound lapped up its contents, spraying water in all directions.

Emerging from the stable, Daniel watched in astonishment as the laughing man and the dripping dog shook the water from their bodies.

"What makes you think Ruth is having a baby?" asked Mariana, as she helped Anica unpack her things into the room's large walnut wardrobe.

"It's just a feeling, but I saw fear in her eyes when you said she would make a good mother. It was as if you had discovered a dark secret. I hope I am wrong. She is so young."

"And very beautiful; always a young woman's curse when she does not have control of her very being." Mariana's face clouded. When she spoke, there was a faraway look in her eyes.

"Before I came to work for your father, I was a servant for a wealthy family in Barcelona. They had two grown sons still living with them. Esteban, the younger brother, was always looking at me, his eyes following me as I worked. I quickly learned to avoid being alone with him, but one afternoon I went into the library to dust, and he was waiting for me. He pushed me against the wall and tore the top of my dress. He was lifting my skirt when his mother came into the room."

Mariana took a breath before continuing. "Esteban said I had seduced him, and despite my torn clothing, his mother believed him. I was let go immediately. The family spread vicious rumors about me. No one would hire me, and my family was so ashamed they could barely look at me. I left Barcelona and made my way to Valencia. That's when I came to work for your family. I never saw my parents again."

Anica embraced Mariana. Holding her tightly, she could find no words to comfort the woman who had comforted her so many times in her life.

Efren stood in the doorway of their room, smiling as Anica, unaware that she was being watched, sat on the floor playing with Isabel. The nine-month-old reached out and patted Anica's cheek, her sweet face crinkled in a drooling smile. Anica laughed and kissed Isabel's hand; the simple gestures between his wife and daughter tugged at Efren's heart.

"Beautiful." It was only when Anica looked up at him with a radiant smile, that Efren realized he had said it out loud.

Anica rose to greet him, her smile quickly disappearing. "You're sopping wet! Did you fall into the river?"

Efren pushed a lock of wet hair off his forehead. "You are looking at a man who just shared a bath of sorts with a mangy old cur, and *that* was the best part of my day." Grinning, he held out his arms for a hug.

"You smell like wet dog," said Anica, taking a step back from him.

Efren pulled off his wet shirt, his grin gone. "We need to talk, but I am starving. Has dinner been served?"

"Not yet, but I think soon. A few minutes ago, I heard Henry call Ruth to come help in the kitchen."

"That girl does a lot of work around here."

"I have much to tell you too."

Philip was seated alone at the dining table, waiting impatiently for the food to be brought to the table, when Efren came downstairs.

A sleepy-eyed boy of six or seven wearing a shirt of rough cloth that reached to his knees, stood near the end of the table, pulling a cord attached to an overhead punkah fan, its soft breeze cooling the air. His shy smile when Efren entered the room revealed a missing front tooth.

"I apologize for being late. Anica will be right down. Unfortunately, Mariana is not feeling well and won't be joining us, and, well, Isabel needed a last-minute change," he said, sheepishly.

"No need to rush. As you can see," said Philip, drumming his fingers and glaring at Silas and Henry as they brought in platters of chicken, beef, and pork, "there is not much to eat on the table. Is there, boys?"

"It looks like there is a lot of food to bring out, and they are doing their best."

Philip looked at Efren with contempt, and spoke as if Silas and Henry were not in the room. "You have a lot to learn about dealing with slaves. They need to be kept in line; know their place. They are devious. You can't trust them, and you can't let them get away with their natural tendency to be lazy."

The boy began to fan faster.

Unable to meet the slaves' eyes, Efren was stunned into silence. Before he could find the words to reply, Anica, Isabel in her arms, made her way to the dining room.

The tension between the two men was palpable; Efren met Anica's eyes and shook his head. Feigning a gaiety she did not feel, Anica pointed to the high chair pushed up against the table. "Did you see what Ruth found in the attic for Isabel? Isn't it beautiful? Wait until you see how much she loves it," she gushed, placing the baby in the chair. When Isabel began to slap the tray as if demanding to be fed, even Philip laughed. Across the table, Efren mouthed "thank you."

Ruth joined Henry and Silas in bringing out bowls of green beans, sweet potatoes, mashed potatoes, collard greens, and plates of cornbread to the long table. Passing Isabel in her chair, Ruth lovingly touched the baby's dark curls, and quickly returned to the kitchen house.

"What a lovely meal, and so much of it. Aren't Charles and Margaret joining us?" asked Anica.

Philip pointed at the platter of beef and then at Henry, who quickly speared several pieces onto his plate. "It appears that Charles is still sulking about my criticism of his apparel this morning, and I haven't the faintest idea of where Margaret is. Nor do I have any idea when she will grace us with her presence again." He craned his neck and surveyed the long table. "Dammit, Henry, where's the gravy?"

The strained atmosphere of the mid-day meal did not ease, and Anica and Efren were grateful for the solitude of their room. Putting Isabel down for a nap, Anica stretched out on the bed next to Efren.

Turning on her side, she rested her head against her hand. "That was almost as bad as supper last night."

Efren faced her and pressed his cheek to hers. "I have so much to tell you, but I suddenly don't feel like talking." Pulling her body close to his, he kissed her neck, and slowly undid the buttons of her dress.

Afterward, snuggled in Efren's arms, Anica told him of her suspicions about Ruth's pregnancy, and of the assault and degradation Mariana suffered in Barcelona.

Efren stroked her hair. "Sadly, it's easy to understand why Mariana has always considered you and your family as her family." He grew quiet for a moment. "About Ruth. After what I saw today, I would not be surprised if she had been taken advantage of."

Anica rested her head on his chest. "What do you mean?"

"After we left the rice fields, Philip insisted I see the slave quarters. All the men and most of the women were in the fields, but a few older women were attending to their tasks around the outside of a dozen or so wooden cabins. They are more like hovels, really. Spaces between the wall boards filled with mud and clay, dirt floors, windows without glass, and little fur-niture—maybe a table, a bench, and mattresses made of burlap bags filled with pine straw on the floor. They have a fireplace for cooking and for heat, but the old women I saw were cooking over open fires in the front of their cabins. It looked like some of the cabins had straw beds for ten people in one small room."

"It gets worse," continued Efren. "Right after we got there, Jesse, the overseer I'd met in the rice field, joined us. I noticed a pretty young girl of about fifteen who was weeding a garden duck back into her cabin as soon as she saw him. From the look on her face, I could tell she was terrified of him. Jesse's eyes were like slits. He smiled at Philip and followed the girl into the cabin. I thought Philip would do something, but he just laughed."

The breath caught in Anica's throat. "Every day brings another reason to abhor your uncle. What have we gotten ourselves into?"

Efren did not answer. His own revulsion for Philip roared to the surface when he thought about his uncle's invitation to visit the slave quarters any time he wanted to.

CHAPTER 19

August, 1785

As Philip predicted, the intense rays of the August sun were unmerciful. The heavy humidity, clinging like a second skin, left the inhabitants of Bending Oaks coated in a perpetual sheen of sweat. With the curtains closed to ward off the sun's hot rays, the house was dark and unwelcoming.

Seeking to escape the unrelenting heat, Margaret and Charles departed for Savannah in the first days of the month. A few days later, Philip set out for his Charleston house and the cooler air of the harbor, saying he had to meet with Captain Lopez about exporting the rice from the upcoming harvest.

Efren paced a circle in their bedchamber. "This is not what I expected. I wanted to meet with Captain Lopez and see for myself how he and the crew were faring. It was his plan to make short trips up and down the coast with whatever cargo he could find until we were ready to ship the rice crop. I pray he was successful, because it's been nearly a month, and I did not leave him with enough funds to sustain the crew for this long."

Efren stopped pacing and stared out the window overlooking the garden. "I don't know how long Philip will be away, and I am not so sure that things will run as smoothly as he thinks they will under Jesse's supervision. I don't trust the man at all."

"I am as anxious as you are about his departure," said Anica.

Efren faced her. "I am almost afraid to ask."

"Ruth told me that the hot months are usually spent in Newport to escape the heat and the risk of malaria and yellow fever. She said your uncle would take most of the house slaves with him. This is the first summer they didn't leave the plantation and remain up north until it got cooler and the danger of malaria passed. She also said that lately it was not uncommon for Philip to disappear for a few days without telling anyone where he is going. When he returns, she said he is always in a terrible mood. She told me when Philip's wife was alive, they had more house slaves, but he sold three right after she died. And Efren, just before we got here, he sold three more. Sally used to be Margaret's personal maid, but now she is needed to help in the house. I'm afraid your uncle is having financial problems, and I can't help wondering what he is up to when he goes off for days at a time. Didn't you say he liked to gamble as a young man?"

Efren pulled at his beard. "If he is gambling again, we have financial problems too."

After two days passed and Philip had not returned, Efren began riding out to the rice fields each morning, first stopping by the slave quarters to confer with Jesse before heading over to the paddies. Despite his deep dislike of the burly overseer, Efren had to admit that he appeared to be keeping the fields and the rest of the plantation running in an orderly fashion. Even with three slaves sick with malaria, work in the paddies was proceeding on schedule.

It also became Efren's habit to bring Daniel biscuits left over from breakfast when he returned his horse to the stables. They would sit under the tree with the old dog—who Efren learned was named Rascal—and talk while the boy ate the small cakes of bread, sharing pieces with the grateful mongrel.

A week after Philip's departure, Efren rode up to the stables and found Daniel waiting for him, his face grim and tear-stained.

Dismounting quickly, Efren went to the boy. "What's wrong? Are you hurt?"

Daniel shook his head, his eyes traveling to the live oak tree. Confused, Efren stared at the empty spot of flattened grass. "Where's Rascal?"

"He must've got some energy in him, 'cuz he took off after a rabbit, and chased it clear up to Mister Jesse's house. I tried to catch him, but he was movin' so fast. He ran through Mister Jesse's missus' garden and tore it up real bad. Mister Jesse, he got hold of Rascal and kicked and beat that old dog 'til he stopped yelpin'. I screamed for him to stop, but he pushed me to the ground. Say he'd beat on me the same way if I didn't shut up. I gots scared and ran away when I shoulda' stayed and helped Rascal." Sobbing, Daniel threw himself in Efren's arms.

Fury igniting every fiber of his body, Efren held the boy until he was too exhausted to cry. "Go into the stables and wait for me. I will be right back."

Efren found Jesse sitting on the front porch of a run-down, white-washed cabin, a rifle across his lap.

"I figured that worthless little brat would come running to you." The overseer stood and grinned, exposing a row of rotted teeth. Pointing his rifle in Efren's general direction, he made a great show of cocking the hammer.

Efren took a few steps toward the porch, and smiled. "You might want to remember who you work for."

Jesse snorted. "You might want to remember who really runs this place."

Efren took one step closer to the porch, the smile gone from his face. "Be that as it may, are you sure you want to explain to Philip why you pointed a loaded rifle at an unarmed member of his family?"

Breathing hard, his flat nose flaring, he stared at Efren for a moment before lowering his weapon. "That damn dog ripped up my wife's garden. If I didn't punish him, he would have done it again."

Efren's face contorted in anger. A vein pulsated in his neck. "You didn't punish him; you killed him, you son of a bitch!" He was on the porch now, advancing on Jesse, his hands curled into fists ready to strike. A sudden movement in the cabin window made him hesitate. The grime-covered faces of two small children stared back at him.

Efren blew out a breath. Dropping his hands to his side, he glared at the overseer. "Don't," he hissed through clenched teeth, "even think about laying a hand on Daniel." Tipping his hat at the children, he turned and slowly walked toward the garden.

Tears puddled in his eyes when he spied the old dog lying on his side, his face a mass of pulp, his golden fur matted with blood. Shooing away the flies that buzzed around Rascal's battered body, Efren wrapped him in his shirt and brought him back to the stables, and to the broken-hearted boy. Together, they buried Rascal in his favorite spot under the live oak tree.

CHAPTER 20

A s the days passed without any indication of when Philip, or Margaret and Charles would return, Anica and Mariana assumed the essential responsibilities of running the household. Leaving the day-to-day require-ments and chores in Mariana's capable hands, Anica turned her attention to making sure Lindy had everything she needed to keep the kitchen in order. The first afternoon she met with Lindy, they escaped the stifling heat of the kitchen, and sat near the herb garden behind the kitchen house to plan the daily meals. When Anica requested lighter fare while the others were gone, Lindy was visibly relieved.

"Thank you, Miss Anica. It terrible hot in there when the fire goin' all the time. Make less iron pots to wash too. Some days I get back to my cabin real late, and my boy is sleeping by then."

Anica's face registered her surprise. "I didn't know you had another child beside Ruth. How old is he?"

"Jonah nine. He work over here sometime gatherin' eggs from the coops or fetchin' water when he ain't needed in the rice fields. His daddy lives over to the Berrell plantation. He a carpenter."

"Jonah is nine years old and works in the fields?"

Lindy nodded. "He scare the birds away so they don't eat the rice, and sometimes he do the hoeing," she said, the lightness gone from her voice. "He been workin' out in the fields since he five. He can be a little devil, though. Already had his hide tanned by Earl for foolin' around 'stead of workin' like he 'sposed to." Lindy sighed. "He a worrisome handful."

No, thought Anica, *he is a little boy.*

It was mid-morning the next day when Ruth knocked on Anica's door, her arms filled with the clean clothes she brought from the washhouse. Up since dawn, she had already helped her mother prepare breakfast, washed the dishes, and hung out all the linens to dry so Sally could keep up with the wash. Greeting Anica with a yawn when she opened the door, Ruth's face flared red. "Excuse me, Miss Anica! I am so sorry."

Anica laughed and stepped aside to allow Ruth to enter the room. "Come in. You just missed Isabel. Mariana took her out for a walk before it got too hot to be outside. And you have nothing to apologize for. I know how long your days are."

Ruth lowered her eyes. More than the long hours, she knew it was the growing life inside her that left her so fatigued, and that she would not be able to hide her pregnancy much longer. She was already tying her apron loosely around her middle to hide her expanding waistline. Soon, even that would not keep the obvious from showing. She felt Anica studying her, and guessed that her pregnancy was not going to be a surprise to her young mistress.

"I'm fine," said Ruth. Turning to put the laundry in the wardrobe, she knocked over the candlesticks hidden at the back of a shelf.

Near tears, Ruth apologized again, her voice quavering with emotion. "I am so sorry. I don't know what's wrong with me. I have been clumsy for days now. Yesterday I spilled a pitcher of milk. I thought Mama was going to take a switch to me."

"No need to be upset," said Anica, taking the candlesticks out of the wardrobe to show Ruth they had not been damaged. "They are brass and will not break."

Ruth took a moment to compose herself. "They are beautiful. If you like, I can bring you some candles to put in them."

"Thank you. I would like that very much." Anica ran her hands over the smooth metal. "They belonged to my mother, and they are very special to me. It would be wonderful to have candles to light in them again."

Ruth's expression brightened. "I'll come by with some later." As she turned to leave, Anica touched her arm. "Forgive me for asking, but when is your baby due?"

"I had a feeling you knew," said Ruth, lowering her eyes and making no attempt to wipe away the tears beginning to spill down her cheeks. "If my figuring is right, the baby is going to be here in about seven months. Sometime in February, I think."

"Is the father someone you care about?"

Ruth stared at Anica in disbelief. "Care about? I could not hate him more! That man forced himself on me, and there was nothing I could do about it. I didn't even fight back, because he has power over every minute of my life."

Anica gasped. "Ruth, is Charles the father?"

Ruth rolled her eyes and snickered. "Charles? He has no interest in me. It's the young boys in the slave quarters who have to worry about him and his nighttime visits." She wiped away her tears with the back of her hand, and looked around as if to make sure no one else was in the room.

Stunned into silence by this revelation, Anica stared open-mouthed at the young girl.

"It was Jesse, the overseer," said Ruth in a flat voice. "He makes the rounds of the slave quarters every night to make sure everyone is accounted for. He just walks right into the cabins like he owns the world. One night, when Mama decided to sleep in the room off the kitchen instead of coming back to the quarters, he barged in and cornered me. I'm just thankful that Jonah didn't wake up while he was…" She stopped, and her face went blank, as if she'd fled to a secret place.

"Oh, Ruth, I am so sorry. I will have him dismissed immediately."

"No! I beg you, please don't make trouble for me. Mister Philip will never get rid of Jesse. He knows what he does in the quarters, and he doesn't stop him." Hollowed out by fear and uncertainty, Ruth began to shake. "He visits the slave quarters sometimes too."

Anica's breathing became uneven, as if all the air was seeping out of her lungs. Her insides churned. She wanted to say something to comfort Ruth, but words deserted her; her thoughts strangled by red-hot rage.

"I thought about using some of Mama's root medicines to stop the baby," Ruth said, clawing her fingernails into the palms of her hands. "I just couldn't do it."

Anica clasped Ruth's hands to keep her from injuring herself. "I have seen how much Isabel loves you. You will make a wonderful mother. Once you hold your newborn in your arms, I promise you will feel an overwhelming sense of love for your baby."

Ruth wrenched her hands from Anica's. "You don't understand. It's not that I don't want the baby. I am afraid I will love the baby too much, and I couldn't bear to lose my child."

Anica blinked in confusion. "Why would you lose your baby?"

Ruth pressed her fingers to her eyes to hold back her tears. "I'm a slave. That means my baby will be born a slave. My child will belong to Mister Philip just like I do. If he decides to, he can sell my baby whenever he wants, just like he sold my little sister Lizzie right before Jonah was born."

"Dear God," said Anica, her mind conjuring up the image of a child being pulled from Lindy's arms.

CHAPTER 21

Efren sat with Anica in the dark of their bedchamber. A silvery beam of moonlight broke through the clouds, playing across Anica's distraught face, and he cursed the day he agreed to come to Bending Oaks.

"We are in a place of hell," said Anica. "It is a good thing your uncle isn't here, because I cannot even bear the thought of being in the same room with him. Not only does he know what goes on in the slave quarters, he is a part of it! We must leave here. I will not stay here one more minute longer than we have to."

"Where would we go?" snapped Efren. "We have no money; no friends to help us. And we wouldn't even be here if you hadn't…"

Anica sucked in a startled breath.

Her tortured expression was an arrow in Efren's heart. "Oh, God, Anica, I am sorry. I didn't mean it."

Turning away from him, Anica stormed out of the room without speaking.

Mariana listened quietly as Anica told her about Ruth's pregnancy, and Efren's unspoken accusation. Holding Anica in her arms until she had exhausted all her tears, Mariana soothed away her anguish.

"*Mi cariña*, every day I see on Efren's face how difficult being here is for him. You know how much he hates Jesse, but he is powerless to do anything about him. It has to be destroying him on the inside. And deep down, you must know that Efren does not blame you for our presence here. His words were from frustration; from his inability to make things right."

Anica rose and went to the window. The moon was nestled in the clouds, and she could only make out vague shadows dancing along the landscape.

Mariana touched her shoulder. "Go back to your husband. He needs you."

Efren was still awake when she let herself into their room. In his arms in an instant, she covered his mouth with hers. Their lips still touching, he carried her to bed.

CHAPTER 22

In the last week of August, the South Carolina breezes deserted Summerville. Silver moss hung limply from branches covered with leaves brown and withered from the blistering heat. With no rain in days, the earth was scorched and dry, the grass making a crunching sound as Efren approached the kitchen house where Anica and Mariana sat in the shade watching Isabel splash about in a washtub.

His shirt wet and sticking to his body, he wiped his face and stared wordlessly at Anica.

Alarmed by his somber look, she rose and went to him. "Did something happen at the rice fields?"

Efren's lips tightened, and he handed Anica an envelope. "It's from Captain Lopez. James had business in Charleston, and at the captain's request he delivered this to me."

Looking from Mariana to Efren, Anica removed the letter and read it aloud.

Charleston, August 25, 1785

Dear Señor Amselem,

I hope this letter finds you and your family well. I apologize for allowing so much time to pass without word of our activities in Charleston, but fortune has smiled on the Águila and her crew, and we have been at sea a

*great deal of the time. In the weeks since you left, we have been regularly
delivering cargo to ports along the eastern coast. Funds from these short
voyages have been sufficient to pay for supplies and the crew's wages, and
I believe you will be pleased with the profit we have reaped. I am hoping
that you will be able to travel to Charleston in the next week, so that we
may discuss future business opportunities.*

*I am afraid there is a second reason for my letter. I regret to tell you
that last week your uncle Philip paid me a visit at the docks and asked for
money. He said you sent him to collect any funds we'd earned on our cargo
expeditions. His appearance was so unkempt and his bearing so unsteady,
that I did not trust his purpose. When I asked him for a note of instruction
from you, he flew into a fury and fled the ship.*

*It is with great sadness that I tell you that one of the crew observed
your uncle's behavior and reported to me that he has been seen in the
French gaming houses. I did some investigating of my own, and I learned
that he is no longer welcome in these establishments, and he is now fre-
quenting the questionable gambling houses on the wharf. It is rumored he
is frequently inebriated, that he consorts with prostitutes, and that he is
deeply in debt.*

*I encountered James by chance in the marketplace, and he agreed to
carry my letter to you. I know this news will cause you grave concern, but I
thought it important to make you aware of your uncle's situation.*

Your friend and ever at your service,
Amadís López

Anica looked up from the letter, her eyes burning with hatred. "We have
put ourselves in the hands of this *cabrón,* and he would have stolen from us
if Captain Lopez had not seen through his pretense. He is even more despicable than I thought possible." On the edge of hysteria, her voice rising in
agitation, Anica shoved the letter back into Efren's hands. "He was supposed
to help us, not put us at greater risk. What if his debt is so large that he will
lose Bending Oaks? What then?"

Frightened by Anica's explosive outburst, Isabel began to cry. Instantly
ashamed of her tirade, Anica lifted her daughter from the washtub, and
hugged the dripping baby. "I am sorry," she cooed as she kissed away the
tears from Isabel's cheeks.

Mariana wrapped Isabel in a towel and took her from Anica's arms. "Come, *niña*, it's nap time. Your mama and papa need to talk," she said, her eyes fastened on Anica's.

Anica crossed her arms over her wet dress and watched them walking towards the house. Her heart splintered when Isabel raised her hand and waved.

"I don't like myself very much right now. I am becoming everything I hate; a whining, irrational shrew."

Efren stood behind her, his arms caressing hers. "I know this news is not good. I am as worried as you are."

"This place is like poison to me. Yet at this very moment I am terrified that we will have to leave, and we will have no place to live. What are we going to do?"

"I am going to go to Charleston. I need to meet with Amadis, and I intend to bring Philip back with me. We should be harvesting the crop soon. I detest Jesse as much as you do, and I don't entirely trust him, but he is critical to getting the rice to market. I will feel a lot better when my uncle is here to be sure Jesse is serving our interests and not his own."

CHAPTER 23

Charleston

Two days later, Efren was sitting in Captain Lopez's quarters on the *Águila*, enjoying his friend's company and his always excellent Madeira. "You have no idea how good it is to see you," he said, raising his glass to the smiling captain.

"And I you, though I hope my letter did not cause you undue worry."

"You did the right thing. I have already sent James to find my uncle. From what you wrote, he said he knew where to look."

Lopez frowned. "Philip has been seen numerous times in the taverns and brothels in an area known as Lodge Alley. Its proximity to the wharves attracts crewmen from the ships that dock here. We did some asking around, and it was not hard to get information about a gentleman who was losing a lot of money at the card tables."

Efren sighed and took a sip of wine, swallowing slowly, savoring its soft burn as it slid down his throat. "I cannot thank you enough for all you have done for me personally and for my uncle. If Philip's gambling continues, or if his debts are worse than we think, we may be at risk of losing everything."

"I pray it does not come to that, and I hope that the good news I have will ease some of your concerns," said Lopez, swirling the yellow-brown liquid in his glass. "In the weeks since you left, I have nurtured contacts with some of the smaller merchants who are in need of a ship to carry their products to the northern states. I have also been talking to some of the cotton growers. There is a great need for transporting their crops to the growing number of textile mills in New England."

Efren put his elbows on his knees and leaned forward. "Go on."

"We have an opportunity here to meet that need while we wait for the rice to be harvested and shipped to England. The Águila is well suited to carrying multiple small shipments along with larger shipments of cotton to Philadelphia, New York, and the New England states. By combining two or three smaller shipments with larger shipments, we can allow the merchants to pay according to the size of their cargo. It costs them less, and we still make a profit even after allowing for the crew's pay, supplies, and ship repairs. We have already made two such voyages at a nice profit." The captain reached into his jacket pocket and handed Efren a pouch filled with cash.

Astonished, Efren stared down at the pouch's contents. Overwhelmed by the captain's honesty and loyalty, his voice was shaky with emotion. "Amadis, you have proven yourself to be a true friend, and once again I do not know how to thank you. You could have kept the money for yourself, and I would never have known."

Lopez stiffened. "Never, Señor Amselem! I am a man of my word. I promised you we would not let you down."

Instantly regretting his choice of words, Efren held out his hand. "Forgive me; I did not mean to imply you would steal from me. You have proven your loyalty to me and my family many times over. What you have done is absolutely brilliant."

The captain's body relaxed. The anger disappeared from his eyes, and he shook Efren's hand. "I am so glad you are pleased, Señor Amselem."

"If we are going to be partners, you should start calling me Efren."

Lopez gaped at Efren. "Partners?"

"Partners. I will draw up the papers before I leave so that we will be co-owners of the Águila and the company we are to form. That way you will be entitled to half of all profits."

"Señor Amselem—I mean, Efren—I am without words. I can only say thank you and hope that you know what is in my heart."

"Amadis, I will always be in your debt for what you have done here. I am afraid all the effort will fall on your shoulders for some time, but I assure you that it is my greatest hope to be able to leave my uncle's plantation within the year, and together we will establish our business here." Efren closed his eyes for a moment. "I do not like the idea of going behind my uncle's back, but for now I think it's wise not to tell him about our business venture. He has already tried to steal from us, and I don't trust him not to try again."

When James returned to the *Águila* later that evening his face was grim. "I think I visited every one of them nasty houses in the Alley 'fore I found your uncle. He sleepin' off a good ole drunk in one of the harlots' rooms upstairs at the Pink House. The woman in the room with him say he owin' her two dollars. I didn't have no money to give her, so I come straight over to here."

Efren let out a harsh breath. "You did the right thing. Now I am afraid I need to ask one more favor of you. I'm going to need your help to get Philip out of there."

"Yes, sir. We should probably get on over there. He ain't lookin' so good to me."

"I'm going too," said Lopez. "I know that place, and things can get rough there very quickly."

The Pink House reeked of whiskey and unwashed bodies. Sailors and dock workers sat crowded around tables, drinking and playing cards. A woman in a dark blue dress, its bodice revealing the tops of her breasts, stood between two men, an arm draped over each of their shoulders. Her red hair was stringy, and even from the doorway, Efren could see the ravages of her profession on her face.

James tilted his chin in the prostitute's direction. "That's the gal right there that say your uncle owin' her money."

"God, I hate this," muttered Efren as he approached the woman. "Excuse me, miss," he said, clearing his throat.

She turned and crossed her arms over her generous chest, her eyes appraising Efren. "Well, hello. I certainly hope there's something I can do for you," she purred, her cheap perfume doing little to disguise the sour smell of sweat and sex that clung to her.

Efren could feel the color rise in his face. "Actually, there is. I understand my uncle is upstairs, and I have come to take him home."

No longer playing the coquette, her lips curled into a snarl. "You mean that son of a bitch who drinks all my whiskey and owes me money. You can have him as long as I get my five dollars."

"You told my big friend over there," he said pointing to James, "that he owed you two dollars."

She glanced over at James and sneered. "Yeah, but he used my services again since then, if you know what I mean."

Efren reached into his pocket and placed two dollars in her hand. His face turned hard. "That's all you are going to get. We're going upstairs to retrieve Philip. I expect there won't be any trouble."

She shoved the money down her bodice and shrugged. "No trouble from me. Good riddance as far as I am concerned."

"It smells like a privy in here," said Efren, gagging and covering his nose with his hand as they entered the upstairs room where his uncle lay sprawled on his back, snoring loudly. His clothes rumpled and filthy, Philip grunted, but did not wake when Efren shook him.

"He is a big man," said Lopez, eyeing the rise and fall of Philip's large belly. It is not going to be easy to get him down the stairs if he doesn't wake up."

Efren looked around the room and spotted a pitcher of water on the dresser. "He's not going to like this," he said, and tossed its contents in Philip's face.

Sputtering curses, Philip roared awake. Sitting up suddenly, he grabbed his pounding head, and squinted through heavy eyelids at the three faces looking back at him. "What the hell…" A wave of nausea hit him, churning his stomach and filing his mouth with foul-tasting saliva. Leaning over the edge of the bed, he vomited whiskey and bile.

"What are you doing here?" he groaned, wiping his mouth with the sleeve of his shirt. His eyes searched the room. "Where's Dolly?"

"If Dolly is the woman we met downstairs, she's busy lining up her next customer," growled Efren, making no attempt to hide his disgust. "Get up. You're coming with us. We'll take you to your Charleston house so you can get cleaned up and get into bed."

Philip dropped his head into his hands and moaned. His head was threatening to explode. His mouth felt like it was filled with sand. "You can't take me to my house."

Efren glared at his uncle. "What do you mean we can't take you to your house? If we have to carry you out of here, we will."

"You don't understand. I lost it in a poker game. I'd already sold everything that was of value from the house, and used the money to try to win back some of my losses. As you can see, I was not successful." His face crumpled, great sobs racked his body.

CHAPTER 24

At first Anica attributed her fatigue to the oppressive heat of the waning days of August. The sultry air and humidity—so unforgiving that she felt like she was drowning—left her sleepless most nights, tossing in sheets damp with sweat until the sun's first golden rays lit her bedchamber. Even when she noticed the tenderness in her breasts, she convinced herself it was a sign that she was close to her monthly courses. But on the morning the smell coming from the kitchen made her stomach contract and threaten to expel what little it contained, she could no longer deny her suspicions.

"I know I should be happy about the baby, but I am frightened of what the future holds for us here," Anica confided to Mariana as they walked in the garden. "We have no idea how much trouble Philip has gotten into in Charleston, or if Efren has even found him."

"Anica, please do not allow your fears to take away from this wonderful news. You should be so happy that Isabel will have a brother or a sister. It is a blessing that your family is growing."

Anica glanced at Isabel asleep in her carriage, her pink cheek pressed against her plump hands. Her eyes welled, and for the first time since they left Valencia, Anica gave in to her deep longing for her home. "It hurts so much that Papa will never see Isabel again, and now he will have a new grandchild that he will never get to hold."

Mariana took Anica into her arms. "Your life is here now. Your papa knows you are safe, and that's what matters most to him. Efren has sacrificed everything to take us from the danger in Valencia. Trust him, *Mi cariña*. He loves you too much to let any harm come to you and Isabel."

Anica reached out and touched the empty side of the bed. It was the first time she and Efren had ever been apart, and the two days since he'd left for Charleston seemed an eternity to her. Anxiety and doubt churned her thoughts, sending them tumbling one over another until nothing made sense. She longed for the reassurance of his arms. She prayed that Philip's debauchery had not cost them everything, and that their flight from Spain had not been a mistake. She hoped Efren would be happy about the baby.

Seized by an unbearable longing for her life before they left Valencia, Anica threw back the mosquito netting, and eased out of bed. Checking on Isabel first, she went to the wardrobe and removed her mother's candlesticks. She ran her fingers over its brass curves, lingering over the traces of candle drippings that clung to the rim, the feel of the metal and wax conjuring recollections of her mother secretly lighting candles on Friday nights. Images of her mother's face emerged from her childhood memories.

Realizing she hadn't lit *Shabbat* candles since the incident in the marketplace, Anica was consumed by shame. "Mama," she said, her voice pleading for forgiveness, "I swear I have not forgotten who I am."

CHAPTER 25

Feigning sleep so he would not have to listen to Efren's harangues, Philip prayed that the swaying coach would not induce another round of retching, though he thought it unlikely there was anything left in his stomach to expel. His mouth was dry, coated in a film of sticky saliva that no amount of water seemed to wash away. The insistent rays of the late afternoon sun seeped through his closed lids, forming a blazing red curtain over his eyes. The humidity, still thick despite the morning rain, magnified his discomfort. His head throbbed with each jolt of the coach.

Efren glowered at his uncle, well aware that his slumber, like so much else about the man, was a sham. Despite Philip's declarations that he was sorry, and his promises that he would right his behavior, Efren feared it was only a matter of time before Philip would return to the gambling tables and brothels. Their only hope was to get the rice crop harvested before he vanished again.

Philip stole a glance at Efren through half-closed lids, only to find his nephew staring back at him. He sat up and ran his hand over his now smooth face, and pulled at the neck of the too-tight shirt borrowed from an *Águila* crewman. He touched his bare head. "Where's my wig?" he whined.

"You didn't have your wig when we found you. I'm guessing your *friend* Dolly sold it to pay for all the whiskey you drank," he answered, unable to hide the contempt in his voice.

"I know you detest me," said Philip. "But keep your righteous indignation to yourself, and remember who is putting a roof over your head."

"Do not talk to me about righteous indignation," snarled Efren. "You're the one who puts on airs and plays the wealthy landowner, lording over everyone as if they are unworthy of your presence. I asked around the docks while James was out looking for you. The ship owners aren't stealing your cargo and selling it for less. They won't deal with you because you owe them money. Clearly, the opulence of Bending Oaks is a pretense." He was breathing hard now; his voice filled with undisguised loathing. "Tell me the truth. Are you in jeopardy of losing the plantation?"

Philip stared out the window of the coach. The muscles around his mouth grew tight as he fought to maintain his composure. "If we don't have a good rice crop, I will have to sell some of the slaves, but I will not lose the plantation."

"Uncle," said Efren, his voice low and steady, "I will do everything I can to make sure we have a good harvest, but I don't have the faith in Jesse that you do. I know he is good at managing the crop and the field slaves, but I don't trust him to do his job unless he knows he has to answer to you. It's not just your interests that are at stake here. My ship is docked and idle in Charleston Harbor waiting for your rice. Swear to me that you will stop this destructive behavior, and do whatever you have to do to prevent the loss of Bending Oaks."

Philip looked down at his trembling hands. "I will."

Efren shook his head. "Not good enough. Look me in the eyes and swear to me that you will do what is necessary. That you will not disappear again, and that the gambling will stop."

Philip lifted his head, his face defiant, "I swear I will stop gambling. I swear I will do everything I can to make sure I don't lose Bending Oaks. Is that what you want to hear?"

"Yes, it's what I want to hear. Just make sure it's what you do."

Nearing the shady bower of trees that led to Bending Oaks, James pushed the horses to pick up their pace. Responding to the urgent flick of the reins, the bays extended their heads, their muscles rippling beneath their smooth brown coats, their hooves kicking up clods of dirt as they sprinted towards home.

Chopping wood alongside the kitchen house, Henry was the first to see the coach advancing up the carriageway. Dropping his axe, he bolted across the lawn into the big house. "Ruth! Ruth! Where you at?"

Ruth came running out of the parlor, a dust rag in her hand. "What's wrong? Is Mama all right?"

Henry looked confused. "Course she be. Why wouldn't she be fine?"

"Because you scared me half to death. What are you yelling about?"

"Mister Efren comin' home. I seen the coach. You got to tell Miss Anica."

Shoving the dusty cloth into Henry's hands, Ruth took the stairs two at a time.

Anica burst out of the house just as Efren helped his uncle step from the coach. Shocked by Philip's disheveled appearance, his unsteady gait increasing her alarm, she remained on the porch. The grim look on Efren's face as he walked toward her meant only one thing. The news was not good.

After supper, when they were finally alone in their room, and Isabel slept curled up in her crib, Efren confessed his doubts about Philip to Anica. "It's even worse than we thought. I have no idea how deep in debt Philip is, but it has to be bad if he was willing to risk the Charleston house to make back his losses. In order for my uncle to get his finances in order, a good harvest is essential."

Her worst fears confirmed, Anica drew in a sharp breath. "We cannot allow our future to be tied to Philip's. We must make other plans. Perhaps we could return to Charleston."

The tight line of Efren's lips stretched into smile, and his eyes lit with excitement. "That won't be necessary. I have good news about my meeting with Amadis."

Listening to Efren's recounting of his conversation with the captain, Anica felt a surge of hope for the first time since their arrival at Bending Oaks. She took Efren's hand and placed it on her stomach. "I have some news too."

She held her breath as a range of emotions played across Efren's face. When his confusion turned to amazement, she began to breathe again. "So, it's good news, then?"

Efren pressed her hand to his lips. "*Mi amor*, it is wonderful news! Isabel is going to have a little brother!"

Anica laughed. "How do you know she won't have a little sister?"

Taking Anica into his arms, he nuzzled her neck; his soft kisses slowly finding their way her mouth. "I just know," he whispered.

CHAPTER 26

They had nearly finished breakfast when Philip entered the dining room. Unshaven and unsteady on his feet, his eyes puffy, his vest not fully covering his bloated body, he mumbled a greeting and took his place at the table. "Fetch me some of Lindy's pennyroyal tea for my head," he ordered Silas, rubbing his temples and pushing away the plate of food the old house slave had set out for him. "And hurry up, dammit!"

Unnerved by Philip's disheveled appearance, Anica pushed back her chair and rose. "I need some fresh air," she said, glancing at Efren. "I'm going to take Isabel for a walk before it gets too hot. Mariana, why don't you join us?"

Grateful for a reason to excuse herself from the table, Mariana lifted Isabel from her high chair and followed Anica out into the flower garden. "Until now, I didn't realize how peaceful the house was while Philip was gone. Just think what it will be like when it gets cooler, and Margaret and Charles return," she said, the corners of her mouth pulling into a frown.

Anica gazed out on the dew-covered lawn, the tiny droplets of moisture glistening in the morning sun. "I am dreading their return. Philip is always at his worst when they are around. Efren said harvesting will begin in two weeks, and his uncle will probably be even more ill-tempered than usual."

Later that morning, Anica stopped by the kitchen house hoping to speak to Ruth about the candles she'd offered to bring her. Relieved that that the smells of breakfast were gone, Anica was surprised to find a young boy, barefoot and wearing shorts held up by a rope tied around his waist, husking corn.

Clearing her throat to make her presence known, Anica was startled when the boy turned, and the large eyes staring back at her were of different colors: one blue, the other brown. "Excuse me," she stammered, disarmed by the intensity of his gaze. "I am looking for Ruth. Do you know where she is?"

The boy studied the mistress he had never seen before, trying to determine if Ruth was in trouble. Unlike Miss Margaret—who was always angry about something, and who Mama had seen spit in the cast iron pots after the meal had been served so she couldn't scrape out the scraps to bring home for his dinner—this lady had a kind face.

"She over to the quarters helpin' Mama help Phoebe have her baby. Been there since after breakfast. I sure do hope that baby born by now. Mama needs to make dinner. Mister Philip goin' to be real mad if she don't."

It took a moment for Anica to realize who the boy was. "You're Jonah!"

Suddenly shy, the boy looked down. "Yes, ma'am, that me. My sister ain't in trouble, is she?"

"Oh, heavens, no. I just need some candles. I can talk to her when she comes back." She started to leave, and then turned and smiled at the boy. "My name is Anica. It was nice to meet you, Jonah."

To Anica's great relief, Silas rang the bell, and the mid-day meal was ready to be served at the usual hour. Looking only slightly better than he did at breakfast, Philip still appeared to be feeling the effects of his final night in Charleston. Sweat coated his face; the dark shadows under his bloodshot eyes a stark contrast to his sallow skin. When Efren tried to engage him in conversation, his uncle glared at him, and resumed picking at his food. His only utterance was directed at the young boy working the ropes of the cloth punkah fan, ordering him to pull faster.

Anica regarded Ruth as she brought food to the table. Her face was fuller, her high cheek bones surrounded by a bit more flesh. Her swelling belly was beginning to push against her loosely tied apron, and she could tell that Ruth was carrying herself differently, instinctively protecting her stomach as she moved about the table.

As if she'd felt Anica's eyes on her, Ruth looked up and smiled. Making sure Philip wasn't watching her, she mouthed, "I'll bring you the candles later."

❧❖❧

Ruth looked on as Anica placed the candles in the candlesticks and put them on the desk by the window. "It's strange," she said. "The candle holders are plain, yet so beautiful. They look very old."

"They have been in my family for generations, but I think of them as just belonging to my mother," said Anica, a memory of her mother lighting the candles darting into her thoughts. "She died when I was quite young."

"I can see that they are very special to you."

"They are. And thank you for the candles. I will be needing two more next Friday."

Sensing Ruth's confusion, Anica quickly changed the subject and pointed to the room's sitting area. "We haven't talked in a while. Isabel is napping in Mariana's room, and Efren is down by the stables, so we have some time together."

Unaccustomed to such familiarity, Ruth hesitated before answering. "I can't stay," she faltered. "I need to catch up on the chores I didn't do while I was in the quarters with Mama helping Phoebe have her baby."

"Does your mother deliver all the babies in the quarters?"

Ruth smiled, her eyes beaming with pride. "Oh, yes ma'am. Her mother delivered babies, and she taught Mama. Now Mama is teaching me. She also takes care of the others in the quarters if they get sick or if they're hurt. Her mother was born in Africa, and taught Mama lots of ways to use roots and herbs for healing. Sometimes Mama is called on to help on other plantations, even when the mistress is having a baby."

Anica folded her hands over her stomach. "And, how are they? Phoebe and her baby?"

"They're both fine. Phoebe had an easy time. She's lucky. She had a boy."

Bewildered, Anica's expression went slack. "Why is she lucky she had a boy instead of a girl?"

Ruth lifted her chin, and feeling the pressure of tears behind her eyes, blinked to push them away. Her jaw taut, she gripped the sides of her skirt to calm herself. "Because now she won't have to worry about Jesse or anyone else messing with her baby girl."

Anica faced Efren. "I promised you that I would never hide anything from you again." She swallowed and waited for the nerve twitching in her neck to stop. "I am going to light the *Shabbat* candles tonight before sundown," she said, trying to keep her voice firm. When he did not reply—and before she lost her resolve—she jutted out her jaw and added, "And I want to light them every Friday night."

The look of determination on her face was so fierce, Efren had to struggle to keep from smiling. *Does she know,* he wondered, *how beautiful she is at this moment?*

Glancing out the window, Anica could see golden orange and pink streaks coloring the sky, heralding the setting sun. Her face burrowed into a frown. "Well, are you going to say something?"

"I think you should do it."

Her eyebrows arched. "Really? You mean you aren't going to lecture me about your uncle forbidding any kind of Jewish observance?"

"I'm not saying you should flaunt it, but it's time you returned to doing something you cherish so much." He stroked her cheek. "I am only sorry that you still have to light the *Shabbat* candles in secret. When we are living in Charleston, you will be able to practice your faith in the open. Amadis said there is a synagogue in the city that was formed by other Jews from Spain and Portugal."

Anica felt a glimmer of joy. To be able to fully embrace her Judaism without fear was more than she had ever hoped for. Retrieving the candlesticks and candles from the wardrobe, she placed them on the desk, and covered her head with her shawl. Mesmerized, Efren watched as she lit the candles. Drawing her hands upward over the flames three times, Anica covered her eyes, and said the familiar prayer spoken by Jews all over the world to welcome the Sabbath.

"*Blessed are you, Lord our God, King of the universe, who sanctified us with his commandments and commanded us to light the Sabbath candles.*"

CHAPTER 27

Daniel was filling the watering trough when he saw Efren approaching the stables. "I gots your horse all saddled up and ready to go," he called out, dropping the half-full bucket of water, and disappearing into the barn. Emerging with Buster, the chestnut gelding he knew Efren liked to ride, a broad grin was stretched across his face, as if he were testing the limits of how wide his mouth could go.

Efren took the reins from Daniel. "How did you know I would need Buster today?"

"It harvest time. They blowed the horn early this mornin' to get everybody up and over to the fields first thing. Mister Philip, he already been here for his horse, so I figured you be comin' by for yours."

"Well, you are ahead of me as usual," said Efren, handing the boy two biscuits and a muffin wrapped in a napkin.

"Thank you, Mister Efren," he said, stuffing the whole muffin into his mouth.

Efren studied the boy as he worked to chew and swallow the mouthful. "Are you doing all right? Getting enough to eat?"

Daniel brushed the crumbs from his mouth with the back of his hand, his dark brown eyes avoiding Efren's. "I all right." His gaze drifted towards the line of cabins. "I gots to get back to fillin' the trough."

When the boy turned to leave, Efren saw the raw slice of broken skin on his back. Enraged, he grabbed Daniel's arm and spun him around. "Did Jesse do this to you?"

Terrified, Daniel started to cry. "No Mister Efren. I swear, it weren't Jesse."

Shaken by the panic-stricken look on Daniel's face, Efren released the boy. "Oh God, I'm sorry, Daniel, I didn't mean to frighten you." Struggling to tamp down his temper, he spoke in low tones. "Who did this to you?"

Daniel rubbed his face against his shoulder, wiping the tears from his cheeks. Sniffling, he stole a look in the direction of the quarters. "I don't want Mama gettin' in no trouble."

"I promise you Viney won't get into trouble. Just tell me who did this to your back?"

"Please don't tell Mister Philip. He gonna' be mad if he find out. A man named Sherman from over the Beckum plantation sneaks into the quarters to see Mama some nights after Jesse checked the cabins. Last night, my baby sister Emmy was feelin' sick and wouldn't stop cryin'. Sherman got mad and started slappin' her. I tried to stop him, and he took his strap to me. Mama yelled at him and told him to leave and not come back. 'Fore he go, he kicked over the pot of cornmeal mush Mama made. She couldn't make no more 'cuz she had to be at the fields when the sun come up, so we didn't have nothin' to eat this morning."

"Put Buster back in the barn. I'll come and get him in a bit. Come with me."

Lindy inspected the wound on Daniel's back and scowled. "Good thing you come to me. This bad enough to need tendin' to. Don't want it startin' to fester." Rummaging through a cloth bag she kept in the kitchen, she removed a jar, its pasty contents dark brown.

"This here made from cinnamon bark. It'll make your back heal better. You gotta come back here tomorrow mornin' so I can put more on. You hear?"

Daniel studied the jar in her hand and flinched in anticipation of the sting. "I hear." He closed his eyes, gritted his teeth, and waited for the medicine's bite.

"Make sure you do," she said, gently applying the herbal paste over the wound. "You all done."

Daniel's eyes flew open. His face brightened, and he smiled the smile that never failed to tug at Efren's heart.

"I have to get over to the fields, but Daniel is a growing boy, and I am sure he wouldn't mind tasting some of your good cooking, Lindy. Anything he doesn't eat, I bet his little sister will."

Lindy put her hands on her hips, and looked Daniel up and down. "This boy needs some fattenin' up! Come on, chile, let's see what we can fix up for you," she said, putting her arm around Daniel's shoulder and signaling to Efren she knew what to do.

Efren came over the small rise leading to the fields and reining the gelding to a halt, took in the grueling start to the days-long process of harvesting the rice crop. The sound of grunting slaves, whooshing rice hooks, and the thud of the blades finding their target mixed with the drone of buzzing flies. In spite of the early hour, the morning sun took no pity on the men and women spread out in the fields of muddy clay. Hunched over and swinging the sharp, sickle-shaped hooks, they lopped off the grain heads of the waist-high rice plants, placing the cut stalks on the remaining stubs to dry out, before moving on to the next row.

Urging his horse forward, Efren could hear Philip and Jesse arguing before the men came into view. By the time he reached them, it appeared as if their disagreement was about to get physical.

"Dammit, there was no need to whip Jed that bad," Philip screamed, spittle flying from his mouth and landing on Jesse's shirt.

Jesse smirked. "Do you want them all trying to get out of work? He ignored the wake-up horn. Lazy bastard was late getting to the fields. He deserved to be punished."

"He may have deserved to be punished, but not whipped nearly to the bone. Now I got one of my best men with the flesh on his back and shoulder torn open and unable to work when I need every available slave in the fields. And who knows if his shoulder will heal well enough for him to have full use of his arm. I pay you to keep things running smoothly, not to order Earl to whip my slaves so badly they can't work. A man with a useless arm is useless to me!"

Jesse's eyes narrowed. The muscles in his cheeks twitched. "Then maybe you should…" His voice broke off when he realized Efren was listening nearby. Throwing a hard look at Philip, he turned and stomped off toward the paddies.

Philip directed his fury at Efren. "I don't want to hear a word about Jesse or Earl. And where the hell have you been?"

"Whoa. You told me you wanted me here after breakfast. So here I am, though I am not sure why."

"You're here because it is important for you to understand every facet of growing and harvesting rice when it's time to negotiate a good market price for the crop. That's why."

Efren held up his hands, palms outward, in surrender. "A good enough reason, Uncle."

His anger dissipating, Philip's breathing returned to normal. "Good. I'm glad we understand each other."

The sun was setting when the men and women of the field, sweat-drenched and muscles aching, slowly began the march back to their cabins, their sixteen-hour day over. Jesse screamed at stragglers to hurry, while Earl jammed the handle of his whip into their backs to prod them along.

"Tomorrow is Sunday and if you want to have time for yourselves, you better get your tails back to the cabins now," bellowed Jesse. "My wife's got dinner waiting for me, and if it's cold when I get home, you better believe you won't be getting any passes to leave the plantation."

Even the weariest slaves picked up the pace.

CHAPTER 28

It was quiet in the quarters, and though the sun was already climbing in the sky, most of its residents slept. High in a tree, a wood thrush trilled its flute-like call, and Ruth's eyes fluttered open. Her lids still heavy with sleep, she closed them again, unwilling to relinquish this rare moment of serenity. Stretching on her pallet of straw, she let her mind slowly come awake. Without the wake-up horn, her mother and Jonah slept peacefully on the other side of the one-room cabin. A soft smile played across Ruth's face. It was Sunday. Although the field slaves had the whole day off, and the domestic slaves had to be in the big house, they were allowed an extra hour of sleep, and their chores would be lighter. By late afternoon she would be able to join the others and enjoy the rest of the day.

Ruth loved Sundays in the slave quarters. It was the one day of the week that belonged to its inhabitants, leaving them free to tend their gardens, or go hunting and fishing, or dance and play outdoor games. It was the day owners issued passes that allowed them to visit family and friends on other plantations or to go into the nearby village to sell food from their gardens, and shop without fear of being rounded up and beaten by patrollers.

But what Ruth really loved most about Sundays was that it was when Brock, Jonah's father, got a pass from his owner to visit her mother and the boy. And when Brock visited, his nephew, Walter, visited too. Ruth's breath quickened at the thought of the tall, muscular nineteen-year-old, with the bold hazel eyes and soft, welcoming lips.

Under Brock's care since his mother was sold to a Virginia planter ten years ago, Walter had diligently applied himself to becoming a carpenter like his uncle. His skills were so highly valued, his owner frequently hired him out, and let him keep a portion of the money he earned. The dusky color of his skin told Ruth his father was white like hers. His soft lips told her he loved her. He said he wanted them to be together, that he would love the baby growing inside of her, and that one day they would make babies of their own. In her heart, Ruth knew it was futile to plan for a future they had no control over. Their fate would always be in the hands of their owners; they could be sold and separated at any time. But when dreams of freedom, and a life without fear with Walter and the baby came to her in these quiet moments, she allowed herself to hope.

Anica sat on the edge of the bed waiting for the room to stop spinning, and the waves of nausea to cease. In the beginning of her pregnancy, it was the cooking smells coming from the kitchen that would make her stomach churn and the bitter taste of bile rise in her throat. Now, late into her second month, she woke most mornings feeling dizzy, her stomach rebelling against the tiny life growing in her womb.

"You look pale," said Efren. "Why don't I take Isabel downstairs for breakfast? I'll have Ruth bring you a cup of Lindy's mint tea. It seems to help you."

Feeling queasy all morning, Anica did not protest. "I don't think I am up to going downstairs yet," she said, holding out her hands to Isabel, and laughing when the child toddled to her, her steps wobbly and uncertain. "Be a good girl for Papa and Mariana," she said, kissing the dark ringlets that spilled onto her forehead.

Anica was still in her dressing gown when Ruth knocked on the door. Balancing a tray laden with a pot of peppermint tea and freshly baked bread, Ruth closed the door with her foot and set the salver on a small side table. Pouring the still-steaming tea into a cup, she handed it to Anica.

Breathing in the strong herbal scent of peppermint, her eyes closed in pleasure. "Thank you, Ruth. This is perfect. Your mother's tea seems to be the only thing that quiets my stomach."

"Mama said you should eat this too to help settle your stomach," said

Ruth, handing Anica a plate with a slice of bread.

Like an obedient child, Anica broke off a small piece. Chewing slowly, her face knitted in concentration, she waited to see if the morsel would stay down.

Ruth laughed. "Look at you, your face all wrinkled up! That tiny bit isn't going to make you sick. You need to eat more. Mister Efren told Mama he's worried that you are getting too thin."

Anica took a small bite of bread, and sipped the tea. Savoring its minty taste, and the soothing effect it had on her queasiness, she could feel her lightheadedness begin to fade.

Ruth put another slice of bread on Anica's plate. "You look better. The color is coming back into your face."

"I am starting to feel better," said Anica, taking several more sips of tea. "This time is so different from when I was carrying Isabel. How are you feeling?"

"Good. No stomach sickness. I'm not even as tired as I was. Good thing too, because Mister Philip told Mama that a messenger brought him a letter from Miss Margaret saying she and Mister Charles will be back from Savannah in a few days. That means there is going to be a lot more work to do around the house."

It was not the news Anica expected or wanted to hear.

After ringing the bell to call the household to an early supper, Silas ducked back into the kitchen. The sounds of music and muffled laughter from the quarters floated through the open door of the kitchen house, making him all the more impatient to be a part of the merriment. Too old for the games and foot races that excited the younger men, he loved to sit with his friends, drop a fishing line in the river, and pass around the jug of berry wine they kept hidden in a nearby spring. He could already feel the cold liquid sliding down his throat, washing down a mouthful of catfish.

"Are Miss Margaret and Mister Charles really comin' back?" he asked Lindy, taking a tray of roasted chicken from the oven, while she ladled green beans into a large bowl and handed it to Henry.

"That's what Mister Philip tole me. Say they comin' home in 'bout four days. You can be sure the nice peaceful house we been havin' ain't gonna be peaceful no more. Them two always makes Mister Philip's mood real nasty."

Henry made a clucking sound. "I likin' the way Miss Anica and Miss Mariana doin' things 'round here. I gonna make sure to have a good time in the quarters tonight, 'cuz I know we gonna be kept late to the house come next Sunday."

"Then you two better go on and get the food out there. The faster they eats it, the faster we can clean up and get ourselves over to the quarters. Brock be comin' visitin' and I wanna get down to the cabins as much as you do."

Walter sat with his back against a live oak tree, waiting for Ruth, his eyes focused on the path leading from the kitchen house to the quarters. Sitting beside him, Brock watched Jonah play with the ball-and-cup toy he'd carved from a piece of oak. Effortlessly flipping the ball attached to the handle by a string into its hollowed-out target, the boy beamed each time Brock praised his success.

Spotting Ruth and Lindy coming their way, Walter nudged Brock. "Now ain't that a beautiful sight." Jumping to his feet, he trotted down the path to meet them.

Ruth began to laugh. "Looks like he's anxious to see me."

Lindy poked her arm. "How you know he ain't runnin' to see me?"

"Because I can see Brock coming up behind him," said Ruth, poking her back. "And hush, now. I don't want you to scare Walter away."

"Chile, from the way he looks at you, I don't think the devil hisself could scare him away."

"That were a mighty good supper," said Brock of the pork bits, rice, and roasted vegetables Lindy and Ruth had prepared over a small cooking fire in front of the cabin. Standing and patting his stomach, he held out his hand to Lindy and pulled her to her feet. His eyes dancing with mischief, he winked and said, "I feelin' like takin' a walk."

As soon as they were out of sight, Walter touched Ruth's cheek and whispered, "I feelin' like takin' a walk too, and I knows a quiet place we can walk to." His lips brushed her neck. Pleasure coiling throughout her body, Ruth took his hand, and they slipped away.

CHAPTER 29

Monday morning the blare of the wake-up horn jolted the slave quarters to life. Barely awake, its inhabitants gulped down cold corn meal mush to fill their stomachs and fuel their energy for the long day ahead. Children old enough to work in the fields rubbed their eyes and begged for more sleep. Mothers still nursing their babies placed their infants in cradles made from hollowed-out pieces of tree trunks and prepared to bring them to the paddies. Toddlers were left in the care of slave women too old to work in the fields. The Sunday spent in leisure a drifting memory, they all scurried to the rice paddies, fearful of Jesse's wrath and Earl's whip.

In the kitchen house, Ruth sang to herself as she stirred the oatmeal while her mother put the biscuits into the brick oven.

"You sure in a happy mood," said Lindy. "Wouldn't have somethin' to do with Walter, would it?"

Images of their bodies pressed together flitted through Ruth's thoughts, and she could feel her face grow warm. "He is a good man, and he sure does make me happy, Mama. He wants me to say the baby is his, so when it's born Jesse can't cause trouble. But feeling this way scares me too, because I know I will never be able to have the happiness I want. Walter is working so hard and saving the money his master lets him keep, but it will take years for him to buy his freedom, let alone mine. And how are we going to be true to each other when the likes of Jesse and Mister Philip can use me any way they want, or Walter's owner can order him to be with another slave woman?

And the babies? They will never belong to us. There is nothing we can call our own. Not our children. Not our bodies."

Lindy's heart ached for her daughter. Her own life had taught her that hope was useless to a slave. She'd met Brock eighteen years ago, when Mary was still alive, and Brock's owner, Clayton Berrell, had hired him out to build a cabinet for her. Brock set up his tools and worked outside near the kitchen house where Lindy's mother was teaching her to cook. It didn't take long for the big, easy-going man with the wide grin, and the pretty house slave with dancing eyes and smooth, tawny skin to discover each other.

Lindy's memories of those early, happy days with Brock were clouded by the realities of her life in the big house. Doe-eyed, with pale brown skin and delicate features, she attracted the attention of Philip's frequent house guests. Weeks after she'd met Brock, a wealthy plantation owner visiting from Charleston followed her when she left the kitchen house. He grabbed her from behind, his hand clamped firmly over her mouth. Enraged when she bit him and tried to get away, he pulled the sixteen-year-old behind the smokehouse and raped her in the weeds.

When Lindy gave birth to Ruth and held the infant in her arms, she wept. Peering into her baby's tiny face, her skin so light it was almost fair, she knew the time would come when her daughter would attract attention too.

"You lucky Walter stand by you like Brock stand by me all these years. It hard for our men to do what right when they always have to answer to a master."

Ruth considered her mother's words, and finally summoned the courage to ask her the question that had been circling in her head for a long time. "Mama, how come you and Brock never got properly married?"

Lindy sighed. "'Cuz old man Berrell wouldn't give Brock permission for us to marry. Besides, Mister Philip, he won't give me permission either. Long as I be his slave, my babies be his and add to his stock. Lizzie, had a white daddy too, and she brought Mister Philip a good price. He done sold her to a fancy lady who wanted Lizzie to wait on her littluns." Lindy's eyes filled. "That's all I knows 'bout what happen to my little girl."

"I still think about her," said Ruth wistfully. "She was such a sweet little lamb; always smiling. Remember how she used to call the chickens in the yard to come to her so she could pet them? She'd get so mad when they ignored her. She just ball her little hands into fists and holler."

"I swear some of them hens stopped layin', she scared 'em so bad."

Laughing at the memory, the two women were startled when Silas poked his head into the kitchen. "Time for the breakfast bell. Y'all ready?"

Lindy's eyes darted towards the brick oven and the forgotten biscuits. Grabbing the baking peel, she placed the long-handled paddle into the oven and rescued the brown dough from the heat. "Go on and ring it. By the time they's downstairs, everythin' be ready."

CHAPTER 30

October 1785

On Lindy's instructions, Daniel ducked into the kitchen house while the family was eating breakfast. Greeting Lindy with a big hug, he took the biscuits and bowl of hot oatmeal she handed him, and retreated to a corner to keep out of the way of Silas and Henry as they hurried food from the kitchen house to the dining room.

Lindy watched Daniel as he wolfed down his meal and smiled. To make sure he was fed at the start of the day, she'd told him to come see her every morning so she could put medicine on his back. The gash had healed weeks ago, but she and the boy kept to the unspoken agreement that it still needed tending to. A co-conspirator in their arrangement, Efren would wait for Daniel in the garden, so they could walk back to the stables together.

"I gots Buster all saddled up for you. Figure you be headin' out to the fields. They's gonna be tying the bundles of rice into sheaves today, and bringin' 'em to the drying barn. Mama said she might be back to the cabin late."

Efren was sure Viney would not be back until after dark. "You going to be all right?"

"Sure. Old Sarah be watchin' my sister Emmy. Emmy walkin' now and gettin' into things, so Mama can't take her to the fields no more. Old Sarah gonna make us some supper if Mama ain't back in time."

Efren considered his next question carefully, unsure of what he would do if the boy answered yes. "Daniel, has Sherman come to see your mother again?"

Daniel stopped and looked up at Efren. "He come around the night after he hit me, but Mama's brother Willy had a pass to come visitin', and he be at the cabin when Sherman come to see her. Uncle Willy bigger than Sherman, and he say he'd knock his teeth out if he ever come around again. Sherman ain't been back since."

Efren felt his body relax. "Good thing your uncle was there."

Daniel's face split into a grin. "Mighty good he were."

The harvest was well on its way when Efren rode up to the paddies. Swatting away swarms of mosquitoes, and already drenched in sweat, the field slaves were fanned out across the rows of shorn plants, binding the cut stalks of rice into sheaves, all under the watchful eyes of Jesse and Earl.

Efren joined the two men where their horses were grazing in the shade of a large oak.

Earl tipped his hat. "Good mornin', Mister Efren."

Working a wad of tobacco leaves wedged between his cheek and gums, Jesse stared steely-eyed at Efren, slices of sunlight seeping through the branches of the old tree casting eerie stripes across the overseer's face.

Ignoring Jesse, Efren spoke to Earl. "It looks like it's going to be another long day."

"Yes sir, Mister Efren. Harvest days always long. Theys gonna be out here all day. The sun gonna set and they still be workin'. They gonna be workin' from can-see to can't-see." The big man looked sideways at Jesse as if they shared a private joke and laughed.

Jesse worked the wad in his mouth, moving it around with his tongue. "Just as long as I get home for my supper, I don't care how long these bastards are out here." Spitting the brown, foul-smelling mixture of saliva and tobacco in Efren's direction, he walked toward the paddies.

"Jesse!"

The overseer turned and glared at Efren. "What?"

Efren flashed a toothy smile. "I just wanted to tell you to have a nice day," he said, relishing the confused look on Jesse's face.

The light was seeping from the sky, the pink and lavender streaks of twilight giving way to the gray hues of dusk when the final rows of stalks were tied off. With piles of sheaves balanced on their heads, the weary slaves brought the bales to the barges that would float the bound stalks to the barn for threshing, and the start of nearly thirty days of dawn-to-dusk labor.

CHAPTER 31

Charles sat sulking in the corner of the coach. His arms crossed, his lips set in a perpetual pout, he glared at Margaret. "I don't know why we had to leave Savannah," he whined. "We were having a wonderful time, and Aaron was happy to have us."

"We left," hissed Margaret, baring her teeth like a snarling cat, "because we have run out of money. Aaron may have been happy to go carousing with you when you were paying for everything, but he made it quite clear to me that he was no longer interested in you or in playing the convivial host."

Charles' face contorted. "Bitch! You did plenty of carousing on your own. I don't know how you kept track of all the men who escorted you around Savannah. You loved how they sniffed around you like you were a dog in heat. It was only after a certain naval captain's ship set sail, that you were so keen to leave. Really, Margaret, who did you think you were fooling?"

Margaret leaned forward, her breath hot on his face. "Do not talk to me about fooling anyone. This marriage has been a sham from the start. You played the ardent suitor and married me to bury the rumors about your trysts with other men. That I choose to seek my pleasure elsewhere is none of your concern. You gave up the right to play the cuckolded husband on our wedding night, and every night after."

Charles slumped, his shoulders curving inward over his chest. She was right. He had deceived her from the very beginning. He'd presented himself as a wealthy Savannah planter, when in fact he had been disowned by his father after he was discovered naked with the young stable hand he had fallen in love with. What he saw in Margaret was a beautiful, naïve young woman who could help him regain his place in society. That her family was wealthy only sweetened the prospect of marriage. But Charles had not anticipated his growing fondness for Margaret, or his unreasonable jealousy when she sought the company of other men.

Regrets and recriminations crowded into the coach, filling the empty space between them with painful reminders of broken promises and unrealized dreams. They did not speak again until they neared Bending Oaks.

"You need to know that there was gossip in Savannah that Philip lost a great deal of money at the gambling tables in Charleston while we were gone," said Margaret, breaking the silence. "There is also a rumor that he gambled away the Charleston house. If all this is true; if things are worse than we thought, and Philip cannot or will not continue to provide for us, my inheritance will be gone within the year."

Charles blanched. "Why do we have to depend on Philip? I thought your mother inherited the plantation when your father died."

"When she was a widow, yes. When she married Philip, he gained ownership under the law. I have no legal claim to the property."

Charles' breathing grew harsh. "Dear God, he could dismiss us from the house if he chooses to."

"That's why we need to do everything we can to be useful to him."

"And just how are we going to do that?"

"I am going to assume more control of the household, and you just need to stay out of Philip's way."

When the carriage bearing Margaret and Charles arrived a day earlier than expected, the house slaves scurried to prepare their rooms, and Silas and Henry abandoned their chores to help the coachman unload the couple's numerous pieces of luggage.

"They been squabblin' with each other the whole time they in the coach," warned the driver. "Nasty, them two."

"Don't we knows it," said Silas. "We been hopin' they like Savannah so much they ain't comin' back."

Agitated about having two unexpected mouths to feed, Lindy was furiously stirring a pot of gravy and muttering when Ruth ducked into the kitchen house.

"Mama, are you talking to yourself?"

"These folk makes me crazy 'nuff to. Comin' back and not givin' us time to prepare for them. And then expectin' everythin' to be like they left it. I swear, since Miss Mary be gone, bless her soul, nothin' been right 'round here."

Before Ruth could speak, Lindy snapped, "And you better not be comin' in here askin' for somethin'."

Hurt by her mother's sharp tone, Ruth stiffened and took a step back. "Mama, it's Friday. I just came in here to get candles for Miss Anica like I always do."

Lindy took a breath. "Sorry, chile. I just gots myself in a tizzy."

Her mother looked so sorrowful, her smooth face haggard after a day in the heat of the kitchen house, it stabbed Ruth's heart. "It's all right, Mama. I'll bring these upstairs and come down and help you."

"You take care of Miss Anica first." Lindy touched Ruth's growing belly. "Miss Margaret seen you yet?"

Ruth shook her head. "Sally told me they were here, and I stayed in the washhouse until they went upstairs."

Lindy raised her eyebrows. "You can't keep hidin' in the washhouse 'til the baby comes."

Ruth laughed. "I can try."

"I'm sorry I am late," said Ruth. "Miss Margaret and Mister Charles are back, and we weren't expecting them until tomorrow. Everybody is running around getting things the way they like them."

Anica glanced at Efren. Charles and Margaret were sure to disrupt the comfortable routine they had grown accustomed to while the couple was gone.

"It's fine, and you're not late," she said, taking the candles from Ruth. "We have enough time before sundown."

The look on Ruth's face told Anica she had let information slip that required an explanation. "It's a tradition in my family to light candles on Friday before sundown."

Ruth lowered her eyes, her fingers toying with the twists in her long braid. "Miss Anica, I have something to tell you, and please don't be mad. When you first came here, I heard Mister Philip tell Mister Charles that you were in trouble in your country for practicing your religion, and that you were running away to save your lives. He told him that if you and Mister Efren were going to stay here, he wasn't going to allow you to follow your traditions. If your candles are part of what you believe, I promise I won't say anything to anyone."

Efren stared at Ruth in disbelief. Anica's face drained of color, and she needed a few seconds to calm her whirling thoughts and make a decision.

"Lighting the candles is part of my religion. I am Jewish, and it's how we welcome the Sabbath as God's special day. In Spain, where we lived, I could not openly practice my faith. It has been that way for hundreds of years. I was suspected of practicing in secret. Efren sacrificed everything so we could escape here. Honoring the Sabbath by lighting the candles is an important part of who I am. I do not want you to get into trouble, but I must ask you to keep your word not to share what you know with anyone. I am afraid Philip will ask us to leave if he finds out."

"Miss Anica, I swear I won't tell anyone," said Ruth, her voice steady, her expression earnest.

Anica squeezed Ruth's hand. "Would you like to stay and watch me light the candles?"

"Oh, Miss Anica, yes!"

CHAPTER 32

Within a day of their return, Margaret was eager to make known her intentions to resume her responsibilities as mistress of Bending Oaks. Waiting for everyone to come down for breakfast, she pounced as soon as Anica and Mariana entered the dining room.

"It appears the house slaves have been lax in our absence," she sniffed, running her finger across the sideboard and holding it in front of Anica's face. "You can be sure that things will be different now that we are back. I won't put up with lazy slaves. You were much too easy on them."

Platters of food in their hands, Ruth, Silas, and Henry froze, and averted their eyes. Stunned by Margaret's affront, Efren took a step towards her, while Philip and Charles looked on in amusement.

Refusing to be provoked, Anica shook her head at Efren, and placed Isabel in her high chair. Turning towards Margaret, she smiled.

"Good morning, Margaret and welcome back," she said sweetly. "There's no need to thank me or Mariana for assuming your responsibilities. We were happy to make sure the house was running smoothly while you and Charles were away enjoying all the social activities and cool air in Savannah. We found the house slaves to be very cooperative. Isn't that right, Mariana?"

"It was truly a pleasure. Lindy, Ruth, Rosie, Flora, Sally, Silas, and Henry all worked hard to keep things in order. They really are very capable, and it was no trouble at all."

Philip began to smirk. Ruth bit the inside of her cheek to keep from laughing.

Spots of red spread across Margaret's face. "Well," she sputtered, "I am sure the house will be back in top shape now that I have returned." Aware that all eyes were on her, she released her anger on the three slaves. "What are you waiting for? Serve the food!"

Ruth, Henry, and Silas barely made it into the kitchen house before they burst out laughing. "Mama, I wish you had been there to see it," said Ruth. "Margaret got all uppity with Miss Anica, and she just smiled and made her appear the fool."

Lindy looked around. "Y'all better hush. I don't want that woman comin' into my kitchen no more than usual. 'Special' now. She gonna be in a mean way. And keep a look out for Daniel. If you sees him, give him some biscuits, but tell him not to come to the kitchen no more 'til I tells him it be safe. Sure don't want Miss Margaret catchin' me feedin' the boy. She have both of us lashed."

Henry picked up a platter of biscuits and headed for the dining room. "Things gonna get ugly for us again."

Efren gulped down coffee and a biscuit, and rose to leave. "If you'll excuse me, I want to go over to the quarters see how the milling is going." Touching Anica's shoulder and kissing Isabel's cheek, he ignored Margaret's smoldering stare.

Margaret's angry expression hardened when Ruth returned to the dining room carrying a silver tray with bowls of hot oatmeal. Watching her like a lioness stalking its prey, Margaret's face widened in recognition as her eyes settled on Ruth's stomach.

"Philip, I see the plantation will soon have an addition."

Annoyed with Margaret's earlier display of arrogance, Philip bit into a biscuit and chewed slowly before answering her. "I don't know what you are talking about."

Anica grabbed Mariana's hand under the table, certain that Ruth was about to bear the brunt of the humiliation she'd caused Margaret.

Smirking, Margaret leaned back in her chair. "It's just as I suspected. You haven't been keeping up with things while we were gone."

Ruth looked from Philip to Margaret, her hands shaking so badly she almost dropped her tray.

Philip's face darkened. "Margaret, I don't know what kind of game you are playing, but whatever it is, you will stop this right now. Haven't you created enough of a stir for one morning?"

Margaret lifted her chin in defiance. "No games, Philip. I am just bringing to your attention a certain swelling of the stomach."

Acting on impulse, Anica stood, and with a forced look of delight, hugged a startled Margaret. "I didn't realize I was showing that much, or we would have announced it sooner," she said, folding her hands over her middle. "Efren and I are thrilled. The baby should be here in March."

Peering at Ruth, Anica hoped that what she was about to do would not create more problems for the frightened girl. "And there is more good news," she added, before Margaret could collect her thoughts. "Ruth is going to have a baby too. Philip, you must be very pleased that your household is growing."

Philip's eyes travelled from Anica to Ruth. His fleshy lips curling into a half smile, he regarded Margaret with disdain. "At least some of the women in this house are producing offspring."

As soon as Margaret was upstairs, Anica rushed to the kitchen house in search of Ruth. "Lindy, I may have done something awful. Where is Ruth?"

"She fine, Miss Anica. Silas tole me what all you did. Thank you for helpin' my girl. Miss Margaret was out to make trouble for her. Ruth down to the dairy house gettin' some butter. She come back anytime now."

Only when the air rushed back into her lungs, did Anica realize she had been holding her breath. "Then she's not upset that I told Philip about her baby?"

"No, ma'am. She relieved that he knowed. She shoulda told Jesse 'cuz he the overseer, and he the one that tells Mister Philip, but she been afraid to."

"And Philip didn't ask about the father?"

Lindy's face tightened. "Not yet."

CHAPTER 33

At the fields, Efren was greeted by the thwacking sound of wooden flailing sticks striking the remaining rows of rice stalks to remove the grains from their stems. Relieved to have escaped the tension surrounding this morning's breakfast, he stopped on his way to the slave quarters to admire the simple grace of the winnowing process brought to America by slaves from West Africa a century ago. Using fanners—flat, shallow-lipped baskets made from tightly woven and coiled sweetgrass—the women tossed the rice into the air, letting the wind blow away the chaff, while the heavier grains fell back into the basket.

Satisfied that the threshing and winnowing were proceeding at a pace that would allow them to ship the crop in November, Efren walked to the quarters where pairs of women working together used long wooden pestles to remove the husks from the threshed and winnowed grains. Pounding the rice in large mortars made from hollowed-out tree trunks, they controlled the pestles with the same tapping and rolling movements as their African ancestors, loosening their grip at just the right moment to ensure the grains of rice remained unbroken. The grueling work meant the women stood for hours lifting and lowering pestles that weighed as much as ten pounds in the unforgiving heat. With daily quotas to meet, and Jesse's menacing vigilance, there was little time for rest, and the women worked well into the night.

Efren's hopes to avoid an encounter with Jesse were quickly dashed when the overseer spotted him. Advancing towards him, his stride telegraphing his fury, Jesse planted himself in front of Efren and scowled. "Did that little bastard Daniel come running to you again?"

Efren felt his heart clutch. "I haven't seen Daniel all morning. What happened?"

Jesse kicked a clod of dirt, sending clouds of dust flying around his feet. "Viney, Daniel's mama, is missing. She was in her cabin when I did the check last night, but she was gone this morning. Daniel has been chasing around the quarters looking for her, but he ain't going to find her. She's run away. I told him not to worry, the dogs will sniff her out, and we'll have her back here in no time." He grinned and rubbed his hands together. "Bitch, thinking she can get away from me. When we find her, she'll curse the day she ever even thought of trying to run."

Jesse's delight at the prospect of capturing Viney sickened Efren. "What's going to happen to Daniel and his sister if she doesn't come back?"

"Oh, we'll get her back. The patrollers and slave catchers are already out searching the swamps and we've alerted the other nearby plantation owners. Word is travelling around the quarters that she's gone. They're all scared. You can see it in their faces. If any of them knows something, we'll find out. Old Sarah and the others will look after Daniel and Emmy until we get her back. One thing about them lazy savages, there's always someone willing to look after the young'uns."

Suddenly aware that the women had stopped pounding the rice and were staring at them, Jesse erupted in anger, his hand finding its way to the handle of the whip tucked into his belt. "What y'all looking at? You think that rice is going to mill itself? Get back to work!"

Efren rushed to the stables. Instead of Daniel, he found Cotter, the blacksmith, filling the water trough.

"Where's Daniel?" he panted. Bending over, his hands on his knees, he sucked in great gulps of air.

Massive as a live oak, his chest straining against his sweat-stained shirt, the veins of his forearms popping against his dark skin, the blacksmith canted his head toward the barn. "In there."

Stepping out of the bright sunshine, Efren waited for his eyes to adjust to the dim light streaming through the spaces between the barn's aged timbers. The musty odors of hay, dung, and barn animals hung in the air and pressed deep into his nose. The horses nickered and stomped their hooves, their large, soulful eyes assessing him as he passed by.

Efren found Daniel wedged into the corner of an empty stall, waves of convulsive sobs ripping through his body. Without speaking, Efren pulled Daniel to him, rocking the terrified boy in his arms.

Daniel clung to Efren, grief and fear leaving him broken and exhausted. Breathing hard, he remained motionless in Efren's arms, his eleven-year-old mind trying to make sense of his mother's disappearance.

Feeling Daniel's body relax, Efren brushed away the boy's tears. "Don't be afraid. I promise you and your sister will be all right. Old Sarah is going to take care of both of you."

"Mister Jesse say Mama run away. I know she ain't gonna come back on her own, 'cuz she knows she gonna be punished if she do. Last time a slave run away, they caught him, tied him to the whippin' tree, and lash him 'til he pass out. Then Mister Jesse put a collar 'round his neck with spikes and a big iron ball on a chain and made 'em work in the fields wearin' it."

Efren felt cold fingers of terror flick along his spine. "Maybe she didn't run away. Maybe she just went to the plantation where her brother lives to visit him."

Daniel shook his head. "I know why she run. Mister Jesse been comin' to the cabin at night and messin' with her. She ain't comin' back unless they catches her. And if they do, he gonna kill her for sure."

By the time Efren got back to the big house, word had spread that Viney had run away with a slave from the nearby Yokes plantation. Philip was fuming, screaming at the cowering house slaves, terrifying them with threats of severe punishment if any of them knew about Viney's escape.

Ducking into the kitchen house to elude Philip, Efren found Lindy working in a cloud of flour, furiously kneading bread dough as if she were beating back an attacker. "You heard," he said.

"The whole plantation heard," she said, angrily sprinkling more flour and rolling the ball of dough on the work table. "Foolish woman ran off with some man she hardly knows, what people sayin'. Filled her head with ideas of goin' North to be free." Lindy wiped the sweat from her forehead, leaving a streak of flour in its place. "Unless they knows where they goin', they ain't gonna get far in them blackwater swamps. If the slave catchers' dogs don't get 'em, the snakes and alligators will. And when they brings her back, she gonna wish she died out there." The anger in her eyes gave way to tears. "She musta' been hurtin' real bad to leave them poor chiles like that."

Before he could answer, Margaret burst into the kitchen. Ignoring Efren, she flew at Lindy. "I know you hear all the slave gossip. What do you know about Vincy running off?"

Lindy's face went rigid. "Miss Margaret, you know the other slaves don't trust any of us what work in the big house. They think we your spies. They don't tell me nothin', and I knows nothin'."

"Margaret," said Efren, "I was at the quarters, and the other slaves are all upset that she left. I don't think any of them knew she was planning to escape."

"I cannot believe you are naïve enough to be fooled by their lies. Deception is at the very core of their being. Someone knows, and the longer it takes for the truth to come out, the harsher the punishment will be."

CHAPTER 34

Three days after she ran off, Viney was marched back into the quarters, a chain attached to a collar around her neck, her arms and legs in shackles. Bleeding from dog bites, her face a mass of bruises, she stared straight ahead, unwilling to indulge either the pity or scorn of the other slaves. It was only when she heard her son's screams, and saw Old Sarah, holding Emmy and struggling to keep Daniel from running to her, that her knees buckled.

Lindy and Ruth were tending to a slave sick with malaria, when Jesse dragged Viney through the quarters. Drawn to the door of the sick man's cabin by the commotion outside, Ruth clamped her hands over her mouth to keep from crying out at the sight of Jesse pulling Viney, beaten and bloody, through the dirt to the whipping tree.

Racing to the big house, Ruth brought the news of Viney's capture to Efren. "You have to do something," she begged. "She has already been badly beaten. Jesse's is going to whip her himself. He's gone crazy. I'm afraid he's going to kill her."

Efren started for the door. "Find my uncle and tell him they have Viney. Tell him to meet me at the quarters."

Jessed had assembled all the slaves to witness Viney's punishment. Her back bare and her hands bound, Viney was hoisted by her arms and left dangling from a thick branch of the whipping tree, her toes barely touching

the ground. In a demonic frenzy, Jesse taunted Viney with curses and promises of the pain he was going to inflict, delivering lash after lash in quick
succession, each bite of the whip flaying strips of flesh from her back and
shoulders.

"Come on, beg for mercy," he screamed, his face red, the excitement
in his eyes betraying his pleasure at her agony. Infuriated when she would
not plead with him to stop, he ordered Earl to pour pepper on her open
wounds. Shrieking in anguish, Viney's eyes rolled back, and she began to lose
consciousness.

"No! No! No!" roared Jesse, grabbing Viney's face. Squeezing her
cheeks, he forced her to look at him. "You are not going to pass out, you
hear me. I have a hundred more lashes for you, and I want to enjoy your
suffering with every single one of them." Running his hands over her bare
breasts, he stepped back and cracked the whip against the ground, making
Viney jump. A grotesque grin on his face, he snapped the lash, the strands of
blood-soaked rawhide gouging another piece of flesh from her back.

Following the sound of Viney's screams, Efren raced towards the whipping tree. Cresting a small hill, Efren was certain he was witnessing the
depths of hell. Viney was barely conscious, her head resting on her bare
chest, blood running down her legs and pooling beneath her feet. Jesse
whooped in glee each time the whip licked her skin.

"Jesse!" screamed Efren. "Stop! No more!"

Fury rippling along every nerve in his body, Jesse whirled and aimed the
tail of the whip at Efren. Flattening himself against the ground, Efren felt the
whip slice the air above his head. Scrambling to his feet, he locked eyes with
Jesse. "You are a big man when you have a whip in your hand. I promise you we
are not done with this. But now, you need to calm down. She's had enough."

"She's had enough when I say she's had enough," he croaked through
gritted teeth. "Bitch ran away. Ran away during harvest! She needs to be
punished good. These black bastards need to see what happens when you
run away."

"You kill her, and you will be putting a slave in the ground Philip consid-
ers valuable. I don't think he is going to be happy with you if you do. As it is,
she doesn't look like she is going to be of much use for a long time, if ever."

His chest heaving, Jesse took a menacing step towards Efren. "I don't
have to listen to you. If your uncle was here, he'd tell me to whip her harder."

"Well, here he comes," said Efren, pointing to Philip and Ruth, running towards them. "Let's see what he has to say about your handiwork."

Philip shoved past them and went over to Viney. Pulling her head back by her hair, he satisfied himself that she was still breathing. "You're lucky I'm not sending you to the Charleston workhouse to be whipped," he screamed, releasing her hair and pitching her head forward. "Jesse, give her fifty more lashes, and let's see if she tries to run away again," he ordered, and stepped aside to watch.

Efren staggered back, his brain struggling to make sense of the savagery before him. Despite everything he had learned about Philip, he had not believed his uncle was capable of such cruelty.

When it was over, Viney was cut down and left writhing and bleeding on the ground. Rushing to help her, Efren was blocked by his uncle. "Don't you ever interfere with my orders to punish a slave again," he snarled.

Efren's rage boiled over. "Or what? What are going to do to me? What happened to the brother my father adored? What would he say if he were to see what you have become? And this mad dog you have unleashed," he spat, pointing to Jesse, gloating in triumph. "He's the one who deserves to be whipped. Do you know why Viney ran? Because this son of a bitch has been raping her for months. You told me she was one of your best field slaves. Well, she's not going to be of much use to you anymore."

Jesse's smirk disappeared. Philip's face turned a mottled crimson, and Efren knew his words had hit their mark.

Cotter rushed to help Efren lift Viney to her feet. Moaning in pain and unable to stand on her own, she let them drape her arms over their shoulders and carry her to her cabin. It was then that Efren saw the three horizontal cuts on her cheeks that would mark her for the rest of her life.

Ruth and Old Sarah were waiting for them. Ruth stepped forward to help maneuver Viney face down onto her pallet.

"Mama is coming," said Ruth. "She went back to the big house to get a poultice and the herbs she needs. She said we should bathe the wounds in salt brine. It's going to hurt really bad, but we have to get the brine on the wounds to clean them out so they don't get infected, and so the torn skin doesn't rot."

Efren stood dazed, still unable to comprehend the evil he had witnessed. It was only when Ruth called his name a second time that he realized she was talking to him. "I'm sorry, Ruth, what did you say?"

"Old Sarah took Daniel and Emmy to the big house so they wouldn't see Jesse whipping Viney. Silas and Flora said they would look after them, but I'm pretty sure Daniel saw Jesse dragging Viney to the whipping tree."

Efren met Lindy as she was hurrying from the kitchen house. "I've never seen so much damage to the flesh before. Her back is covered in welts and flayed skin. Are you going to be able to help her?"

"Mister Efren, I gonna do everthin' I can. But we gots some prayin' to do for that poor girl, and her chiles. Flora and Miss Anica took little Emmy outside to play with Miss Isabel, but Daniel, he just cryin' his eyes out, and he won't talk to no one. Silas in the kitchen tryin' to get him calm."

The old slave sat with Daniel in his arms, stroking his back and letting him cry, great heaving sobs ripping through his small body. When Silas looked up, he blinked away his own tears. "Mister Efren, no chile should ever see what he seen done to his mama. He sufferin' real bad."

"Daniel," Efren called softly, placing his hand on the boy's shoulder.

"I wanna see my mama," he said between sobs.

"Lindy and Ruth are with Old Sarah, and they are taking good care of your mother. She's resting now, but I promise I will take you to see her as soon as Lindy says it's all right."

Daniel peered over Silas' shoulder at Efren. His sobs slowing, and his breathing becoming more regular, he slipped from Silas' arms into Efren's.

A deep sadness pressed down on Efren's chest; a weight so heavy it felt like it was crushing his soul. *This America, this land of promise, was no different than Spain. Intolerance. Hate. Torture. Women raped and beaten. Children made to witness unspeakable acts.* Holding Daniel in his arms, Efren feared he had escaped one maelstrom of horror only to be sucked into another.

CHAPTER 35

A pall hung over the big house in the days following Viney's whipping. Philip's stubborn refusal to dismiss Jesse intensified Efren's animosity towards his uncle, his resentment festering like a thorn wedged deep in his skin. Barely acknowledging each other at meals, they spoke only when they needed to address matters that concerned getting the harvested rice to Charleston and loaded onto the *Águila* for shipment to England.

Fearful of Philip's dark mood and Margaret's constant scrutiny, the slaves scurried to get their work done. When whispers of Efren's efforts to spare Viney further punishment reached the big house, they offered their silent thanks with nods and looks of admiration.

In the quarters, Jesse's unrelenting wrath fueled a constant tension. Humiliated by Efren, and aware that the man had now attained greater stature in the eyes of the slaves, the hot-tempered overseer was quick to use his whip or the butt of his rifle for the smallest infractions.

Despite the unrest swirling throughout the quarters, Lindy and Ruth took turns caring for Viney and sleeping in her cabin, while Old Sarah took Daniel and Emmy to her quarters at night. Feverish and delirious for days, Viney slipped in and out of consciousness, screaming in pain each time Lindy or Ruth applied a poultice of flowering yarrow to the torn flesh of her wounds. Worried about infection, Lindy would return to the quarters after each meal at the big house to change the bandages and layer them with Spanish moss to absorb the fluids seeping from her ravaged flesh.

When Viney's fever broke five days later, Lindy said a silent prayer of thanks that the worst days were behind them. Still troubled in her sleep, Viney called out in terror, and Lindy knew bad days were still to come.

The acrimonious chill in the big house gradually subsided, replaced by a general civility, such as one extends to an unwanted, but necessary guest. Still angry about his uncle's defense of Jesse, Efren fled the house each morning after breakfast, stopping by the stables to spend time with Daniel before checking on the progress of the threshing. As the lacerations that crisscrossed Viney's back and shoulders began to heal, Efren was pleased to see the fear disappear from the boy's face.

"Mornin' Mister Efren. Mama doin' better, and gettin' a little bit stronger. She askin' for you. She say she wanna see you. Can do?"

"Can do. I'd be happy to see your mother."

Daniel's face brightened, and Efren could feel his spirit lift.

"I done fed the horses, so we can go now, if you want."

Indicating Daniel should lead the way, Efren followed the boy through the quarters. As he passed the slave cabins, men and women too old to work in the fields stopped their tasks to nod and smile his way.

Daniel tugged his hand. "Mister Efren, they all thankin' you, 'cuz they knows what you did for Mama."

Lindy finished cleaning Viney's wounds while Efren and Daniel waited outside the cabin. Covered in sweat, Viney bit down on her lower lip, lines of pain etched on her face as Lindy applied a fresh poultice and bandage.

"I knows it hurts. I done now," murmured Lindy, helping her sit up. "You needs to drink all the burdock root tea I leavin' you. It keeps the fever away and helps the healin'. Promise me you gonna drink it."

Viney made a face. "Promise."

"Good. I'm gonna start bringin' you some decent meat from the big house if I can get it out without being noticed. You need to start eatin' to get strong. You hear?"

"I hears."

"All right then. Daniel brung Mister Efren over to see you. You ready for him?"

"Tell Daniel he need to get back to the stables, so there ain't no trouble with Jesse. I wants to see Mister Efren alone."

Lindy raised her eyebrows. "He be a good man. Don't go doin' nothin' stupid."

"I knows he a good man. That why I wants to talk to him."

Viney was sitting on the edge of her pallet, a piece of rough muslin cloth over her lap, when Efren entered the cabin. Her face gaunt, the bruises and cuts on her cheek still visible, she offered him a weak smile.

"I thanks you for you comin'. And thanks for what you done, tryin' to help me, and for your kindness to Daniel. He talk 'bout you all the time. He say your wife been lettin' Emmy play with your little girl."

Her words were a torment to Efren. The stain of guilt over his failure to spare Viney further punishment was like a poison eating away at his insides. The earthy smells of Lindy's medicinal herbs and the heat in the cabin closed in on him. Sweat coated his skin, pooling under his arms and trickling down the hollow of his back. He felt dizzy and squeezed his lids shut, trying to blot out the image of Jesse flaying the skin from Viney's back. When he opened his eyes, she was staring back at him.

"Viney, you owe me no thanks. I wish I could have done more," he said, his voice husky with regret. "Daniel has been a great help to me, and my daughter Isabel loves playing with Emmy. You don't have to worry about them. You just need to get better."

Tears slid from her eyes. "What if I ain't better? Mister Philip, he have no use for slaves what can't work." A ragged cough rumbled up from her chest, and she took a moment to catch her breath. "I gots caught 'cuz I turned back. I just couldn't go North without my babies. I be runnin' towards Bending Oaks when the dogs catch up to me. I be such a fool for thinkin' Jesse go easy on me if I come back on my own. Now I worth nothin' to Mister Philip. And Jesse, he gonna keep coming at me, only worser. I beggin' you, if I sold, or if I die, please don't let nothin' happen to my babies."

Viney's plea hit Efren like a blow to the chest, sucking the air from his lungs. *How could he promise Viney he would protect Daniel and Emmy when he had no power to do so? They were Philip's property.* The realization that there was always the danger that they could be sold at any time made his heart pound.

"Viney, I will always fight for what I think is right for your children. But you have to understand, I do not have the authority to make final decisions about their welfare or service here."

Viney bowed her head for a moment. When she looked up, her dark eyes were dull, defeat casting a shadow over her face. "I understands. But it give me comfort knowing you and your wife lookin' after Daniel and Emmy best you can."

Efren stood at the edge of the flower garden, looking on as Anica sat with Isabel and Emmy on her lap, a drowsy child curled under each arm. Mariana crooned a Spanish song he remembered from his childhood. He smiled when Anica joined in, softly singing the refrain about baby chicks chirping when they were hungry and cold.

"*Los pollitos dicen,*

pío, pío, pío,

cuando tienen hambre,

cuando tienen frío."

Within moments of each other, Isabel and Emmy were asleep, their heads resting close together on Anica's chest.

Greeting Mariana with a hug, Efren kissed Anica's cheek, lightly touching the heads of the sleeping toddlers. "I see you have become mother hen to two chicks. I hope it isn't too much for you. It won't be long before there is another one in the nest."

"I'm fine, and they really are no trouble. They play well together, and Isabel adores Emmy."

Efren lowered himself into a chair. "I just came from the quarters." Recounting his conversation with Viney, he became agitated, ashamed that he was not able to assure her that he would protect Daniel and Emmy from harm.

"The poor woman," said Mariana. "Lindy said some of the slaves have been judging her for running away and abandoning her children. The real shame is that she was punished so horribly for coming back to them on her own."

"I don't think there is any worry that Viney will be sold," added Anica. "Ruth told me the scars on her face and back mark her as runner. She said no one will buy her because of the fear that she will run away again."

Efren sighed. "I am not sure if that's a good thing for Viney. I worry about what Jesse might do to her. And my uncle has proven he will not step in to stop Jesse's cruelty."

CHAPTER 36

November 1785

The milling finished, the bushels of rice were stored in barrels and loaded onto the flatboats that would carry them to Gibbes Wharf in Charleston Harbor. There, the *Águila* waited, moored and ready to deliver its cargo to England.

The morning Efren was to leave for Charleston to attend to final arrangements for the shipment, the air was crisp and tinged with an early November chill. Waking slowly, he turned to his side seeking the warmth of Anica's body, and found her propped up on her elbow, smiling at him. Her hair loose and draped over her breasts, she moved closer to him, nuzzling into his neck.

"And what are you smiling about?" he asked, trailing his fingers along her naked shoulder.

"At you. You were smiling in your sleep."

"Ah, that was only because I was remembering last night." In one quick motion, he pulled her on top of him. Brushing her lips lightly at first, his kiss became a hunger that begged to be sated.

Anica's eyes widened. "Again?"

"Again," he whispered, his touch igniting her skin on fire.

Anica clung to Efren one last time before he stepped into the coach. "Come back to us safely, *mi amor*."

Efren ran his hand along the smooth skin of her arm before kissing her hand. "I promise I will. I should only be gone four days. I'll be with Amadis on the *Águila,* so I will be well taken care of."

"Just don't enjoy too much of his Madeira," said Anica, managing a smile.

One of the horses whinnied, scraping the ground with his hoof to make known his impatience with prolonged goodbyes. Efren drew Anica to him for one last kiss, and signaled to James he was ready to leave.

Anica stood watching the coach lumber down the carriageway. When it finally disappeared from sight, she joined Mariana and Isabel on the front portico.

"He will be back before you know it. Now, come," said Mariana, putting an arm around Anica's shoulder, "Ruth is bringing Emmy over from the quarters so she and Isabel can play."

They found Ruth in the kitchen, Emmy perched on her lap, covered in biscuit crumbs. "This child sure does love Mama's biscuits. This is her third one," laughed Ruth, kissing her forehead, as Isabel rushed to hug her new friend.

"Hello, little one. Here's one for you too."

Taking the biscuit Ruth offered in one hand, and Emmy's hand in the other, Isabel tugged her friend towards the garden. "Mariana, too?" she asked, her brows knitted, her crinkled face irresistible.

"Of course, I will come, *mi ángel*," said Mariana. "Let's go see if we can find that silly old cat in the garden."

Ruth lingered at the kitchen house door, watching Emmy and Isabel holding hands and calling for Tabby, the skinny orange cat who prowled the garden for mice. "Old Sarah told Mama that Emmy is always asking for 'Isa.' From what I can tell, it looks like the feeling is mutual."

"Isabel adores Emmy. Daniel too. How is Viney?"

"She is getting better. Her wounds are starting to close up, but she is still weak."

"I know Efren is very concerned about her. He's worried about what will happen to her if she can't work in the fields the way she did before."

Ruth did not answer right away. Studying her hands, she faltered for a moment before summoning the courage to present the plan she and Lindy had been considering for days.

"Miss Anica, Viney is in real danger in the quarters. Jesse is sniffing around her cabin again, and the only thing that's keeping him from bothering her is Mama. She's been sleeping over there, and Jesse knows better than to tangle with her because she's Mister Philip's favorite cook, and Mister Philip is still angry with him…" Her voice trailed off as she chose her next words carefully. "I know I have no place asking this," she said, "but is there a way Viney could come work in the house when she gets better? Mama doesn't use the room off the kitchen much. Viney could stay there with Daniel and Emmy, and she would be safe from Jesse."

When Anica didn't answer, Ruth pressed her case further, her words coming in a rush. "It would be good for Daniel and Emmy. And this way, Isabel could play with Emmy every day."

Anica held up her hand to slow Ruth down. "You don't have to convince me. I think it's a wonderful idea. I just don't know if we can convince Margaret and Philip that it is."

Ruth's mouth curved into a sly smile. "When Mama thinks Viney is healed enough, she is going to tell Mister Philip she needs more regular help than Sally in the kitchen, and suggest Viney. That should make Miss Margaret happy because it will free Sally from her kitchen chores, and then she can serve as her personal maid again."

Anica regarded this fierce version of Ruth, so confident that her plan would work. "I am impressed that you seem to have this all worked out."

Red blotches blossomed on Ruth's cheek. "Miss Anica, I hope I wasn't too forward, but Mama and I are afraid for Viney."

"You are right to be concerned about Viney. Just let me discuss your plan with Efren when he returns from Charleston. We are going to need his help if we are going to make this work."

Anica measured the days of Efren's departure by the passage of daily events, each one bringing him closer to home. Two breakfasts without him meant only one more remained. Three sleepless nights, and his side of the bed would no longer be empty. Lighting the *Shabbat* candles on Friday marked his return the next day.

As she had done every Friday since she first observed the simple beauty of the *Shabbat* candle-lighting ceremony, Ruth joined Anica as she lit the candles. When the wicks caught, and the flickering flames reached upward in an arc of bright light, Ruth felt her soul lift and fly unbound.

"I always feel at peace when you light the candles," said Ruth after Anica finished saying the Sabbath prayer. "I can see the tranquility in your eyes too."

Anica grew wistful. "The women of my faith have welcomed the Sabbath this way since biblical times. My mother taught me that lighting the candles on the Sabbath brings peace to the home; that their flames illuminate the darkness and make room for joy to enter the house. For many years after she died, I prayed, but did not light the candles because it was forbidden, and I was afraid of discovery. I had almost forgotten how sweet these moments are. Now, when I say the prayer, I feel connected to the generations of women in my family who had the courage to pray in secret." Anica's voice broke. "When I pray, I hear my mother's voice whispering the prayer with me."

CHAPTER 37

The clatter of the coach and the pounding of the horses' hooves announced Efren's return as James steered the team along the carriageway. Spotting their approach from her bedchamber window, Anica was in Efren's arms as soon as he stepped from the coach.

Seated at her dressing table, Margaret watched the scene playing out below in contempt, the happiness of the couple's reunion mocking her own loveless marriage. Seething with rage, she threw her hand mirror against the wall, its thud and the sound of breaking glass bringing Charles scurrying from the adjacent sitting room.

"What the hell?" he bellowed, appraising the shattered pieces of coated glass clinging to the flocked wallpaper and covering the floor. "What's gotten into you now?"

"Them," she said, pointing outside, just as Isabel dropped Mariana's hand and ran towards Efren and Anica. "Look at them. The perfect family, all happiness and smiles."

Incredulous, Charles bit back a sneer. "That's why you are throwing things? Because they're happy?"

Margaret made a growling sound that always reminded Charles of a wild creature. "Don't you see? Everything has changed since they got here. We have lost control of the household. The house slaves are much more willing to please them than us. Efren is handling all the details related to selling and shipping our crop. He's even managed to convince Philip that he didn't have

to accompany him to Charleston. Soon that bitch will bring another screaming brat into the house. And in case you haven't noticed, Philip is drinking
more than ever. The one thing that hasn't changed is you," she said lashing
out. "You do nothing around here but preen and disappear most nights to
God knows where."

Charles' eyes filled with hate. "The only bitch in this house is you," he
shouted, slamming the door behind him.

Philip asked Efren to meet him in his study before supper to discuss
the events of his trip. By the time Efren joined him, the half-empty whiskey
decanter on his uncle's desk explained his glassy-eyed stare.

Philip handed Efren a glass. "Pour yourself a drink."

Efren placed the empty glass back on the desk. "No thank you. I've had
a long day. I am tired, and my back aches from bouncing around in the carriage for hours. I am afraid a drink will put me to sleep."

Shrugging, Philip refilled his glass. "So, tell me, was our agent able to
sell our crop at the price we were asking?"

"Close enough that when you consider the Águila is mine, and we are
not paying a fee for the ship, we should make an excellent profit."

Philip studied Efren through half-closed eyes. "Don't start counting
your money yet. Our profit depends on many things we have no control
over. Everything will depend on the weather and on Captain Lopez's ability
to deliver the shipment safely to England."

Efren did not need his uncle to remind him of the treachery of the sea.
"The Águila is as sound as any ship on the ocean. I have complete faith in
Captain Lopez and the crew to make the voyage and return to Charleston
safely."

"I hope you are right," said Philip, emptying his glass in a single gulp.
"We cannot afford a mishap of any kind."

"I understand," said Efren. Turning to leave, he was nearly knocked over
by Margaret's sudden entrance into the room.

"If you are talking about the shipment to England, I would like to join
you," she said, focusing a steely glare on Efren.

"It's all been discussed, and it is of no concern to you," snapped Philip.
"You would do better to spend more time running the household and less

running off with your emptyheaded friends."

Margaret's eyes narrowed. "And you would do better to spend less time with a drink in your hand."

Philip pounded his desk, his empty glass crashing to the floor, shards of glass covering the marble tile. "Let me remind you who puts a roof over your head and the food in your stomach. My promise to your mother to provide for you only goes so far. Am I being clear?"

Margaret's mouth twitched. Without a word, she whirled and left the room.

Efren was grateful for the end of the long day. Stretched out on their bed, he told Anica about his encounter with Margaret and his uncle as she placed Isabel in her crib and covered the sleepy child with a blanket.

"From the very first day we arrived here I sensed that Margaret resented our presence," said Anica, lying down beside him, and tucking herself under his arm. "Since her return from Savannah, she has made a point of letting me know she is in charge of the house slaves. I am convinced she hates us, and I am afraid of what she is capable of."

Efren yawned and shifted his weight to accommodate the pain in his back. "I am hopeful that we won't have to stay here much longer. The rice sold for a good price. If all goes well, we should be able to establish ourselves in Charleston within a few months after the baby is born. The new venture with Amadis looks promising. He was able to take one more shipment to Boston before he moored the *Águila* to wait for Philip's crop."

Giving in to the tug of exhaustion, Efren mumbled something unintelligible, his hand slipping from Anica's shoulder.

Anica lightly brushed his lips. "Sleep, *mi amor*."

CHAPTER 38

December 1785

Wrapped in a thin blanket and listening to the sounds of the quarters coming to life, Viney gratefully accepted the cup of tea Lindy offered her. With the harvest completed, the field slaves had returned to the paddies to prepare the ground for the next season's crops. Starting before sunrise in the cold mist of December Lowcountry mornings, they labored in the mud, burning away the stubble of the old rice plants. Using their hands, a few simple tools, and buckets, they worked to dig new trenches, and clear the rubble from the existing ditches. It was back-breaking work, and for the first time that she could remember, Viney was not among them.

Taking a cautious sip of the tea, she closed her eyes, and let the hot liquid warm her from the inside. "You know Jesse gonna be stickin' his head in here to see if I can work today, just like he do every morning. He not gonna put up with me stayin' out of the fields much longer. I keep tryin', but I still can't raise my arm much higher than this," she said, barely bringing her hand to her face.

Lindy stirred the pot of cornmeal mush hanging over the fire and ladled the thick yellow porridge into a wooden bowl. "You need to eat this to get your strength back. Your back and shoulders mostly healed. Now you need to start movin' around more to get your arms and legs strong again."

Viney grimaced. "It still hurt to move. Everthin' feel tight, like I got bands stretched across my back."

"I knows it hurt, but you got to keep your shoulders from tightenin' up, or you'll never be able to move your arms all the way. You'll be no use…"

Both women jumped when the cabin door burst open. Viney pulled the blanket around her chest and looked at Lindy.

Jesse stood in the middle of the cabin, his hands on his hips. "How much longer you think you can stay holed up in here? You ain't fooling me. Drop that blanket so I can see your back."

Viney began to shake. Lindy moved in front of her, blocking the overseer's view. "You can look at her back all you want, but you ain't gonna see the problems. Them scars are thick and pullin' tight on the skin so she can't move real good." Lindy shifted her stance in defiance. "I'm guessin' she never will."

A muscle twitched in Jesse's face. His hand dropped to the whip hanging at his side. "I said I want to see her back."

Lindy moved slowly towards Viney. "It all right," she whispered in Viney's ear as she bent and carefully lowered the blanket, exposing only her shoulders and back.

Jesse smiled at the sight of the constellation of thick cords of raised flesh that traversed the length of Viney's torso. "Looks like I did a mighty good job."

Lindy replaced the blanket around Viney's shoulders. "All them scars around her back and shoulders makin' it hard for her to move her arms. She need some time to stretch the skin out."

Jesse squinted at Lindy, deciding what to do. "All right," he said at last. "She got till next week, but no more. I don't care if all she can do is tote water like the damn brats, but she's gonna be back in the field." He moved towards Viney and laughed when she drew back.

"Good. Now you know I mean what I say."

As soon as Jesse left for the fields, Lindy hurried to the kitchen house. Stopping at the door to catch her breath, she was relieved to find that Ruth had started preparing breakfast without her.

"You all right, Mama? I was getting worried about you."

Tying on her apron, Lindy stepped in beside Ruth and began rolling out the biscuit dough. "I was with Viney. Jesse came to the cabin like he always do to see if Viney ready to go to the fields. He give her a week more, and he gonna put her in the field even if she not up to it." Lindy shook her head.

"She not gonna be ready. We gotta talk to Miss Anica and Mister Efren about gettin' Viney here to the big house. Quick."

Days later, Viney, Emmy, and Daniel moved into the room off the kitchen. Efren had patiently waited until he found Margaret and Philip together in the parlor before suggesting that Viney would be an excellent addition as a house slave and a great help to Lindy. Philip's reticence to lose a field worker was easily overcome by Margaret's enthusiasm for the chance to have Sally back as her personal maid.

"I could see Philip had no appetite for a confrontation with Margaret," Efren told Anica after their meeting. "He was much more interested in the bottle of whiskey on the table by his chair than in what I had to say."

Anica's face hardened. "In spite of his promise to you, his behavior is becoming more reckless. While you were in Charleston, he would leave right after supper and come creeping home in the morning looking disheveled and reeking of alcohol. He'd sleep all day, and we wouldn't see him again until supper."

Efren's shoulders drooped. "I can't say I am surprised."

"Lately, he seems absent even when he is here. I'm glad you are taking a more active part in managing the day-to-day affairs of the plantation. I worry that Philip will try to steal from us again."

"You are the only one who is glad. Margaret is fuming that I am looking at Philip's records. I think my uncle agreed to let Viney leave the fields and free up Sally to appease her."

"Whatever Philip's reason for consenting, having Viney here in the house will keep her and the children safe from Jesse."

Efren grew thoughtful. "I worry she's still not strong enough to do a full day's work. I spoke to Ruth and Lindy about making sure Viney always has chores to do. If Philip sees her being idle, he'll put her back in the field, regardless of what Margaret wants, and that would put her in peril. Jesse is furious about Philip letting them leave the quarters. It makes him look weak to the other slaves, and that makes him dangerous."

On their first night away from the quarters, Viney lay on her pallet watching her children sleep. A thin shaft of moonlight spilled through the boards of the tiny room off the kitchen, its pale glow soft on their sweet faces. In the half-light she saw that they slept holding hands, and she smiled. *Her babies were safe. Jesse would not come bursting through the door. Darkness would no longer be her enemy.* Her lids heavy with sleep, Viney closed her eyes.

As the days passed, Viney grew stronger. Grateful to be in the big house, she no longer complained about Lindy's potions, or resisted her prodding to lift her arms to regain the motion she'd lost. The fiery pain that coursed its way along her back to her shoulders began to subside. Within weeks of her arrival, Viney was working alongside Lindy in the kitchen house peeling potatoes, and chuckling at the sounds of Emmy and Isabel playing outside in the herb garden.

Lindy rolled pieces of chicken in flour and smiled at Viney. "It good to hear you sounding happy."

"My heart is full hearin' them little ones together. Soon as Emmy up, she wantin' to be with Miss Isabel. And Daniel, he his ol' smilin' self again. I knows I here because of all you and Ruth did for me. I would be dead by now and my babies sold, but for you takin' care of me, feedin' me, and gettin' Mister Efren and Miss Anica to help. It mean everythin' to me to be here with Emmy and Daniel and not be fearin' Jesse every night. I ain't gonna let you down, I promise."

"I gonna keep you to that promise," said Lindy, glancing sideways at Viney. "Just don't get it into your head to run again."

Ruth stopped at the top of the stairs to catch her breath. She had been busy all day helping to decorate the house for Christmas, and nearly forgot that it was Friday. Bent over and sucking in a lungful of air, she felt the baby kick, as if to remind her it was almost sundown and Anica was waiting for her to light the *Shabbat* candles.

"You have no mercy," she said to her bulging belly. "Moving around at night so I can't sleep, poking me all day long. You better calm down by the time you're ready to come into this world or else you are going to have one tired mama. Now, settle down, please."

Anica stood in the doorway smiling. "If your baby listens to you, will you have a talk with mine?"

Ruth jerked her body upright.

"I didn't mean to startle you," said Anica, stepping aside so Ruth could enter the bedchamber. "You are just in time. The sun is almost ready to set."

Ruth set the tapers in the candlesticks. As Anica lit the candles, she pulled the shawl from her shoulders and covered her head. Bowing her head, Ruth mouthed the words as Anica prayed over the candles.

"You learned the prayer," murmured Anica, as they stood watching the flames gutter.

"Oh, Miss Anica. I meant no disrespect. I just learned it from hearing it. Please don't be angry."

"Angry? I am not angry. I cannot tell you how moved I am that you have taken the prayer to your heart."

"Some of the masters let their slaves pray. They even let preachers come to the quarters to give sermons. Mama said before Miss Mary married Mister Philip, she had an old freed slave come to the quarters on Sundays to preach the gospel. Mister Philip doesn't allow any preaching. I never knew what it was like to talk to God. The prayer and lighting the candles are a comfort to me. It's something that has become a part of me now; something that can't be taken from me. It makes a piece of me feel free, like I am standing in freedom's light."

CHAPTER 39

Christmas Day 1785

The slave quarters hummed with excitement. Christmas morning marked the beginning of a three-day celebration. Three days of respite from the fields. Three days of feasting, music, dancing, and jugs filled with whiskey. Three days when passes to go into town or to visit spouses, families, and friends on other plantations, were easier to come by. Three days of enjoying a tiny taste of liberty.

Just before dawn, their breath forming plumes of vapor in the cold air as they worked, Silas and Henry delivered cuts of chicken, butchered beef, and a whole hog for the slaves' Christmas feast. By mid-morning, the meat would be slow roasting over open pits, saturating the air with a smokey, mouthwatering aroma that tormented empty stomachs.

Also up and at work well before the sun rose, Lindy, Ruth, and Viney were preparing breakfast so it could be served early, and the holiday celebration could begin. It was the custom at Bending Oaks to invite the slaves to gather outside the big house on Christmas morning to receive gifts of tobacco, small jugs of rum, extra molasses, and butter, as well as their yearly allotment of shoes, clothing, and blankets. Ginger-cakes and stockings filled with candy, slices of oranges and apples, and small toys awaited the children. A tradition established by Philip's wife Mary, it was one of the few remaining traces of the regard she had for the people who worked her land.

"We got to get right to makin' dinner as soon as breakfast over," Lindy instructed Viney, putting biscuits into to the hot oven. "Brock is comin' over to the quarters with Walter. I ain't seen him since…" She stopped herself before she said "you ran away."

Ruth sighed, running her hand over her stomach. "I've gotten much bigger since the last time I saw Walter. I don't think he's going to find what he was expecting."

Lindy hugged her daughter. "Jus' more of you to love."

Viney reached for the plates to bring to the table. "My brother comin' over. He got no one else to celebrate with. I jus' hates for him to see me like this." She ran her fingers along the thick scars on her face, the slices of pulpy skin ragged to her touch.

"He gonna be happy to see you and the children. And help empty them whiskey jugs," said Lindy, coaxing a smile from Viney.

"Y'all go on ahead," said Viney, "I knows I slowin' you down. My brother already gots the kids up there, so he knows I comin'."

Ruth wanted to run not walk to the quarters. "You sure you'll be all right?"

"I be fine. You go on."

Ruth looked at Lindy, and they both picked up their pace, the sounds of music and laughter coming from the quarters urging them on. "I don't think I'll be dancing much," said Ruth, looking down at her stomach.

"That's all right. Me and Brock be dancin' enough to make up for you and Walter."

"Just remember your age. You don't want to hurt yourself," teased Ruth.

"Just remember I your mama and can still…" The words stuck in Lindy's throat, when she saw Brock standing alone in the path, a pained look on his face.

He slowly walked towards them, every step increasing the sorrow in his expression. "Ruth, honey, I gots some bad news."

Ruth began to shake; the ground beneath her started to spin. She reached for Lindy's arm to steady herself. Her eyes darted around, but she knew she wouldn't find who she was looking for. "Walter?"

"Chile, I so sorry." His voice broke. His shoulders heaved and sobs tore through his body. "He dead."

Ruth heard screams and only realized they were hers as she tumbled into inky darkness.

When she woke, Ruth was in Lindy's cabin, her mother holding her hand, Brock sitting at her side. Confused by the noise and merriment outside, she blinked, her eyes coming to rest on Lindy's worried face.

"Mama, it's not a bad dream, is it?"

"No baby, it ain't. I so sorry."

Ruth stared numbly at Brock, fighting to make sense of the chaos in her head. "What happened?"

"Walter, he always suspected that Mister Berrell his daddy. He never knowed for sure, but Mister Berrell always kind to him. Mister Berrell got a son, name of Edgar, who go away to some fancy school most of the year. He come home for Christmas and seein' how Mister Berrell treat Walter so good, he get jealous and real mad. Whenever Mister Berrell ain't around, he sayin' nasty things to Walter, pushin' him around and trippin' him. Walter knowed better than fightin' back. But Edgar, he call Walter's mama a whore. Walter just couldn't hold back no more. He jumped on Edgar and started beatin' on him real good. I pulled them apart and make Walter cool down; Edgar screamin' and cussin' the whole time, sayin' he gonna kill Walter. We walkin' off, when Edgar come from behind and shoot him. I couldn't do nothin'. Walter bleedin' bad. Blood comin' from his back, bubblin' from his mouth. I carried Walter to the big house as fast as I could, but he dead by the time I get there."

Brock wiped away his tears with his sleeve. "Mister Berrell scream at Edgar somethin' terrible. The house servants said he slapped his son and pushed him down, but Mistress Berrell, she jump in and protect the boy. She never been happy about Walter. She probably knowed Mister Berrell his daddy. She sendin' Edgar back to that fancy school to keep him safe from Mister Berrell. She know the law ain't gonna do nothin' about a white man killin' a slave."

Ruth grew quiet. Despair swallowed her, carving a hollow place in her heart. She felt empty, bereft of substance. Afloat in a sea of sorrow, she was surprised she was still breathing.

CHAPTER 40

February 1786

The second month of the new year was colder than Ruth ever remembered. Her thin sweater offered little protection from the icy chill of the relentless wind that tugged at her skirt, catching its hem, and threatening to wrap it around her ankles and trip her. Her head lowered and her arms pulled tightly around her chest, Ruth felt big and ungainly walking as fast as she could from the quarters to the big house. Protesting the constant jostling, the baby kicked and shifted, pressing down on her bladder. Hastening her steps, she grabbed a bucket as soon as she entered the kitchen house and disappeared into the side room, the panicked look on her face all the explanation Lindy and Viney needed.

Viney chuckled. "That baby better come soon. She lookin' like she 'bout had it."

"It's not jus' the baby. She ain't herself since Walter got killed. It like she here but she ain't. There ain't no light in her eyes. I worried 'bout her. Miss Anica worried too. Ruth carryin' low now. That baby comin' any day."

Ruth returned to the kitchen and stood in front of the oven to get warm, her hand pressed against the ache in her lower back. When the women suddenly stopped their chatter, she knew they'd been talking about her.

"What are you two hatching up?"

Viney looked down and kept rolling the dough for biscuits.

Lindy wiped her hands on her apron. "We sayin' it lookin' like that baby gonna be born soon. How you feelin'?"

Ruth's chin quivered. She wanted to tell them that a profound sadness left her in a world so dark she was without hope. She wanted to tell them that grief clung to her skin and echoed throughout her body. She wanted to tell them that every memory of Walter made the hole in her heart bigger.

Instead, she said, "I hope you're right about the baby coming soon, because I feel like a melon ready to split open. I'm not sleeping much. I can't find a comfortable position, and when I finally do, I have to use the bucket. I am so ready to have this child."

Lindy placed her hand on Ruth's stomach and felt the baby kick. "My grandbaby jus' say hello. We gonna get along jus' fine," she said, the corners of her mouth lifting into a broad smile.

Ignoring the persistent ache in her back as she climbed the stairs to Anica's bedchamber, Ruth stopped mid-way to catch her breath. "You need to move so I can breathe better," she instructed the baby. "I have to get the candles to Miss Anica before the sun sets, though I don't know how anyone can tell when that is, it's so gray outside." Breathing hard, she waited for a response. When the baby did not change positions, she moved awkwardly to the top of the stairs.

"Sorry I didn't get here sooner," said Ruth, handing Anica the candles. "I went to the cabin to rest and fell asleep."

Anica drew Ruth into the room and assured her there was time before they had to light the candles. Her ragged breathing and drawn look worried Anica.

"I'm glad you decided to join me again," she said. I missed you all those weeks you stayed away."

Ruth pressed her hands into the small of her back, the ache becoming a dull pain. "I didn't feel like talking to God for a while. I didn't think He would listen to me while I was so angry, and my heart was emptied of everything but hate."

"I am glad you're back."

"My baby brought me back. I don't want to bring my child into this world with my heart filled with so much poison. It's just that my baby's worth will always be measured by the amount of work it can do or how much money it will bring on the auction block." Ruth clasped her hands over her stomach. "I know God is listening when you pray over the candles, and my baby is going to need every blessing possible."

A lump lodged in Anica's throat. She'd lived on the plantation long enough to know that Ruth's fears for her baby were well-founded. Reality had already shown her that Ruth would never know a day when she would not worry if her child would be sold away from her, or if she would be sold away from her child. Ruth's entire life would be spent at the mercy of Philip's whims, or of any man who lusted after her.

Hoping to give Ruth the comfort she sought, Anica raised her shawl over her head and lit the candles. After she'd recited the prayer and lowered her hands from her eyes, she found Ruth staring horrified at the small puddle at her feet.

CHAPTER 41

"You gots a girl." said Lindy. "I knows how you worrin' and hopin' it a boy, but listen to this baby cry. She fierce."

Too exhausted to respond, Ruth let Viney tend to her, while Lindy cleaned the baby and cut and tied the umbilical cord. Once the infant's navel had been taken care of and a belly band secured around her middle, Lindy placed the squalling infant in her daughter's arms. Ruth's face softened, and she kissed the baby's cheeks, all the sorrow and emptiness of the past months replaced by a burst of love so strong it hurt.

When the infant's hands flailed and her cries grew sharper and angrier, demanding to be fed, Lindy laughed. "That little girl already gots a mind of her own. She gonna be a handful. You mark my words."

Ruth studied her baby's tiny face before taking her to her breast. "Mama," she said, in a voice so soft Lindy strained to hear her, "she's beautiful and light-skinned."

The smile disappeared from Lindy's face, and her eyes clouded. "I knows, chile. I knows."

The following morning, Lindy stoked the fire in the cabin before she left for the kitchen house, and set a bowl of cornmeal mush on the chair next to Ruth's pallet. "Old Sarah gonna come stay with you while I at the kitchen house. She good at carin' for new mamas and new babies, and I wants to make sure someone here with you, in case Jesse come pokin' around. You makes sure you eat that mush, and keep that chile close to you so's you both stay warm."

Ruth rolled her eyes. "Mama, I know what to do. We'll stay warm, I will eat, and she will be fed."

"Well, she sleepin' now, so you should sleep too, 'cuz she gonna get hungry again real soon," said Lindy, stroking the infant's head, her hair soft as down.

"Mama," said Ruth as Lindy started to go, "I want to give her your mother's name. The one she was given when she was brought to Charleston from Africa. I want to call her Hannah."

Lindy's eyes grew moist. "You never gots to know your grandmother, but she a proud woman. Smart and strong too. It the perfect name for my granddaughter. Don't you worry none about this baby no more. My mama's spirit gonna protect her."

The cabin door flew open, a gust of cold air swooping into the cabin. Expecting Old Sarah, Lindy and Ruth were stunned by the appearance of Lucinda, the overseer's wife. Tall and boney, her black stringy hair was pasted flat against her head, giving her gaunt face and deep-set eyes a skeletal look.

"I heard there was a new baby girl in the quarters," she said, her stare never leaving Ruth's face. "Jesse sent me to see if she was healthy."

Ruth pulled Hannah closer to her as the woman approached.

"The baby sleeping," said Lindy, stationing herself between Ruth and the overseer's wife.

"I'm not going to wake her. I just want to look at her." She pursed her thin lips, the lines etched around her mouth folding into each other. "Or is there a reason you don't want me to see her?"

"I have nothing to hide," said Ruth, pulling aside the blanket draped around Hannah's head.

Peering into the baby's face. Lucinda's beady eyes became slits. "She is very light, isn't she?"

"Black babies born lighter than they gonna be," said Lindy. "This baby's daddy the slave that got killed over to the Berrell plantation."

"Well, we'll have to see, won't we? You take care, now Ruth," said Lucinda, her mouth twisting into a smirk.

As soon as the woman left, Ruth felt like she could breathe again. "Mama, she knows."

"'Course she does. Jesse didn't send her. She know what Jesse doin' when he go prowlin' around at night."

Anica cradled three-day-old Hannah in her arms. The infant's light brown eyes were bright and probing, intent in their contemplation of her face. "I hope you are being a good girl for your mother and letting her rest," she cooed.

Ruth shifted on her pallet trying to find a comfortable position. "She had a mind of her own before she was born, and she's just as fiery now. She gets furious when she's hungry, and her face gets all red if she doesn't latch on right away. I just nursed her, so you're seeing her in one of her better moods."

"She a good baby," said Old Sarah. "She just spirited, that's all."

"Spirited is going to be a good quality for such a beautiful child," said Anica, meeting Ruth's eyes as she placed Hannah back in her arms. "She will be the daughter you raise. I have no doubt that she will be as strong as her mother."

Before she could respond, someone rapped three times on the cabin door. Old Sarah flinched, and fear tracked across her face. "She comin'."

Bewildered, Anica looked at Ruth. "What's happening? Who's coming?"

"Mama told anyone who sees Jesse's wife coming this way to knock on the door three times. She came here the day after Hannah was born to look her over. She's coming back to see if Hannah's skin has gotten darker."

Rigid with rage, Anica turned toward the door. Arms folded, she waited.

Within minutes, the overseer's wife came barging into the cabin. "Let me see..."

"Let you see what?" asked Anica in clipped tones.

Lucinda took several steps backward, nearly tripping over the small pile of logs near the door. "I... I came to see how Ruth was feeling," she stammered.

"As you can see, she is fine, so there is no need for you to disturb her or the infant again."

Lucinda stared defiantly at Anica, her eyes lingering on her swollen belly. "Are you saying I can't come around again?"

"I'm saying I don't think you want your husband to know you're nosing around in the quarters."

The momentary flash of anger that flickered across Lucinda's face before she brought it under control did not go unnoticed by Anica.

"Ruth needs to rest, so it's best if you leave."

Her lips tightening into a thin line, Lucinda nodded and left the cabin.

"She is more dangerous than Jesse," said Anica. "Ruth, you and Hannah are going to stay at the big house."

"You told her what?" shrilled Margaret, shaking with rage. "I don't care who has been bothering Ruth. How dare you presume she and her squalling brat are welcome to stay in the house. I won't have it!"

Anica nestled her arms around her stomach, as if she were cradling the child within. "Will you throw me out when my 'squalling brat' is born?"

Margaret's lips twitched into a sneer. "I will admit I am not happy there will soon be a screaming infant in the house keeping us up at night."

Inwardly seething, Anica kept her face serene. "I guarantee that after the first few sleepless nights, you will be so tired you won't even hear the baby crying."

"Enough! Stop this ridiculous bickering," commanded Philip, bolting from his chair. "Anica, Margaret is right; there is no place for Ruth and her baby in the house."

Anica made a pretense of being lost in thought for a moment. "What if I can find a suitable space in one of the outbuildings near the house? Could Ruth and the baby stay there?" she asked, ignoring Margaret's smug expression.

Philip drew his hand over his face, and licking his dry lips, eyed the decanter of brandy on the side table. "Fine," he answered, willing to agree to anything to be rid of the two women.

Anica ducked her head so they could not see her gloat. Anticipating a negative response, Lindy had shown her the room off the side of the washhouse. Once the living quarters of the slave who did the laundry, it had remained empty since Philip sold the young girl to another plantation owner.

Margaret glared at Anica. "Just keep the brat out of my sight," she said, stomping out of the sitting room.

"Thank you for letting Ruth and Hannah stay closer to the house," said Anica. "And I'm sorry if I caused a problem between you and Margaret."

Philip shrugged. "There is always some kind of problem between me and Margaret. Just make sure she has no reason to be upset with Ruth or the baby." His eyes remained on her face. "Tell me, is Jesse the baby's father?"

Anica returned his gaze. "No, it's Walter, the young slave who was shot by Clayton Berrell's son," she said, hoping she hadn't answered too quickly.

"A shame about the boy. He was a good carpenter. Made a lot of money for Clayton." Philip poured a glass of brandy and swirled the golden-brown liquor. "No matter, Ruth's baby still adds to my stock of slaves."

CHAPTER 42

March 1786

Sounding far away at first, the knocking at her bedchamber door grew louder. Startled awake, and disoriented by the golden streaks of afternoon sun pouring through the window, it took Anica a few seconds to realize she had fallen asleep in the rocker where she sat reading. Taking deep breaths to calm her pounding heart, she heaved herself out of the chair and waddled across the room.

"Thank goodness you are all right," said Ruth when the door opened. "I hadn't seen you all morning and I was afraid something was wrong. It's almost time for dinner, and Mister Efren sent me looking for you."

Anica rubbed the sleep from her eyes. "Sorry. Mariana took Isabel to play with Emmy so I could rest, and I must have dozed off."

"No need to explain to me," said Ruth, peering at Hannah, asleep in the sling fastened crosswise to her body.

Anica sighed, the dark circles under her eyes testimony to her fatigue. "It's been weeks since I've had a good night's sleep. If it's not leg cramps keeping me up, it's the need to use the chamber pot. A lot."

"You know you're not going to be any less tired after the baby is born," said Ruth as Hannah stirred in the sling and tucked her hands under her chin.

"I do know. But I'd rather be exhausted from having the baby than waiting for it to get here."

Three nights later, Efren was pounding on Mariana's door. "For God's sake, Mariana, wake up! The baby is coming!"

The door flew open and Mariana stood staring at Efren, his shirt half tucked into his breeches, his uncombed hair a mass of unruly curls. "Are you sure? You thought it was coming last night," she said, struggling to find the sleeve of her dressing gown.

"It's real this time. Please, come stay with her while I get Lindy. After last night, I asked her to sleep in the kitchen house with Viney so she would be close by," said Efren, already descending the stairs.

Mariana entered the room just as Anica felt the bottom of a contraction begin its steady, wave-like roll. Grabbing the sheets, she rocked back and forth, a guttural sound escaping through her clenched teeth as the pain crested, its touch red and hot, sluicing through her like molten steel. Her body limp and slick with sweat, she was left gasping for air when the contraction finally abated.

Mariana's cool hand stroked her cheek. "Efren went to get Lindy, *Mi cariña*. Soon you will be holding your beautiful baby."

Anica grabbed her hand. "I am so afraid," she rasped. "I keep seeing Mama's face, like she is waiting for me to join her."

Mariana pushed the damp hair from Anica's face. "*Cariña,* she's not waiting for you. She is watching over you."

Lindy emerged from Anica's bedchamber, her expression unreadable.

Efren's heart began to race. "What's wrong? It's been hours. Why is it taking so long?"

"Don't you get all upset. Miss Anica fine, but she tired and the pains slowin' down. I gonna boil up some blue cohosh tea to get them started again. Don't want that baby waitin' too much longer to get born. Viney stayin' with her, and she restin' a bit."

"I don't like this," said Efren after Lindy left. "I should have insisted on having a doctor here."

Mariana placed a reassuring hand his arm. "You know Anica wanted Lindy to deliver the baby. She is in good hands. I'm going to sit with her until Lindy comes back. Isabel is still sleeping. I checked on her a few minutes ago."

Efren stood staring at the closed bedchamber door, consumed by a panic he could not keep at bay. Hours of listening to Anica cry out in pain seared his heart. Fear that he could lose her coursed through his brain like a surging sea. Shaking his head to chase away the terror, he was surprised to find Ruth standing at the top of the stairs, Hannah nestled in the sling across her chest, and Sally right behind her.

"Mister Efren, Mama is coming with the blue cohosh tea. Sally is going to take care of Hannah, and Isabel when she gets up. I am going to help Mama, so Viney can get some sleep."

Efren stared numbly at the two women.

"Mister Efren," said Ruth, her voice soft and certain, "Miss Anica and the baby are going to be fine. Mama promised me they would be."

The day was just breaking free of darkness when the wails of a new life beginning pierced the early morning quiet. Bursting from the room, joy radiating across her tear-stained face, Mariana threw her arms around Efren. "*Es un niño*. You have a beautiful son!"

Efren swallowed the sob rising in his throat. "Anica. How is Anica?"

"She is fine, but very tired. Your son is a much bigger baby than Isabel was."

"But she is going to be all right?"

Mariana hugged him again and kissed his cheek. "She's just going to need some time to regain her strength. Lindy and Ruth are tending to her and the baby. As soon as they are done, you can go in and see them."

Anica was barely awake when Efren brushed his lips against hers. "You were right," she said, her eyes half-closed, her voice hoarse and barely above a whisper. "We have a son. He is healthy and beautiful, and he already has a head of curly hair like yours."

"I was so afraid I was going to lose you." Efren took Anica and the sleeping baby into his arms and wept.

Anica stroked his head, her fingers smoothing his rumpled curls. "Shh, *mi amor*. We are both fine. I am just very tired, that's all." She closed her eyes. Within seconds her hand stilled, and she was asleep.

Efren lifted his son and cradled him to his chest. The infant stretched and came awake. The two studied each other, the baby's expression so serious, his dark eyes pondering the face before him so intently, that Efren laughed.

"*Hola, niño,*" he whispered. "I'm your Papa. Your Mama is sleeping now. She is very beautiful and worked very hard to bring you into this world, so you must be a good son to her. Your big sister Isabel is going to be very happy that you are here. You, *mi hijo*, are Benjamin, named after your mama's father. It is a strong name, and he is a good man. I hope you will come to be proud that you share it with your grandfather."

The room began to lighten, and Efren walked to the window to watch the sun lift from the horizon, its rays casting hues of yellow and orange across the pearly gray sky.

"Look Benjamin," he said, kissing his son's curls. "The world is welcoming you."

⚜

"Can't you do something to shut that baby up?" Margaret stood in her dressing gown, the straps of her night cap dangling along the sides of her face. "He kept us up all night. Again."

"Margaret," said Efren, the veins on his neck forming pulsing cords, "if you mean Benjamin, I sleep in the same room with him, and I can assure you he wasn't crying all night. In fact, this was one of his better nights."

"Well, it felt like all night. How much longer is this going to go on?"

His patience cracking, Efren let out a long breath. "I don't know, Margaret. We're hoping it stops by the time he starts to shave."

By breakfast the following morning, Margaret and Charles were dressed for travelling, a trunk and several satchels sitting by the door.

"We're leaving. I will not go another night without sleep," announced Margaret, as Efren helped Mariana settle Isabel in her high chair, and they took their places at the table.

"Amen to that," sniffed Charles, adjusting his wig.

Mariana held her breath, hoping Efren would remain civil.

"I hope you have a safe trip," said Efren, nodding his head when Henry approached with a tray of warm biscuits.

Philip sat back, his hands folded over his stomach, his expression dark. "I presume you are staying with friends in keeping with your monthly allowance. Let me be clear; there will be no advances."

Charles stopped chewing, and looked at Margaret.

"We sent word to our Savannah friends, the Appletons, days ago," she said, her brows knitted in a scowl. They sent a return message indicating that they are happy to host us."

"Good. I just want to make sure we understand each other," said Philip, signaling to Silas to ladle more pork sausage gravy over his biscuits. "Stay away as long as you like, but Sally remains here."

After Charles and Margaret departed for Savannah, and Mariana excused herself to take Isabel upstairs to be with Anica, Efren remained seated with his uncle. "I'm sorry," he said, aware that he was apologizing a lot lately.

Philip wiped a spot of gravy from the stubble on his chin. "No need to be sorry. In case you haven't noticed, it's always calmer around the house when they are gone." He pointed to the empty chair next to Efren. "Anica is still taking her meals in her room?"

"She needs a few more days of rest. Actually, we could all use a few days of rest. Benjamin works so hard nursing that he exhausts himself before he is full and falls asleep. He wakes up two hours later because he's hungry. Lindy thinks…"

Philip frowned. "I don't want to hear the details."

"I think things will be better. Ruth started nursing Benjamin a few times during the day to let Anica rest, and we're hoping he'll start sleeping longer between feedings. I don't know what we would do without her."

Philip shifted his girth in his chair. "I can see that your wife and Mariana have grown very fond of Ruth. I would even go so far as to say you are protective of her. Overly so. I want to remind you that she and her baby are my property. Do not get too attached to them."

Efren's body stiffened. "Philip, are you telling me you plan to sell Ruth and her child?"

"Not at this time. But if we don't see a good profit from the shipment, I will have to sell more slaves. Ruth is young and fertile, and her daughter is going to be a real beauty. They will bring a handsome price." Philip glared at Efren. "And Daniel too. He's scrawny, but talented with the horses."

Efren never hated anyone as much as he hated his uncle at that moment.

CHAPTER 43

June 1786

The cool, early morning mist had turned to humidity so stifling it was hard to breathe by the time Efren joined Philip and Jesse at the drained rice field. Dozens of slaves stood ankle-deep in the mud, hoeing around the young rice plants and preparing the fields for the second flooding of the season.

"We are going to need at least another week before we finish weeding and can flood again," said Jesse, slapping a mosquito on his arm.

"What the blazes is the hold up? We should have been flooding the fields days ago. We cannot afford to fall behind," snarled Philip.

"We need more slaves in the fields. We got six out with malaria, and Lindy is treating three more for yaws. Damn fools didn't tell me when the first sores showed up on their feet. Now they are raw and spreading, and are so bad the bastards can hardly walk."

His face dark as thunder, Philip turned his fury on Efren. "And why the hell haven't we heard from Lopez? He should be back by now."

Efren's face remained expressionless, refusing to give Philip the satisfaction of responding to his anger. "I would remind you," he said in a quiet voice, "of our conversation about the uncertainty of the weather and the sea. It's not unreasonable to assume that Lopez may have encountered bad weather and rough seas on his voyages to and from England. I am confident he will arrive safely in Charleston."

Philip's countenance turned cruel. "If he doesn't sail into Charleston soon, you won't be so smug when I start selling slaves to meet expenses."

"Wait," sputtered Jesse. "Fewer slaves won't help get the crop to market."

Spittle foaming in the corner of his mouth, Philip jabbed his finger hard into Jesse's chest. "I want the fields ready for flooding in two days. Get it done. That's what I pay you for."

Grateful his long day was over, Efren sat propped up on the bed watching Anica nurse Benjamin, the *Shabbat* candles casting her in a gentle glow. Even in the dimming light, he could see she was growing stronger. Her skin, once so pale it was nearly translucent, had returned to its golden color, and a touch of rosy pink bloomed across her cheeks.

Anica could sense his eyes on her. "Our son has gotten hungrier," she said, meeting his gaze with a smile. "And bigger," she added, shifting Benjamin from her breast to her shoulder and patting his back. The infant's hearty expulsion of air made them both chuckle.

"It's good to hear you laugh," said Anica, settling Benjamin in his cradle. "I've sensed something has been bothering you for days."

Efren opened his arms to her, and she got into bed beside him. "I won't admit it to Philip, but I am worried about Amadis and the shipment," he said. "He is two weeks overdue. My uncle needs the proceeds from his crop to keep the plantation going, and I am counting on the profit from the sale of the cargo Amadis is bringing from England to help us establish our business in Charleston. I know you are not ready to travel yet, but I have become as anxious as you to leave this place; everything about my uncle and the way of life here sickens me."

The following morning, Ruth met Efren as he was coming down the stairs. "I'm sorry I'm late, Mister Efren. Hannah was fussy this morning," she said, balancing Anica's breakfast tray.

"It's all right. Mariana and Isabel are with Anica and the baby."

Turning to go up the stairs, she hesitated and looked back at Efren.

"What's wrong, Ruth? Has something happened?"

Ruth looked around and stepped closer to Efren. "Mister Philip told Viney last night that she was going back to the fields this morning. Daniel has to leave the stables and go into the fields too," she said in a low voice. "Mister Philip said they have to move back into the quarters. Mama tried to tell him

Viney wasn't as strong as she used to be, but Mister Philip wouldn't listen."

"Where are Viney and Daniel now?"

"They're already in the fields. Jesse showed up to get them before the sun was even up. He wouldn't let Viney leave Emmy here. He said he would get Old Sarah to watch her." Ruth's eyes shone with tears. "Mister Efren, Viney said she would rather die than let Jesse touch her again."

Keeping a grip on the anger roiling through him like a tidal wave, Efren strode into the dining room and faced his uncle. "We need to talk."

Philip peered at him over his cup of coffee. "Word travels fast in this house."

Efren leaned over him, his hands resting on the table, his voice taut. "I know you need more people in the paddies, but Viney is not the field slave she was, and Daniel serves you better in the stables."

Philip took a sip of coffee. "Stay out of this, Efren. They are my property not yours."

Efren could feel his grip slipping. "Viney is a human being, and she would still be a valuable worker if you hadn't turned that animal on her."

Philip pounded the table with his fist, rattling the plates and silverware, and overturning his coffee cup. When Silas rushed to clean up the spill, Philip pushed him away, sending the old slave stumbling backwards.

"Efren, I warned you before not to interfere with the way I run my plantation." His mouth twisted into a cruel smile. "If you are so offended by how we do things here, perhaps you should consider leaving after Lopez returns, and we've settled the finances from the shipment."

Seething, Efren glared at Philip. "Uncle, I was just about to suggest the same thing."

His entire body throbbing with rage, Efren ran to the stables. Cotter was leading a horse from its stall when Efren burst into the barn.

"He ain't here, Mister Efren. I heared he back in the quarters and workin' in the fields now." The big man's face grew solemn, his hands squeezing his hat as he fought to regain his composure. "I'll get Buster for you," he said, and disappeared into the barn.

Efren guided the gelding to a small hill overlooking the final paddy remaining to be hoed. Swatting away a swarm of mosquitos, he stood in the stirrups and scanned the field below looking for Viney and Daniel. Staring down at the backs of the bent-over slaves, he flinched when he spotted Earl atop his horse, riding along the rows, and flicking his whip whenever he thought a slave wasn't working fast enough. Scanning the field again, Efren felt the cold clutch of fear. Viney and Daniel weren't at the rice field. Nor was Jesse.

Dismounting Buster before he came to a complete stop, Efren ran to Viney's cabin, the sound of wailing nearly stopping his heart. Cotter sat with his arms around Old Sarah, her keening rising above the cries of the others. "They all dead," he said without looking up.

Pushing past the frightened slaves standing near the door, Efren nearly plowed into Jesse. "What have you done?" he roared, grabbing the overseer by his shirt and pushing him against the wall.

Pale and sweaty, Jesse held up his hands to protect his face. "I swear I didn't do this. I left Viney and the kids to go get Old Sarah. I couldn't have been gone more than ten minutes. When I got back, I found them like this. Efren," he begged, "you have to tell Philip I didn't do this."

Shoving him aside, Efren stepped into the cabin and staggered back. His legs turned rubbery, and he leaned against a wall to keep from falling. Gulping for air, he stumbled into the room where Viney dangled from a rope tied to a rafter, a stool overturned beneath her feet, her lifeless body still swaying. Daniel and Emmy were lying side-by-side on the bed, their vacant eyes staring into nothingness, their bodies carefully arranged so that Daniel's arm encircled Emmy, and her head rested on his chest. Reaching to close their eyes, Efren's fingers grazed their faces, the feel of their still-warm skin crushing his heart. *She loved her children. How desperate she must have been to be free of this life, and Jesse, and my uncle to do this.* Broken, Efren slid to the floor and wept.

Viney and the children were buried the following night in the small slave cemetery at the edge of the swamp. Lindy came to Efren with word that he was welcome to attend.

"They knows you cared about Viney and the children. It going to be late tonight, 'cuz they gots to do their field work 'fore they can dig the graves and bury 'em."

A chill clung to the air, and gauzy clouds muted the moonlight as Efren,

Lindy, Ruth, and the other house slaves joined the solemn procession to the burial grounds. Some crying, some softly singing hymns, the mourners followed the horse-drawn cart carrying two rough-hewn coffins. The light from their torches cast the live oaks in eerie shadows, tendrils of Spanish moss seeming to float unattached to the overhead branches.

The woods came to life as the inhabitants of the quarters made the slow march to bury their friend and her children. Fireflies flitted through the trees. Leaves rustled as tiny creatures scurried to safety; twigs snapped as larger animals retreated. Wings flapped and frogs croaked, protesting the presence of the intruders. Something slithered over Efren's boot.

"Why are there only two coffins?" asked Efren, carefully picking his way along the dirt trail to the graveyard.

"Emmy in her mama's arms," said Lindy, looking past Efren into the night, her voice husky with grief. "She poisoned 'em. With pokeweed. I seen Emmy when they take her from the cabin. Her lips be dark purple. Viney gave her pokeweed berries to eat. It grow all over here, and Viney smart enough to know berries kill a small chile quick. She musta' gotten Daniel to eat the root somehow; it gots the most poison in it. He big enough it would take a whole lot of berries..." She shivered as cool breeze whispered through the trees.

Ruth put her arm around her mother. "Mama, Viney's happy now. She told me she would rather die than have Jesse rape her again."

Efren pushed aside a low-hanging branch, unable to rid his thoughts of Viney's plea the day Daniel brought him to her cabin. *Please don't let anything happen to my babies.*

"Why the children? We would have looked after them."

Lindy's eyes filled. "'Cuz she got no hope, and she didn't want her babies growin' up slaves."

The marshy odors of decaying vegetation and swampy water reached their noses before Cotter brought the cart to a stop near the burial site. Forming two lines on either side of the crooked path to the cemetery, the mourners raised their torches to light the way for the coffin bearers, falling in behind the caskets as they passed.

Located on a ragged plot of land at the edge of the swamp, the slave cemetery was covered in deep underbrush and surrounded by ancient cypress and palmetto trees. Sweating despite the cool night air, Efren's step faltered at the sight of the open, side-by-side graves waiting to receive Viney and her children. The nearby graves were unmarked by headstones. Instead, broken or pierced pieces of pottery, cups, shells, stones, dishes, bottles, and bowls sat upside down on top of the earthen mounds.

Sensing Efren's puzzlement, Lindy explained, "'Fore they brung here as slaves, it the way our people buried their dead. Them things put there to keep spirits of the dead from wanderin' in search of them in the livin' world. Things have a spirit too. They's broken to release their spirits so they stay with the dead 'stead of comin' back to the livin'."

Cradled in ropes, the coffins were positioned next to the graves. Old Sarah's soulful voice called out in song, quickly joined by the others. Clapping in an ancient rhythm, their words rose up to the heavens.

> *O who will come and go with me?*
> *I am bound for the land of Canaan.*
> *I'm bound fair Canaan's land to see,*
> *I am bound for the land of Canaan.*
> *I'll join with them who've gone before,*
> *I am bound for the land of Canaan.*
> *Where sin and sorrow are no more,*
> *I am bound for the land of Canaan.*

Pushing down the storm of emotions threatening to break free, Efren bowed his head as first Daniel's, and then Viney and Emmy's coffins were lowered into the ground and buried, each thud of the dirt against the pine boxes widening the crack in his heart.

After the graves were filled and the last person had placed an item on the fresh mounds, Efren, Lindy, and Ruth walked behind the others, each lost in their memories of the family buried in the desolate patch of earth near the swamp. A sudden movement stirred the trees; the piercing kee-aah call of a hawk blotting out their thoughts. Barely visible in the watery moonlight, the large bird spread its broad wings and soared over the tops of the marsh's towering cypress trees.

Lindy's eyes lifted skyward, a joyous smile lighting her face. "It a sign from Viney. She tellin' us her and her babies goin' home. They flyin' free now."

CHAPTER 44

July 1786

A heavy mantle of gloom settled over the big house in the days following the funeral. Anger mingled with grief; unspoken accusations and simmering resentments threatened to boil over at the slightest provocation. Always attuned to the mood of the household, the house slaves scuttled about attending to their chores, doing their best to stay out of Philip's way.

"He in a temper this morning," said Silas, carrying a tray of dishes cleared from the table. "He not happy 'bout the biscuits. Say they too dry."

Lindy rolled her eyes and snorted. "He complainin' 'bout everthin' these days. Yesterday he grumblin' about Ruth spendin' too much time upstairs with Miss Anica. Day 'fore that he angry 'cuz Ruth spendin' too much time in the kitchen nursin' Hannah. Wouldn't mind him disappearin' for a few days like he do."

"Mister Efren probably feelin' the same. Mister Philip lit into him 'bout that ship being late. Mister Efren, his face get angry, but he don't say a word. He jus' get up from the table and leave. Miss Mariana finish up feeding Miss Isabel, and they leave too."

Lindy wiped her hands on her apron. "Poor chile. Ruth say she keep cryin' for Emmy." Her throat tightened. "I do miss hearin' the sweet sound of them two little ones playin' and laughin' in the garden."

"I seen some awful bad things here," said Silas, sadness playing over his worn face. "But Viney and them children dyin' the way they did hurt my heart somethin' terrible. I close my eyes at night and their faces right there, smilin' at me. I knows they happy now, but I sadder than I ever be."

Efren made his way to the stables where he knew Cotter would have Buster saddled and waiting for him. Every morning since the deaths of Viney and the children, he would ride aimlessly for hours, seeking an escape from his uncle, the rice fields, Jesse, and everything else about the plantation he had come to hate. This morning, with Cotter's help, he had a destination and a purpose.

Efren let Buster set the pace as they made their way along the narrow path to the slave cemetery. Moving slowly, the gelding raised his head and snorted as they neared the swamp, the loud vibrating sound of his fluttering nostrils scattering a flock of fish crows foraging at the edge of the marshy water. Cawing their indignation as they flew away, the large birds formed a black, ink-like stain against the flawless blue sky.

Efren tightened his hold on the reins as Buster whinnied and tensed. "It's all right; just some birds. We only have a little further to go," he said, stroking the horse's neck.

Within minutes, the forlorn burial ground came into view. Tethering Buster where there was shade and ample grass to nibble, Efren grabbed the cloth pouch Cotter had hung from the saddle. Stepping carefully around the other graves, he knelt between the mounds of newly turned earth that covered Daniel, and Emmy and Viney, hoping to find some solace in the quiet of the burial ground.

The crushing weight that settled in his chest that tragic afternoon in Viney's cabin would not leave him. Their faces haunted his nights. His inability to change everything that led to their deaths tormented his days. Grief ringed his heart. He could not banish the memories and images of Daniel's smile, or the sound of Emmy's laughter, or Viney's new-found happiness working in the kitchen house. Tears did not come; he had no more to spill. Instead, Efren was consumed by the overwhelming fear that if they did not leave Bending Oaks soon, the evil that permeated every corner of the plantation would never leave them. And despite his daily assurances to his uncle that all was well, he could not quell his deep fears that something had happened to the *Águila*.

Buster whinnied impatiently. Rising, Efren took a worn and frayed bridle from the pouch Cotter had given him, and placed it on Daniel's grave.

"Now you won't have to go searching for one," he said.

Coming down the path from the stables, Efren was surprised to see a coach making its way around the carriageway towards the big house. Certain it was James bringing word from Amadis, he broke into a run, reaching the portico just as the coach pulled to a stop. Squinting into the sunlight, he did not recognize the driver stepping down from the coach's box seat. His breath coming in choppy bursts, he leaned against a column and watched Margaret emerge from the passenger compartment.

"Dammit," spat Efren, as much from disappointment as from his contempt for Margaret. It was only when Silas and Henry came scurrying from the big house to retrieve Margaret's trunks that Efren realized Charles had not accompanied her home.

The mystery of Margaret's unexpected arrival without Charles was quickly explained when Margaret announced she was going to stay in Charleston at a home provided for her by Ned Blaylock, the naval captain she'd met during her previous stay in Savannah. That a scandal around her living arrangements was already brewing in the port city seemed not to bother her at all.

"Do you realize your reputation is going to be as tarnished as that of a common whore?" sputtered Philip, his face inches from Margaret's.

Calmly smoothing a crease in her yellow traveling dress, Margaret held his stare, a brittle smile playing across her lips. "If anyone knows about common whores, I suspect it is you, Philip. And why should you care about my reputation now or, for that matter, anything else about me, when you never did before?"

Philip returned her smile with a villainous one of his own. "I actually care very little, but I owe it to the memory of your mother to point out that you will find the society you are so fond of may not be as welcoming as you think if you enter into this arrangement."

Margaret rose, her body erect, her chin jutting out in defiance. "I am quite comfortable with 'this arrangement' as you call it. And you needn't worry about Charles. He's found someone who returns his affections. Since we cannot end our marriage legally, we have simply agreed to part with no claims to each other, financial or otherwise. I have it in writing that he has agreed to relinquish any rights that may be his as my husband. In truth, we are both relieved to put an end to this charade. I need a few more days to get my things in order, and to arrange to send Charles' belongings to Savannah, and then I will be gone. I doubt you will miss either of us."

The morning of Margaret's departure, the bell summoning the house slaves rang incessantly as Rosie and Flora hurried back and forth attending to her demands. Pressed into service for the last time, Sally tended to Margaret's hair, artfully arranging her coiled braids into an intricate bun. Stepping back to allow Margaret to inspect her handiwork in a hand mirror, Sally stood looking down, still anxious to avoid her displeasure. She had been Margaret's personal slave since they were both fourteen, assuming the role after the death of the old nurse who had taken care of Margaret since she was born. Always the slave to Margaret's mistress, Sally held no misconceptions about her place in the household or in Margaret's heart.

Margaret inspected the braided bun and handed the mirror back to Sally. "You can go now. You can all go now," she said waving her hand dismissively. "Tell Henry and Silas to come get the rest of my things and bring them downstairs."

The quiet of the house was shattered by the clatter of horses' hooves announcing the arrival of Margaret's coach. Straining under the weight of Margaret's trunks, Silas and Henry passed James as he approached the big house.

"Mister Efren here? I got a message for him from Captain Lopez."

"You gonna make that man real happy," beamed Silas. "We almost done here. I'll send Ruth to get him for you."

Bolting out of the house, Efren greeted James with a wide smile. "You have no idea how good it is to see you," said Efren, slapping the driver on the back. "You have word from Amadis?"

James removed a letter from the pocket of his coat. "Yes sir. He told me to wait for an answer."

Efren broke the seal on the envelope and scanned the letter. His solemn expression slipped into a smile that widened into a grin. "James, will you be available to take me to Charleston in a few days?"

"Yes sir. I takin' Miss Margaret today and then comin' back to spend some time with my wife and children. Send word over to Mister Tobias' plantation in Goose Creek when you ready to go, and I come get you."

"Good. Please tell Captain Lopez he brings the news I was hoping for, and that I will come to Charleston before the end of the week."

"James!" called Margaret, her voice shrill and demanding.

Efren shook James' hand. "You'd better go. She is not someone you want to have angry with you."

James ran his hand over his face to hide his smile. "No sir. I sure don't want that."

Efren lingered on the portico, waving as the coach pulled away. Margaret sat staring straight ahead, never glancing back as James guided the horses past the gardens and away from Bending Oaks.

CHAPTER 45

Charleston, July 19, 1786

My Dear Friend,

I apologize, for I know the delay in our return must have caused you great worry. It is my hope that the news this letter brings will allay your fears about our business venture and lighten your heart.

Our voyage to England turned perilous mid-way to our destination, when we encountered a monstrous storm that tossed the Águila about as if it were straw in the wind. Fortunately, the cargo hold remained dry, but damage to the one of the masts, and then a stretch of demonic days without so much as a ghost of a breeze, slowed our journey to London. When we finally arrived in port, we had to remain in dry dock for weeks while the mast was repaired.

However, this seeming set-back proved to be most fortuitous. The extra days in port afforded me the opportunity to spend time in the delightful Charleston Coffee House on London's Birchin Lane, where businessmen go to meet with ship captains arriving from Charleston. It was there that I was able to arrange for a rice agent to represent us in England, and to make new contacts with men of means eager to export their goods to our great city. As soon as the Águila was repaired, we set sail with contracts for future shipments, and a hold filled with woolens, linen goods, and porcelain.

I am pleased to assure you that despite the time lost to the storm and the cost to repair the ship, the voyage was a profitable one. I hope you

believe as I do that the business venture we are embarking on has the po-
tential for great success. We have much to discuss.

James was kind enough to inform me of the birth of your son. Please
accept my fondest congratulations to you and Anica. It seems we have many
reasons for celebration.

Your devoted friend,
Amadis Lopez

His spirits soaring, Efren read the letter one more time to assure himself his fears of ruin were unrealized. If the profits were as Amadis indicated, he could begin to make arrangements to leave Bending Oaks, and finally provide the life he envisioned for his family.

Eager to share the good news with Anica, Efren found her in the bed-chamber, nursing Benjamin. Putting his finger to his lips to signal he would be quiet, he sat beside her on the bed.

Anica nuzzled her shoulder to his. "He should be done soon and ready for his nap," she said, her smile as radiant as the sun streaming through the window, flecks of gold dancing in her dark eyes.

"I am happy to wait and observe the view," said Efren, his own eyes bright with merriment.

"I like this Efren much better than the one who has been moping around for days," teased Anica. "What happened to change your mood?"

He took the envelope from his coat pocket and placed it in her lap. "A letter from Amadis saying he'd returned safely, and that the voyage was a success."

Savoring the opportunity to prove to his uncle that he had been right about the *Aguila's* safe return, Efren entered the parlor expecting to find Philip enjoying his usual afternoon brandy. Instead, he startled Flora, nearly toppling her from the stool she was standing on to dust the portrait over the fireplace.

"Flora, I am so sorry if I frightened you. I was looking for my uncle."

Her legs wobbly, she placed her hands on the mantle to steady herself before climbing down from the step stool. "He gone. I seen him go off in a carriage a bit ago with Mr. Conroy," she said, her eyes lowered, her fingers nervously twisting the corner of the dust rag in her hand.

Efren's high spirits plummeted. *Dammit, Philip, what are you up to?*

Two days later, James pulled the coach to a halt at the Charleston wharf where the *Águila* was moored. Efren stepped from the passenger compartment and inhaled deeply. The salt air filled his lungs, reminding him how much he missed the smell of the sea. Taking in the swirl of activity on the wharves, he tried to imagine how different their lives would have been if they had remained in Charleston.

"Mister Efren," said James, "if you all right, I gonna leave, so's I get back 'fore it dark. I don't want to take a chance of runnin' into no patrollers."

Despite James' freedman badge, Efren knew he would be in danger if he was out after dark. Reaching into his coat pocket, he withdrew an envelope and handed it to James. "I hope you won't need this, but just in case, I've written out a pass. Journey back safely, and I will see you back here the day after next."

A sea breeze ruffled Efren's hair as he watched the coach make its way from the docks. Turning to board the *Águila*, he spotted Amadis waiting for him on the deck.

Racing up the ship's ramp, Efren was engulfed in a hug, Amadis nearly lifting him off his feet. "What took you so long to get here?" asked the laughing captain.

"I could ask you the same thing," said Efren in mock seriousness.

"Fair enough, my friend," said Amadis, grinning broadly. "Let's go below so we can talk."

Settled in his quarters, Amadis filled their glasses with Madeira. "I am glad you are here. You look worn, my friend, and I sense that you are troubled. Are Anica and the children well? Mariana?"

"Anica and the children are fine. Mariana too. Isabel is like a little mother hen with Benjamin. If I look tired, you can blame my son; he does not seem to need as much sleep as I do. I am concerned about my uncle, though."

"Is he ill?"

Efren responded with a snicker. "There is nothing wrong with him that less brandy would cure. He disappeared again three days ago. When I left Bending Oaks this morning he still hadn't returned, and I have no idea where he is, or why he left. I do know he is having financial problems, and I am concerned about his mental state. One day he threatens to sell off some of the slaves; the next day he rants about the crop being late because he doesn't have enough slaves in the fields. He appears to me to be desperate. I am worried that the crop won't be harvested in time to ship in November, and that will have disastrous consequences for him—and us if we depend on him to fill the hold of the *Águila* for the next voyage to London."

"It would be a problem only if we were too late to find other growers or exporters. There is a great demand for other products in England—lumber, tobacco, cotton, sugar, fur. We do not have to rely on Philip's rice crop."

"I am ashamed to admit that I have been thinking the same thing. I despise the man Philp has become. I certainly don't trust him. Yet, I feel a sense of obligation to him—he is still my uncle, and he provided us with a place to live when we had nowhere to go."

Amadis took a moment to take in all Efren had told him. "Will a month be enough time for you to determine if the rice will be ready to ship in November?"

"I think so. It will certainly be enough time to see if Philip is up to something."

"Then we have a plan. We will wait a month. If you determine that the work in the fields is not going well, we can begin to seek out other planters and exporters. I am sure I don't need to remind you that in order for our business to flourish, we must have a full hold of cargo for each leg of the round trip."

Efren drained his glass. "I just wish I wasn't so bothered by the thought of what my father would think if he knew I was considering abandoning his brother."

"Perhaps that won't be necessary. If it is finances that are at the bottom of Philip's problems, this may help," said Amadis, placing a leather-bound ledger on the table.

There, in Amadis' elegantly written script, were meticulously recorded columns of the voyage's expenses and collected payments. Efren ran his finger down the rows of numbers, his smile broadening with each turn of the page. Amadis had been right. Despite the delay, the cost of repairing the ship's mast, and English tariffs, the profit from the rice crop was a handsome one. Efren felt a flicker of hope.

"Amadis, your skills as a captain are only exceeded by your business savvy. This is beyond my expectations. What you've done here," said Efren holding up the ledger, "is extraordinary. If we have another successful voyage like this, our company will surely attract investors, and we will have the capital we need to expand our operations."

Amadis ducked his head in acknowledgement of Efren's praise. "You honor me with your trust."

"Amadis, I would trust you with my life."

Driven into a wharf-side tavern by an afternoon thunderstorm, Efren and Amadis sat hunched over mugs of ale, surrounded by an assortment of sailors, merchants, and other refugees from the deluge.

"I didn't think it would be this difficult to obtain warehouse space," said Efren, raising his voice to be heard over the din in the tavern and the driving rain pounding the roof. "I'm afraid that we'll have to settle for smaller space than we hoped for."

Amadis wiped the foam from his upper lip. "I agree it is our wisest course until we have investors backing us. The warehouse we looked at on Gibbes Wharf should be adequate. The scale-house at the end of the wharf will make it convenient to weigh crops when they arrive and immediately load them onto the ship."

"It's settled then. Tomorrow we will arrange for the space. Philip knows I am not happy at Bending Oaks. He actually told me we should leave if I did not like the way he runs the plantation. Still, he said it in a moment of anger, and I have some misgivings, even feelings of guilt, about making the move to Charleston."

"You will serve him just as well by continuing to ship his rice crops," said Amadis. "Your absence from the plantation may even improve your relationship with him. And you have your growing family to consider."

"Wise counsel, my friend," said Efren, raising his mug. "To our successful venture."

"To the A & E Eagle Shipping Company," said Amadis, touching his mug to Efren's.

CHAPTER 46

Anica had just finished nursing Benjamin when she heard the familiar sound of an approaching coach. Hoping it was Efren returning early from Charleston, she peered out the window and was startled to see Philip, disheveled and grim-faced, step out from the carriage, followed by a well-dressed man she did not recognize. Tall and thin, his gray hair was tied back in a ribbon at the nape of his neck. A large, aquiline nose dominated his face, accentuating his pointed chin. Smoothing his bushy mustache, he adjusted his elegant frock coat, and took in the surroundings before following Philip down the path to the slave quarters.

Remembering the last time Philip returned looking so unkempt, Anica grew alarmed. Placing Benjamin, already drowsy, in his crib, she hurried downstairs.

Henry stood at the doorway, staring at the coach. "Miss Anica, Lindy ain't here to make refreshments for Mister Philip's guest. Ruth say she over to the quarters lookin' after Sawyer; he down with malaria. Flora went to fetch her."

Anica nodded absently, more concerned about why Philip led his guest to the slave quarters than with making sure he was provided refreshments. "Do you know who he is?" she asked.

"He Mister Jedidiah Conroy. He own a plantation in Moncks Corner, and come here sometime to play cards when Mister Philip has his friends to the big house. He ain't been here in a long while."

The minutes ticked by and when Flora did not return with Lindy, Anica's unease increased. Stepping out into the late afternoon sun, she walked slowly in the direction of the quarters, her skin prickling in a sudden sense of dread.

The sound was so distant at first, Anica was unsure she heard anything at all. Her uneasiness growing, she picked up her pace. When the unmistakable sound of keening reached her ears, she began to run.

The horror of the scene before her left her frantic with fear. A group of older slaves huddled together, terror marking their faces like grotesque masks. Lindy was on her knees, her arms wrapped around Philip's leg, begging for her son, as Jonah, screaming "Mama," struggled to escape Philip's grip.

"Please, Mister Philip, don't take another baby from me. He a good boy. He work hard for you in the fields. If he givin' Mister Jesse trouble, I whup him to make sure he listen. Mister Philip, please," she sobbed.

"Lindy, don't make this so hard," hissed Philip, shaking his leg to dislodge her. When Lindy would not let go, Conroy pulled her off and kicked her, sending her sprawling in the dirt.

"Stop it," screamed Anica, rushing to help Lindy to her feet. "Philip, what is this madness? Where are you taking Jonah?"

Philip was breathing hard, his face florid. "It is none of your damn business. Now get out of the way."

"Let go of him," demanded Anica. Shaking with fury, she stepped towards Philip.

"Get this bitch out of here, and let's get this done," snarled Conroy, stepping between Anica and Philip. "We had a wager. You lost. I won. The boy is mine."

Conroy wrenched Jonah from Philip's arms. His eyes bulging with anger, he slapped the kicking boy.

Stunned, blood trickling from his nose, Jonah stopped struggling, his arms outstretched towards his wailing mother.

Conroy's thin lips curled into a brutish smile. "That's more like it. Good thing for you that you're a fast learner." Cuffing Jonah in the face one more time, he held him by his shirt and shoved the crying boy onto the path leading to the big house, Philip trotting after him like an obedient puppy.

Alerted by Henry that they might have a guest, Ruth was in the kitchen house preparing tea, when Silas burst through the door. Gasping for air, he grabbed her by the arm. "Ruth, he sellin' Jonah! That Mister Conroy takin' him away."

Ruth could not remember leaving the kitchen house or how she got back. What she would never forget was Jonah's terrified face; his arms reaching out of the coach for her as she chased it down the carriageway screaming his name.

Anica stayed with Lindy until the sedative effects of Old Sarah's yellow jasmine tea eased her to sleep. Unsure how much time had passed, and anxious that Benjamin would be awake and hungry, she hastened back to the big house, nearly bowling over Mariana and Isabel at the end of the path.

"*Gracias a Dios*, you are all right," gasped Mariana, as Isabel threw herself into Anica's arms. "Flora came back after that man took Jonah and told us what happened. *Dios mio*, Lindy. How is she?"

Anica lifted Isabel. Hugging her tight, she felt the pain of Lindy's empty arms. "Like a mother who has lost her child. Her second child. Old Sarah gave her something to help her sleep. And the awful truth is that all she can do is wake up tomorrow, accept what Philip has done, and behave like it never happened." Her chin began to tremble. Biting her lip to keep from crying, she kissed Isabel. "We'd better hurry. I don't know how long I've been gone. Benjamin must be hungry."

Sally greeted them at the door, her eyes red and swollen. "Miss Anica, Ruth scaring us. She actin' real strange. She not lettin' anyone near her. She just' sittin' by herself in the kitchen house with Hannah in her arms. When Flora offered to take the baby, Ruth screamed and pushed her away."

"Go," said Mariana, taking Isabel's hand. We'll look in on Benjamin."

When Anica found her, Ruth sat unmoving, her eyes glazed and flat, a large knife on her lap.

"Ruth," said, Anica, her heart hammering; her eyes darting around the kitchen. "Where's Hannah?"

Ruth looked up, her eyes lifeless and unseeing. "He took Jonah," she whimpered. "Before that, he took my little sister Lizzie. He can't have Hannah."

Panic pressed down on Anica's chest. "Ruth! Where is Hannah?"

Ruth blinked. Still not acknowledging Anica, she glanced towards the dark room off the kitchen.

Anica flew into the room, almost falling over the basket where Hannah slept; her face peaceful, her thumb in her mouth. Weak with relief, Anica pulled back the light blanket covering the infant to assure herself that Hannah was unhurt.

"She is too beautiful," croaked Ruth, standing in the doorway, the knife in her hand. "If she were ugly and scarred, she would be safe from Jesse and Philip, and the men who come here and think because we are slaves we exist for their pleasure."

Anica's stomach tightened with fear. Pushing the basket to the side with her foot, Anica stepped towards Ruth. "Please give me the knife, and then we can sit and talk."

"Talk! What good is talk? Will talk protect my daughter? Will talk give my mother back her children? Will it stop Jesse from raping me? Will it keep Philip from selling me and my child when he needs more money?"

Sobbing now, Ruth swayed and leaned against the door frame. Anica lunged for the knife, and wrestling it from Ruth's hand, kicked it across the room.

Ruth's body sagged. Clinging to Anica, she wept, and Anica wept with her.

CHAPTER 47

Word of Philip's gambling debt and payment to Jedidiah Conroy had reached Charleston the next morning, quickly becoming the main topic of conversation among the wealthy planters who resided in the city's opulent mansions on East Bay Street. It did not take long for Efren to hear of the gossip. He and Amadis were signing papers to lease wharf space when the owner divulged what he knew about the incident. "I hope your finances are not tied to your uncle's," he said.

Efren fought to keep his expression unchanged. "I can assure you that the A & E Eagle Shipping Company is solely owned by me and Captain Lopez. My uncle holds no interest in our enterprise. And as you have seen for yourself, we have ample funds to ensure our financial obligation to you."

"Good, that is what I was hoping to hear. Just be diligent about paying your rent on time."

As soon as they were away from the wharf, Efren gave in to his anger. "Damn him. He promised me he would stop gambling. And my God, to offer a child as payment."

Amadis regarded his friend. "If he relinquished a slave when he is need of more in the field, I am afraid it is because he has nothing else to offer."

The pulse in Efren's throat quickened. "I need to get back to Bending Oaks."

James had barely reined the horses to a stop when Efren sprang from the coach and raced into the house. "Philip!" he roared as soon as he entered the house.

Rosie darted from the parlor and pointed towards Philip's study. "He in there," she said, her voice trembling, her eyes fixed on his clenched fists.

Efren relaxed his hands. "Please tell my wife that I've returned, and that I will join her shortly," he said, forcing the anger from his voice.

"Yes, Mister Efren. Her and Miss Mariana takin' Miss Isabel and the baby for a walk. I'll find 'em for you and let 'em know."

His anger bubbling just below the surface, Efren stomped down the hall. About to barge into the study, he stopped at the sound of shouting coming from behind the closed door. It took him only a moment to recognize Jesse's muffled voice.

"We can't get the rice to harvest without more slaves. Instead of adding more, we're losing them," shouted the overseer. "*You're* losing them!"

"Dammit," Philip shouted back, "keep the bastards in the fields longer if you have to. I don't care what you do, just get the weeding and second seeding done so the fields are ready for the next flooding. Now get out of here and go do your job."

Efren stepped out of the way just as the door flew open. Startled to see Efren in the hall, Jesse looked him up and down and grumbled, "He's all yours." Pulling his hat low on his forehead, he fled the house.

"What the hell do you want?" demanded Philip, his eyes glassy and laced with red, the stench of liquor and sour sweat clinging to him like the fetid stink of decay.

"I want to know what the hell is going on," clipped Efren through gritted teeth. "You swore to me that you would stop gambling."

Philip gave a quick bark of laughter. "That's true, but I also swore I would do anything to save Bending Oaks."

Efren's skin grew clammy. Amadis had been right. "How bad is it?"

His defiance cracked, and Philip looked away. "Bad. The plantation is heavily encumbered. I have not been able to keep up with what I owe. I've been entering false payments in the account ledger to keep the debt from you. When Lopez was late returning, I panicked."

"You should have had more faith in Lopez. He arrived the day after you disappeared." Efren reached into his frock coat and removed an envelope.

"Your profits. I only deducted the amount we agreed on for expenses and to pay the crew."

Philip squared his shoulders; his eyes fastened on the envelope in Efren's hand.

Tossing the money on Philip's desk, Efren stalked out of the room.

Anica was waiting for Efren upstairs. "I am so glad you are home," she said, kissing him and folding herself into his arms.

"I left Charleston as soon as I heard what happened. Are you all right? The children?"

"They're fine. Benjamin fell asleep in his carriage while we were out walking. I asked Mariana to take him and Isabel to her room so Isabel could nap, and we could talk. She will be so excited to see you when she wakes up."

"I've missed her; missed all of you. I don't like being away from you and the children. I worry about your safety the whole time I am gone."

"I'll admit it's been a difficult two days. I barely slept at all last night. Every time I closed my eyes, I saw Jonah struggling with that horrible man and screaming for Lindy. I don't think I could go on living if someone took Benjamin and Isabel from me."

Anica was crying now, her words coming in bursts. "Lindy begged Philip not to let Conroy take Jonah, but your uncle just stood there and let him kick Lindy to get to the boy."

"How is Lindy?"

"She didn't come to the kitchen house last night. Ruth and Flora made a hasty supper. Philip was the only one who really ate, and if he noticed the cold meal, he didn't say anything. Lindy returned this morning, but she hasn't said a word to anyone. She is so quiet, it frightens me. We heard this afternoon that when Brock, Jonah's father, found out, he went crazy and had to be restrained. His owner won't let him come see Lindy because he is afraid of what Brock might do to Philip."

Anica stopped to wipe her eyes. "I am worried about Ruth too. She's so full of rage, I'm afraid she'll do something drastic."

Efren could feel his own anger igniting, gaining heat like a slow-burning flame. His uncle's callousness and reckless behavior disgusted him. His decision to leave Bending Oaks was no longer hindered by his feelings of guilt over deserting Philip.

Efren stood outside of the kitchen house, fully aware that there was nothing he could say to Lindy that would ease her pain or convey his own heartbreak. He remembered Jonah as a lively boy, his open face always smiling, his eyes, so startling and bright. His thoughts wandered and grew jumbled; images of Viney, Daniel and Emmy mingled with those of Jonah, leaving him frozen in sorrow in front of the kitchen house door. When it opened and Ruth stepped out, he stared dumbly for a moment before speaking.

"Ruth, I was coming to see your mother. I am so sorry about..."

Ruth shook her head, unwilling to hear Jonah's name for fear of falling apart. "Thank you, Mister Efren. We know how much you and Miss Anica and Miss Mariana care, but this isn't a good time. If you'll excuse me, I have to get some butter," she said, pushing past Efren, never meeting his gaze.

Efren watched Ruth make her way down the path to the spring house. His chest tight with sadness, he entered the kitchen house. Lindy peered up at him, her face twisted in anguish. Wordlessly, he reached for her hand and squeezed it.

Her eyes filling, Lindy closed her hand around his. "Mister Efren, that devil Conroy took Jonah. My chile out there with no one to look after him. No one to love him or care for him if he sick or hurt." She looked at him, broken by despair. "This worse than him bein' dead. Least then I knows he at peace and they ain't hurtin' him no more."

CHAPTER 48

The day after his return, Efren rode to the rice fields. When he reined Buster to halt in front of Jesse, the overseer sneered. "Come to see if things were as bad as you heard?"

Efren dismounted and watched the activity below. Instead of hoeing to the rhythm of their usual call-and-answer songs, the slaves worked at a furious pace under the merciless July sun. "Tell me the truth, are you going to be able to stay on schedule?"

"I am pushing these bastards as hard as I can. They're working hard from sunup to sunset," he said, a hint of respect in his voice. "I have everyone I can find out here. I even have some of the slaves from the quarters toting water to free up a few of the older children to work in the field," he added, nodding towards two elderly men, yokes across their shoulders, their backs bent under the weight of the dangling buckets. "But all it's going to take is an injury or two, or a few more cases of malaria, or even a couple of days of rain, and we are done for."

Efren looked around. "Where's Earl?"

Jesse pointed to a big man swinging a hoe at the far end of the field. "Right there. When I said everyone is in the fields, I meant it."

By the time Efren returned to the big house, his decision to leave Bending Oaks as soon as possible was sealed.

"I have to return to Charleston for few days to arrange for a place for us to live," Efren told Anica that night. "I am afraid that Philip is deeply in debt.

He may be able to manage for a little while longer with the profit from the last crop, but there is a good chance he won't be able to meet his financial obligations even if Jesse can bring this year's crop to harvest on time."

"Does he really owe that much money?"

"I am pretty certain he does. Philip is getting desperate. He is drinking more and still gambling. I do not trust him to make sound decisions going forward. From what I saw at the rice fields today, we cannot depend on the crop coming to harvest to fill the hold of the *Águila* in November. I am hoping to find potential customers while I am in Charleston." *And secure additional financing.*

The day after Efren left, Ruth came to Anica's room for the first time since Jonah had been taken by Conroy. The natural liveliness gone from her hazel eyes, she managed a half-smile when Isabel threw herself into her arms.

"Me miss you," squealed Isabel, holding tight to Ruth's neck.

"Oh, little one, I've missed you too."

Anica could see the despair in Ruth's face, and her heart ached. "I am glad you are here. I'm…I'm so sorry about Jonah."

Ruth's gaze seemed far away. "You did a brave thing trying to keep them from taking my brother. But no one could have stopped them. It's useless to resist." The smooth contours of Ruth's face contorted in unsuppressed fury. "We are nothing to Mister Philip. He owns us just like he owns the cows, and hogs, and goats on the plantation. He can do whatever he chooses to us. Sell us or slaughter us; it doesn't make any difference to him as long as he can profit from us."

The stark truth of Ruth's words stunned Anica. Her lips moved, but she made no sound. When Ruth withdrew two candles from her apron pocket, Anica stared at them.

"For the Sabbath. Tonight."

"Of course," said Anica. "I hope you will join me."

Ruth held Anica's gaze. "I will," she said, the fire returning to her eyes. "I may be Mister Philip's slave, but he doesn't own my soul."

CHAPTER 49

The following morning dawned wet and dark. Ominous black clouds released bullet-like pellets of hard-driving rain that pitted the dry ground. The rain quickly became a deluge, the dry, powdery soil turning to mud and forming crevices filled with streams of water. Lightening knifed the dark sky, and seconds later deafening thunder rolled across the marshes. Eerie sounding and high-pitched, the wind rattled the windows and bowed the trees surrounding the big house.

Philip stood at the windows of his study watching the avalanche of water cascading down the terraces of the ornamental gardens like an angry river, and calculated the damage the torrential downpour and wind were doing to the rice fields. When a thunderclap accompanied by a strong gust of wind hammered sheets of rain against the window pane with an explosive roar, he jumped back in terror.

Looking behind him to make sure none of the house slaves had seen his fear, his glance was met by his grinning overseer.

"I didn't see Silas or Henry, so I just let myself in," said Jesse, water dripping from the brim of his hat.

"Those damn fools are useless. What the hell do you want?" snapped Philip.

"I went down to the fields, and the water is near flood level. The rivers are so swollen we can't drain the paddies."

Philip's face darkened. "Where are the field slaves?"

Jesse looked down; his eyes glued to a rivulet of rain that rolled down the front of his oilskin poncho onto the carpet. "In the quarters."

Philip's pupils became snake-like slits. He turned and stared out the window. "Get them into the fields as soon as the rain starts to let up," he bellowed.

Jesse did not bother to point out that there wasn't anything the slaves could do until the rivers began to recede.

Upstairs, Anica also stood watching the rain waiting for it to abate, and for a chance to escape the four walls of her room. Benjamin had been fussy all morning, and now Isabel sat on the bed crying because they could not go outside. Anica knew how she felt.

"Please, Mama, we go play," begged the toddler, her shoulders rising and falling with each sob.

The plaintive sound of Isabel's little voice, and the serious look on her face made Anica smile. "We have to wait for the rain to stop and the ground to dry a bit, and then we can take a walk to the stables to see the horses. How does that sound?"

Isabel grew thoughtful, her expression a study in concentration. "Mariana and Benjamin too?" she asked, wiping her cheeks with the back of her hand.

Anica scooped Isabel into a hug. "Mariana and Benjamin too."

Carrying a basket of vegetables, Ruth hurried from the garden to the kitchen house. Putting the cabbage, peas, and corn near the wash basin, she checked on her sleeping daughter.

"I can't believe she slept through that storm."

"Hmm," responded Lindy, absently prodding the coals under a pot of simmering carrots and onions.

Ruth scrutinized her mother's worn face. What she saw was a woman finally broken by all that had been taken from her, and she knew her mother would never be the same again.

"I have to get over to the big house, but I'll be back in a little while to nurse Hannah," Ruth said, hugging her.

Lindy looked up as if she suddenly realized Ruth was there. "That fine," she said, stirring the carrots and onions.

Isabel tugged Mariana's hand, propelling her through the mud toward the stables. Anica followed with Benjamin asleep in her arms. Clearing the bower of trees that lined the footpath, they were surprised to see Cotter leading the horses from their stalls and releasing them into the fenced-in pasture.

His expression troubled, Cotter greeted the visitors in the stable yard. "Afternoon, Miss Anica, Miss Mariana. I ain't sure this is a good time to see the animals," he said, dipping his head towards Isabel. "The horses actin' like another bad storm comin'. Whinnyin' and kickin' at the sides of the stalls. These two here the last horses to turn out. The others already done run down to the lowest part of the field. The dogs actin' funny too, whinin' and all skittish."

As if to verify Cotter's concern about the weather, the sun disappeared behind blue-gray clouds. Nodding, Anica handed Benjamin to Mariana and lifted Isabel. "Cotter has to put the horses in the pasture. Why don't you pet them now before he lets them go?"

Isabel reached over and stroked their faces, giggling when the roan made a soft blowing sound through his nose.

The wind was picking up again as Ruth stepped out of the kitchen house. Walking with her head lowered, she was near the big house when the air turned ominously still. The sky darkened; one side a pale gray, the other amassing a wall of greenish-black clouds along the horizon. In a blur of yellow, Tabby, the garden cat, startled her, bolting from a bush and burrowing into a small space under the portico. Pea-sized hail began to pelt the ground.

In the few moments it took Ruth to realize what was happening, Anica and Mariana, each clutching a child screaming in terror, burst from the stable path, running towards the house. In the distance behind them, a giant column of violently twisting air and debris jutted down from the sky like a dagger speeding toward them, it's rumble growing louder as it approached. Increasing in intensity, the wind snapped branches and sent leaves flying as if they had been shot out by cannons. Lightning bolts streaked the sky in rapid succession, eerily absent of thunder.

Buffeted by the wind, Anica and Mariana struggled to stay on their feet.

"Get into the root cellar," screamed Ruth over the heightening roar.

Anica and Mariana veered toward the side of the house. Clattering as the wind passed under it, the oak door to the underground storage room shot open when Anica unbolted the latch, releasing a damp odor mixed with the smells of spices and rotting food. Looking into the dark hole that yawned in front of them, its steep wooden steps leading to the infinite blackness below, she hesitated.

"Anica!" shrieked Mariana, pointing at the whirling funnel gobbling up and hurling anything in its path, peeling the bark from the trees, and turning snapped limbs into deadly projectiles.

"Go," yelled Anica, holding the door open with one hand and clutching Benjamin against her body with the other.

It was only after Mariana and Isabel began their descent that Anica realized Ruth was not behind her.

Leaning into the wind, her skirt whipping around her legs, and dirt burning her eyes, Ruth fought her way back toward the kitchen house, praying her mother and Hannah were safe. Hail bit into her face, pinpricks of blood dotting her cheeks. The roaring sound, like a herd of thundering horses, grew louder, and she knew, without looking back, that the tornado and its field of flying debris were bearing down on her. The kitchen house in sight, Ruth ran to a low spot between it and the washhouse. Lying flat, and using her apron to lash herself to a tree, she wrapped her arms around the trunk and waited.

Within seconds, the pea-sized hail turned egg-sized, and debris showered down on her; rocks, twigs, and wood propelled by the vortex pummeled her body. Flying leaves became sharp slivers, cutting into Ruth's arms and legs. Twisting around her, the tornado's monster-like force lifted her off the ground, suspended her mid-air her for seconds, and slammed her back into the dirt. Barely conscious—the breath whooshing from her lungs, and blood gushing from a wound in her scalp—Ruth raised her head and screamed as the tornado moved over the kitchen house, and stripped off its roof. Blowing out an exterior wall, the maelstrom toppled the chimney and sucked up strips of siding, splintering them into kindling, and flinging them over the fields like swarms of angry locusts.

❧✦❧

Anica scanned the field, her desperate cries for Ruth swallowed by the roar of the tornado cutting a large swath through the trees and coming directly toward her. Pulses of lightning ripped jagged slices in the black sky. The saturated ground loosened its hold on trees; the force of the rotating air ripping them from the earth and spitting them out as if they were twigs. A limb snapped with a deafening crack, and flew past Anica, narrowly missing her head. Shaking, she wrestled the wooden cellar door closed. Descending the stairs into the inky darkness, she felt for the edge of each step with her foot, while trying to soothe Benjamin's screams of terror. Overhead, the door rattled relentlessly, its metal latch groaning under the strain, threatening to unleash the portal. When Anica's foot hit the soft dirt floor, she was drenched in sweat.

"Mariana? Where are you?" she shouted, disoriented in the dark and trying to follow the sound of Isabel's sobs.

A hand touched her arm. "We're here, *Mi cariña*. Thank heavens, you are safe."

"It's right on top of us," cried Anica. The ceiling above them vibrated, sending dirt and dried spices and vegetables raining down on them. Something crashed into the north wall, its thud rocking the house like an explosion.

Her eyes grown accustomed to the darkness, Anica pulled Mariana and the terror-stricken children under the stairs. Huddled together, with Isabel and Benjamin cocooned between them, they felt a change in the air pressure as the latch tore free and the cellar door flew open.

The roar of the storm and pounding hail sounded like thousands of horses stampeding over them. The walls of the cellar shuddered, and the wind swooped down into the subterranean room, creating swirls of dust clouds that clogged their noses and ears with dirt. Shelves collapsed, and casks of preserved fruit scattered across the floor. A squall of heavy rain followed, pouring down the stairs into the cellar, water coursing along the earthen floor and swirling around their feet, licking at the tops of their shoes, and turning the dirt into a morass of mud.

Anica kissed her children and whispered Efren's name. Mariana—her fingers tracing along an invisible rosary—prayed that their deaths would be swift, and that the children would not suffer.

Pronged lightning flamed in the sky, casting the cellar in a spectral glow. Suddenly, the terrifying whooshing became a murmur. The sky began to lighten, and the air grew unnaturally calm, leaving them suspended in an unearthly silence as terrifying as the howling wind.

Creeping out from under the cellar stairs, Anica sloshed through the mud and floating debris, and slowly climbed the flight of steps to the surface. The cellar door was gone, its metal hinges dangling from its frame, a terrifying reminder of the tornado's strength. Peering out of the opening, Anica gasped, her mouth frozen in stunned surprise at the destruction left in the wake of the storm. In less than two minutes, the tornado had rampaged through the gardens and brought down ancient, forty-foot live oaks, their expansive root balls rising in the air like gigantic fists. A palmetto tree crashed through a side window of the big house, half of its trunk disappearing into the residence. Household goods were strewn everywhere. A rocking chair from the portico stood absurdly upright and unscathed in the middle of the carriageway, while the other chairs had been tossed about and splintered by the wind.

Its roar fading, Anica watched the tornado spin away to the northeast, and returned to the cellar to help Mariana and the children up the stairs. In the glare of daylight, she inspected Isabela and Benjamin to assure herself that they weren't injured, and circled Mariana so she could be certain she too was unharmed.

"I am fine," assured Mariana, stamping her mud-caked feet.

Anica looked toward the kitchen house, hoping to catch sight of Ruth, and her face stiffened in horror.

Mariana followed her gaze and sucked in a sharp breath, "*Dios mio!* You go. I'll take the children inside."

Taking off on a run, Anica called over her shoulder, "Send help!"

Anica had only gone a few yards when she caught sight of movement under a stand of trees.

"Ruth!" she screamed, running towards a mound of dirt and leaves. Climbing over a downed tree, she found Ruth, mud and grit embedded in her skin, blood caked around her scalp.

Anica dropped to her knees and wiped the mud from Ruth's face and body. "Thank God, you're alive."

Ruth grabbed Anica's arm. "Mama? Hannah?" she croaked. "The kitchen house…"

Anica glanced past Ruth at the partially caved-in outbuilding and didn't answer.

"Leave me." She tightened her hold on Anica. "Please," Ruth begged, her eyes wild with pain and terror.

Her heart pounding, Anica ran toward the kitchen house. *Please God, let them be safe*, she prayed as she picked her way through the shattered wood, chimney bricks, and cooking utensils littered throughout the yard. Approaching what was left of the building, Anica was seized by a feeling of dread so strong, she staggered back. Her chest heaving, she gulped in a lungful of air, and ducking under a fallen timber, stepped into the rubble.

Frozen in place, Anica could hear Hannah's wails. "Lindy!" she screamed. Frantically pushing aside splintered furniture, baskets of food, pots, and pans, she stumbled blindly towards the side room where Hannah usually slept. Shoving aside the broken door frame that blocked her entry, she recoiled in horror; her knees buckling. Draped over Hannah's basket, Lindy's body lay crushed beneath a fallen beam.

CHAPTER 50

The coach rocked to a sudden halt, the horses rearing in confusion as the driver suddenly reined them in to avoid a large tree lying across the carriageway. Efren sprang from the passenger compartment and ran towards the big house, fear churning his stomach as he drew closer to the residence. Splintered branches, uprooted trees, and roof shingles covered the sloping lawn. Part of the roof was peeled back. The head of the iron rooster weathervane that sat atop the stable barn was embedded in the north side of the house. Curtains caught in the wind fluttered through shattered windows like large flapping tongues. Broken glass covered the portico steps, crunching under his feet as he bolted into the house.

Efren looked in disbelief at the devastation all around him. Shattered glass from the arched window and crystal chandelier carpeted the parquet floor in the entrance hall. The marble-topped table that stood at its center was pitched on its side, broken into jagged pieces. Brown, withered rose petals clung to the flocked wallpaper like slowly dying moths. The crimson velvet settees lining the foyer were soaked with rain, dripping water and coloring the shards of glass beneath them a dark red.

In a panic, his heart pounding, Efren stood in the entrance hall shouting Anica's name. The door to the parlor swung open and his heart soared; she was unharmed and in his arms.

"Thank God, you are all right. I was crazy with worry," he said, caressing her face. "We heard about the tornado this morning, and I got here as fast as

I could. The children and Mariana? Are they safe?"

"They're unhurt. We were safe in the root cellar, but..." Her face crumpled in anguish.

"But what?" asked Efren, his voice shaky.

Anica took his hand. "The storm hit with no warning. It had rained and then cleared. The workers were in the field. Ruth was near the big house, but Hannah was with Lindy in the kitchen house."

Efren closed his eyes. From what he'd seen of the destruction in and around the big house, he knew the outbuildings could not have withstood the tornado's fury.

"Ruth tried to reach the kitchen house before the tornado hit, but she was trapped in the storm. She tied herself to a tree, and by some miracle survived, though she is badly cut and bruised." Anica could feel her throat constricting. Swallowing hard, she continued, her words halting. "Lindy covered Hannah's body with her own to protect her. The roof collapsed. Hannah was unscathed, but a support beam fell on Lindy."

Efren held her tight, sorrow humming through his body. His mind flew to the last time he spoke to Lindy. The sadness in her eyes, and the feel of her hand in his were carved into his memory.

"There's more you need to know," said Anica easing herself out of Efren's arms. "Your uncle was seriously injured when a tree crashed through the window of his study. His face was badly cut by flying glass, but the worse injury is to his right foot. When the tree came through the window, it toppled his desk, crushing his foot. Doctor Andrews, the doctor from Summerville, left just before you arrived. He gave Philip laudanum for the pain and to help him sleep, but he said the damage was so great his foot has to be amputated. Philip screamed at him and told him to never come back."

Efren started to speak, but Anica held up her hand. "Wait until you've heard it all. The quarters are all but gone. The tornado missed three cabins, but the others are rubble. We are still trying to determine how many injuries and deaths there are. We don't know for certain because so many slaves ran off after the storm. Most of the slaves who remained are the older ones. Some crowded into the three remaining cabins last night; others slept outside. Jesse's house took a lot of damage, but they are all safe and can still live there. I'm not sure what condition the rice fields are in."

Efren rocked back on his heels, dazed by the quick succession of catastrophic news. "Is everyone in the house all right?"

"Thank God, they are safe. Silas steered them into the dining room, and they all got under the table. Except for some minor cuts and bruises from flying glass and debris, they are all right."

"I should go out and check the fields, but I want to see the children and Mariana first. Are they up? Are we able to stay in our rooms?"

"Yes, and yes. The roof was damaged over the wing where Margaret and Charles stayed. There's a lot of destruction in those rooms, but repairing the roof is all that matters for now. Just go upstairs quietly. Ruth is resting in the room next to Mariana's."

"How is she?"

Anica lowered her head, her mouth dipping into a frown. "Her physical wounds will heal, but she blames herself for not being at the kitchen house. I think the only thing keeping her going is Hannah."

That night, their love-making was raw and desperate, their hunger for each other leaving them exhausted. Efren wrapped Anica in his arms and nuzzled her neck.

"And I thought I was tired before," she laughed, raking her fingers through his curls.

Efren kissed the top of her head. "Don't fall asleep yet. We have to talk."

Stifling a yawn, Anica rolled to her side.

I went over to the quarters while you were helping Old Sarah get dinner ready," said Efren rising up on his elbows. "From what I saw, most of the slaves used the confusion after the storm as cover to disappear into the swamp. Just as you said, the elderly slaves didn't try to escape. Cotter didn't run either. When I asked him why, he said Olivia, one of the field slaves, was going to have his baby any day now, and he wouldn't leave her."

Anica sat up, her hair tumbling around her shoulders. "Is she all right?"

"I assume so. I didn't see Jesse, or ride out to the paddies. I'll do that first thing in the morning. Cotter said he was going to try to round up the horses he let loose before the tornado hit. I need to see my uncle, but I want to assess the condition of the fields first. If there is as much damage there as here at the house, and if most of the slaves are gone, I don't see how he can recover from this."

"Are you saying he could lose Bending Oaks?"

"Depending on how much money he owes, I think he could."

Sunlight was just breaking through the ash-gray sky when Efren left the big house. A thin mist rose off the warm earth. Tiny beads of dew dotted the fallen trees and debris that blanketed the property, prisms of color captured like hunted prey in the drops. Despite evidence of the storm's havoc everywhere he looked, Efren was comforted by the rhythms of the new day—the dawn chorus of bird songs that filled the air; the stirrings of small creatures as they came awake and scurried through the underbrush to fill their empty stomachs. He could feel his mood begin to lift, the natural push and pull of the morning a salve to his flagging spirits.

His improved disposition vanished when the stable yard came into view. The roof to the barn was gone, and one wall was partially caved in, leaning precariously against an adjoining wall. In the distance, Efren could see Cotter leading two horses back to what was left of the stables and hurried to join him.

The doleful look on the blacksmith's face said it all. "I only found these two. I goin' back and lookin' again. They'd go to low spots to protect themselves from the storm." He took off his hat and mopped the sweat from his close-cropped hair with a torn red bandana. "The fence, it down in spots, and I fears they gone for good."

"All of them?"

"I sure hopes not." Cotter's gaze swept the open field. "I ain't even started lookin' for the cows and the hogs. If you needs a horse, you can take one of these here, but first I gots to see if I can find a saddle and bridle. Stable gear be blown all over the place."

"I have to ride out to the rice fields, but I want to get another look at the quarters first. Do you think you can get one of these horses saddled for me in the next half an hour?"

"I sure gonna try."

Efren turned to leave.

"Mister Efren," said Cotter, "it bad in the quarters. Some gots injured, and last count, three dead in the quarters and seven out in the fields. We spent most of the day yesterday burin' them. The old folks all scared. They sharin' what left of their gardens, but it ain't gonna last long. It gonna start gettin' cold at night, and they ain't got no place warm to sleep."

Efren ran his hand over his face. *Ten dead.* "I am going to see what they need. I will try to do everything I can to make sure they are safe."

The flesh around Cotter's large eyes crinkled, and a slow smile rippled across his face. "Thank you, Mister Efren."

"Don't thank me yet," said Efren, unsure of how much he could get Philip to consent to, or Jesse to oversee.

Efren walked slowly through what was left of the quarters, his despair growing with each step. Evidence of the tornado's ferocity was everywhere.

Picking through the caved-in walls and piles of shattered boards that used to be their cabins, the young slaves who hadn't run off, and the old slaves who had no place to go, searched for their meager belongings.

An elderly man, sitting on the ground, his head wrapped in a bloody bandage, called to Efren as he approached. "Mister Efren, we'd sure 'preciate it iffn you could spare Lindy and send her on over here. We gots some folk needin' tendin' to."

Efren felt his chest tighten. Meeting the injured slave's gaze, he sat down beside him. "I'll send Old Sarah down to see if she can help. I'm sorry to tell you Lindy was killed in the tornado. She was protecting Ruth's baby and a kitchen house beam fell on her."

The old slave closed his eyes. When he opened them, they were wet with tears. "She was a mighty good woman. I remember her and her mama on the Ball plantation before we sold to Miss Mary when Mister Duncan still alive. Please tell Ruth that Alfie mighty sorry to hear about her mama."

"I will tell her. Are you all right? Your head looks like it's bleeding badly."

"I done looked worse, and I done felt better, but I can manage."

"I'll send Old Sarah to help here as soon as I get back to the big house. I just need to see Jesse."

Alfie's face twisted at the mention of the overseer's name. "Good luck findin' him. He ain't been around here since the storm fire up. I heared his house gots lots of damage, but his family be all right, just some bangs and bruises."

Efren found Jesse standing in front of his house, rifle in hand. "You expecting trouble?" he asked, keeping his hands loose and away from his body.

Jesse scowled and lowered his weapon. "Just making sure them black bastards don't take it into their heads to raid my garden. It's all I got to feed my family."

Efren surveyed the damage to Jesse's cabin. Part of the roof was gone, windows were shattered, and the front door hung loosely by its hinges. Bricks from the chimney lay scattered around the yard. "Is your family all right? Do you need anything?"

The overseer eyed Efren suspiciously. "My wife got some cuts, but the young'uns are good," he stammered. "Might need some boards for the roof."

"I'm glad they are unhurt. I'll see what I can do about the boards." Efren's tone changed. "I heard most of the slaves have run off. Is that true?"

"They're gone. Ran into the marsh, probably to join up with other runaways living in there in the settlements. They got encampments so deep in the swamp even the dogs can't find 'em. Some been living out there since the Brits left after the Revolution."

"Where's Earl?"

Jesse's lips stretched over his decaying teeth. "The son of a bitch ran off too."

"And the fields?"

"Not good. I was out there this morning. They're all flooded. In about half of 'em, the stalks are flattened and soaking in the water. They're ruined; the grain is washed away. In the other half, some of the plants are squatted, but most are still standing. Once they dry out, they can be harvested, though it means poorer grain quality and smaller yield. But all that don't mean nothing if we don't have the slaves to do the work. You can try looking for 'em and bringing 'em back, but if they're in them runaway settlements, you ain't never gonna find 'em."

Standing in Jesse's debris-strewn yard, Efren could feel his plans to leave for Charleston in the upcoming weeks slipping away.

CHAPTER 51

"Why don't you go upstairs and get some rest?" said Efren. "I'll stay with Philip, just tell me what to do."

Anica had been dozing in a chair at Philip's bedside, the room darkened by the boards Cotter placed over the broken window. An oil lamp sat on a small table, its flame casting sinister shadows on the walls. Exhausted and craving sleep, she did not protest.

"I'm too tired to argue with you. His fever is high. Keep cold compresses on his forehead to bring his temperature down." She pointed to a small bottle on the table beside Philip's bed. "The doctor left laudanum for the pain and to help him sleep, but he's asked for it so often, it's almost gone. His foot looks infected, and it's starting to smell. It needs to be amputated."

Efren glanced at his sleeping uncle. His face was a mass of cuts. A gash on his forehead seeped blood into the bandage wrapped around his head. "I am going to send for the doctor. I don't care what he says. Does he know about Lindy?"

"He called for her to come treat him as soon as Doctor Andrews left. I told him what happened, but the laudanum was taking effect, so I'm not sure if he understood what I was saying."

"Has she been buried?"

Anica's arms encircled his waist. "Yesterday. I'm sorry, Efren, we couldn't wait. Mariana went to the cemetery with Ruth. She said they buried Lindy next to Viney." Anica grew silent. When she spoke again, her voice was heavy with anguish. "Brock doesn't know. Jesse wouldn't let anyone go to the Berrell plantation to tell him."

"He loved her. It's wrong that he doesn't know she's dead."

Pressing her cheek against Efren's chest, Anica could feel the anger fueling his pounding heart. "We all miss her," she said, lifting her head to kiss him. "I am going upstairs. Benjamin is sure to be hungry. I'll ask Sally to take Isabel, so Mariana can get some rest too."

Alone with his uncle, Efren's thoughts were beset by images of the damaged rice fields, the devastation in the quarters, and the damage to the big house, all melding into a haunting collage that mocked his helplessness and stoked his fears that recovery was impossible.

Philip moaned and pushed himself up into a sitting position. Weak from the effort, he began to cough, his breath coming in short, quick gasps. Groggy and glassy-eyed, fever flushing his cheeks, he regarded Efren with obvious scorn.

"So, you are back," he croaked, his battered face contorting in pain.

Efren poured his uncle a glass of water and held it to his lips. Philip took in long gulps, drops dribbling down his chin and wetting the front of his shirt. He drew his arm across his face and wiped his mouth on his sleeve, wincing as he irritated the cuts on his cheeks.

"I got back as fast as I could after I heard about the storm. I arrived yesterday afternoon."

"How nice of you," Philip sneered, and pointed to the brown bottle of laudanum on the bedside table. "Give me some."

Ignoring his uncle's sarcasm, Efren placed a cool cloth on his head. "There's not much left, and if you want more, you are going to have to be seen by Doctor Andrews again."

Philip batted away Efren's hand. "I do not want that charlatan coming near me. Get Lindy in here with her roots. She'll fix me up."

Efren blew out a breath, puffing out his cheeks. "Lindy was killed in the tornado."

Philip's mouth went slack, his stare vacant and uncomprehending. "Did you say Lindy is dead?"

"I'm sorry," said Efren, repeating how Lindy died. "She was buried in the slave cemetery the day before I got back."

Philip looked away. "I took two of her children from her. Lizzie was just a baby when I sold her. I always felt bad about that." Shrugging off his moment of remorse, he scowled at Efren. "Who's going to fix me up, if she is gone?"

Efren steeled himself for what was to come. "I sent Cotter to get Doctor Andrews."

Philip pounded the bed with his fist. "Why the hell did you do that? He wants to cut off my foot! I'd rather die than be a damned cripple."

"Because if you don't let him amputate you might get your wish. You're running a fever and your foot is starting to smell, which means it's badly infected. Besides, you are going to need more laudanum, and he is the one who provides it."

Defeated, Philip fell back on his pillow, too tired and weak to resist, and too fearful of being without the bitter, reddish-brown liquid that quieted his pain and induced peaceful slumber. "Just as long as you understand I will not let him take my foot. Now, give me the damn medicine."

"I will, but first we need to talk, and your thoughts need to be clear. I've been to the rice fields, and at least half of the crop is destroyed. The other half has some substantial damage, and the paddies are flooded."

Philip waved his hand dismissively. "So, we get the field slaves out there, and we salvage what we can. Even damaged grain will bring in a small profit."

"That's not all of it. Most of the slaves ran off as soon as the storm pulled away. Jesse said they're probably deep in the swamp in slave encampments. Only Cotter, a few of the younger slaves, and most of the older ones stayed behind. They are all living in the three cabins that didn't blow away."

Philip pulled the cloth from his forehead and threw it across the room. "Are you telling me that son of a bitch let them all get away?"

"I don't know if Jesse could have done anything to stop them. The patrollers and dog handlers were all dealing with the aftermath of the tornado and keeping track of their own slaves."

Efren edged his chair closer to the bed. "There's also a lot of damage to the big house. Windows are blown out, some of the furniture is ruined, and part of the roof is gone. Rebuilding the quarters and the repairs to the big house are going to be costly." Efren cleared his throat. "You need to be honest with me about how much money you owe."

Shivering with fever-induced chills, Philip pressed the covers around his heated body. "I am months behind on the bank loan on the property, and my gambling debts total nearly two thousand dollars. There's barely anything left."

⨼❖⨽

Doctor Andrews signaled Efren to join him outside Philip's room. "His foot is badly infected. I cleaned the open wound as best as I could, but the injury is so extensive that blood flow to his foot is poor. The flesh on his foot is starting to rot. That's why the skin around his toes is beginning to smell and blacken. If we don't amputate his foot, the infection will spread throughout his body, and kill him."

"Philip is adamant. He won't allow it. I've tried talking to him, but he won't listen."

"Then there is nothing I can do for him." Reaching into the worn brown leather bag at his side, the doctor produced two bottles of laudanum and gave them to Efren. "If your uncle continues to refuse amputation, he will die a painful death. Ration the medicine as much as you can, because in the end, he will be begging for it, and it will take larger doses to control the pain. And Efren, if I may, a word of advice. Now is the time to send for his lawyer, and make sure your uncle gets his affairs in order. If the infection spreads as quickly as I think it will, it could only be a matter of days. In fact, if he is up to it, I would talk to him now." Tipping his hat, he shook Efren's hand. "Send for me if he changes his mind."

Efren knew his uncle had given up; he was a beaten man long before the tornado ripped into Bending Oaks. Squaring his shoulders, he prepared himself for the conversation he had been dreading since Philip told him his money had run out.

"Is that bastard gone?" grumbled Philip.

"You should listen to him," said Efren. "The infection is starting to spread. Andrews is convinced that if you do not allow him to amputate, you may only have a few days to live."

"You think I don't know how bad my foot is?" Philip cast a weary look Efren's way. "I'm going to lose Bending Oaks; everything will be gone. I'd rather be dead than be a penniless cripple depending on the kindness of others. And don't try to give me some noble speech about starting a new life. We both know I'll be back at the gambling tables first chance I get. I knew the minute the tornado hit it was over for me. I just didn't expect it to end this way."

Overcome by warring emotions, Efren struggled to find a way to broach the subject of finalizing Philip's affairs.

"I want you to send Jesse to get Elvin York, my lawyer," said Philip as if he had been eavesdropping on Efren's conversation with the doctor. "My creditors are going to descend on Bending Oaks like a pack of jackals. They'll seize everything and put it on the auction block to recoup their losses. I can't do anything about the rest of the property, but I can keep the bastards from getting the slaves."

Efren's confusion was so obvious, Philip laughed. "I'm going to manumit them in my will; free all of the slaves who didn't run away, so they can't be sold to pay my debts." His gaze grew distant, his voice soft and wistful. "Besides, it's what Mary would want me to do. She never felt right about owning slaves. I owe her that much."

"You would do that?"

Philip ground his teeth in pain. "Isn't that what I just said I would do?" he snapped. "Just make sure you get York here fast, and give me the damn laudanum."

Stooped with age, his powdered wig slipping down his forehead, Elvin York leaned heavily on his ebony cane, the shine of its silver elephant-head grip a sharp contrast to his aged, brown-spotted hand.

"I have been taking care of this family's legal matters since before Duncan Hagret married Mary." He fixed his rheumy eyes on Efren. "She was a fine woman, and Duncan adored her. I never knew why she married Philip. I urged her to protect herself with a written agreement that would permit her to retain her personal property and dispose of it to her heirs, but she wouldn't hear of it. Within a year of marrying Philip, I think Mary knew she'd made a mistake. Now the damn fool's gambling habit has destroyed everything Duncan built."

Efren bridled at the lawyer's condemnation of Philip. "I don't condone his actions, but I truly believe my uncle loved Mary."

York's lips stretched into a straight line. "If you say so. He certainly has no feeling for Margaret. He made no allowances for her in his will. Claimed she'd already received her inheritance along with all of Mary's jewelry, and that she didn't even deserve that. At any rate, you are his only heir, and he named you executor of what's left of his estate." Tugging his wig back into place, he indicated he was ready to leave. "I will file the will immediately.

I agree with Doctor Anderson's assessment. I don't think Philip will live much longer. I am at your service if you need me. Good day."

Philip died four days later. Buried in the family cemetery next to Mary, the graveside mourners were dry-eyed and few. Margaret declined to attend, sending word that she was sure she would not be missed. Jesse, his hair slicked back and wearing an ill-fitting waistcoat, tugged at his tight shirt collar, looking like a trapped animal desperate for a way to escape. Jedidiah Conroy appeared seeking to collect the money Philip owed him. Efren informed him he would have to wait along with the others, and asked him to leave. Only Amadis Lopez, Doctor Anderson, and Attorney York came to pay their respects.

With Anica and Mariana at his side, Efren offered a brief prayer for his uncle's soul. As they turned to leave, a cool autumn breeze rustled the leaves of the surrounding live oaks. Efren cupped his hand over his eyes and looked skyward. *Lindy would have found a spiritual meaning in the swirling air*, he thought, and a deep sense of sorrow overtook him—not for his uncle, but for the wise and gentle woman he considered his friend.

CHAPTER 52

February 1787

Efren stood looking out at the weed-choked rice fields for the last time. After months of legal wrangling, the bank had finally taken possession of the property and everything on it. The manumission papers had been certified and were in the hands of the freed slaves.

The plantation was desolate. The slaves gone, Jesse left to oversee a plantation in Goose Creek. Only Cotter, Olivia, and their infant son remained, hired by the bank at Efren's recommendation to look after the property and the livestock that was left until everything could be auctioned off.

The big house was empty too. With Amadis' help, Efren was able to secure employment for the house slaves and Old Sarah as servants with several merchants in Charleston. Ruth and Hannah were now a part of their family.

Efren retreated from the fields of ruined rice, relieved to be free of the honor-bound entanglements that had kept him tied to Bending Oaks, to his uncle, and to a way of life he abhorred.

Up before dawn the following morning, Anica eased out of bed, careful not to wake Efren and the children. It was Anica's favorite time of the day. Pure and quiet, it belonged to her alone, and she savored its solitude as a welcome start to the day. Wrapping herself in her dressing gown, she moved to the window, luxuriating in the splendor of the pre-dawn sky. Still visible in the dark above the horizon, the moon was fading even as the sun began its ascent.

Sitting in the semi-darkness, Anica grew pensive, mixed feelings of excitement and apprehension coloring her thoughts. Eager to put the unhappiness of the past months behind her, she looked forward to their new life in Charleston. Efren had leased a house on Broad Street; a temporary arrangement until they could purchase a home of their own, a place where Isabel, Benjamin, and Hannah could grow up together, and where she could openly observe her Jewish faith.

But the promises Charleston offered did not quell her anxieties over what awaited them in the city. Too many of their hopes had been dashed for her to ignore the uncertainties of their new life. The destruction of Philip's rice crop was a devastating blow to Eagle Shipping's business on both sides of the ocean. In the months following his uncle's death, Efren spent several days each week in Charleston with Amadis, reassuring the bank and planters that their company was solvent and could meet their needs. It was only when a ship bound for London needed repairs and could not set sail on time, that Amadis was able to secure enough goods to fill the *Aguila's* hold and make the trip across the Atlantic profitable.

Taking the *Shabbat* candlesticks from the chest where they remained hidden, she ran her fingers over their smooth brass curves, and an unexpected peacefulness settled over her, as if she had been wrapped in her mother's arms. "Mama, I haven't forgotten," she whispered as she nestled the pair into her travel satchel.

Down the hall, Ruth was also awake. Too excited to sleep, she'd spent a fitful night waiting for the new day; the day that she would leave Bending Oaks a free woman. And like Anica, she was afraid to give full rein to her dreams. Instead, she had approached her new freedom with a plan, heeding the words her mother whispered to her when she visited her in her dreams: *Your African ancestors were all healers. Your path is clear.*

With Lindy's voice as her guide, Ruth had recovered her mother's bag of roots and herbs and salves from the ruins of the kitchen house. Relying on what Lindy had taught her, and with Old Sarah's help and Efren's encouragement, she committed the use and doses for her mother's herbal remedies and balms to memory and began caring for the remaining slaves in the quarters. When word spread of Ruth's success as a healer, planters from nearby plantations began requesting her help in treating their slaves. Sent for when births turned difficult, Ruth delivered healthy babies, including the son of a wealthy Summerville planter, and her reputation as a midwife spread.

Ruth reached for the cloth pouch tucked under her pillow, and fingered the folded bills and coins she'd been paid for her healing and midwifery services. Unlike the pittance her mother received after Philip took most of the payment, the entire amount she received was hers. Deep in thought, Ruth closed her eyes, and conjured her mother's face. *Mama, I know you are with your mother. Watch over us.*

Her reverie was interrupted by the burbling noises that always signaled Hannah's waking moments. Ruth watched her daughter curl her body and then stretch, rubbing her eyes with her plump, dimpled hands. At the sound of Ruth's voice, she began to coo, extending her arms to be picked up.

Ruth lifted Hannah, unable to remember ever being this happy. "We're leaving this hell today," she said, kissing her daughter's soft cheeks. "You will never know what it's like to be a slave. You will never have to answer to a master, or fear being whipped, or endure the desires of strange men," she said, hugging the child tightly, her arms forming a protective wall. "You will be able to love whomever you want, and you will never have your babies taken from you. From now on, you are Hannah Amselem, and you are free."

PART III

CHAPTER 53

Charleston, November 1804

"Hannah Amselem, we need to leave. You know we have to get there before the sun goes down to light the *Shabbat* candles!"

"I know, Mama! I'll be right there. Just give me another minute," Hannah shouted back, tucking her hair into a lace-trimmed bonnet. Examining the results in the mirror, she nodded at her reflection, satisfied with the face staring back at her.

Ruth knew how carefully Hannah had chosen her dress for the evening, certain the eighteen-year-old's sudden interest in her appearance was prompted by Benjamin's return from his Virginia boarding school. Inseparable as children, Hannah had been heartbroken when Efren decided Benjamin wasn't learning enough from the tutor hired to educate him, and sent the boy to boarding school. Isabel and Hannah had flourished under the instruction of their tutor, but Benjamin's quick mind went unchallenged by the education he was getting at home. Hannah was inconsolable when he left, even when Ruth pointed out that she should be grateful Efren and Anica feared for Benjamin's safety on a cross-Atlantic voyage to England, and chose a Virginia school instead.

"Hannah! Now!" demanded Ruth, the tone of her voice clearly conveying it was time to go.

Breathless, Hannah appeared at the top of the stairs. "I'm coming!"

Ruth knew she looked beautiful even before she gazed up at her. Taking in the sight of her daughter as she descended the stairs—the simple empire lines of her pale blue dress revealing the curves of her body—she felt the tug of time, and with it the realization that her child had become a woman. The old fears haunted her. Even when Hannah was small, her startling beauty had attracted attention, and now men appraised her openly, their eyes betraying their thoughts.

"You look lovely. If you are trying to get Benjamin's attention, I am sure you will."

Hannah ducked her head, ragged splotches of pink spreading across her tawny cheeks. "I thought we had to go," she said, grabbing her cloak. Standing at the front door with her hands on her hips, she set her mouth in a frown, and scolded, "Why do I always have to wait for you?"

Laughing, Ruth led the way. Gripping the medical bag she carried with her at all times, she paused to look back at the house on Tradd street for a moment. Three stories, with a stucco façade of pale pink, its long and slender street-facing frontage was typical of Charleston's single-house architecture. It always amused her that the door facing the street only allowed entry to the piazza that ran down the side of the house, and that the actual front door was located near the middle of the structure. *A far cry from the slave cabins and the old washhouse*, she mused, as they let themselves out through the ornate wrought iron gate and stepped onto the street.

Hannah knew what her mother was thinking. She'd seen the rapt expression on her face many times. "Still can't believe it's yours?"

Ruth tightened her cloak around her body to ward off the November chill. "Memories of life on the plantation and all the people I lost are not easily forgotten. So, yes, it is hard for me to believe that we have come this far. But it also reminds me of how glad I am to have the family we have now."

Hannah grew quiet as they walked. "I know that Efren and Anica gave us a start, and you know how much I love them," she said, breaking the silence as they walked, "But you've made your own way here. All those times when people banged on the door in the middle of the night because someone was sick, or having a baby, or there was a fight on the docks and someone needed stitching up, it was you who left your bed to take care of them. And look at you, always carrying your bag of roots and herbs just in case someone needs you. You are well respected here. I hope you know how proud I am to be your daughter."

They were standing in front of Efren and Anica's stately East Bay Street mansion, the brisk wind coming from the harbor plucking at their clothes. Such praise from her daughter was so unexpected that a sob caught in Ruth's throat. Tucking a loose strand of hair under Hannah's bonnet, she kissed her cheek. "We'd better go in," she said, tilting her head towards the horizon. The sun is almost setting."

They had just given their cloaks and Ruth's medical bag to Robert, the Amselem's longtime butler, when Isabel burst into the entrance hall and greeted them with warm hugs. At twenty she was even more beautiful than her mother, her dark hair piled in a halo of curls, her startling emerald green eyes highlighting her exotic looks. Tall and lanky as a child, she had acquired a gentle gracefulness in womanhood. It was no surprise to Ruth that she was being pursued by a number of Charleston's most well-to-do, eligible young men.

"I am so glad you are here. Benjamin has been literally pacing in anticipation of your arrival," she said, raising her eyebrows in delight and looping her arms through Hannah's. "Come, everyone is in the dining room."

Ruth followed the girls, admiring as she always did the exquisite décor of Anica and Efren's home. The Italian marble floor of the entrance hall; the ballroom with its azure blue cove ceiling; the elaborately decorated Georgian mantles and wainscotting; the Waterford crystal chandeliers, their candles enclosed in etched globes casting circles of light. It was a home that reflected Efren's hard-earned success.

No longer burdened by the weight of Bending Oaks, Efren had quickly returned to the world he knew best, and along with Amadis, built the A & E Eagle Shipping Company into a thriving business. After constructing their own wharf with stores and shops for lease, they extended their interests to include land speculation. Along with their shipping business and fleet of ships crisscrossing the seas, wise investments and the company's real estate holdings had made them wealthy men.

"Here they are!" exclaimed Efren, stepping forward to greet them. The intervening years had been good to him. At fifty-six, he still maintained the looks and vigor of a younger man. With only slight threads of gray in his beard and curly hair, his face remained smooth; the faint, spidery lines around his eyes bearing testimony to his kind and gentle nature.

Ruth glanced over at Anica as she approached, warmed as always by her friend's welcoming smile.

Kissing the women on both cheeks, Anica held Hannah at arm's length. "You look lovely. And someone over there," she said, inclining her head towards Benjamin, "is very anxious to see you."

Peering at Benjamin, Hannah caught him looking her way, an impish grin on his handsome face.

Hannah pointed to the fading light outside. "Um, isn't it time to light the candles?" she stammered, desperately hoping to escape the moment.

"Nicely done," whispered Efren, steering Hannah to a spot next to Benjamin. After exchanging quick hugs with Mariana and Amadis, Ruth joined the others as they gathered to watch Anica light the *Shabbat* candles.

The brass candlesticks were set out on an intricately carved sideboard, their smooth lines elegant in their simplicity. Placing a shawl over her head, Anica lit the candles and recited the ancient prayer that ushered in the Sabbath.

Staring into the dancing flames, Ruth mouthed the words of the prayers along with Anica, savoring the serenity that encircled her like a loving embrace. And as she had done since that first time years ago at Bending Oaks, she met Anica's eyes, and joined her in saying, "Amen."

Shabbat dinners with their family of friends had become an Amselem tradition since their arrival in Charleston. Anica cherished these Friday night gatherings. An open affirmation of her faith and her pledge to her mother's memory, they also quieted her disappointment over *Beth Elohim's* stand that she could not be recognized as a member of the synagogue because her marriage to Efren had not been performed according to Jewish law. The irony of the ban in the synagogue's constitution did not escape her. Although Efren lacked the inclination to reclaim his own Jewishness, he relished the Friday night gatherings that brought together the people he loved most as much as she did.

Seated at the head of the table, Efren's eyes swept the faces of his little family, taking in the snippets of conversation and the easy laughter of Isabel, Hannah, and Benjamin. Tipping his glass to Ruth and then to Amadis and Mariana, his glance settled on Anica at the far end of the table. Untouched by time, her beauty still left him breathless.

Sensing Efren's gaze, Anica smiled coquettishly, her dark eyes twinkling, teasing him with the promise of more to come.

Observing this intimate exchange, Amadis covered Mariana's hand with his, delighted by the instant smile that danced across her face. *This is all I want,* he thought, his mind drifting back to his years of loneliness. Convinced that his life at sea left no room for love, he had grown accustomed the hollow emptiness that accompanied his solitude. When Mariana came back into his life, what had begun as the rekindling of the friendship that had developed on the voyage from Valencia to Charleston, turned into something deeper. Not the blind passion and desperate need of young love, but the growing recognition that everything was better when he was with her. They'd married sixteen years ago, and he'd found a contentment he never dreamed possible. Each day he woke with Mariana by his side he was happier than the day before.

Efren rose from his chair. Clapping his hands to get everyone's attention, Efren raised his glass. "I would like to propose a toast, but first I want to tell you how happy it makes me to have you all here tonight, and especially to have Benjamin home. Now that he has finished his studies in Virginia, he will be entering Litchfield Law School in Connecticut to prepare to join Amadis and me at Eagle Shipping," said Efren, beaming at his son. "And so, here's to our family being one again; to Benjamin, and to my beautiful wife for bringing us together every Friday night to share the friendship and love that has kept us together all these years."

Benjamin's smile faded and his body stiffened. Disquieted by his father's words, he stared down at his plate. Sensing his dismay, Isabel squeezed his hand and glanced sideways at her mother to see if she had noticed too.

Her son's discomfort had not escaped Anica. He'd been quiet since his return, and his reaction to Efren's toast only confirmed her suspicion that something was troubling him. He'd chafed at being sent to Virginia for his schooling. Now, it was obvious to her that Benjamin was unhappy about Efren's plans for his future.

CHAPTER 54

Benjamin liked the feeling of Hannah's arm looped through his. "Did your mother really have to look in on a sick patient?"

Hannah shrugged her shoulders. "I'm not sure, but I am glad she asked you to escort me home."

He pulled her closer. "Me too. I wanted to see you before tonight, but my father insisted I go down to the wharf and spend the day in the office with him and Amadis." He sucked in his breath and slowly blew it out. "It was the longest day of my life. I would much rather have been with you."

"It's all right. I was with Mama most of the day helping her deliver Missus Jacoby's baby. It was her first baby so it took a little longer. And even though she is a friend of your mother's and knows we are…well, family, you should have seen the look on her face when Mama promised her she would have the baby in time to light the *Shabbat* candles."

Hannah's chuckle exploded into laughter. Not the soft sound of tinkling of bells, but a full-throated rumble so infectious that Benjamin snorted and laughed, his misery disappearing into the thin fog purling in from the harbor.

"You always could draw me out of a bad mood," he said, pressing her hand to his lips.

The whisper of Benjamin's lips still soft on her palm, Hannah struggled to slow her breathing. "I saw your face when your father made his toast. What did he say that upset you so?"

Benjamin's smile vanished, and his mouth tightened. His voice was low and anguished. "Ever since I can remember, Papa and Amadis have made it clear that they expected me to take over the business someday. I never spoke up against their plans, hoping that they would see I didn't have a head for the intricacies of importing and exporting goods. I even persuaded my last tutor to speak to my father on my behalf, to point out how inept I was when it came to figures. But all that brilliant idea of mine did was to convince my father I would learn more in boarding school. And Litchfield Law School in Connecticut? This evening was the first I'd heard of it. I can assure you I have no interest in overseeing the legal concerns of Eagle's shipping business."

His despair broke her heart. "What do you want to do?"

"I want to do what you and your mother do."

"You want to deliver babies?" she sputtered.

"No. Well yes, if I had to. Hannah, I want to be a doctor. I've seen how you and your mother comfort and heal people. I see how much you both love what you do. It's what I want to do."

A memory flicked through Hannah's thoughts triggering others of Benjamin when they were growing up. The bereft child crying over the dead rabbit they'd found in the woods. The gentle boy who tended to wounded birds and was inconsolable if they died. The quiet friend who snuck food from the house to feed the stray cats and dogs that darted about the wharfs. *Of course, he wants to comfort and care for the sick.*

"There's something else," he said. "I don't ever want to be apart from you again. I hated being in Virginia for a lot of reasons, but most of all, I missed you." His eyes locked on hers. "I love you."

Hannah began to tremble. Her heart somersaulting in her chest, she tried to speak, but the words froze in her throat.

Taking her silence as a rejection of his feelings, Benjamin dropped his hands to his side and looked away. "I'm sorry, if I ..."

Hannah touched his cheek and brought his face close to hers. "Benjamin, I have loved you for so long, but I never dared to hope that you would love me the same way; that you would ever think it was possible for us to be together."

Now it was Benjamin who was voiceless. Letting his heart speak for him, he kissed her gently, her lips as sweet as he had dreamed they would be.

❧❖❧

"Somebody slept late," said Isabel, placing a buttered biscuit on her plate.

Benjamin went to the sideboard and poured a cup of coffee. "Somebody didn't sleep at all."

Surprised by his tone, Isabel measured her next words carefully. "Did you and Hannah have a fight last night?"

"A fight?" he asked, surprised at the very idea. "No, of course not. Why would you think that?"

"Because you look terrible, and you are in a sour mood."

Benjamin ran his hand over the stubble on his face, and pointed to the empty chairs around the table. "Where is everybody?"

"Mama is in the garden. Papa left for the wharf a few minutes ago."

Benjamin pulled up a chair next to his sister. All his life, it was Isabel he'd turned to when he was troubled. She was his confidant, the keeper of his secrets. He breathed in the nutty aroma of the coffee and took a sip. Staring into his cup, he blurted, "I don't want to go into Papa's business and I don't want to go to law school. I want to be a doctor."

Stunned, Isabel sat back in her chair. "A doctor? I'll admit I am not surprised that you do not want to go into business with Papa and Amadis, but when did you decide you wanted to be a doctor?"

"I've been thinking about it for a long time, but because it seemed to mean so much to Papa that I join the company, I didn't want to disappoint him. But I can't do it—I can't spend my whole life doing something I hate."

"Then you need to tell Papa."

Benjamin sighed. "That's what Hannah said too. I just dread telling him."

"Dread telling him what?" Anica stood in the dining room doorway, her arms full of pink hydrangeas from the garden.

Benjamin peered over his coffee cup at Isabel, his eyes beseeching her for help. She returned his gaze with a barely perceptible nod of encouragement.

Anica recognized the conspiratorial look as the same one that passed between them when they were children hiding some mischief they had gotten into. And just as when he was a child, Benjamin's face betrayed his feelings. A single glance told Anica how miserable he was.

"Here," said Anica, handing the hydrangeas to Isabel. "Please have Cora put these in a vase."

Nestling the flowers in the crook of her arm, Isabel touched her brother's shoulder and made her way to the kitchen.

Benjamin sat slumped in his chair, his head bowed. His emotions jagged and barely under control, he folded his hands to keep them from shaking. *How do I tell my mother that I am going to break my father's heart?*

Anica reached across the table and covered his hands with hers. "This is about what Papa said last night, isn't it?"

His eyes were swimming in tears when he looked up. "I can't do what Papa wants me to do. I know I am letting him down, but my plans for my life are different from what he expects of me."

His pain was so raw, so palpable, it tore at Anica's heart. "Perhaps you are not giving your father enough credit. It's true he has always thought you would take over the business, but he loves you enough to want you to do what makes you happy."

"That's not what it sounded like last night. He made it pretty clear what he expected my future to be."

Ignoring the bite in his words, Anica kept her voice calm. "I will admit that Papa surprised me when he announced you were going to law school, but in fairness to him, you never objected when he spoke about you joining Eagle Shipping."

"I didn't want to hurt him. And the truth is I didn't know what I wanted to do."

"And now you do?"

Benjamin met his mother's gaze. "I want to be a doctor."

If Anica was surprised by his declaration, she did not show it. "Then you must tell him."

"And, I'm in love with Hannah."

"I know," she said, stroking his cheek.

CHAPTER 55

Benjamin ambled along East Bay Street toward the harbor. The sound of each footfall jangling his nerves, he rehearsed in his mind what he would say to his father. It was only when two women whispered and laughed as they passed by, that he realized he had given voice to his thoughts. Increasing his pace, he pulled the brim of his hat low on his brow, and made his way to the docks.

The wharf was teeming with stevedores loading rice and cotton onto vessels destined for European markets. Dodging the burly dockworkers, and averting his eyes from the unbearable misery of hundreds of slaves being removed from moored ships, Benjamin hesitated beneath the large carved eagle that marked the warehouse and office of the A & E Eagle Shipping Company. Dreading the confrontation with his father, yet desperately needing to rid himself of the great weight of guilt bearing down on him, he blew out a breath and squared his shoulders as if to affirm his decision.

Pushing open the entry's heavy oak door, Benjamin stepped into the vast warehouse, crinkling his nose at the pungent odors of spices, tobacco, and fish that mingled with the building's always-present musty smell. He stood for a moment watching the thickly muscled men who were loading barrels of rice and other goods to be transferred to the company's ships moored along the quay. One of the workers waved and shouted, "Your father is in his office with Captain Lopez."

Benjamin smiled. Amadis had not captained a ship in years, but he would always be Captain Lopez to the workers and ships' crews. Still lean and muscular, he maintained the bearing of a sea captain. But it was his concern for the men who worked in the warehouse and the crews on Eagle's ships that earned him their respect. Benjamin sighed. *I am going to disappoint Amadis too.*

"This is a nice surprise," said Efren, coming up behind Benjamin and throwing his arm around his shoulders. "You are just in time. Amadis and I are going over to McCrady's Tavern. Join us. We have much to talk about."

"It's the damn British and French war," declared Efren, raising his voice to be heard over the conversations of the other patrons in the crowded tavern dining room.

When Amadis shot a look at the young man approaching the table with their food, Efren took a sip of his ale, resuming his tirade as soon as the fellow finished placing steaming bowls of stew on the table. "English press gangs are boarding our ships at sea and forcing British deserters and British-born naturalized citizens into the Royal Navy. The British are outnumbered by the French Navy, and they are seizing our men to bolster their manpower at sea. Last month they boarded one of our ships and took so many men, there was barely enough crew left on board to make it back to port. Other merchants have reported that they are also taking cargo."

Amadis dipped a thick slice of bread into his stew. "I am afraid the British are emboldened by their success, and it appears we can expect little help from Secretary of State Madison. He seems to think America's neutrality protects us."

"Madison is a fool."

Amadis quickly glanced around the room to see if anyone overheard Efren. McCrady's Tavern was a well-known gathering place for businessmen and dignitaries of diverse political views and loyalties. He had no taste for engaging in a confrontation with supporters of James Madison. Eager to shift the topic of conversation, Amadis turned to Benjamin. "How does it feel to be home?"

Benjamin sat pondering the bowl of stew before him, his appetite and the opportunity to talk to his father rapidly fading. "Um, good. It feels good," he answered, avoiding his father's gaze.

Efren sat back in his chair and lit a cigar. "I know you want to visit with

Hannah, but I'd like you to spend a few days each week with us in the warehouse so you can see how the business is run. There are many important facets to learn."

Benjamin felt his stomach knot. *Tell him now.* Swallowing hard, he forced himself to speak. "Papa, there's something we need to discuss. I hope you and Amadis will…" His words died in his throat as a man Benjamin recognized as a business associate of his father's approached their table.

"Jonathan, how good to see you," said Efren, rising and offering his hand. "You know Amadis, and this is my son, Benjamin. He is going to be joining the company soon. Benjamin, this is Jonathan Timort."

Towering over Benjamin, he wrapped his paw-like hand around Benjamin's and shook it vigorously. "Nice to see you again, Benny. I think the last time I saw you, you were going off to boarding school. I see you're shaving now," he said, letting out a deep bass guffaw and slapping Benjamin's shoulder.

Benjamin winced. "Nice to see you too," he said, his feigned smile barely disguising his loathing of the man. "Papa, I need to…"

"What are you doing about the British taking your men?" interrupted Timort, pulling up a chair. "Damn bad business this impressment. It has to be stopped. I cannot afford any more delays in delivering my rice."

Benjamin stiffened and rose. "If you will excuse me, I have several errands to attend to. Papa, I will see you at home tonight."

Efren regarded his son across the table. "Can't you stay a bit longer? This is an important discussion."

Benjamin withdrew his pocket watch from his waistcoat and checked the time. "I told Hannah I would meet her in the park, and if I leave now I will just about make it on time."

"A lady friend too!" boomed Timort. "The boy really is growing up!"

Maintaining a pretense of politeness, Benjamin nodded toward Timort and took his leave.

Benjamin sat with Ruth in her garden. He inhaled deeply, letting the soft, spicy perfume of gardenias and the earthy smells of Ruth's medicinal herbs wash away the odors of the harbor that clung to him.

Ruth stretched and arched her back. "I think I am getting too old to be bending over these plants," she laughed. "Hannah should be back soon. I sent her to the Marketplace to get some fresh meat and vegetables for dinner. You know you are welcome to join us."

"Thank you, but I need to talk to my father and I am afraid if I put it off…" Hunched over, his elbows on his knees, Benjamin covered his face, embarrassed by the tears rimming his eyes.

Ruth placed her hand on his back. "Whatever it is that you need to tell your father, I know he will understand. He's a good man, and he loves you very much."

Tears blurring his vision, Benjamin wiped his eyes with the back of his hand. "I know he does and that's what makes it so hard. I am going to disappoint him; I just don't want the same things for me that he does."

"Benjamin, look at me. I was there when you were born, and I can tell you Efren was proud of you from the moment he saw you. I know in my soul that your father only has your happiness at heart. Now you need to tell him what's in your heart."

Benjamin's face softened. "There's something I need to tell you too. I am in love with Hannah. I have always been in love with her. I know we have to wait, and I know it won't be easy, but I will find a way to marry her."

A faint, weary smile flit across Ruth's face. "I was wondering how long it was going to take you to openly acknowledge your love for Hannah. Anyone who has watched you two grow up could see how you felt about each other." She folded her hands in her lap, her fingers interlaced as if in prayer. "Benjamin, I have always thought of you as a son, but I have to ask you. Are you strong enough to face the people who will treat you with scorn for marrying a Negro woman? Will you be able to protect Hannah from the hatefulness she will encounter, because even though she is light-skinned, she will always be looked upon as a Negro woman? And are you prepared for your children to be considered Negroes and face the hate that is out there?"

"Ruth, I know full well the hurts we will encounter. Hannah knows too. I just cannot bear the thought of my life without her. I want to have a family with her. And I swear to you, I will always take care of her."

"I look at you and I see the little boy who took the blame when Hannah broke one of your mother's vases. I see the child who wrapped Hannah's bleeding leg in his shirt and carried her home when she cut it on a jagged rock. And now, I see a young man who adores my daughter, and I know I don't have to be convinced of your intentions. I just pray that both of you will have the strength to withstand the difficult times that are sure to find you."

CHAPTER 56

Benjamin let himself into the house just as supper was being served. "I'm sorry I am so late," he said, taking his seat and spreading a napkin across his lap. "I went to see Hannah and lost track of time."

Efren eyed his son across the table. "I thought you were meeting her in the park."

Benjamin lowered his eyes. "I'm sorry, Papa. It was an excuse to get away from Mister Timort. He was absolutely odious. Benny! He called me Benny like I was still a child in knee breeches."

Efren's mouth tightened into a grim line. "You damn well behaved like one. You may think Jonathan Timort is odious, but he owns a large plantation in Monck's Corner, and he ships a lot of rice. You were rude."

"I'm sorry Papa, I didn't mean to offend anyone. I just needed to leave."

"And did you have errands to run? Or was that an excuse to leave too?"

Isabel stared down at her plate, wishing she could make herself disappear, while Anica tried to get Efren's attention in an attempt to calm him down.

Surprised by the sting in his father's tone, Benjamin retorted, "Actually, I'd come to the docks to talk to you, but captured crews and Mister Timort appeared to be more important, so I left. I understand business comes first."

Efren glared at Benjamin. "Do you?"

"More than you know." Benjamin folded his napkin and placed it on his empty plate. "I didn't sleep well last night and I am very tired. If you will excuse me, I am going to bed."

Stunned by Benjamin's exit, Efren fought to keep his temper under control. "What was that all about?"

Anica leaned forward and touched his arm. "I think we should finish dinner, and then you and I need to talk."

They ate in silence so thick it felt as if the air had left the room. Anxious to go to Benjamin, Isabel gulped down her supper and asked to be excused.

Efren shoved his plate aside, and refilled his glass with Madeira, taking several sips before he spoke. "I am sorry I lost my temper with Benjamin. He did say he had something to tell me, but surely he can see that there are problems with the business that could ruin us. I am only trying to ensure that he will have a company to inherit."

Anica sighed. "He does have something important to tell you. He is unhappy and trying not to show it, because he doesn't want to disappoint you, and because he loves you very much. He finally worked up the courage to talk to you today, and obviously, it didn't go as he intended. Efren, go to him and listen to him with an open heart."

Relieved to see the light seeping under Benjamin's door, Efren wasn't surprised when Isabel answered his knock. "I can come back if you two aren't done talking."

Isabel stepped aside and gestured for him to come in. "I was just leaving." Rising on her toes to kiss his cheek, she whispered, "Please, don't be angry with him. He has been troubled for days."

Her words sliced through him. Filled with remorse, Efren faced his son, desperately wanting to undo the damage his words had done. "I want to apologize for what I said. I was in a foul mood, and I took it out on you. I am truly sorry. You came to me to talk, and I let my preoccupation with the business get in the way. I am here to listen to what you have to say."

Benjamin felt his shoulders tighten. "Papa, I never meant to be rude or embarrass you in front of Mister Timort. And I do understand the reasons for your concern about the business. I hope you know that. I just really needed to talk to you. I still do."

The plea in Benjamin's voice deepened Efren's shame. "Your mother thinks you are going to disappoint me. I promise you, nothing you do or say could ever make me stop loving you."

"It seems I was the only one who didn't know that Benjamin had other plans for his future," said Efren, watching Anica brush her hair, still thick and lustrous as polished onyx.

Anica studied his reflection in her dressing table mirror. Fatigue etched his face. "He wanted to tell you himself," she said, turning to face him. "It was important to him that you understand how much he wants to be a doctor."

Efren sat down on the bed and patted the spot next to him. "You are too far away from me."

Smiling, Anica sat beside him, and rested her head on his shoulder. "Now that you know, how do you feel about Benjamin's plans?"

Efren nuzzled her hair, breathing in its sweet scent. "I am not going to lie. I am disappointed that he won't be a part of Eagle Shipping. From the day he was born, I dreamed of him taking over the company. Amadis, I might add, felt the same way. Now, I wonder what all the hard work was for. But I did listen with my heart, and you know I only want him to be happy. He has such a passion for wanting to heal and care for the sick, I would hate myself for standing in his way. Tomorrow I will arrange for Benjamin to meet with Doctor Harrows to see if he would be open to having him serve as his apprentice. I cannot imagine that he will refuse the generous fee."

CHAPTER 57

March 1805

"I thought by now that I would be accompanying Doctor Harrows when he sees patients, but so far all I've done for the last four months is read the journals and medical books he has in his library and then we go over what I've read. I admit he is a good teacher, and I am learning a lot, but I want to put what I've learned to use," said Benjamin as he and Hannah walked along Market Street. Unable to hide his petulance, he added, "And did I mention he also has me running errands for him and cleaning his office?"

Hannah suppressed a smile. "Don't be so eager. I would suggest that it's not a bad thing to know what you are doing when you are with a patient."

"I know," he said sheepishly. "But until I can apply what I've learned, or at least see how Doctor Harrows treats his patients, it's just a lot of memorized facts rattling around in my brain. I want to do what you do. You actually help people get better."

"I understand, but I've been going with Mama to treat her patients for as long as I can remember, and I am still learning as an observer. I am happy to wait until she feels I am ready to step in and provide treatment, because taking care of someone who is sick or having a baby is not the time to find out what you don't know."

Benjamin raised his hands in mock surrender and laughed. "I can see I'm not going to get any sympathy from you."

The sudden raspy sounds of hissing and grunting muffled their voices, and they drew back as they came upon a pack of buzzards fighting over the scraps of meat the butcher had tossed outside his shed.

Putting his hand on Hannah's back to guide her away from the frenzy, Benjamin bridled at the look of contempt from a passer-by. Before he could challenge the man, Hannah tugged at his arm. "Don't," she begged. "You will only make it worse."

The fear in her eyes fueled Benjamin's anger, his conversation with Ruth resounding in his ears.

Isabel found Anica in the dining room polishing the *Shabbat* candlesticks. "I see you still insist on cleaning them yourself."

"It's an act of love," said Anica, tenderly holding a candlestick to the light to be sure it was clean. Replacing it on the sideboard next to its mate, she gestured to Isabel to join her on the settee. "So, Richard Nottem, the young man who is joining us for *Shabbat* this evening, he must be important to you. You've never invited any of the others who have come to call to dinner."

"That's because unlike the others, Richard is not infatuated with himself. He listens to what I have to say and values my opinion. More than that, he has a gentle heart, and he genuinely cares about the well-being of others."

"You sound very taken with him. We're glad you've asked him to join us tonight. I just want to be sure Richard will be comfortable with our family. All of us," she said pointedly.

"Of course, he will. Do you think I would bring anyone to our home who did not accept us as we are? Or that I could care for anyone who thought otherwise?"

"Isabel, I did not mean to upset you. I just want to make certain there will be no awkward moments for Richard or the rest of us. You have to admit, our *Shabbat* dinners do not represent typical Charleston gatherings."

Isabel took a moment to consider her mother's words. "I should not have snapped at you that way. I'm sorry. And yes, I do understand your concerns. It's just that once you get to know Richard, you will see for yourself what a good man he is. Except for Papa, he is the most caring person I know. I told him about our family, and he is eager to meet everyone. His parents are dead and he has no siblings. He's been on his own since he was nineteen. He began working as a clerk for a merchant, and now he keeps all the company's financial records. And before you ask, I did explain to him that we always welcome the Sabbath by lighting candles."

Anica slipped her hand into Isabel's. "You love him, don't you?"

Surprised by her mother's directness, Isabel sputtered, "I think I do."

Anica kissed Isabel's cheek. "I hope you will let us know when you are sure."

Waiting for Richard, Isabel paced the piazza, her eyes darting from the street to the sky where the sun was beginning its tranquil descent. Just as she was about to give in to her anxiety, Richard exited a carriage and made his way up the path to the house.

The sight of him left her nearly breathless. Tall and lean, his light brown hair parted to one side, a strand falling over his forehead, he waved and smiled when he saw her standing there. "Mister Parkson insisted on going over the ledgers with me." Richard glanced up at the sky. "Am I too late? You said the candles had to be lit before sunset."

Isabel wished her mother could see his earnestness. "You made it with a few minutes to spare, but we'd better go in," she said, as they hastened toward the house. Pausing before she opened the front door, she rested her hand on his arm. "Are you ready for this?"

Richard puffed out his chest in mock bravado. "For you my lady, I would face dragons."

"Dragons might be easier to face than this group," she said, stepping into the brightly lit foyer.

Sitting in the comfortable silence shared by old friends, Efren and Amadis puffed contentedly on their after-dinner cigars, stretching their legs to better enjoy the warmth of the glowing coals in the fireplace.

"Richard seems like a nice young man," said Amadis. Filling his mouth with smoke and blowing it out, he savored the Panetela's earthy flavors.

"I agree. We had a chance to talk for a bit, and he seems level-headed. He keeps the books for Garrett Parkson. Garrett is a hard man to please, so it speaks highly of Richard that he is in his employment."

Amadis nodded. "Did you notice how his eyes followed Isabel as she moved about the room? He certainly made no attempt to hide his feelings for her."

Efren watched the smoke rise from his cigar. "I remember when I held Isabel for the first time. My joy turned to an icy fear that I would not be able to protect her and keep her safe. She's grown into a beautiful, fiercely independent young woman, but I still feel that way. I can see that she cares for him, and she is certainly old enough to know her own heart. It's just hard for me to step back and let another man take my place as her protector."

Amadis regarded his friend, unsurprised by Efren's melancholy confession. Family, Amadis knew, was what Efren valued most. "Be happy that of all the callow young men who thought themselves worthy of Isabel's affections, she has chosen one who truly is."

CHAPTER 58

A rare June breeze wafted through the house carrying with it the perfume of the gardenias, azaleas, and roses artfully arranged around the parlor. Relishing the cool air, Efren and Benjamin exchanged grins as Richard nervously pressed his fingers against the pocket of his waistcoat to be certain the ring was still there. Reassured that it was, he began to pace around the room.

Benjamin leaned in close to his father. "That's the third time Richard checked his pocket for the ring in the last ten minutes. Were you that nervous when you married Mama?"

"I was a mass of nerves. I was terrified your mother would change her mind. She was so beautiful and there were so many young suitors eager to pursue her hand in marriage. I still couldn't believe she favored me over them. I don't think I started breathing normally again until after the ceremony was over," said Efren, his features softening at the memory. "Go talk to Richard. He looks like he needs to be distracted."

"He looks like he's in love. And Papa, she's still beautiful," said Benjamin, inclining his head in Anica's direction as she entered the room.

Efren turned and felt the same stirring he always did when she approached. She smiled at him, her lips slightly parted, the tiny lines forming at the corners her mouth the only sign of the passing years. With her hair drawn back off her face and falling in a cascade of curls down her back, she was once again the sixteen-year-old beauty he'd fallen in love with.

"What were you two up to? You were both grinning like a pair of fools."

"I was just telling Benjamin how nervous I was on the day of our wedding."

Anica looked over at Richard, glad to see Benjamin chatting with him. "Grooms are supposed to be nervous."

"And how is the bride?"

"She's nervous too. Hannah is putting her hair up. Ruth and Mariana are keeping her calm."

"And what about you? Are you at peace with Isabel's decision to follow Richard's faith and become a Unitarian?"

Surprised, Anica drew back. "Why would you think I wouldn't be?"

"Because I know how much your Judaism means to you."

"It is important to me, but I respect Richard's beliefs, just as he respects mine. Isabel told me he wants her to continue to light the *Shabbat* candles. He has even learned the prayer," she said, glancing in his direction and offering him a smile. "But above all, he makes Isabel happy. What more could I want from a son-in-law?"

Efren took her into his arms. "I hope he knows what an extraordinary mother-in-law he is getting."

"I am counting on you to remind him," she said playfully, smoothing the lapel of his frock coat.

The sound of voices in the entry hall drew them apart. "That must be Amadis. He went by the church to bring the Reverend Keith here," said Efren.

"Then I had better go upstairs and make sure the bride is ready."

Efren grasped her hand and kissed it as she turned to leave. "You know, it's not fair to look as beautiful as the bride."

"Isabel is almost ready," said Mariana, as she, Ruth, and Hannah joined the men downstairs. "She just wanted a few minutes alone with Anica. I promise it will be worth the wait," she said to Richard.

Richard's face turned ashen. "I hope she isn't having second thoughts," he blurted, setting off laughter throughout the room.

"I know the feeling," said Efren with a reassuring pat on his back.

"No need to worry." Smiling broadly, the minister gestured towards Isabel descending the stairs. "Your lovely bride awaits."

Her hair swept up into a braided bun wrapped in sprigs of flowers that matched the delicate floral designs on the skirt of her pale blue gown, Isabel stood at the foot of the stairs. Her eyes were fastened on Richard, her face glowing with unmasked love.

Efren offered Isabel his arm, his throat tight with emotion. Escorting her to Richard's side, he stepped back to stand beside Anica. The small group drew closer, treasured memories of Isabel softly flitting like butterflies through their thoughts. Listening to the couple say their vows, Hannah slipped her hand into Benjamin's, wondering when the same happiness would be theirs.

CHAPTER 59

August 1805

His skin slick with perspiration, Benjamin could feel the sweat dripping down the nape of his neck and dampening his collar. It was the end of his third day accompanying Archibald Harrows to the Charleston Dispensary for the Sick and Indigent, and he was not sure which was worse, the incessant heat or the rank smell of bodily functions that permeated the air.

Charleston was in the middle of its sick season—the hot months that saw a rise in malaria and diseases that thrived in its moist heat and marshlands—and the dispensary was filled with the sick and dying. Harrows and Benjamin stood at the foot of the cot of a young man delirious with fever and soaked in his own sweat. Semi-conscious and groaning, his legs drawn up to his chest in pain, the patient's skin had the unmistakable pallor of yellow fever.

Harrows pointed to a basin filled with dark bloody vomit on a side table. "His body is trying to rid itself of the disease. We need to help it along." Reaching into his leather medical bag, he withdrew a scalpel. Signaling Benjamin to get a clean basin, he approached the young man and without a word to the patient, made a quick cut in a vein in the man's arm. Unable to hide his surprise, Benjamin rushed to catch the flowing blood in the receptacle.

As the basin filled, Benjamin felt a mounting sense of alarm watching the blood flow from the moaning patient's arm. A slight nervous tic stuttered around the side of Benjamin's mouth; each minute the blood continued to drain making him more anxious.

"You getting queasy or something? You look like you're not too sure of yourself. Bloodletting cleanses the disease from the body. You'd know that if you read the books I gave you," said Doctor Harrows, his voice sharp with distain.

"I did and I'm fine. I'm afraid the basin is going to overflow."

Harrows eyed the nearly full vessel. "All right, that's enough for now. If he isn't doing any better tomorrow, I'll give him calomel to purge his bowels and then drain more blood to deplete the disease. Go on, bandage his arm. Just make sure you wrap it tightly so there is plenty of pressure on the wound to stop the bleeding. I'm going home for supper."

His eyes boring into Harrows' back, Benjamin's jaw was set in outrage. *You never offered him a comforting touch or a kind word.*

Lingering to be certain that the bleeding had stopped, Benjamin stood watching the irregular rise and fall of the man's chest. In the month he had been accompanying Harrows on patient visits, it had become clear to him that the well-to-do received better care and attention than the wounded and sick Harrows treated at the Charleston Dispensary.

Sitting with Hannah, Benjamin closed his eyes as the cool breeze flowing through the piazza washed over him. "After a day in the dispensary, I can't tell you how good that feels," he said, filling his lungs with fresh air.

Hannah touched his face. "Do you want to talk about it?"

"Talk about what?"

"Whatever it is that has been bothering you."

"I didn't think it was that obvious."

"You haven't been yourself for days. I thought you would be ecstatic now that you are finally seeing patients with Doctor Harrows."

"I don't know how to explain it. I feel like I am a constant annoyance to him. He's short with me. He grows impatient when I ask questions and refers me to one of his medical books for answers. Yesterday he became apoplectic when I mentioned that one of his private patients appeared to be taking a lot of laudanum even though his fractured arm had healed months ago. And that's the other thing. His well-to-do patients receive special attention and his best care, but he has no compassion for the poor wretches in the Charleston Dispensary. Harrows is well-educated and loves to flout his European medical degree, but he is not a man I want to emulate. He's not the kind of doctor I want to be."

"What kind of doctor do you want to be?" Unnoticed, Ruth stood framed in the archway, her medical bag in her hand.

"Not like Archibald Harrows," answered Benjamin, rising to make room for her to join them.

Ruth stole a quizzical glance at Hannah and settled into a chair. "He is well-respected in the community, and your father thinks highly of him," she said, her voice solemn.

"That's because my father is a successful businessman, and the community Harrows is respected in is made up of wealthy planters. If my father was a dock worker or a seaman, Harrows would not provide him the same kind of care. I just came from the dispensary where we saw a man with yellow fever. He was in obvious pain, but Harrows did nothing to try to alleviate it, or offer any comfort. Instead, he sliced a vein in his arm to 'deplete' the disease. If I hadn't called his attention to the nearly full basin, I don't know how much longer he would have continued the bloodletting." Benjamin paused to cool his indignation. "Ruth, I've seen how you and Hannah care for patients. Whether they are planters' wives giving birth, or a dock worker cut up in a tavern fight, you see no difference in your patients. You care about them. That's the kind of doctor I want to be."

Ruth's mouth twisted into a frown. "I will admit I do not like this business of bleeding patients, but Benjamin, you must learn what you can from Doctor Harrows. When you are on your own, you can decide how you want 𝑡𝑜 treat your patients."

Benjamin leaned forward in his chair, his dark eyes entreating Ruth. "I am going to continue with Harrows, of course, but if you will teach me, I want to learn how to use roots and herbs too."

Ruth looked at Hannah and smiled.

Up early the next morning, Benjamin shaved and dressed quickly. Haunted by the suffering of the dispensary patient with yellow fever, he'd stayed up late studying the medical books Doctor Harrows had given him, hoping to find something he might have missed that would alleviate the man's pain. To his frustration, he'd found none, and the night of fitful sleep that followed left him with a vague sense of unease he could not shake.

Treading down the stairs as lightly as he could so he wouldn't wake the rest of the family, Benjamin was surprised to find his father sitting at the dining room table, *The Charleston Daily Courier* spread out before him.

Peering at his son over his reading glasses, Efren pointed to the silver server and plate of biscuits on the sideboard. "The coffee should still be hot. Cora is making porridge if you want some."

"This is fine," said Benjamin pouring a cup of coffee and drizzling honey over his biscuits. "You're up early."

Efren folded his newspaper and set it aside. "I was about to say the same of you."

Benjamin took a sip of coffee, trying to decide how much to tell his father. "Yesterday, Doctor Harrows and I saw patients in the Charleston Dispensary."

Efren's eyebrows arched. "Not a very pleasant place, I would imagine."

"It isn't. So much misery. The last patient we saw was a young man probably about my age with yellow fever. His suffering was horrible to see. Doctor Harrows bled him, but when we left, he looked worse than when we got there. I am bothered by the fact that no attempt was made to ease his pain."

"Perhaps Archibald thought pain medicine would have made the man worse."

"He has no problem giving laudanum to his wealthy patients," said Benjamin, his voice heavy with contempt.

Efren glowered at Benjamin. "I would remind you that Archibald Harrows is a well-respected doctor and much-admired member of the community. I would also caution you to show him the utmost respect and do nothing that causes you to lose favor with him. That you are apprenticed to a man so highly esteemed reflects well on you. If you truly want to be a doctor, I advise you not to squander this opportunity."

"I won't," said Benjamin, smarting from his father's reproach. "Please excuse me. I got up early so I could stop by the dispensary before I went to Doctor Harrows' office. I want to see how the patient is doing."

"You keep calling him the patient. Doesn't he have a name?"

Benjamin faced his father. "I'm sure he does, but I don't know it. Harrows never inquired about who he was."

By the time Benjamin reached the dispensary, the early morning sunlight had given way to the first strong rays of the day, and the heat inside was already stifling. Pulling at his damp collar, Benjamin walked between the rows of cots with a rising sense of panic. *Where is Harrows' patient?* A noise behind him made him jump. Turning, he stared down at an elderly man mopping the floor, his back bent so badly his body seemed to be folded in half.

"I'm looking for a man with yellow fever. He's about twenty years old with dark hair. He was here yesterday. There, I think," said Benjamin, pointing to an empty cot. "Do you know what happened to him?"

"I heard someone with the yellow plague died during the night. He's probably been hauled off to be buried in pauper's field by now. Sorry about your friend," he said, plunging his mop into a bucket of dirty water and moving on.

My friend? I did nothing for this man to ease his suffering. He died alone, anonymous to everyone and now buried in an unmarked pauper's grave. Where did he come from? Did he have parents who are worried about him? A sweetheart who is waiting for his return?

Benjamin looked out over the roomful of cots, the sounds of suffering flooding the room like a roaring wave, and his despair turned to resolve. *I do not know your name, but I will not forget you.*

CHAPTER 60

August 1806

"They've been in Papa's office for a long time," said Isabel, rocking two-month-old Leah in her arms. "Richard only told me that Papa and Amadis wanted to talk to him. It's about the business, isn't it?"

"It is, but let's wait until the men are done talking, so Richard can tell you himself," said Anica. "They shouldn't be too much longer; it's almost time to light the candles. Now, let me hold my granddaughter, while you set out the candlesticks."

"Just don't keep Leah all to yourself," said Mariana. "I want to kiss those cheeks too."

Isabel relinquished the sleeping infant into her mother's arms. "I can see where I am going to have to work very hard to keep the two of you from spoiling her."

"We aren't spoiling her. We are just giving her lots of love, aren't we, Leah?" cooed Anica. Sliding her pinkie into the baby's open palm, she smiled in delight when Leah curled her tiny fingers around hers and slumbered on.

Isabel shook her head. "I think we have different definitions of spoiling," she laughed. "I'll get the candles ready."

By the time Isabel returned to the sitting room, Benjamin had joined the group, and Efren, Amadis, and Richard were waiting for her. All of them wore broad grins.

"You are back just in time to join us in toasting the newest member of

Eagle Shipping. Richard has agreed to join us and take charge of all the company's accountancy responsibilities. To Richard," said Efren, raising his glass in his son-in-law's direction.

"Thank you for your confidence in me. I will always do my best for you," he said, peering sidelong at Isabel's beaming face.

Amadis refilled their glasses. "Just make sure Garrett Parkson doesn't come after us for stealing you away from him."

"I don't think he'll mind. Mister Parkson has not been particularly receptive to my objections to his decision to shore up his finances by allowing his ships to bring slaves to Charleston from Africa. He puffed up with righteousness, and said that my distaste for slavery was hypocritical given that I had married into a family of slave owners. It gave me great pleasure to see his face drop when I pointed out that your household servants were all paid workers."

Efren put down his glass. "I had no idea. We've all been hurt by Britain's impressment of sailors, but I thought better of Garrett."

"Things will only get worse once President Jefferson's ban on certain British imports takes effect," said Amadis. "We will have to be very careful about the goods we fill our ships with. It's that or run the risk of having our shipments impounded."

The mood in the room shifted, and the men grew quiet.

"Enough talk of business. It's time to light the candles," said Anica, unwilling to let the celebration of Richard's new position in the company, and the joy of the Sabbath slip away.

"I'm afraid Ruth and Hannah are going to be late," said Benjamin. "They're with a woman in labor over on Boundary Street in the Neck. They should be here in a little while."

Anica frowned. "The Neck?"

"Mama, Ruth and Hannah are the sole source of medical care for most of the people there. They are all very protective of them, and it's probably the safest place they could be."

It was nearly nine o'clock when a mule-drawn wagon brought Ruth and Hannah to the house on East Bay Street. The young driver helped them alight from the wagon seat and handed Ruth her medical bag.

"Isaac, are you sure you know what you need to do to keep Jane and your new son healthy? Jane had a hard time, so she is going to need her rest.

And you have to make sure the baby gets enough milk. If Jane can't nurse, see if one of the new mothers in the Neck will nurse him. And put a wet cloth on her forehead to keep her cool. Jane worked hard to give you a son. Now you need to take good care of her. If she has any problems during the night, you come and get me right away."

Isaac's head bobbed up and down. "Yes, ma'am, I will. I gonna boil some of the burdock root you left for Jane's fever and make her some tea soon as I get back. And I ain't gonna let no harm come to my son," Isaac said so solemnly, Ruth smiled.

"Now, you hurry home. Even though you've got your freeman's papers, it's not safe for you to be out this late."

"All right. I goin'. And I be mighty grateful to both of you," he said, climbing onto the wagon.

Their late arrival and tired faces told Anica everything. Hugging Ruth and Hannah, she asked, "A difficult delivery?"

Ruth rubbed her aching shoulders. "It was bad. She was in labor for most of the day. We gave her blue cohosh tea to speed things up, but it didn't help much. She lost a lot of blood. The baby is fine, but he's big and she's small in the hips. "

Anica, put her arm around Ruth. "You both look exhausted, and you must be starving. Come have something to eat."

Crushed by a profuse sense of helplessness, Ruth was far away, her thoughts drifting. "She couldn't have been more than fourteen or fifteen years old," she mumbled. "Kept screaming for her mama." Ruth closed her eyes, willing the images trapped in her brain to disappear. "I'm sorry. It's been a long day. What did you say?"

"Just that you should have some supper, and then Benjamin will walk you and Hannah home," answered Anica, saddened by her friend's despair.

⌘

Saying good night to Ruth, Hannah and Benjamin lingered in the piazza under the half-light of a milky crescent moon. The night was airless; silent lightning from a distant storm streaked the sky at the horizon.

"I hope some of that rain is coming this way. Mama's garden needs a good soaking," said Hannah, stifling a yawn.

"You're tired," said Benjamin. "Get some to sleep. I'll come by tomorrow morning. There's something we need to discuss."

"Stay," said Hannah, placing her hand on his arm as he turned to go. "I missed seeing you, and now you've got me too curious to sleep. What is it we need to talk about?"

"Us."

"Us?" she echoed, struck by a sudden coldness, uncertainty flickering in her eyes.

"My apprenticeship with Doctor Harrows will be up in three months. I've learned a lot from him, but I've been reading the most recent medical journals, and there is so much more out there than what he is teaching me. I've discussed it with my father, and he has given his blessings to my plans. I want to study with the medical professors at the University of Pennsylvania. And," he said, taking her hand, "there are no laws forbidding our marriage in Pennsylvania. We can be together there." He clasped her hands in his. "That is if you will marry me."

Realizing she had misinterpreted his intent, Hannah gaped at him open-mouthed.

"Should I take your silence to mean you don't want to marry me?" stammered Benjamin, his heart sinking.

"What? No! I love you. Of course, I want to marry you. It's just a lot to consider. I never thought about having to leave Charleston. And Mama," she added, her eyes welling. "She'd be all alone."

"I know it's not the same as having you here, but she's not alone. She has my parents and Amadis and Mariana. We can visit when my classes are on break."

There was a long, awkward silence. Benjamin's nerves grew taut, a knot formed in his stomach. "Please, say something."

Hannah leaned against him, resting her head on his chest. The feel of his body soothing her senses and loosening the grip of the disquieting thoughts that gnawed away at her. "I love you," she whispered.

Folding her into his arms, Benjamin's lips traveled slowly to her mouth, kissing her softly at first, and then with a desire long denied.

Hannah clung to him, his kiss obliterating all thought except her need for him.

≈❖≈

Hannah was surprised to find Ruth sitting in the parlor, a pot of tea and two cups on the side table. "I thought you would be asleep by now," she said, sinking into a chair.

"I'm exhausted, but not sleepy. I brewed some chamomile tea. It will help both of us sleep."

Hannah filled the cups, breathing in the tea's sweet, apple-like aroma. "You're worried about Jane, aren't you?"

"I am. She has a long way to go to regain her strength. And she's too young to be having babies."

"You weren't much older when you had me. And at least Jane has Isaac. You were alone."

"I wasn't alone. I had my mother and Mariana, and Efren and Anica. The other house slaves also helped take care of both of us when you were a baby. We were a family."

Hannah peered at her over her cup. Her mother rarely talked about her life as a slave, but Hannah had pieced together enough bits of information to know that it had been one of degradation and heartbreaking loss.

"Mama, why didn't you ever marry? You've certainly had several opportunities over the years."

"It's simple. I was in love once with a slave named Walter," she said, her eyes shining, memories of him lighting her brain. "I just haven't found anyone I loved as much as I loved him, or the way you love Benjamin." She placed her cup of tea on the table beside her chair. "Now, do you have something you want to tell me?"

"Mama! Were you eavesdropping on us?"

Ruth gave her a coy smile. "Benjamin told me he was going to ask you to marry him. He also told me his plans. He wanted to make sure he had my blessings."

"And does he?"

"He does."

"Mama, you realize if I marry Benjamin and go to Philadelphia, it means we will be hundreds of miles away. I can't bear the idea of you being alone," she said, her lips trembling.

"You know I'm not alone. I have our family here, just like we had on the plantation. And Eagle's ships go up and down the coast all the time. I can come visit you and Benjamin in Philadelphia whenever I want."

Hannah slid to Ruth's feet and laid her head on her mother's lap. "It's hard for me to think about being away from you."

Ruth stroked Hannah's hair, glad she couldn't see her tears. "It is for me too."

CHAPTER 61

Philadelphia, January 16, 1807
My Dearest Hannah,

I arrived safely after a rather pleasant voyage up the coast, and any concerns about the British boarding the ship to impress sailors were unfounded. Papa will be pleased to know his newest addition to the fleet, the Falcon, performed beautifully. Captain Larkin was most congenial, welcoming me to his quarters for every evening meal. His companionship over the course of our nine days at sea was most appreciated, and I will be sure to tell my father of his graciousness.

As I suspected they would be, my lodgings are spare; a narrow bed, a chest, a chair, and a pitcher and basin for washing. Still, the room is clean, the landlady is a cheery sort, and the food is satisfactory. There is a roaring fire in the parlor; a welcomed sight given the bitter cold that envelopes the city. There are other medical students leasing rooms here, including a number from South Carolina and other southern states. They are friendly enough, though more inclined to visit the taverns of the city than I am.

My studies begin in three days, and I am eager to get started, not only for the knowledge, but also to occupy my days and ease the emptiness that has set in since we parted. I know we agreed that I should get settled here first and find suitable living accommodations for us before we wed, but I regret the decision. Being apart from you is agony. I miss our talks. I miss seeing your face and hearing your voice. I miss kissing your lips. I want you here as my wife, and I will make every attempt to quickly find suitable living quarters so that we can begin our life together.

Yours for always,
Benjamin

Charleston, February 24, 1807
My Beloved,

I miss you so. My heart nearly burst with joy when Captain Larkin brought me your letter. He apologized for the three-week delay in delivering it to me, explaining his return trip to Charleston was postponed until the ship was fully loaded with cargo.

What a long three weeks it has been! Despite your father's assurances that all was surely well, I could not quiet my fears that something terrible had happened to you. I thought myself stronger than this, but find I am not well-suited for this separation. Unlike the years you were away at boarding school, being apart is harder to bear now that I know we are meant to be together.

To keep myself occupied and to make the days pass quickly, I continue to accompany Mama on all her patient visits. But where I once observed in silence, I now assist with examinations and delivering babies, under Mama's supervision, of course. What an exhilarating feeling! I know now that this is what I want to do. Dare I hope that after we marry I may find a way to continue to practice midwifery in Philadelphia?

I trust that your studies are going well. I want to hear everything about them, and I am curious to learn if your apprenticeship with Doctor Harrows has been helpful.

I close this letter with all my love and prayers for your safekeeping. I long for the day when we are together again.

With all my love,
Hannah

Philadelphia, March 10, 1807
My Dearest Hannah,

Imagine my delight when I returned from my anatomy lecture and found Captain Larkin waiting for me in the parlor, your letter in his hand. The good man lingered for an hour, keen to convey news from home. I must confess that as much as I enjoyed his company, I could not wait for him to leave so I could read your letter. I can only hope he did not sense my eagerness for his departure.

I read your letter twice, so great is my need to feel your presence. It pleases me to hear that your days are spent adding to your skills. There is no finer teacher than your mother. If you desire to continue to practice midwifery, I dare say you will find that just as in Charleston, there is always a need here in Philadelphia for someone skilled in delivering babies.

My studies are going well. I've had to spend some time revisiting my Latin, but I have had no difficulty keeping up with my anatomy, physiology, and pathology lectures. I am a bit dismayed, however, that we use diagrams, preserved specimens, and wax models of body parts in our laboratory assignments. I find this method of learning less than satisfactory. In truth, I have only just begun to appreciate how fortunate I was to have been apprenticed to Doctor Harrows, and to have had the opportunity to participate in the treatment of patients.

I apologize for prattling on this way. I fear I have revealed more about my studies than you wanted to know. If I have blathered on, it is because burying myself in my books is the only way to deal with my constant longing for you.

Please forgive me for saving the best for last. The first term ends in two months, and I will have a few days off before the second term begins. I have secured a lease on a small rowhouse that will be available at that time, and I hope you will agree that this is the perfect time to marry. Please say yes.

I await your answer.

Yours for Always,
Benjamin

Charleston, March 22, 1807
My Beloved,

Yes!

I love you,
Hannah

Philadelphia, April 10, 1807
Dear Mama and Papa,

I hope you are both well. I apologize for the long weeks between my letters, but as the academic term nears its end, I have been keeping to my books in preparation for my subject examinations. In a way it has been a blessing, for the days rapidly disappear one into another, bringing my marriage to Hannah closer.

I am so thankful that the family will be coming to Philadelphia for our nuptials. As soon as we agreed upon May 17 as our wedding date, I began inquiring about accommodations for everyone for the duration of your stay. To my surprise and abiding disgust, I have discovered an aspect of the North I had not expected. There may be no laws against our marriage, but the city's public accommodations are less than welcoming to Ruth and Hannah. To ensure the family has a place to stay, I have taken the liberty of renting rooms in a home owned by a lovely older widow who also owns the nearby rowhouse I have leased for our residence. A Quaker and an abolitionist, Nella Hinshaw does not appraise her guests by the color of their skin, and I am certain she will make you all feel most comfortable in her dwelling. I told her about our family, and she is eager to meet you all. So eager, in fact, she insisted that we have the ceremony in her beautiful garden. One thing to keep in mind when you and the family meet the dear lady: Quakers, do not use the titles Mister or Missus. Hence, she prefers to be addressed as Nella Hinshaw, or Nella.

I have missed you terribly, and long to see you again. Though I understand that Isabel's condition and the imminent arrival of her second child prevent her from traveling, I cannot help but be saddened by her absence *on the happiest day of my life. Please tell her how much I love her and miss her.*

I pray you have a safe voyage, and count the days until you, Amadis and Mariana, and Ruth and Hannah are here.

Your loving son,
Benjamin

CHAPTER 62

Philadelphia, May 17, 1807

"Nella, I don't know how to thank you for your gracious hospitality, and for offering your beautiful garden for the ceremony," said Ruth, hugging the tiny woman.

"You've made this day perfect," added Hannah, "and I can't thank you enough."

Her robin-egg blue eyes merry behind wire-rimmed spectacles, Nella Hinshaw beamed. "It is truly my pleasure. My dear husband Cyrus and I weren't blessed with children. Thou honor my house by having the wedding here. And, I have grown quite fond of Benjamin in the months that he has been in Philadelphia," she said, her lined face lighting up at the mention of his name. "He told me so much about his family and thee, of course, Hannah, that I feel as if I know ye all. And now that we've met, I can say that everything he said was true."

Smiling to hide her anxiety, Hannah fidgeted with the bodice of her cream-colored dress, pulling it one way and then the other until she was satisfied it revealed her shoulders evenly.

"You are going to stretch it out if you're not careful," warned Ruth, plucking at the frock's short sleeves to puff them out. "There, it looks beautiful and so do you."

"Thou are a lovely bride, my dear," said Nella, her dress of olive-green silk bereft of all ornamentation other than a white lace kerchief at her neck.

"I agree," said Efren, stepping into the parlor. "The minister is here, and Benjamin is growing anxious, so I think we'd better go rescue him."

A moment of panic flickered across Hannah's face. "Mama," she said, hugging Ruth tightly.

"Go to Benjamin," whispered Ruth, clinging to her a moment longer before letting her go.

"Are you ready to become Missus Benjamin Amselem?" asked Efren, offering his arm.

Glancing back at her mother, Hannah nodded and slipped her arm through his. Placing his hand over hers, Efren kissed her cheek. "My son loves you very much. I hope you know that Anica and I do too."

Hannah and Benjamin stood before the minister, marveling that this day, so long dreamed of, had finally arrived. In Nella Hinshaw's resplendent garden, under a cloudless sky that stretched to infinity, and in the presence of those they loved most, they promised to love, comfort, and honor each other for the rest of their lives.

⌁❖⌁

After well wishes, lengthy goodbyes, and many tears of joy, they were finally alone in the Elfreth's Alley rowhouse that would be their home. Benjamin studied Hannah's face as she glanced around the parlor, her slow smile easing his concerns about its small size and sparse furnishings. "I wish I could give you a palace," he said.

"Shh," she said, pressing her fingers to his lips. "It's perfect. It's not a palace I want; I only want to be with you."

Without a word, Benjamin took her hand and led her up the winding stairs to the bedroom. In the dim light of the fading colors of the day, he removed the pins from her hair, and drew in a sharp breath as her dark curls spilled around her shoulders. "I love you," he murmured. His thumb stroking her cheek, he pulled her close and kissed her.

Hannah gasped as his lips traveled to her neck and breasts. Every fiber of her body responding to his touch, she raked his hair, unleashing the ferocity of her desire. Pent-up longing obliterating all modesty, she slipped out of her dress, her fingers working the buttons on Benjamin's waistcoat.

Fumbling out of his clothes, his desire matching hers, Benjamin pulled her hips to him. Driven by their desperate need for each other, they tumbled onto the bed. Their bodies intertwined, and drowning in exquisite pleasure, they lost all thought of everything but each other.

Lying in the dark, Benjamin curled his body around Hannah's. "I wish we could spend endless days just like this," he said, kissing her shoulder.

"Mmm," she purred drowsily. "Nice, but not very practical. Besides, I haven't eaten since breakfast and I'm hungry."

"So am I," said Benjamin, rolling her toward him.

Laughing, she ran her fingers over his chest as he covered her mouth with his.

The group huddled together on the dock until Captain Larkin inclined his head toward the harbor pilot who would navigate the ship down the Delaware; the man's presence signaling they could no longer delay their departure. The hurried farewells prompted hugs and tears, and as Benjamin embraced Amadis and Mariana first and then his mother and father, Hannah clung to Ruth.

"Take care of yourself, and be sure to write me," said Ruth.

Feeling as though a piece of her heart was being sliced away, Hannah swallowed hard to keep from sobbing. "I will Mama, I promise. I am going to miss you so much."

"And I will miss you, but knowing how happy you are to be beginning your life with Benjamin gives me great joy. Now, say goodbye to everyone and let me hug your husband one last time before Larkin comes down here and drags us onto the ship," she said, pointing to the captain standing at the top of the ramp.

Larkin's stern demeanor clearly conveyed his readiness to leave. Amid a flurry of last-minute embraces, kisses, and wishes for a safe journey, the small group made their way up the ramp, turning and calling out their good-byes one last time.

Waving to their family as they stood at the rail of the departing ship, Hannah and Benjamin remained on the dock watching the *Falcon* unfurl its sails and make its way toward the Atlantic Ocean.

Hannah stared out on the harbor until the ship was a speck on the horizon. "I miss them already," she said, her voice quavering. "When will we see them again?"

"I am sure they will miss us as much as we miss them. I urged Mama and Papa to plan for everyone to return as soon as Isabel and the baby are able to travel. She promised they would."

Managing a faint smile, Hannah took his arm. It wasn't until they turned onto Elfreth's Alley and the block of rowhouses came into view that she spoke.

"I feel so foolish. I didn't think saying goodbye to everyone would be so hard."

"Farewells are always difficult, especially to the people you've spent your whole life with."

"But you are the one I want to spend my life with," she said, searching his face for a sign that he hadn't misread her despondency for regret.

"I'm glad to hear it. Ours would be the world's shortest marriage if you didn't," he said, laughing.

The sound of his laughter swept over her like a cooling breeze, stripping away the sadness from her heavy heart. "I'm ready to go home now," she said.

CHAPTER 63

Charleston, June 21, 1807
Dear Hannah and Benjamin,

Wonderful news! Your new niece arrived squalling and healthy early this morning, perfect in every way. Isabel is well, thank God, and of course, it was Ruth who helped to bring another of our babies into the world.

Richard and Isabel have chosen to call their second daughter Elizabeth, a beautiful name for a beautiful baby. She is tiny, and dark-haired like Isabel, with Richard's brown eyes. We are, of course, overjoyed by the gift of our second grandchild, and so grateful for Isabel's good health. All our happiness is diminished, however, by the miles that separate us and keep you from sharing this wonderous occasion with us. It is our most fervent hope to gather our growing family and bring them to you in the coming months.

Papa and I send our love to you both, along with prayers for your good health and happiness,

Mama

Philadelphia, July 13, 1807
Dear Mama and Papa,

    Captain Larkin brought your letter to us today, and we are beyond happy over this extraordinary news. We are also relieved to learn that Isabel is doing well, though as Hannah pointed out, she was in Ruth's exceptionally skilled hands.

    My classes have resumed, and as you would expect, my days are filled with lectures, laboratory work, and studying. Although I did not always approve of Doctor Harrows' demeanor and methods, I continue to find new respect for the experience I gained as his apprentice. Classroom learning is important, but I have so much more knowledge to draw upon as a result of all that I saw and did under his tutelage.

    Hannah's days are busy as well. Nella Hinshaw has informed the ladies of her church and several charitable organizations of Hannah's midwifery skills, and she has been caring for several women who are with child and delivering their babies. With Nella's encouragement, Hannah is also growing herbs in the small plot of land behind the rowhouse to care for the ill and injured.

    I hope this letter puts your minds to ease. We are well and happy, but I confess, we miss you all terribly, and share your sorrow at not being present for Elizabeth's birth. We will be counting the days until Isabel, our new niece, and all of our beloved family will be able to make the voyage to arms that long to embrace them.

Your loving son,
Benjamin

CHAPTER 64

Philadelphia, September 1807

The dusky hues of evening were filling the sky when Hannah let herself into the house. Dropping her medical bag, she closed her eyes and leaned against the door. Unable to stifle her grief any longer, she slid to the floor and sobbed.

Startled by the sounds of crying downstairs, Benjamin found Hannah in the entranceway, staring into the semi-darkness. "Hannah! Hannah, what's wrong?" he gasped, sinking to his knees beside her.

She turned to look at him; her expression vacant. "The baby was born dead," she answered, her voice flat, her eyes red and unseeing. "I tried everything I could think of to start his breathing, but I knew it was hopeless. He was so tiny; he just came too early."

Benjamin took her into his arms, and rocked her until the spasm of tears subsided and her breathing slowed. Helping her into a chair, he wrapped a shawl around her shaking shoulders.

"A man from the Friends Meeting House came to the door while you were at your lecture. He said Nella Hinshaw had sent him; that there was a woman—her name was Frances—who was having a baby. He led me to an airless shed, a hovel really, on German Street." She shuddered and tightened the shawl around her body.

"She was alone with no other women to help her, and I should have realized something wasn't right as soon as I saw her. She was so thin her skin appeared stretched tight over her bones. Her face was gaunt and her eyes were like sunken lumps of coal. When I approached her, I could smell whiskey, and I knew it was slowing down the birth. She couldn't tell me how many months along she was, or how long she'd been in labor. She just kept cursing and screaming at me to get the baby out. Nothing I gave her to help things along worked. It was hours before he was born, and when he was, his skin was peeling and so badly discolored I knew he'd been still in the womb for days."

Hannah leaned into Benjamin, and was so quiet, he thought she'd fallen asleep. When she finally spoke, it was in a raspy whisper. "You know what broke my heart? His eyes were shut so tight his lids formed tiny creases as if he were laughing," she said, choking back a sob. "The only emotion Frances showed when I told her the baby was dead was to call me a black bitch. After I tended to her, I went to wash the baby's body and wrap him in a blanket for burial. When I got back, she'd left." Resting her head on Benjamin's chest, Hannah closed her eyes. "He had wisps of red hair..."

Benjamin tightened his arms around Hannah and waited for her breathing to slow to be sure she was sleeping. Stroking her face, he kissed her, and carried her upstairs.

Hannah woke cradled in Benjamin's arms.

"You cried out in your sleep," he said, pulling her closer.

"A bad dream," she mumbled. Her tongue felt thick, the sour taste in her mouth unsettling her stomach. Half-awake, her thoughts foggy and disoriented, she struggled to clear her head. "I don't feel as if I slept at all. Is it morning?"

"Almost. It will be light soon. Stay in bed a little longer. I'll make some tea."

When he returned from the cellar kitchen, Benjamin was surprised to find Hannah sitting in the parlor, the flame from a single candle casting the room in a yellow glow. Even in the pale light, he could see her fatigue; the dark circles under her eyes hollowing out her cheeks. "I thought you might want something to eat," he said, placing cups of tea and a plate of cheese and sliced bread on the table.

"Thank you," said Hannah, suddenly aware of her empty stomach. "I am hungry. And I'm sorry I was in such a bad state last night."

"You had every reason to be upset," said Benjamin, sitting beside her. "I just hope you aren't blaming yourself."

"I did last night. But this morning, I am angry. I'm angry about the squalor Frances lived in. I'm angry that she was emaciated and drunk, and had bruises all over her body. I've witnessed stillbirths before, but I am angry because this one could have been avoided. If she had taken better care of herself her baby would be alive. The charitable societies that are meant to help destitute women need to do more than tend to their souls when they seek help. They need to reach out to the poor—the prostitutes too—and teach these women about the importance of taking care of themselves to protect their unborn children." She hesitated and added, "And how to prevent having babies."

Benjamin straightened in his chair. "Hannah, I am not saying you are wrong, but if you are contemplating what I think you are, you are wading into dangerous waters. There are important people who will be outraged if you pursue this. You could even be putting yourself in danger."

Hannah's eyes darkened. "I cannot ignore what I know in my heart is the right thing to do. If I make a few people angry, then I will have succeeded in drawing attention to the misery of the city's poor, especially the women."

"You are being incredibly naïve. You have no idea how much trouble you will stir up if you pursue this. We're not talking about antagonizing a few people. You will be going to war with the clergy, the local politicians, and even the existing charities. I agree with everything you are saying, but I am more concerned about your welfare. You are in no position to battle the people you will be going against."

Hannah laced her fingers through his. "The women in my family had to be strong to overcome the horrors they endured as slaves. My great-grandmother was kidnapped in Africa and brought to this country. My grandmother had two of her children ripped away from her. My mother was raped, and your mother risked her life to practice her faith. I would dishonor the women who raised me; the women I love and respect most, if I did not stand up for what I believe in."

"Why are you being so stubborn? Your cause is a noble one, but there is always a price to pay. I would remind you that my parents had to flee their home and leave behind all the people they loved because my mother practiced Judaism in secret."

"Can you honestly tell me that you do not admire your mother for the bravery it took to honor her mother's wish that she remain faithful to her heritage? On Friday night when I light the candles, are you not proud of the sacrifices your mother made so that we can continue to welcome the Sabbath as her ancestors—*your* ancestors—did?"

His anger spent, Benjamin bowed his head in defeat, and in some small part, admiration. Her fiery defense of her beliefs did not surprise him. Even when they were children, Hannah felt compelled to right every perceived wrong, no matter the consequences. He suppressed a laugh when an old memory surfaced.

"Do you remember the time we were playing in front of our old house on Broad Street, and a man started beating the dog he was dragging by a rope around the poor creature's neck? You flew at him, screaming like a wild banshee."

Hannah's face lit with a smile at the recollection. "I frightened him so badly, he dropped the rope and ran off and never came back for his dog. The poor thing was so ragged, we named him Scruffy. Mama and I loved that old hound. I seem to recall you did too."

"Oh, I did," he said, locking eyes with her. "But not every effort to do good will have the same happy ending. You can't save all the Scruffys of this world."

Nella Hinshaw tugged at the plain Quaker cap that left on a snippet of her white hair uncovered, and listened quietly as Hannah related the events of the previous day. "I am so sorry about the dear little infant, and the vile way thou were treated." She paused and knotted her hands in her lap. "I am not unsympathetic to thy concerns, but I feel I should warn thou that efforts to educate the women thou attend to about their bodies will not be well received by many in the community. We've already seen that some members of the medical profession see their instruments and methods of delivery as superior, and are not welcoming of the city's midwives."

"Benjamin said the same thing. But poverty here in Philadelphia is no different than poverty in Charleston. I have been called to too many squalid dwellings where too many poorly clothed and underfed women and children live in the most deplorable conditions. The doctors at the Almshouse only see these women when they are ready to give birth—if they come to the Almshouse at all. I want to see them while the baby is developing. I want to make sure they understand that taking proper care of themselves and avoiding whiskey helps their babies. And," she added, in a low voice, "I can also advise them about methods they can use to avoid having babies in the first place."

The old woman's eyebrows arched, and the corner of her mouth began to twitch. "Hannah, thou will incur the ire of the church, the city's leaders, and, I am quite certain, the husbands of the women thou treat."

Hannah sulked. "Benjamin said that too."

"I would hope so! And I hope thou will listen to reason, and abandon all thought of such a pursuit."

Hannah sighed. "I understand your concerns, but most of these women have eight or more children, and their lives are at risk each time they are with child."

"I appreciate thy good intentions, but I beg thee not to insert thyself into matters that will focus attention on thine activities and surely cause great difficulties. Thy midwifery and healing skills have gained thee the confidence of not only the poor women in the community, but also those who are well-to-do. Please do not do anything that would put their esteem and support in jeopardy. It is because of their largesse that we are able to sustain our charitable efforts."

Oh, Nella, if you only knew it's the well-to-do women who inquire about ways to prevent future births. Grinding her teeth to keep from speaking her thoughts, Hannah assured her distraught friend that she would not do anything to imperil the good will of her patrons.

"I thank thee," said the old woman, a gentle smile replacing the disconcerting twitch.

"But, I still intend to visit the poorer neighborhoods. I don't know how I will be received, but I feel it is my responsibility to reach out to the women and talk to them about their health and the health of their families. I hope you understand that I do not wish to cause you anguish, but I cannot ignore the conditions that led to that sweet infant's death."

The corner of Nella Hinshaw's mouth began to twitch again.

✦

Philadelphia, October 23, 1807

Dearest Mama,

We were distressed to learn that Leah was sick with measles. We pray that by the time you are reading this letter, she is well again. We are, of course, disappointed that her illness means putting off the family's visit to Philadelphia, but our main concern is for our young niece. I hope that no one else fell ill.

I wish I could report that my attempts to inform the destitute mothers I see of the importance of proper diet and rest to the well-being of their unborn children has been successful, but I fear I am making little progress. The poverty that assails these poor women appears to have consigned them to hopelessness. In truth, I can see that there is scarce money and opportunity to access healthy food, and there are so many children to care for, rest is impossible. Several of my patients are recently arrived from Germany, and have yet to master the English language. My efforts to communicate with them would be laughable were it not for the seriousness of their needs. I have also come to see that fear of government interference in their lives keeps many of the women from seeking assistance from the Almshouse and many of the city's worthy charitable organizations. Nella Hinshaw has been a huge help in arranging for donations of food, but we are reaching only a small number of those in need. I will admit to feeling frustrated, but I am not yet ready to give up this endeavor.

Benjamin continues to be absorbed in his studies, though I sense a certain restlessness on his part to leave his books and return to actual patient care. It will please you to know that he is more inclined toward the healing practices he observed you use than he is to some of the methods being taught at the university. He has great disdain for the practices of bloodletting and purging.

I worry the coming winter months will make sailing from Charleston to Philadelphia a difficult voyage for our nieces. Benjamin will have some extended time off from his studies at Christmas, and we are hoping to return to Charleston for the holidays. We are desperate to be with our family.

I am going to close for now. The sun is sinking in the sky, and the

Sabbath is almost here. As I always do, when I light the candles, I picture the family gathered together, and I feel the presence of all my loved ones. Please send them my fondest regards.

Your loving daughter,
Hannah

CHAPTER 65

Charleston, November 12, 1807

Ruth hunched down into her cloak, and tightening the bow of her hood, lowered her head as she walked into the cold November wind. "Babies always seem to decide to come into the world when the weather is too hot or too cold," she muttered to herself. After a night spent waiting for Priscilla Graden's baby to arrive, she longed to be home, sitting in front of a roaring fire and sipping a hot cup of tea. Instead, she turned towards the harbor, intent on placing her letter to Hannah in Efren's hands so it could go out with the next shipment to Philadelphia.

The biting wind bore down on Ruth as she neared the wharves, sudden gusts sending dirt and fallen leaves pirouetting in an impromptu aerial ballet. When she finally reached the Eagle Shipping Company office, she was shivering and gulping for air. Standing inside the warehouse, she leaned against a wall and waited for the erratic pulsing of her heart to slow down.

"Ruth, is that you?" called out Efren, rushing towards her. "Are you all right?"

"I'm fine. The wind is blowing so hard it literally took my breath away."

Efren put his arm around her shoulders. "Come into my office where it's warm."

Ruth sat in front of the wood-burning stove and offered no resistance when Efren handed her his coat to drape across her lap.

"What brings you to the wharf? Anica said you were delivering Priscilla

Graden's baby," said Efren, lifting the kettle warming on top of the stove and pouring Ruth a cup of tea.

Gratefully accepting the hot brew, Ruth inhaled the rising steam. "I was with her all night. Her first. A boy. I can tell you Hiram was one happy man." She reached into the pocket of her cloak and retrieved her letter to Hannah. "I wanted to get this to you so it could go out on the next ship to Philadelphia."

"The *Falcon* should be ready to sail in a few days. Let me call one of the men to take your letter to Captain Larkin. I think the new worker is still here. Amadis hired him today. He's a freed slave; been sailing up and down the coast on any ship that would hire him. Amadis said his eyes are different colors."

Ruth's hands began to shake, the cup of tea rattling in the saucer. "Did you say he has different color eyes?"

"Yes. Amadis said one was blue, the other brown." Efren gasped. "Oh my God, Ruth! How could I have been so stupid? Amadis said his name is Calvin. It never occurred to me."

Ruth began to rock back and forth. "Sometimes new owners changed slaves' names."

Efren wrenched open the door. "Calvin!"

"Yes, sir! I right here." Stepping from behind a row of cotton bales, he wiped his hands on a rag and stuffed it into his pocket. "I just gots the last of the shipment ready to go," he said, rolling down the sleeves of his threadbare shirt over arms as thick and scarred as an old oak tree. "What else you needs me to do?"

"I just need you to step over here to the office."

Efren studied the big man as he came toward him, surprised by the agility of his movements. *If it's not him, it will break Ruth's heart.*

"Did I do somethin' wrong, sir?"

"No. No, everything is fine. I just need you to take a letter over to the *Falcon* and give it to Captain Larkin."

Ruth stood with her back to the door. Her hands clasped over her chest, her lips moving in soundless prayer. *Please, God.*

"Calvin, I am going to step outside for a moment, but this is Miss Amselem, and she would like to meet you."

"Sir?"

Ruth turned. The trembling woman and the dazed young man stared at each other. Seconds passed. Seconds that felt like hours.

Taking a deep breath, Ruth stepped closer, studying his chiseled features for any signs of the nine-year-old boy that had been ripped from her mother's arms. The eyes were right, of course, but she could not find any semblance of the boy she remembered in the man's jutting jaw and sharp cheekbones.

Growing uncomfortable under the strange woman's intense scrutiny, he shifted his weight from one foot to the other, angling his head to one side to avoid her gaze.

Ruth clasped her twitching hands, unsure if it was real or if she wanted it to be there so badly, that she imagined it. She reached up, her fingers tracing the small curved scar on his cheek, a lasting reminder of the overseer's displeasure with an impudent, strong-willed boy who wouldn't do his chores. "Jonah," she intoned, her voice hushed, as if in prayer.

Flinching, his hand flew to his face, his fingers brushing hers. *Jonah?* A moment of recognition flickered behind his eyes. His heart began to thud against his ribs. Long-buried memories flooded his brain; shadowy images of faces that once haunted his dreams faded in and out. There was a roaring in his ears. He staggered back, struggling to stay on his feet. *No one had called him Jonah since...* His eyes grew wide.

"Mama?"

Ruth pictured the screaming boy taken from them. She mourned all the years he'd been denied their mother's love, and the comfort of her tender care. She imagined his terror and loneliness, and how much he must have longed for her, and she knew what she was going to tell him would break his heart.

"Jonah, it's me, your sister, Ruth." She touched his hand. "I'm sorry. Mama died many years ago."

His expression blank, he stood so still, Ruth thought he hadn't heard her. "Jonah?"

Staring at her as if he was seeing her for the first time, his face crumpled. His strangled cries filling the room, Jonah dropped to his knees. Weeping, he sank to the floor, and pulling his legs to his chest, curled his body into a tight ball.

⚜

"I been moving around for so long, it's hard for me to remember it all," said Jonah, tearing off a piece of biscuit and wiping the gravy from his plate. "Old man Conroy, he only kept me for a few months. I thinks he only wanted me so's he could sell me. He the one who changed my name. At first I wouldn't answer when he call me Calvin. He beat me so much, I finally gave in. That man was the devil hisself. There was an old house slave name of Ruben. He kinda looked after me. Would sneak me food, 'cuz I was always being punished for somethin'. If Ruben couldn't bring me nuthin', I be hungry for days. I gots real skinny. Then one day Ruben, he say the master want me to be eatin' good. That's when I figure out he fattenin' me up to get me ready to sell."

Ruth sat moving her uneaten stew around the plate, Jonah's words like hot stones on her soul. "When Mister Philip died and the bank took Bending Oaks, Efren tried to find you. But you'd been sold by then, and Conroy didn't know, or wouldn't tell him where you were. Efren still tried to find you, but all the information he gathered led nowhere."

Jonah scowled. "Conroy, he sold me to a cotton plantation owner in Jonesboro, Georgia. That man worse than Conroy. We out in the fields from the time the sun poke through 'til there ain't no sun no more. Made me wish I was harvestin' rice again," he said, chuckling. "I be in Jonsesboro 'til I be about twelve or thirteen, then I gots sold to another cotton plantation. The master there weren't so bad, but his wife be shriekin' and hollerin' at me all the time. I be there 'bout four years. There was a girl there, Tenah. She took a shine to me, and I sure did like her. Her daddy be a carpenter like my daddy, and he taught me to be one too. I was pretty happy there, but a drought damaged most of the master's cotton, and he had to sell some slaves, me along with 'em."

Jonah glanced at Ruth's full plate, and she pushed it towards him. Wolfing down his second helping, he leaned forward, resting his forearms on the table.

"This time, I be outside of Savannah on a cotton plantation, but it make no mind to me, 'cause I doin' carpentry, helpin' Mister Fulton, my new master, build his house. He and Missus Fulton, they treats me real good. Mister Fulton, he loan me out to other plantation owners, and even let me keep some of the money they pay him for my work. I be with him the longest of anybody, and I was savin' my money to buy my freedom. But then he and his wife got sick with the yellow fever. First she dies, and then days later he dies. I cried like a bitty baby when he go to his maker. Then his brother tell me Mister Fulton set me free in his will. That man kinder to me than anyone in my life, since…" He grew silent and bowed his head. When he looked up, his cheeks were wet.

"As soon as I could, I headed back to Jonesboro to get Tenah, hopin' I could use the money I saved to buy her freedom. But she be gone, when I get there. Her daddy say she be sold not long after me. I just started movin' around then, taking whatever jobs I could get. Signed on to a ship in Savannah as a carpenter, and been sailin' ever since. I landed in Charleston two days ago and gots hired by Captain Lopez today." He studied the callouses on his hands. "You know where my daddy be?"

Ruth covered his hands with hers. "James, the coach driver, used to come see Efren whenever he was in Charleston. A few years ago, he brought us the news that your father was sick with malaria. A couple of weeks later, James came by to tell Efren that Brock had died. James is gone now too; died last year."

A shadow passed over Jonah's face, and his eyes flattened. "I used to have dreams about you and Mama and my daddy. But as time go by, it got harder and harder to remember what you all looked like. Somewhere along the way, I stopped dreamin' and stopped hopin' we be together again."

Smoldering embers were all that remained of the once roaring fire in the fireplace. Ruth patiently answered all Jonah's questions, filling in the gaps in his memories of their time at Bending Oaks, and relating all that had happened in the intervening years. His emotions careened wildly, from deep despair over the deaths of his mother and father, to pure joy at discovering he had a niece.

"I named her Hannah, after Mama's mama. Our grandmother was captured in Africa and brought here as a slave. She was a healer and a midwife. She taught Mama to be one. Mama taught me, and I taught Hannah. She's married to Efren's son, Benjamin. They live in Philadelphia where he's studying to be a doctor."

Jonah shook his head from side to side, the pain of the lost years in his eyes. "She all grown up and I didn't even know 'bout her." He hesitated. Deep lines furrowed around his mouth. "She light like you?"

Ruth knew he was asking a different question. "Yes. Yes, she is."

CHAPTER 66

Philadelphia, November 15, 1807

Despite the free-flowing wine and excellent food, Benjamin was a reluctant attendee at the regular gatherings hosted by members of the medical school faculty. Meant to foster bonds between the students and the professors, many of the young men viewed the get-togethers as an avenue for developing social and professional connections. A good word from a revered faculty member, or the friendship of a student from an influential family could propel a young doctor into a position of esteem.

It was a world Benjamin wanted no part of. With no interest in joining his classmates when they frequented the taverns and brothels of the city, it was not long before invitations to accompany them ceased, and he soon found himself excluded from the camaraderie the other students shared. His outsider's status was further solidified among the southern students when he made no effort to hide his support for the efforts of the abolitionists.

"I hate going to these things," complained Benjamin, bending down so Hannah could adjust his cravat. "I am no good at idle conversation, and there aren't many of my classmates I choose to talk to," he said, omitting the fact that most of the students chose not to converse with him.

"Then don't go."

"I wish it were that simple. We are expected to attend, and I cannot afford to offend this evening's hosting faculty member. It's James Woodhouse, my chemistry professor."

Hannah brushed a piece of lint from his waistcoat, and tried one more time to straighten his cravat. "You look very handsome, but you would be much more approachable if you'd stop scowling."

"Is this better?" he asked, stretching his mouth into a grotesque grin.

By the time Benjamin arrived at the professor's elegant Georgian row-house, his classmates were clustered in groups, chatting and laughing as faculty members circulated among them. Stuffing his sweaty palms into the pockets of his frock coat, he stood in the doorway of the parlor, scanning the room for a friendly face. Finding none, he was surprised when Doctor Woodhouse, who was engaged in conversation with Casper Macy, his anatomy professor, beckoned him over.

"I was hoping you would attend this evening," said Woodhouse. "In fact, Doctor Macy and I were just talking about you."

Benjamin felt the heat rising in his face, his posture angling with tension. "Oh?"

Macy clasped his shoulder, the snow-white brows framing his gray eyes rounded in amusement. "I can assure you it's all good things. I was just telling Doctor Woodhouse how attentive you are in my lectures."

"Thank...thank you," he stammered, his muscles going slack.

"I don't mean to take you away from the others, but I'd like to talk to you someplace where it is less noisy. Doctor Woodhouse has graciously offered his study. Do you mind leaving the gathering for a short while?"

"Not at all," answered Benjamin. The noise of the room had quieted to a low hum, and he could feel the stares of his classmates as he followed Doctor Macy out of the room.

Lined with floor-to-ceiling shelves heavy with leather-bound books, Woodhouse's study smelled of cigars and ancient volumes. A fire burned in the fireplace, and the two men settled into the gold damask-covered chairs facing the hearth. Macy remained silent as Benjamin's eyes traveled around the room.

"This reminds me of my father's study," said Benjamin wistfully.

"Is your father a doctor?"

"No, sir. He owns a shipping business in Charleston. He and his partner import and export goods, mostly to and from England, though the recent hostilities between the British and the French have limited his sailing routes to cities along the East Coast." He paused and added, "I was supposed to take over the company."

"I see. How did your father feel about you wanting to be a doctor?"

A gust of November wind shook the limbs of a large oak, its bare branches making scratching noises against the rattling windows.

"He did not take it well at first, but once he understood how much it meant to me, he gave me his blessing and supported my decision."

Doctor Macy stared into the orange flames. "Your dedication to your studies has not gone unnoticed by your professors. Nor has the compassion you show the patients in the Philadelphia Almshouse's hospital when you accompany Doctor Parrish on his visits to the wards. You do not exhibit the hesitancy around the ill and injured that many of the other students do."

"I had the good fortune of apprenticing with Doctor Archibald Harrows for two years. As part of my studies, I accompanied him when he visited patients at the Charleston Dispensary for the Sick and Indigent. I do not presume to know everything I need to know to be a good doctor, but those visits convinced me that kindness and respect for one's patients can play a part in treating and easing suffering."

"I can see why Nella Hinshaw thinks so highly of you," said Macy.

Benjamin gawked at the professor. "Nella? You know Nella Hinshaw?"

"Oh yes. We are both members of the Pennsylvania Abolition Society. She also told me that your wife Hannah is a midwife."

That's what this is about. Benjamin stood. The contours of his face hardened, anger burning in his chest. *He's praising my work because he wants me to force Hannah to stop hers.*

"Not only is my wife an excellent midwife, she also goes into the poorest neighborhoods to teach mothers how to take better care of themselves and their children. Before you ask, I will not keep her from doing what she loves."

The old doctor rose and warmed his hands over the fire. "I admire your loyalty to your wife, and your passion for her skills. I'm sorry you think my intent was to discourage her good work. On the contrary, it is precisely because of her talents and yours that I wanted to talk to you."

His anger quickly giving way to shame, Benjamin bowed his head, too embarrassed to speak. *I am an idiot.*

"Not every member of the faculty," said Macy, "harbors ill will towards midwives."

Benjamin's face flushed red with humiliation. "Doctor Macy, I cannot apologize enough for my outburst. I will understand if you wish me to withdraw from the University."

"Withdraw? I don't want you to withdraw. I have a proposal I want you to consider. Please, sit," he said, gesturing towards the chair.

When they were both seated again, Macy said, "Many of your classmates are hoping to establish their own medical practices or find positions with private hospitals that treat the wealthy among us. Have you given any thought to what you want to do when you complete your studies in March?"

After a long moment, Benjamin turned to his professor. "My wife is of African heritage," he said, looking directly at Macy. "Our plans are largely dependent upon settling in a place that will welcome us a couple. We would like to return to Charleston to be with our families again, but we do not believe we will be well received by many of the city's citizens."

Holding Benjamin's gaze, Macy nodded. "I know that there are also Philadelphians who are not accepting of marriages such as yours. I hope you and your wife have not been subjected to their cruel bigotry."

Only if you ignore the stares and looks of repugnance. "We have not been openly accosted, if that's what you mean," said Benjamin.

"I take it then, that you've had unsettling encounters."

The corners of Benjamin's mouth tightened. "We have."

Macy rose and stood in front of the fireplace, his hands clasped behind his back. "I hope you will still consider remaining here. The Almshouse's hospital is in need of doctors. Yes, its wards are filled with sailors, prostitutes, alcoholics, and the aged. And yes, its patients are diseased, blind, deaf, and mentally incompetent. But they all are entitled to good medical care. I know that such a posting has neither the prestige nor the financial rewards your classmates seek, but I sense that you are more interested in caring for the sick than you are in material gains. Were you to agree to becoming a house physician for a year, you would receive a stipend, of course, but you will also have the opportunity to gain skills far beyond those we teach in our lectures and laboratories. In addition, the medical school faculty would be there to support and advise you."

Benjamin sat in silence trying to assemble his thoughts. His memory was still raw with images of the suffering patients he saw in the Charleston Dispensary. Nor did he forget the callousness of the doctors, and the futility of caring for patients who only sought treatment when they were beyond help.

A log in the fireplace slipped off the andirons, sending embers sparking and popping. Macy flinched, barking a mortified laugh. Regaining his composure, he cleared his throat and asked, "I hope your hesitancy doesn't indicate a lack of interest in my proposal."

"No, sir. I am just surprised by your offer. Confused too. Although I've never considered being a physician in the wards of an almshouse hospital, I am drawn to caring for those who are most in need. It's the reason I decided to become a doctor." He absently tugged at his ear. "I'm curious, though. Earlier, you mentioned my wife's talents. May I ask what you have in mind?"

"Her efforts in the poor neighborhoods are starting to make a difference. I am hoping you will agree to my offer, and that you will both continue to carry on your good work here in our fair city."

Relishing the feel of the cold air on his face, Benjamin hastened his steps as he navigated his way along Mulberry Street toward Elfreth's Alley. A steady wind fluttered the candles' flames in the street lamps, casting ghostly shadows on the brick houses standing like silent sentinels in the night. Somewhere in the distance, a shutter slammed shut, and a dog barked its displeasure. Smoke curled from chimneys, and the comforting smell of burning logs permeated the air. Benjamin slowed his pace and blew out a breath, watching it condense into a tiny cloud and disappear. Perplexed by his conversation with Macy, his thoughts were disjointed and roiled by doubt. *Could he be the doctor he wanted to be in the Almshouse? Is it even possible to make a difference? What would Hannah want?*

They talked for hours, sitting in the semi-darkness of the parlor, slender ribbons of amber flames in the fireplace forming soft shafts of light.

"I know I should be grateful that Doctor Macy has so much faith in me, but, I do not share his confidence in my abilities. Why would he look to someone who has so little experience to tend to the most wretched of patients; patients who need the benefit of a seasoned doctor?"

Hannah curled herself under his arm. "I don't think your lack of experience is the issue. The real question to ask yourself, is do you want to do this? It's your decision."

"I confess I am torn," he said, tightening his arm around her. "If I decide to accept, it will be for the chance to learn treatments for a variety of illnesses and injuries, and possibly to do some real good. But that's being optimistic, and I should add, selfish. It's not just for me to decide. You have as much to say about this as I do. Accepting Macy's offer will mean that we remain in Philadelphia and away from the family for at least another year."

Hannah shifted her body so she was facing him. "We both know there are those in Charleston and in the rest of Lowcountry who are unwelcoming to us. Despite some unpleasant encounters here—and as much as I miss Mama and the family—I believe we are safer if we stay in Philadelphia."

He knew she was right. They could visit Charleston, and it would always be home to them. It just would never be *their* home.

CHAPTER 67

Charleston, December 22, 1807

The *Falcon* glided past Sullivan Island, and eased into Charleston Harbor, its sails snapping in the bitter wind whipping over the deck. Ominous, metal-colored clouds blanketed the sky. Sensing the coming storm, seagulls were flashes of white and gray beating their wings and riding the wind to the safety of the shore.

Ignoring the bite of frigid air on their faces, Benjamin and Hannah stood at the rail, scanning the wharves for sight of the Eagle Shipping Company's warehouses. When at last they came into view, Benjamin was unprepared for the sudden surge of exhilaration that jolted through his body. His heart racing, his blood thrummed in his ears like the incessant murmuring of a thousand voices. "It's good to be back," he said, wrapping his arm around Hannah.

"I think someone has been anxiously awaiting our return," she said, pointing to Efren leaning against the warehouse wall, blowing into his hands to warm them. Turning at the sound of the *Falcon's* approach, he began to wave furiously when he spotted Benjamin and Hannah huddled together on the deck.

"Thank God you are safe," said Efren, embracing first Hannah and then Benjamin, then engulfing them again, his hugs—usually warm and comforting—tight and tense with fear. "You are a day later than expected, and there's been more news of ships being boarded by the British, and then the weather has been bad, and the embargo, and I was getting concerned," he said in a rush of words that left him breathless.

Benjamin placed his hand on his father's shoulder to calm him. "We were delayed a day in Philadelphia waiting for cargo to be loaded. The voyage was fine, Papa. No sign of the British."

"Forgive an old man his foolishness," said Efren. "Come, let's get out of the cold while we wait for your luggage to be taken off the ship. I told Amadis to go home before the storm hit. Richard too. I can't have Isabel blaming me if her husband catches a cold because I kept him here too long," he laughed.

Inside the warehouse, workers storing the crates of flour, furs, tobacco, and lumber unloaded from the *Falcon* moved the heavy cargo with surprising speed.

"You two go ahead to my office and get warm," said Efren. "I need to check on the cargo, and I want to send a messenger to Anica and the others to let them know you arrived. I'll join you in a few minutes."

Benjamin's glance lingered on his father's face. His beard was shot with gray, and deep lines were etched around his eyes. Watching him as he made his way toward where the men were working, Benjamin detected a slight hitch in his gait.

Hannah noticed too. "Your father does not look well to me," she said, warming herself in front of the woodburning stove in Efren's office. "His face looks drawn, as if his vitality has seeped away."

Benjamin sighed. "I am fairly certain he has more on his mind than our safe arrival. The warehouse is half empty. When we were boarding the *Falcon*, I saw the crew adding stones for additional ballast, and that means the hold wasn't filled with enough cargo to stabilize the ship. I knew the embargo on British and French goods was carving deep cuts into the company's trade abroad, but I thought Papa's East Coast business was sufficient to balance his losses. It doesn't appear to be the case."

"Hopefully, our visit will raise his spirits," said Hannah, sliding into his arms only to jump back at the sound of Efren clearing his throat, a deep shade of crimson overspreading her cheeks.

"Perhaps we should have made more noise as we approached," said Efren, addressing the grinning man standing next to him. "Hannah, there is someone I want you to meet," he said softly. "This is Jonah. Your Uncle Jonah."

Bewildered, Hannah blinked and stepped back in surprise. Her mother had told her stories of the half-brother who had been taken from the plantation when they were slaves, weeping at each telling of the last time she saw the frightened little boy.

Jonah took a small step toward her, his features wavering between uncertainty and hope. "I been lookin' forward to meeting you," he said, casting his misty eyes at the floor. You as beautiful as your mama."

"Uncle Jonah," she said, enfolding him in an embrace that felt to him like home.

By early evening, a drop in the temperature turned the storm's diminishing rain drops into snow flurries, the tiny flakes dancing in the glow of the street lights. Inside Efren and Anica's brightly lit house, the joy of reuniting bubbled up as each member of the family arrived. Ruth first, rushing into the house and into Hannah's arms. Amadis and Marianna, their smiles and tears flowing in equal amounts, then Isabel, Richard, and their daughters. Tender kisses were bestowed on six-month-old Elizabeth, asleep in her mother's arms. Eighteen-month-old Leah, shy at first, followed Hannah like a devoted puppy. Finally, Efren and Jonah. The family was together at last.

CHAPTER 68

December 23, 1807

Benjamin rose early the following morning. Dressing in the dark, he kissed Hannah as she slept and hurried downstairs, hoping to get a moment alone with his father before he left for the warehouse. Relieved to find him in the dining room having his breakfast, Benjamin joined him at the table.

"I expected you to sleep late," said Efren. "Though I must admit, I am glad to have your company. I've missed you."

"I've missed you and Mama as well," he said, leaning forward, his arms crossed. "Is everything all right? Are you feeling well?"

"Why wouldn't everything be all right?"

"Because you look haggard. I saw the half-empty warehouse, and the newspapers are full of reports of privateers and the British boarding merchant ships. I can tell you are worried about the business."

"I feel fine. Fortunately, we have not had any problems with privateers. But, yes, British impressments and the embargo are having a negative effect on business. Still, it could be worse, and although it will take time, we are building relationships with merchants along the East Coast, extending all the way up to New England. Even as our shipping interests are undergoing what I believe to be a temporary decline, our real estate holdings continue to be profitable, and Richard keeps a sharp eye on company expenses. So, stop worrying. Now, should I have Robert bring you some breakfast?"

"Thank you, but I'll wait for Hannah." Benjamin traced his finger along the tablecloth's damask print. "Papa, there is something else we need to talk about."

Efren's calm, open expression gave way to concern. "Is something wrong? Hannah?"

"We are fine," assured Benjamin. "It's just that I have been presented with an opportunity, and I wanted to discuss it with you."

Efren listened intently as Benjamin related his conversation with Casper Macy. Studying his son's face for any clues that might indicate his true feelings about the position he was offered, he saw only confusion.

"What is it that makes you so hesitant about this opportunity? It appears that your professor has a great deal of faith in your abilities, and as you pointed out, it provides an excellent occasion for you to learn many new skills."

Benjamin hunched his shoulders. "I am concerned about how much good I can really do in the Almshouse. I didn't choose medicine as a profession to watch people die. I know from experience that the patients who are seen in almshouses are too often beyond saving by the time they seek treatment. I am also concerned that accepting the position means remaining in Philadelphia far away from you and Mama and Ruth."

"You may not be able to save everyone you treat in the Almshouse hospital, but isn't it just as important to provide the dying with compassion, comfort, and dignity in their final hours? I seem to remember your disdain for Archibald Harrows centered on his seeming callousness towards his less fortunate patients. What if you could set an example for other doctors and change all that? And what of Hannah's good work in Philadelphia? Even from my brief conversation with her last night, I can see how much pride she takes in what she has accomplished. Benjamin, I believe you both have much good left to do there."

"But, Papa, what about the miles that will keep us apart for months at a time?"

Efren's gaze grew intense. "We all understood when you and Hannah married, that it would be difficult for you to make Charleston your permanent home. And as much as it pains me to tell you this," he said, his eyes fastened on his son's face, "we do not think it wise that you do."

CHAPTER 69

Assembled in the dining room, they were a complete family for one last night.

Bathed in the soft glow of the tiny flames, Anica drew her hands over the burning candles three times, and covering her eyes, recited the *Shabbat* blessing. Lowering her hands, her loving gaze traveled from one face to another, its warmth spilling over each one as they joined her in saying, "Amen."

"I dare say there are not many homes welcoming the Sabbath in a parlor festooned with garlands of ivy and sprigs of holly," said Efren, wryly, pointing to the Christmas decorations still adorning the room.

"And I think there are not many homes fortunate enough to have a family such as ours," said Anica, putting her arm through Efren's. "That *Shabbat* falls on the start of the new year, and that we are all together to celebrate both occasions make tonight even more special."

A blend of savory aromas stirred memories of long-ago holiday celebrations with each platter of food brought to the dining room table. Sipping a glass of sparkling white wine, Benjamin closed his eyes, imprinting on his memory the faces of each member of his family as they were at this moment. It was then he knew that no matter where he and Hannah were; no matter how many years passed or miles separated them from their loved ones, home and the family would call to his heart as surely as the sun called to the flowers in the field.

The last barrels of rice loaded and stowed in the cargo hold, the *Falcon* stood ready to leave the harbor bound for Philadelphia.

Hannah clasped Ruth tightly. "I miss you already," she murmured, finally stepping out of her mother's arms, the heaviness on her chest making it hard for her to breathe.

His arm around his mother, Benjamin was also struggling to say farewell to his parents. "I don't know when we will be back again. When my studies are over I will begin my duties at the Almshouse. It just feels like we didn't have enough time together."

"No matter how much time we have together, it will never be enough," said Anica. "But delaying your departure will not make it any easier to say goodbye. Your life is elsewhere and you leave with our love and blessings, and our prayers for a safe trip."

Efren moved away from the group and beckoned Benjamin to his side. "There is something you need to know," he said, his voice so low, Benjamin could barely hear him over the clamor of the docks. "Remember James, the old coach driver? Gideon, James' youngest son, came to me last month with a pass I'd written for James years ago to prove that he was who he said he was. James told Gideon to come to me if he ever needed help. He fled his master's plantation after he was falsely accused of stealing a chicken. I've been hiding him in the warehouse while I waited to hear back from Nella Hinshaw. She sent word with Captain Larkin that she would help Gideon get to Canada. Gideon is on the ship. I wanted to be sure he was safely onboard before I told you. He will remain in a cabin away from the crew. Only a few trusted men know he is on the ship. Larkin will be sure he is safe."

Benjamin stared at his father. "You've been harboring a runaway slave? Are you saying Nella helps runaways?"

"Lower your voice," hissed Efren, looking around to see if anyone was nearby. "I thought you knew. Nella discussed it with me when we were there for your wedding. She is a part of a small network of Quakers who help slaves escape to Canada. Once she knew we had ships leaving Charleston for Philadelphia on a regular basis, she asked if I would be willing to transport escaping slaves if ever the need arose. I discussed it with Amadis, of course, before giving her an answer, but I knew he wouldn't object. As it turned out, I approached her about Gideon, before she ever asked us to bring an escaped slave north."

"Papa, if you are discovered helping a runaway you and Amadis could be imprisoned."

"We have considered the consequences, but James was a good friend to our family. There were many occasions when I asked for his help, sometimes putting him in danger, and he never refused. Over the years he earned enough money to free his wife and daughter. His oldest son died of yellow fever, and when James tried to purchase Gideon's freedom, his owner wouldn't sell him." He paused and looked out over the blue-green water at the ships dotting the harbor. "There is hope for Gideon in Canada. Would you deny him the opportunity to live the rest of his life as free man?"

Benjamin did not hesitate. "I would not."

"I didn't think so. And now you understand why it's a risk Amadis and I gladly take."

"Does Mama know?"

"She does. Her memories of why we left Spain and our time at Bending Oaks remain vivid."

"And Isabel?"

"Her too. She's been bringing Gideon his meals, and gathering the warm clothes and other supplies he will need for the trip. She is eager to help other travelers as well."

Benjamin pulled his father into a rib-crushing hug. "I love you, Papa."

"Then you are not angry with me for entangling you and Hannah in this plan?"

"Papa, I have never been prouder of my family than I am at this moment."

As soon as the *Falcon* was moored, Captain Larkin dispatched a seaman to inform Nella Hinshaw of the ship's arrival. An hour later, a wagon arrived to receive ten barrels of rice, all loaded with great care under Captain Larkin's supervision.

"Well done," said Benjamin, shaking the captain's hand, as they watched the horse-drawn dray rumble down the dock to the cobblestone street.

Larkin's gaze remained on the wagon. "Godspeed. He has a long way to go until he is truly safe."

"Pennsylvania is an anti-slavery state," said Benjamin. "I don't understand why he can't just stay in Philadelphia. I thought he was free here."

"Free yes; safe no. Slave catchers are always lurking in the city, hoping to round up runaways and bring them back to their owners to collect the reward. Gideon will only be safe if he can get to Canada. Once there, he'll be beyond the reach of those bastards, and settled in a country that does not recognize the law that sanctions the capture and return of escaped slaves."

"Gideon asked that I thank thee for the kindnesses thou showed him," said Nella Hinshaw the following afternoon, as Hannah poured cups of tea. "It was very caring of thee to see to his needs."

Benjamin shrugged, embarrassed by Nella Hinshaw's praise. "Even though it was for his own safety, it bothered me that he had to remain in his cabin the entire voyage. I merely stopped by to make sure he was comfortable, and to keep him company for a while."

"I can't even imagine how frightened Gideon must have been," said Hannah. "Is he staying with you?"

"He's with a Quaker family that harbors escaped slaves until they can continue their journey. They have a small hidden room upstairs; its entrance is covered by a bed. It's not the most comfortable accommodations, but Gideon is safe there until we can provide him with the provisions he will need for the next leg of his journey. He will be harbored at safehouses, but we still have to be careful. He's been gone long enough that his owner has begun placing newspaper advertisements offering a reward for his return." She spread a copy of the previous day's newspaper on the table and pointed to the bottom half of the page.

> TWENTY-FIVE DOLLARS REWARD
> RUN AWAY from my plantation, in Goose Creek, South Carolina on the first of December last, a Negro man named Gideon, twenty-four years of age, five feet eight or nine inches high, of a dark complexion, is well made, a long scar on his right arm, and missing two bottom teeth. Whoever delivers said Negro to me at my plantation in Goose Creek or my residence in Charleston shall receive twentyfive dollars reward. – T. Hudson

Hannah shuddered and shoved the paper aside. "What happens next?"

"We wait for word that the next hiding place is safe and clear for Gideon. Then he and his guide will set out. The exact route will depend on available safehouses along the way, but it should take him from here to Buffalo. Passage will be arranged for him to cross Lake Erie into Canada."

Benjamin, raised his cup of tea to his mouth, and set it back in the saucer without drinking. "It sounds dangerous."

"It is."

A quick glance at Hannah, and Benjamin nodded. "How can we help?"

PART IV

CHAPTER 70

Philadelphia, April 20, 1808
Dear Mama and Papa,

    *I hope you are both well, and that you will forgive the tardiness of
this letter. My first weeks at the Almshouse have passed in a blur of patients
requiring treatment from diseases and injuries ranging from pneumonia
and typhus to broken bones and severe burns. Nor am I the only Amselem
tending to the needs of Almshouse patients. Hannah has been called upon
to deliver two babies in the short time I have been on the wards. Despite
constant exhaustion, I can say that my initial fears about my work here
have been unfounded. My days are full, and I can see that I am able to a
make a difference, even if it is only to provide comfort to a patient in the
last moments of life. Thank you, Papa, for reminding me that compassion is
an essential part of healing.*

    *Hannah is beginning to gain the trust of the impoverished women
she sees, finally realizing the rewards of her efforts to educate them about
better health habits for themselves and their families. The number remains
small when compared to the need, but Hannah is encouraged by the progress she is making.*

    *I hope to set your mind at ease with this news: We received word last
week that our cousin arrived safely at his destination, and is settled in his
new home. I am sure Uncle James would be pleased.*

    I must confess that after seeing everyone in December, we miss the

family more than ever. Please convey our love to Richard, Isabel, and the
girls, and to Amadis, Mariana, and Ruth. To you, Mama and Papa, prayers
for your well-being from a heart filled with love.

Your devoted son,
Benjamin

July 1808

The honeyed-colored rays of dawn were spreading across the sky when Benjamin let himself into the house on Elfreth's Alley. Too tired to climb the stairs to the bedroom, he stretched out on the parlor sofa, closed his eyes, and welcomed the oblivion of sleep. He woke with a start two hours later, Hannah staring down on him.

Benjamin held up his hand to ward off the questions he knew Hannah was about to ask, and rubbed his temples, the drumming pain in his head making it feel as if his skull was gripped in a vise.

"It was a bad night in the wards," he said, his voice hoarse with fatigue. "A ship returning from Jamaica docked yesterday afternoon with sixteen crewmen sick with malaria. They have been ill for at least a week, shaking with chills and complaining of headaches and muscle pain. Some are vomiting. Others are in advanced stages, showing signs of yellowing skin. The embargo is affecting our supplies, and we don't have enough quinine to treat the men. We have to ration the medicine, and only give it to those we think have the best chance of survival. Three men died during the night. I fear there will be more deaths today."

"Dear God," gasped Hannah. "I'm so sorry."

Benjamin rose suddenly. "I have to go back."

"I know you are needed there, but you're not going until you've had breakfast," insisted Hannah. "Go wash up and change your clothes. I'll make you something to eat."

The mention of breakfast reminded him that he hadn't eaten since yesterday morning. When he returned downstairs, the sight of slices of buttered bread and cheese on the table prodded his hunger, saliva filling his mouth.

"I'll eat on the way to the Almshouse," he said. Kissing Hannah, he scooped up his breakfast and was out the door before she could protest.

❧✦❧

Standing at the entrance to the ward, Benjamin watched Barrett Burward, a doctor he recognized as a former classmate, moving down the rows of cots, never stopping to examine or offer comfort to patients begging for something to ease their pain. Infuriated by the man's callous indifference, Benjamin blocked his way as he attempted to leave. His arms folded tightly across his chest, he glowered at the man. "Didn't you forget something, Burward?"

Confused at first, Burward smirked in recognition. Irritation crossing his corpulent face, the veins in his thick neck becoming livid ridges, he regarded Benjamin with disgust. "Amselem! What the hell are you talking about?"

"I am talking about your negligence and total disregard for the welfare and suffering of these men," fumed Benjamin, poking him in the chest.

Burward shoved his hand away. "Don't get all righteous with me. You may think practicing in this hellhole is a noble calling, but I'm only here because no one else was around to fill in for a ward doctor who got sick. The quinine is gone, and there is nothing more to be done for these filthy bastards, so why even waste laudanum on them? Now get out of my way," he bellowed, pushing past Benjamin.

Fatigue and contempt fueling his outrage, Benjamin grabbed Burward's arm, and whirled him around. "These men have families and people who love them. *Nothing more to be done!* You could show them some compassion. You could offer them the kindness of sitting and talking to them. You could comfort them so they do not die in fear." Benjamin dug his fingers into Barrett' soft flesh. "You could be a decent human being, for God's sake!"

Burward yanked his arm free of Benjamin's grasp. His eyes murderous, he sneered, "You just made the biggest mistake of your life."

The summons from the Manager of the Almshouse Hospital two days later was not unexpected. The Burwards were among Philadelphia's oldest and most influential families. Well-regarded for their philanthropic endeavors, they were feared for their political connections.

His hooded eyes fixed on his desk, the hospital administrator spent a few minutes organizing stacks of papers before acknowledging Benjamin's presence.

"Doctor Amselem," he said, still averting his gaze, "it seems that we no longer require your services in the Almshouse Hospital. Your employment here ends as of today."

Taking devious pleasure in the man's obvious discomfort, and curious to hear the justification for his removal, Benjamin pressed him for a reason for his dismissal. "I don't understand. Just last week you praised my efforts in the wards. Have you had complaints from the patients?"

More shuffling of papers. "I ask that you not make this more difficult than it already is," he said, finally facing Benjamin. "I will deny saying this, but you tangled with a member of one of the city's most powerful families."

"And one whose financial support of the Almshouse you depend upon," sniped Benjamin, exploding out of his chair.

"And *you* should be grateful they aren't bringing you up in front of the Board of Health, retorted the Manager, his mouth twisted in barely controlled rage.

"With all due respect, *sir*," sputtered Benjamin, his fists clenched so tightly his fingernails bit into his palms, "it's Barrett Burward who should be answering to the Board. Now, if you'll excuse me, I have patients to attend to before I leave."

They sat in the tiny garden behind the Elfreth's Alley rowhouse, the fragrance of lavender blooms mixing with the earthy smells of Hannah's herbs.

"I brought this on myself," admitted Benjamin. "I stood there watching Burward ignore the suffering right in front of him, and something inside of me snapped. The cold look on his jowly face; his calculated indifference to their pleas for help infuriated me. Even as I was reviling him, I knew I was making a dangerous enemy. I knew it was a mistake. I just didn't care."

"You were right to react the way you did. His lack of concern for the patients under his care is inexcusable."

"His actions may have been inexcusable, but mine were reckless. All the reasons I chose to accept Doctor Macy's offer were valid. I have thrown away an opportunity to gain invaluable experience, and I may have tarnished my reputation as a doctor as well. Worse, I let Casper Macy down. I dishonored his faith in me. I don't have the courage to face him."

"He already knows what happened," said Hannah in a low voice.

Benjamin scowled. "I should have known that Burward would make sure the news reached Macy. I will go see him first thing tomorrow and apologize to him."

Hannah studied her hands. "That won't be necessary. Nella Hinshaw invited us for tea tomorrow afternoon. Doctor Macy will be there too."

"Do you know something I don't?" he spat, his tone hard and accusing.

"No, of course not," sputtered Hannah, the sting of his words making her flinch. "I met with Nella this afternoon about a young woman who is in need of care. She told me she had spoken with Doctor Macy, and that she knew what had happened at the Almshouse. She said he wanted to talk to you, and suggested it would be best if we came to her house. I didn't know what to say, so I accepted."

Hannah looked so miserable, Benjamin instantly rued his words. "Hannah, I am so sorry. I didn't mean it the way it sounded. Please forgive me. For everything."

Casper Macy was seated in Nella's parlor when Benjamin and Hannah arrived. Rising to greet them, the doctor's firm handshake and warm smile deepened Benjamin's shame.

"Professor Macy," he blurted, "I want you to know how much I regret…"

Macy patted Benjamin's shoulder. "There is no need to apologize, and there is plenty of time for you to tell me what happened. At this moment, I would like to meet your lovely wife," he said, turning his attention to Hannah. "Nella Hinshaw has kept me informed of the good work you are doing with the city's women in need, and of your help in our particular efforts. I am so glad to finally meet you."

"Thank you for your kind words. Benjamin speaks of you often. I am grateful to Nella for bringing us together."

The tiny woman beamed. "It is truly my pleasure. And if ye will excuse me, I'll go brew the tea."

"Please let me help you," said Hannah quickly, following their host to the attached kitchen.

Benjamin barely concealed his smile. "I hope Hannah's sudden departure wasn't too obvious."

"She is a very perceptive young woman," chuckled Macy. Indicating they should sit, his smile faded. "As you have probably surmised, Barrett Burward made sure news of his dispute with you reached my ears. I would like to hear from you what happened."

Benjamin took in a deep breath and slowly exhaled. When he finished his recounting of the confrontation with Burward, he felt unburdened; buoyed by relief. "I take full responsibility for everything that happened. I just couldn't ignore his calculated indifference to the suffering of those men."

Macy sat back in his chair, his thumbs hooked in the pockets of his waistcoat. "As I suspected, Burward was not entirely truthful in his telling. You should not have any misgivings about your actions. His callousness is unforgivable."

"Still, I fear that my anger at his negligence will reflect poorly on you."

"I hope it would take more than the rantings of a universally recognized spoiled member of the Burward family to challenge my standing in the medical community. However, I am concerned about how it will affect your reputation. Word of Barrett's humiliation is spreading throughout the medical community. In some quarters, I dare say it has gained you a high degree of respect. Still, the Burwards hold great sway in the state. I fear that they will use their connections to keep you from gaining privileges to treat your patients in the city's hospitals."

Benjamin stood and looked out the window. "We were married right here in this garden. I felt like the happiest man alive. Hannah was finally my wife, my studies were going well, and I had my father's blessing to pursue my dream to become a doctor. I remember thinking nothing could stand in the way of achieving all I had set out to do. Now, it appears I have thrown it all away."

"My boy, it is not as dire as you make it seem. Pennsylvania is not the only state in which to practice medicine. There are many areas—small towns and newly formed communities—that are in need of doctors. Midwives too. If you and Hannah are willing to consider such a move, I think I can help."

"We are," said Hannah, standing in the doorway, a tray of teacups and scones in her hand. Mortified by her outburst, she added, "I'm sorry. I didn't mean to eavesdrop."

Looking from his wife to his mentor, Benjamin fought the urge to hug them both. "It appears Hannah and I are in agreement."

The lines on Macy's face folded into a broad grin. "Excellent. I will reach out to some of my colleagues on your behalf."

Sweeping into the parlor, teapot in hand, Nella regarded the smiling faces of her guests. Her smile matching theirs, she began pouring tea.

CHAPTER 71

August 1808

Weeks went by without word from Casper Macy. Weary of the waiting, his patience worn thin by days of idleness, Benjamin was grateful each time Hannah requested he accompany her when she visited an expectant mother and there was a sick child or family member to be seen. No longer able to access the drugs and elixirs he'd had at his disposal at the Almshouse, he turned to the roots and herbs growing in Hannah's garden to treat congested lungs, skin irritations, headaches, and stomach problems. With his gentle manner and easy smile, he chased the fear from his patients' eyes.

"You like doing this, don't you?" asked Hannah as they left a crowded, two-room apartment on Water Street.

Benjamin, touched her elbow and guided her past a filth-filled puddle. "I do. It's more of what I'd envisioned myself doing as a doctor than the time I spent treating patients at the Almshouse."

"You're good at this. If I even came within a foot of little Albie he would start to scream, but you won him over in a matter of minutes."

"He's just a good judge of character," teased Benjamin.

Hannah rolled her eyes, secretly delighted to see Benjamin's playful side again.

"Actually," he said, his tone tentative, "I've been doing a lot of thinking, and what happened at the Almshouse might be a good thing after all. Maybe it took Barrett Burward to open my eyes to what I truly love to do."

Hannah felt her soul lift. "Mama always says that things work out for the best. I do believe that good will come from all this. Perhaps we are meant to take a path we never anticipated. We may not see it right away, but I believe there is a purpose we are meant to follow."

The pounding on the door the next day brought them both scampering down the stairs. Reaching the entry first, Benjamin faced a small boy who shoved a note into has hand and dashed away.

"It's for you. It looks like Nella's handwriting."

Breaking the wax seal, Hannah read the note, her hand flying to her mouth. "It is from Nella, and I have to go," she said, handing the note back to Benjamin. "It will explain everything." Grabbing her medical bag, she kissed Benjamin and barreled out the door.

Ablaze in a cloudless, cornflower-blue sky, the August sun was like a fire-breathing dragon, its scorching rays penetrating down to Hannah's bones. Propelled by the urgency of Nella Hinshaw's note, she hurried across the searing cobblestones to Mulberry Street. Checking to be sure she was at the correct address before she knocked, she jumped back when the door to the large red-brick house swung open with a thud.

"Are thou Hannah?" asked the man standing in the doorway, his craggy face framed by a bushy beard reaching to the top of his chest.

"I am. Nella Hinshaw sent for me. Where is the mother?"

"This way. We have to hurry," he said, leading her to the back of the house and the door to the cellar.

"We were not informed she was with child when we agreed to hide her and her brother until they could be moved to the next haven," he said, his agitation mounting. "She's young. Around fourteen or fifteen is my guess. My wife is with her in the room tucked under the cellar staircase." He raked his fingers through the thick growth of his graying beard, and shook his head. "Now I don't know how long it will be before they can be transported to the next safehouse. And how are we going to keep an infant quiet?"

Her sense of urgency growing, and anxious about her young patient, Hannah ignored the good man's question. "I'll need boiled water and some clean rags. Can you get them for me?"

"I can," he answered, appearing to be glad to have something to do. He started for the outdoor kitchen and turned. "I am Wilfram Smedley. My wife's name is Minna. Minna Smedley. Our thanks to thee for coming."

"I am glad I could help," said Hannah, moving quickly towards the entrance to the cellar. Descending the old wooden staircase, the worn steps creaking with each footfall, she was grateful for the cooler air of the underground room.

Minna Smedley, her Quaker cap untied, its ribbons dangling loosely over her shoulders, emerged from the tiny space under the stairs, visibly relieved to see Hannah. Much younger than her husband, her face pale with fatigue, she placed her hand against the wall to steady herself, and fought back tears.

"I am so glad thou are here. Until her brother Ned came to get me, we didn't know Celia was having a baby. I don't know how long she's been in labor, but her pains are coming closer together," she said, clearly as frightened as the young girl lying on the thin straw mattress.

Two hours later, Hannah left Celia dozing, her newborn son fully sated and asleep beside her. Waiting for her at the foot of the cellar stairs, Celia's brother Ned blocked the way.

A faint hint of facial hair above his curled lips, he snarled, "She say the baby not comin' for another month. Sez we be in Canada by then. I knew I shoulda left without her, but she beg me to take her along, and our mama make me promise to take care of her so her baby be born free." His face hardened. "Now we ain't never gonna escape old man Roberts and his whip."

"Babies have a way of coming when they are ready," said Hannah, hoping to calm the agitated boy. "Judging by his size, his time to come was now. Celia is going to need to rest for a few days. The Smedleys are good people. They will make sure you and your sister and the baby are safe."

His feigned bravado slipping, Ned dropped his head to his chest. "Wilfram, he already say he worried we be found out if the baby cryin' all the time. He be right to worry."

Hannah silently agreed.

"I know it seems like an impossible situation," said Nella Hinshaw, "but I think we have found a solution to Celia's and Ned's changing situation.

I've sent word to Jethro and Carrie Hoopes in Byberry. They have harbored escaped slaves before, and have a large farm, so their nearest neighbor is miles away."

"Where a crying baby won't be a problem," added Hannah, smiling for the first time that day.

"Exactly. I am certain they will agree to take Celia, Ned, and the baby, though I will admit—for obvious reasons—the infant complicates the transport process. Some would say, endangers it."

"I suspect Celia realized she would not have been helped to escape if the network knew about the baby. Still, it's hard to be angry with her when you consider the circumstances she and Ned are fleeing."

"True, but we cannot ignore that good people risk their lives to help, and any misjudgment or betrayal puts the whole network in danger. That's why we have to move the three of them out of the city to Byberry as soon as possible."

"Unless there is some complication with either Celia or the baby, they should be able to travel in a few days," said Hannah.

"Good. Once we receive word that the Hoopes will harbor them, we can arrange for the three of them to leave. Will thou be able to look in on them to make sure Celia and the child are well enough to travel?"

"Of course. I just wish I didn't feel so uncertain about their chances for success. Celia is very young. Ned looks like he is only two or three years older. He strikes me as unreliable; he appears to have temper that flares easily."

Nella made a clucking sound with her tongue. "In that case, I share thy concern."

Six days later, Ned and Celia, baby Lewis in her arms, stood behind the Smedley's house readying to board Jethro Hoopes' wagon for the eighteen-mile journey to Byberry.

"Give Lewis the cloth I soaked in chamomile tea to suck on if he starts to get fussy," instructed Hannah. "It will calm him and make him sleepy."

Looking every bit like the terrified fourteen-year-old girl she was, Celia hugged Hannah. "Thank you for takin' care of me and Lewis," she said, fear clouding her dark brown eyes. "I wish we could stay here so you could look after us some more. I worried 'bout takin' good care of my baby."

"Once you get to Byberry, Carrie Hoopes will be there to help you if you need it," assured Hannah.

"We ain't gonna get to Byberry 'less you gets in the wagon," grumbled Ned, pushing past them, a small cloth bundle draped over his shoulder.

"Go on," said Hannah, stroking the top of the infant's head. "Just remember everything we went over, and you will do fine. And don't forget to take care of yourself too," she added, as Celia climbed onto the wagon and joined Ned in the cave-like space created by bags of grain stacked on top and alongside of a makeshift ledge over their heads.

"We will make sure they are well and safe," said Jethro Hoopes, covering the opening of the hiding place and filling the wagon with more bags of grain. Mounting the wagon's spring seat, he flicked the reins and the horses jolted forward.

A week later, a messenger brought word from Jethro Hoopes. Celia and the baby were safe and doing well. Ned had disappeared sometime during the night of their arrival. Attempts to locate him were unsuccessful.

CHAPTER 72

October 1808

"I think that's all of it," said Benjamin filling a second barrel with what remained of their few belongings. There's room for any last-minute items, but it looks like we're done. The barrels will be picked up tomorrow and taken to the docks. I've arranged to have them stored in a warehouse until we are settled in Buffalo."

Circling her arms around his waist, Hannah detected a note of sadness in his voice. "You're not having second thoughts are you?"

Benjamin buried his face in her loosened hair. "It's not that. I'm looking forward to working with Macy's former colleague, Doctor Strand, while he prepares to retire. Buffalo is more like a village now, but it is growing, and its proximity to Canada positions us well to be a part of Nella's network if we are needed. It's just that this is where we began our life together. We've made a lot of wonderful memories here."

"Memories we will take with us."

He closed his eyes for a moment, deep lines rippling along his forehead. "I feel like my actions have taken you from what you love to do most. You're leaving behind all your good work."

Hannah took his face in her hands. "And I will continue to do the same work in our new home. Please Benjamin, stop torturing yourself with guilt. The past few months have been wonderful. We were able to work together. You found your passion for medicine again. This new start will be good for both of us. And now we can spend the next few weeks in Charleston with the family before we have to be in Buffalo."

Benjamin kissed her tenderly. "I love you."

"And I love you," she said kissing him back. "But," she said, pointing to the candles in the ceramic candlesticks on the table, "the Sabbath waits for no one, and it's almost sunset."

Despite his long and exaggerated sigh, Benjamin treasured the Friday evening tradition. Each time Hannah lit the candles and recited the ancient prayer in observance of *Shabbat*, he imagined the family gathered around his mother in the glow of the candles. It comforted him to know that even though they were separated by hundreds of miles, they were bound together on this night by the sacred act of welcoming the Sabbath.

The silvery-white light of a full October moon sliced through the bedroom window, illuminating their naked bodies in a pale glow. Lying in each other's arms, their need for each other demanding to be satisfied, they made love with desperate urgency. Seductive words of love and longing whispered in the darkness. Fevered hands and lips discovering new delights. Smooth, silky skin sliding against each other in perfect rhythm. Frantic for release, Hannah arched her back and surrendered herself to Benjamin's body.

It was still dark when Hannah woke in the tangled sheets, memories of the night before making her smile. Stretching languorously, she kissed Benjamin's shoulder, gently trailing her finger down his back, his muscles rippling under her touch. "Are you awake?"

"I am now," he yawned, rolling towards her, and kissing her breasts. "You know," he said, slowly moving his hands down her body to her hips, "we don't have to meet Nella and Doctor Macy until late this morning."

"Then we have hours to ourselves," she answered, her body eager for his.

Nella Hinshaw's chin began to tremble as soon as Benjamin and Hannah stepped through the door. "Forgive an old woman," she said, taking an embroidered handkerchief from the sleeve of her dress and dabbing the corners of her eyes. "I do not mean for this to be an emotional parting. Ye have so much to look forward to."

Struggling to stifle her own tears, Hannah hugged the tiny woman. "We're not saying goodbye yet."

"Not for a little while, at least," she said, sniffling. "Casper Macy is waiting for thee in the garden. The air is a bit cool, but it would be a shame to waste such a beautiful day."

They sat in the warmth of the sunlight that filtered through the brilliant orange and gold leaves of the surrounding oaks, dappled shadows playing across the garden. Benjamin and Hannah listened intently to Casper Macy's advice and insights into what awaited them in Buffalo. They reminisced with Nella about their wedding and the happy times they'd shared. When words could no longer postpone the inevitable, their anguished hearts heavy with sorrow, the four friends said goodbye.

CHAPTER 73

Charleston, November 1808

Afterten days at sea, Benjamin and Hannah stood at the *Falcon's* bow, scanning the wharf for sight of Efren at his usual spot. As the ship pulled alongside the quay, they were surprised to see Jonah waving at them instead.

Looking uneasy and shifting his weight from one foot to another, Jonah waited for Benjamin and Hannah to disembark from the *Falcon*.

"Jonah, it's good to see you," said Benjamin, searching the wharf for sight of Efren. "Is my father at the warehouse?"

Growing more apprehensive, Jonah looked past Benjamin, unable to meet his eyes. "Uh…he at home. I so sorry to tell you this, but your mama be real sick."

Hannah felt her legs grow weak.

The color left Benjamin's face. "What do you mean she's real sick? What's wrong?"

"I don't know 'xactly. She take to her bed a few days ago. Efren, he say to bring you right away. I gots the coach yonder to take you right to the house. I gonna come back to get your bags."

Jonah drove the horses hard, his urgency heightening their fears. As soon as he brought the matched team to a halt in front of the East Bay Street house, Benjamin and Hannah bounded from the coach.

Efren met them at the door, his hair and clothes disheveled, his face pale and etched with exhaustion. "Thank God you are here," he said, embracing them both.

"Papa, what's wrong with Mama? How long has she been sick? I want to see her."

Efren wiped his red-rimmed eyes with the heel of his hand. "She came down with a cold last week that seemed to be getting better. Four days ago, she became feverish, and started coughing up thick, yellow phlegm tinged with blood. Then she had trouble breathing, and it became painful for her to take a deep breath. Doctor Harrows came, and said it was winter fever; that there had been an outbreak of the disease over the past few weeks. He wanted to bleed her, but you know how strong-willed your mother is, and she wouldn't allow it. She did finally submit to cupping to draw the illness from her lungs, but she continued to worsen. Ruth has been caring for her all along; she hasn't left her bedside in days. Her root medicines bring temporary comfort, but," he said, his voice breaking, "Anica is getting worse."

Pneumonia. Hannah stifled a sob. Benjamin looked away, hope fading from his eyes. "I want to see her," he repeated.

Swaying dazedly, Efren bowed his head, suddenly seeming smaller, shrunken.

Benjamin reached out to steady him. "Papa, are you all right?"

"I...I haven't been sleeping much. We have all been taking turns sitting up with Anica at night. Isabel just left a little while ago to spend some time with Leah and Elizabeth and to get some rest. I think I will go lie down for a bit." He hugged Benjamin and Hannah and shuffled slowly towards his study.

The sound of footsteps on the stairs made Hannah and Benjamin turn. In an instant, Hannah was in her mother's arms.

"I am so glad you are here. Anica has been asking for the both of you," said Ruth, her eyes revealing what she was too heartbroken to say aloud.

Benjamin's glance shifted from Ruth to Hannah.

"Go to her," said Hannah. "I will be up in a few minutes."

Benjamin hesitated at the top of the stairs, dread knotting his stomach. When he entered Anica's bedroom, the curtains were slightly parted, a sliver of daylight playing across the darkened room. Mariana dozed in a wing-backed chair beside Anica's bed, her gray hair undone, her face troubled even in slumber.

Anica slept too, her chest rising and falling erratically, her breath coming in rapid, shallow bursts, rattling as her inflamed, fluid-filled lungs battled to provide oxygen to the rest of her body.

Shocked by how small and thin she appeared, Benjamin lowered himself into a chair alongside the bed. Assessing her gray pallor and strangled breathing, he knew. *She is dying, and everything I have learned is useless. Harrows' barbaric treatments. Ruth's roots and herbs. Useless.* Hot tears of grief tumbled down his cheeks unchecked. Taking his mother's hand, he startled when she squeezed it.

"Benjamin," she wheezed, "is that you?"

"Mama."

"Shh, don't cry. I am sorry I am ruining your visit with this illness. I know everyone is worried about me. I just need to rest." Anica's eyes drifted around the room. "Where is Hannah?"

"She is downstairs with Ruth. She'll be right up."

"I have missed you both so much," she said, a cough starting low in her throat, feebly at first, and then in convulsive spasms that shook her body. When at last the spasms subsided, she fell back on her pillows, exhausted and gulping for air, grimacing at the pain ripping through her chest.

Springing awake, Mariana held a glass of water to Anica's lips, pushing the damp curls from her face, while Benjamin propped her up into a sitting position. "*Mi cariña*, you must rest."

Anica nodded and closed her eyes. "I do tire easily," she mumbled, sleep overtaking her.

"You look exhausted too," said Benjamin, opening his arms to Mariana.

"*Nieto*," she wept, "I am afraid we are losing her."

Downstairs, Ruth looked past Hannah, her gaze haunted. "I have failed my dearest friend, my heart's true sister. I've called on all my skills and all my knowledge. I've prayed to my ancestors. I've prayed to the God Anica showed me how to love." She faced Hannah, her eyes wet, "And still, she grows weaker."

"Oh, Mama, it's a disease we do not know how to cure. It strikes the rich and the poor with equal ferocity. Surely, you have seen its scourge among your patients. Some survive..."

"But, most don't," said Ruth, finishing Hannah's sentence, her voice flat.

"Please, Mama. Don't blame yourself."

"It's not blame that is torturing me. It's this feeling of total helplessness."

Insisting that Ruth and Mariana go home and get some rest, Benjamin and Hannah took up the nighttime vigil. Her sleep fitful, Anica would wake for short periods, smiling weakly, and telling them how much she loved them. By morning, her breathing was more labored, her lips tinged with blue.

Dozing, his head resting on Anica's bed, Benjamin startled awake when Isabel entered the room.

"Benjamin, I was so afraid you wouldn't get here on time," she said, pulling him close and resting her head on his chest. When his loose hold on her tightened, she let herself cry for the first time since Anica fell ill. "I am sorry. I didn't mean to do that. It's just that each day Mama seems to be weaker, her breathing worse. Ruth is downstairs. She and Hannah were brewing burdock root tea to help break up the congestion," she said, peering at her mother.

Benjamin followed her gaze. He'd heard the gurgling sound of Anica's infected lungs too many times in the wards of the Almshouse to hold out any hope she would get better.

Anica drifted in and out of broken sleep, only vaguely aware of the changing faces at her bedside. Unable to fight off the slumber that came unbidden, and unfettered by time and place, she floated in a sea of fragmented images. Efren when she first met him. Isabel, Hannah, and Benjamin playing together. Her mother's face smiling down at her. *Mama!*

Her eyes flew open, and like a swimmer surfacing from the depths of the ocean, Anica gasped for breath.

"I'm getting Benjamin," said Mariana, already at the door.

Efren grasped her hand. "Anica, are you in pain?"

"No pain, she said. "Just dreams. Good dreams." She caressed Efren's face. "Do you remember the first time we met?"

"Of course, I do. It was at my parents' Christmas Ball. You were there with your father. You were so beautiful. As soon as you arrived you were surrounded by every eligible young man at the party. I remember thinking you would never entertain the attentions of an old man like me."

"But I only had eyes for you. In truth, I'd loved you from afar well before that night. I would stay out of sight and watch when you came to our house to conduct business with my father." She smiled at the memory, and took his hand. "Efren, I know how sick I am. I will leave you soon. Promise me you will not let the life we shared keep you from being happy again with someone else."

Efren's face contorted, anger mixing with grief. "This is not the way it was supposed to be! You were supposed to outlive me." His eyes filled. "Anica, there is no one else for me. I cannot bear to think of my life without you."

"Please, Efren. Let me leave knowing you will do as I ask. Promise me," she begged, her chest heaving as she strained to take in gulps of air.

Nodding, Efren kissed her, his mouth warm on her cool lips, his tears mingling with hers.

"I have one more request," she said.

Wrapped in blankets to ward off the crisp November air, Anica draped her arms around Benjamin's neck as he lifted her and carried her downstairs to the garden where everyone waited.

Sorrow weighing down on them like a heavy cloak, the family watched as Efren placed cushions on a garden bench. Moving it into the sun, he positioned it so Anica could look out on her treasured rose bushes. When Benjamin placed his cheek against Anica's and tenderly nestled his mother in Efren's arms, Mariana turned her head and wept, grief crushing her heart.

Anica closed her eyes and tilted her face to the sun, welcoming its warmth on her skin. A cardinal perched on limb above her trilled its sweet song, and her eyes fluttered open. As if a curtain had been parted, Anica's jumbled thoughts unraveled, a quiet serenity enveloping her like a loving embrace. She smiled radiantly at the faces around her. Tears brimmed in her eyes. "You have filled my life with more happiness than you will ever know. I love you all."

Isabel came to her. Sinking to her knees, she rested her head on her mother's lap. "I love you, Mama. Please don't go. You still have so much to teach me. There are so many things left for us to share."

Anica's cool fingers stroked Isabel's face. "My darling, you will have a wonderful life with Richard and the girls, and I promise I will be there with you for all your joys. Please tell Leah and Elizabeth how much I loved them. Don't let them forget me."

Her voice growing hoarse, Anica began to cough. Her breathing became hitched; the space between each breath longer. Her hands began to shake. Isabel rose in a panic. Benjamin hurried to his mother's side.

Anica could sense the curtain closing. The bright sunlight began to dim, its warmth fading. She felt Efren's arms tighten around her, his wet cheek against hers. *It is so hard to leave you, my love.* Hands roughly pulled her upright. *Why is Benjamin shouting? So much noise and crying.* She heard her name called from a distance. Arms open, her mother beckoned her. *I'm coming, Mama. I lit the candles, Mama. I know you are waiting for me, Mama.* Her arms curled into an embrace and she smiled.

CHAPTER 74

A black-ribboned wreath hung on the entry door. Inside, the mirrors were draped in black cloth; the curtains were drawn, the usually vibrant rooms shrouded in gloom. The servants moved quietly about the house, averting their red and swollen eyes when the mourners returned from the cemetery.

No one spoke as they gathered in the parlor at Ruth's request, their grief deafening. *Together, but not,* thought Ruth, scanning the doleful faces of their little family.

"As she always did, our beloved Anica was thinking of others—of us—even as she knew she was dying," said Ruth, her voice wavering. "During the nights I sat with her, she fought her fatigue and summoned the strength to write down her thoughts and wishes. She asked that I read them to you upon her death."

Ruth took a folded, cream-colored letter from her pocket; Anica's once beautiful handwriting a shaky scrawl. Inhaling deeply, she began to read:

My Dearests,

If Ruth is reading this to you, you are gathered in the house that witnessed so many happy times, and it saddens me to know that this occasion brings you together in sorrow.

I know that this illness will take me from you. I have never been fond of goodbyes, but the realization of one's mortality brings with it a certain clarity. Life is precious…and precarious.We do not know what each day will bring.We do not know how many days we have left to share with each other.Words are left unsaid, and I do not want to leave this world without saying these words to you.

I foolishly thought my years on this earth stretched before me. I thought I would be granted the joy of watching my granddaughters grow up, and cuddling Benjamin and Hannah's babies. I thought I would have many more years of loving Efren, years spent together in ease and tranquility. I thought I would grow plump and gray-haired, and die a contented old woman. Now, it seems God has other plans for me.

I have had a full and wonderful life, made all the richer by you, my cherished family. I have loved and been loved by the most extraordinary man. I watched Isabel, Benjamin, and Hannah grow into caring adults who made me proud every day. I lived to see the miracle of Jonah's return to us, and to welcome Richard into our family. I held my two beautiful granddaughters in my arms. I was granted the good fortune of having the love and treasured companionship of Mariana and Ruth. I have been blessed to have each one of you in my life; to have had the privilege of friendships that surpassed the bonds of bloodlines to form our remarkable family.

Please do not let grief consume you. Carry on your lives and live them to the fullest. Hold tight to each other. Find strength in each other. Continue to gather here on Friday evenings and welcome the Sabbath together.When you think of me, know that I am at peace.When you remember me, remember how much I loved each of you.

I will never be far from you,
Anica

The last to leave, Mariana and Amadis lingered in the piazza with Efren. "Do not worry about the business," said Amadis. "Spend time with Isabel, Benjamin, and Hannah. Richard and I can handle things until you are ready to come back."

Efren stared hollow-eyed. "I still cannot believe she is gone. I hear her voice. I see her everywhere." His eyes flared and he exploded in anger. "Why couldn't she be made well again? How will I even exist without her?"

Mariana held him, smothering her own grief to absorb his. "*Mijo*, Anica loved you so much. She fought so hard not to leave you. Grieve for her, yes, but also let the healing come. It is what she wanted for you. Please, for her, leave room in your heart to one day find happiness again."

Efren's body sagged. "How can I be happy when she took my heart with her?"

CHAPTER 75

Benjamin sank down on the bed beside Hannah. "My father is going to be lost without her. I found him downstairs wandering from room to room, as if he were looking for her. When I called to him, he didn't seem to hear me at first."

Hannah laid her head on his chest. "He adored her. It is going to take some time for him to accept that she is gone. You know my mother and the rest of the family will make sure he is well."

She sat up and faced him. "There is something else we need to talk about. I have something to tell you."

Panic flashed across Benjamin's face. "What's wrong?"

She took Benjamin's hand. "Do you remember our last night in Philadelphia? And the morning after?"

His panicked look turned to puzzlement and then to recognition. He began to laugh. "Are you saying...?"

"I am saying we weren't exactly careful."

Bringing her mouth to his, he kissed her tenderly and held her face, his forehead pressed to hers. "Are you sure?"

"I'm sure enough that I told your mother. She knew before she died, Benjamin. She knew, and she was so happy for us."

Benjamin took Hannah into his arms and wept.

A week later, the family huddled on the quay in the chill December wind, the *Falcon* bobbing up and down in the choppy water.

Hannah and Benjamin said their goodbyes to the family. Mariana and Amadis clung to them, unsure of when they would see them again. Jonah and Richard murmured their sympathies and good wishes, and embracing them, took their leave. Only Efren, Ruth, and Isabel remained.

"It seems like we spend too much time on docks saying goodbye," said Hannah, holding fast to Ruth's hand. "You will come to Buffalo when the baby is due?"

"I will be there the month before so I will be sure to deliver my grandchild. It's a promise I made to Anica before we even knew we had a grandchild coming. I also promised her I would give you this," she said, handing Hannah a small satchel.

Surprised by its weight, Hannah gasped when she looked inside. With shaking hands, she removed the cloth-wrapped object, its shape unmistakable. "Is this what I think it is?"

"It is. Anica wanted you and Isabel to each have one of her mother's candlesticks to welcome the Sabbath, but also to keep her mother's memory alive."

Hannah glanced at Isabel and Efren, her gaze questioning.

"It's what Mama wanted," said Isabel. "She told me her plans, and I agreed. It is important to me too that our children and their children know about the courage of the matriarchs of both of our families. The candlesticks—even separated from each other—will always be a reminder of where we came from and of the risks our mothers took so we could live in freedom." She took a note from her reticule and handed it to Hannah. "From Mama."

Peering over at Ruth, Hannah untied the blue ribbon curled around the letter.

My Dearest Hannah,

This candlestick is for you. I know that you will cherish it as I have. It is my hope that when you welcome the Sabbath, you will tell your children and their children the story of my mother's candlesticks; how they brought us to America, and how they bound our two families to each other. It is my

wish that the candlesticks will continue to pass from generation to genera-
tion, so that the courage of the women in your family and mine will never
be forgotten, and that the stories of our brave mothers and grandmothers
who stood up for their faith and freedom will inspire our future daughters
and granddaughters to do the same.

My sweet Hannah, I loved you from the moment you were born. That
you and Benjamin found happiness together brought me more joy than I
can ever convey.

My deepest love,
Anica

Efren put his arm around Hannah and kissed her forehead. "You leave
with all my love," he said, straining to keep his voice even, "and Anica's as
well."

Benjamin held his father close. "I hate leaving you. Promise me you will
take care of yourself. You know what Mama wanted for you. Please allow
yourself to find happiness again."

Efren kissed Benjamin's cheek. "It appears we cannot delay your departure much longer," he said, pointing to the harbor pilot boarding the ship.

A sudden sense of urgency seized them, embraces and goodbyes mixed
with tears and wishes for safe travel. Half way to the ship, Hannah ran back
to hug her mother one more time.

Ignoring the cold wind, Hannah and Benjamin remained on the deck of
the *Falcon*, waving goodbye, until the pilot eased the vessel away from the
quay. Benjamin leaned his arms on the rail, and gazed out over the rough
water. "It is still hard for me to believe she is gone," he said at last. "All I can
think of is that she will never hold our child or see our family grow."

"I believe that she will find a way to be with us just as she promised."

Benjamin watched the pilot steer the ship past the sand bars and skirt
along Sullivan's Island where he disembarked. "I wish I believed as strongly
as you do."

Hannah did not respond, her attention drawn to a cardinal nestled high
in a pine tree on the island. As if the tiny creature knew it was being observed,

it took flight. Swooping low over the deck, the bird circled the vessel, and returned to its perch, its ebony eyes seeming to lock onto Hannah's.

Hannah grabbed Benjamin's arm, pointing to the red tail feather at her feet. Stooping to retrieve it, she nodded towards the cardinal as it bobbed its crested head and flew away.

Hannah handed the scarlet plume to Benjamin. "For you, from Anica, with all her love."

EPILOGUE

Buffalo, November 24, 1848
My Dearest Isabel,

Your letter arrived yesterday, and we were delighted to learn that
Abigail and her new daughter are well. I do not know which is harder for
me to comprehend: that Leah is a grandmother, or that you are a great-
grandmother! I will write to Leah and Abigail too, but I want you to know
how touched we both are that Abigail chose to name our new great grand-
niece Anica Ruth. I am certain our mothers are together, smiling, their arms
entwined as they always were when they stood next to each other.

We too, have some good news to share. Anna's oldest, Lindy, is expecting, and we will be great-grandparents in May.

Our dear son Edward remains a bachelor, but we hold out hope a
young woman will come along to steal his heart and bring us more grandchildren. As you can imagine, his protests that he is too busy overseeing the
Buffalo branch of the A & E Eagle Shipping Company to wed do not fall
on sympathetic ears! Still, as Richard can attest, the opening of the Erie
Canal has certainly been a boost to the business...and to our once quiet
little village. Buffalo is fast becoming a bustling commercial center.

Benjamin remains busy too, splitting his time between treating his
regular patients and teaching students who attend the new University of
Buffalo Medical School. He is delighted that instruction takes place at
Buffalo General Hospital, and that he is able teach in a practical setting.

He is content; happy to be doing what he always wanted to do. Happier still to see his family happy and well.

Anna has taken over my midwife practice. I step in only when she is unavailable. I am not idle, however. I continue to help where I can when a traveler needs assistance. As you know from your own efforts, these troubling times have seen the demand for our help increase daily.

Tonight, we light the Shabbat candles. Do you remember when Anna was little she called them Granny's freedom candles because my mother said they cast freedom's light? As always, your grandmother Debora's candlestick will be joined by the ceramic candle holders we used when we were first married. Our children and grandchildren will gather here to welcome the Sabbath, and we will remember them all: Anica and Efren, my mother and Uncle Jonah, Amadis and Mariana, and the family will be together again.

My love to you and Richard,
Hannah

AUTHOR'S NOTES

Three years ago, at a dinner party I'd attended somewhat reluctantly, I found myself seated next to a delightful young woman who, in the course of our conversation, mentioned that she had just received her results from a DNA testing company. Given her Catholic family's long history as residents of Charleston, South Carolina, she revealed how surprised she was to learn that she was of Iberian and Jewish descent.

Intrigued, I asked her if any of her family members engaged in any practices associated with Judaism. She thought for a moment, then responded that her father had a great aunt on his mother's side of the family who lit candles on Friday nights, and who would not eat pork, but no one, including the great aunt knew why. The elderly woman could only explain that she performed the ritual of the Sabbath candles and did not eat pork because they were family traditions observed by her great-grandmother, grandmother, mother, and aunts for as long as she could remember.

I was fascinated by the fact that my young dinner companion had no idea that she most likely had ancestors who were Spanish or Portuguese conversos—descendants of Sephardic Jews who were forced to renounce their faith during the Spanish Inquisition, but who continued to practice Judaism in secret. I was especially struck by her family's continuation of traditions out of respect for previous generations. That night the seed was planted for what would become *In Freedom's Light*.

While *In Freedom's Light's* characters are of my creation, and the Amselem family's flight from Valencia in 1785 is fictional, the circumstances prompting their journey to Charleston are not.

The fourteenth and fifteenth centuries heralded a rise in the persecution of Jews and increased demands for them to renounce their Judaism and convert to Catholicism. Faced with the choice between Baptism, torture, or death, thousands of Jews opted for conversion. Jews who fled Spain and settled in Portugal to avoid conversion, found themselves facing the same choice when the Inquisition took root there five years later.

Legally considered Christians, conversos—also called crypto-Jews or secret Jews—were subject to the Church's Inquisitional laws of heresy and apostasy if they practiced Judaism after conversion. Converts who adopted Christianity and denounced their Jewish faith were under constant suspicion. Suspected conversos were carefully watched for signs of Judaizing: forgoing pork, avoiding work on Saturdays, or keeping Judaic symbols in their homes. Conversos—both men and women—accused of practicing Judaism in secret, were arrested and tortured until they confessed to the crime of being a practicing Jew.

The reach of the Spanish Inquisition extended into the nineteenth century. Its last victim, a Valencia schoolteacher, was hung for heresy in 1826. By the time the Inquisition came to an official end in July 1834, an estimated one hundred fifty thousand Jews had been burned at the stake or died in prison as the result of torture or maltreatment, and thousands of crypto-Jews and their descendants—many unaware of their Jewish ancestry—were scattered around the world, including in the American colonies.

ACKNOWLEDGEMENTS

It is the nature of historical fiction to address difficult topics. Because it deals with the Spanish Inquisition and America's history of plantation life and enslavement, *In Freedom's Light* is no exception. I have made every effort to ensure the accuracy of the places, times, and events the novel depicts. A complete list of resources can be found on my website, sharonglogerfriedman.com. I am particularly indebted to Juan Marcos Bejarano Gutierrez for his expansive discourse on conversos and the Spanish Inquisition in *Secret Jews*. The depiction of the lives and experiences of the enslaved people of the fictional Bending Oaks plantation are based in part on the recollections recorded by interviewers for the *WPA's Federal Writer's Project Slave Narratives*. Other helpful sources include, *Charleston! Charleston!* by Walter J. Fraser; *Born in Bondage,* by Marie Jenkins Schwartz; and *This Happy Land*, by James William Hagy. In addition. I am grateful to the respective staffs of Charleston's Middleton Place Plantation, the Old Slave Mart Museum, and the College of Charleston's Marlene and Nathan Addlestone Library for their invaluable help and expertise.

Once again, I owe a huge debt of gratitude to Kim Lazarovich and Bernice Cozewith for embracing a roughed-out first draft and helping to turn it into a cogent manuscript. Thank you both for your invaluable insights.

Endless thanks to author Nancy Carey Johnson for her willing ear, pep talks, and inspiration. Much gratitude to friends Steve Stone, Jerry Greenfield, Ruth Benson, Bonnie and Steve Salamon, Connie and Bob Stern, and Gail and Steve Simon for their unfailing support. Thank you too, to Dawnny Ruby and Denise Birt for their constant encouragement.

My good fortune in friendships is only exceeded by the rich blessings of my family. To my daughter Jenna, son-in-law Kyle, son Jamie, daughter-in-law Kelley, my grandchildren Kate, Sam, Jack, and Colton, and my brother Kenny, thank you and more love than you can ever know for being the cheerleaders on my team.

In Freedom's Light would never have made it to the page without the love and support of my husband George. I am so grateful for the alphabetical seating that brought us together fifty-eight years ago in a University of Florida Freshman English Writing Lab. Thank you for your unwavering belief in me. Thank you for propping me up on the days when the words would not come, and for celebrating with me when they did. Thank you for your patience, and for making me laugh when I needed to most. Above all, thank you for being you. You are my for-always love.

And finally, to the always-present spirits of my beloved parents and grandparents, thank you for keeping me company as I wrote.

QUESTIONS AND TOPICS
FOR DISCUSSION

1. The act of lighting *Shabbat* candles is Anica's enduring link to her faith and to her mother. "When I pray, I hear my mother's voice whispering the prayer with me," she tells Ruth. Explore the significance of the observance of the candle lighting ceremony and how it connects generations of Amselem women to come. How does lighting the candles strengthen the bond between Ruth and Anica? Does your family observe traditions that have been handed down from one generation to another?

2. Many of the novel's women display extraordinary strength and fierce independence in the face of overwhelming societal obstacles. Consider their courage within the context of the male-dominated society in which they lived. Which female character did you like most? Least?

3. When Anica sympathizes with Margaret about losing a parent at a young age, Margaret responds, "Yes, well these things happen." What does the exchange reveal about Margaret? Did your feelings change toward her when you learned the circumstances of her marriage?

4. Discuss Viney's reason for ending her life and the lives of her children.

5. Does Philip's final act of freeing his slaves change your opinion of him or redeem him in any way?

6. Upon returning from boarding school, Benjamin is blindsided by Efren's plans for his future. What are your impressions of Efren as a father? How would you describe the relationship between father and son?

7. Consider the role spiritual connections to the dead play in the novel. Do you believe in omens and signs?

8. When Benjamin tells Ruth he wants to marry Hannah, she asks: "Are you strong enough to face the people who will treat you with scorn for marrying a Negro woman?" Reflect on the challenges facing Benjamin and Hannah in 1808. Would they face the same challenges today?

9. Think about Nella Hinshaw's reaction when Hannah reveals she wants to educate the destitute women she treats about birth control. Is she right to discourage Hannah?

10. Benjamin challenges a doctor from a prominent family for his lack of compassion for Almshouse patients, and loses his position as a staff physician. "Even as I was reviling him I knew I was making a dangerous enemy. I just didn't care," he tells Hannah. Was Benjamin's stand against indifference admirable or reckless?

11. Consider Mariana's devotion to Anica, and the unwavering bonds of friendship between Anica and Ruth, Efren and Amadis, and the family they create. Discuss the difference between having relatives and being a part of a family.

12. How is *In Freedom's Light* relevant today?